ONE MAN WAS THE PRINCE OF DEATH.
THE OTHER WAS KNOWN AS GRANDMASTER

Alexander Zharkov and Justin Gilead. All their lives
they had been trained to believe their destinies were
forever intertwined. They were to fight the battle of
the gods against each other and die together. For
one lifetime, good and evil would merge, repel, and
connect again. It was a spirited game and a deadly
one—for it was a game played with lives. . . .

HIGH PRIEST

"COMPELLING AND EXCITING . . . it tops its
predecessor, the Edgar-winning *Grandmaster*!"
—Max Allan Collins, author of *The Quarry Series*

"A DIVERTING ADVENTURE!"
—*Publishers Weekly*

"An unusual spy thriller . . . enjoyable reading!"
—*Roanoke Times and World News*

HIGH PRIEST

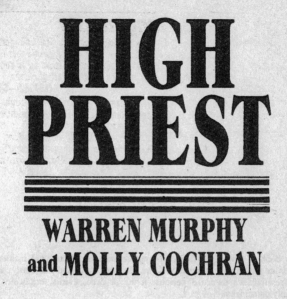

WARREN MURPHY
and MOLLY COCHRAN

A SIGNET BOOK

NEW AMERICAN LIBRARY

PUBLISHED BY
PENGUIN BOOKS CANADA LIMITED

PUBLISHER'S NOTE

This book is a work of fiction. Names, characters, places, and incidents either are the product of the author's imagination or are used fictitiously, and any resemblance to actual persons, living or dead, events, or locales is entirely coincidental.

NAL BOOKS ARE AVAILABLE AT QUANTITY DISCOUNTS WHEN USED
TO PROMOTE PRODUCTS OR SERVICES. FOR INFORMATION PLEASE
WRITE TO PREMIUM MARKETING DIVISION, NEW AMERICAN LIBRARY,
1633 BROADWAY, NEW YORK, NEW YORK 10019.

High Priest previously appeared in an NAL Books edition published by New American Library.

First Signet Printing, February, 1989

2 3 4 5 6 7 8 9

SIGNET TRADEMARK REG. U.S. PAT. OFF. AND FOREIGN COUNTRIES
REGISTERED TRADEMARK — MARCA REGISTRADA
HECHO EN WINNIPEG, CANADA

SIGNET, SIGNET CLASSIC, MENTOR, ONYX, PLUME,
MERIDIAN and NAL BOOKS are published in Canada by Penguin
Books Canada Limited, 2801 John Street, Markham, Ontario,
Canada L3R 1B4
PRINTED IN CANADA
COVER PRINTED IN U.S.A.

For Devin Buckaroo,
who knows what the wild birds say

HIGH PRIEST

BOOK ONE
THE PLAYERS

CHAPTER ONE
ANDREW STARCHER

Sasha Kaminskaya was on the trapeze when the old man entered the amphitheater.

"Watch out," he grunted, barging through a row of spectators sitting in the darkness. Overhead, the girl twirled like a spinning Christmas ornament as the people seated around the old man strained to see past his voluminous coat, stiff with dried vodka and urine.

"Sit down, you stinking pig," someone hissed behind him.

"*Idi cortu,*" the old man answered in gutter Russian, stomping on a woman's foot as he shuffled past. "Go to hell." He chose a seat beside a small boy who was too enraptured with the sight of the flyer on the trapeze to notice the old man's presence.

Without fanfare, La Kaminskaya spun into a perfect triple somersault. The crowd cheered. Even the eyes of the impassive and omnipresent police were momentarily riveted on the diminutive blond woman hurtling through the small round spot of light high above them.

Four at the west exit. The old man's gaze swept over the bulky-suited men at the main entrance. *Militsia,* he decided. Plainclothesmen on riot duty or pickpocket de-

tail. Standard. And two more at the south end, cops in
uniform, carrying stun guns. All routine.

The clown selling sausages down near ringside was
another matter. Natural red hair stuck out from under
his blond curly wig. A pair of highly polished black shoes
with gum soles shone beneath his polka-dotted panta-
loons. The old man was amused for a moment. The
Committee never did seem to get their disguises quite
right—not in Moscow, anyway.

A weeknight at the circus shouldn't rate the Committee's attention. Why was there a KGB man there? And if
there was one, there were probably more. Why?

The ringmaster announced the trapeze artist's specialty,
the quadruple somersault. Before Sasha Kaminskaya, only
three trapeze flyers in the world had managed the quadruple. La Kaminskaya had changed all that. Every night
she performed the quadruple without a safety net, high
above the sawdust-covered stone floor, soaring fearlessly
where the slightest error meant death.

The feat made her a national star, the headliner of the
Russian State Circus. Word had even leaked to the West
about the beautiful young woman who could fly better
than any man in trapeze history, but Sasha Kaminskaya
was kept strictly inside the Soviet Union. No tours were
allowed, no interviews with the foreign press were permitted, and only the occasional smuggled photograph of
Sasha performing her amazing act appeared in the West.

Among circus aficionados it was rumored that the
twenty-four-year-old woman had refused to teach her
training methods to the Russian Olympic team. She had
similarly declined a "suggestion" that she teach young
gymnasts the tricks of her extraordinary speed, strength,
and balance.

Because of her uncooperative attitude, Sasha Kaminskaya was denied the privilege of touring with the circus
on its infrequent excursions to the West. Her name rarely
appeared in *Pravda* or *Izvestia*. Still, people flocked from
as far away as Minsk and Kazakstan to see her perform.
The popular gossip was that it didn't matter if the gov-

ernment seemed to disapprove of her because La Kaminskaya had very important friends in very high places.

The auditorium lights dimmed. Silence dropped over the red-seated amphitheater as the musicians in the balcony lowered their instruments. The audience was glued to the movements of the blonde woman in the center of the spotlight.

Suddenly the old man's breath caught in his throat. Something was moving behind him. There was a change in the air, a feverish intensity that was more than anticipation of the event in the center ring. The old man recognized the feeling. It was almost a smell, as if the air around him had suddenly become ionized, electrically charged.

In the early days of his career he had believed the reaction was caused by his own nervousness. But he had tested it again and again, in crowded rooms, in one-on-one meetings. The feeling was not a perception of himself but a communication with death.

The man was sixty-eight years old and had learned when death was coming. He had learned to sense its presence. It was an instinct he never ignored.

As the auditorium slid into darkness he bent over and slipped his hands into a pair of gloves made of steel-reinforced American pigskin.

There was a burst of applause as one lone spotlight suddenly caught the small figure of the girl on the trapeze. The old man straightened up, his hands held stiffly in front of his chest.

Now, he thought. He felt his bowels melting. It was the signal. If he ever failed to feel that rush of pure fear, if he ever ceased to tremble at the moment when death sprang claws-out at him, it would be his last moment on earth.

The wire came down as softly as a whisper. The old man saw the thin glint of metal looping gracefully over his head.

Of course it would be a wire. He had guessed as much

before it happened. They were quiet, easily concealed weapons that the KGB loved. Their training camps devoted a half year or more to "silent removal" techniques, the cornerstone of which was the wire. This wasn't the first time the old man had made use of the steel-reinforced gloves.

He caught the wire at eye level and yanked it down hard. Then he turned and shot his left elbow straight back into his assailant's throat. He heard the crack of cartilage from the man's Adam's apple and felt the warm spray of blood on his neck.

No one else noticed at first. The people around him were staring at the trapeze high overhead. Then the woman next to the old man screamed as the KGB man's body fell forward into her lap. The old man saw her leap to her feet, hands flailing, her skirt bloodied as the corpse slid off her. The dead man's face was long and horsey, probably younger than it looked, judging from the taut skin around the bulging eyes. Two streams of blood snaked from the man's sloping nose into the crack between his lips and pooled there.

The tableau lasted only a moment. The body was then on the floor, and the people surrounding it jumped to their feet, shouting wildly. The sausage vendor in the clown suit stared for a moment at the old man, then crashed through the crowd, taking the steps three at a time, a pistol suddenly appearing in his hands.

The woman kept screaming and the lights came on, flooding the auditorium. The music stopped abruptly. The audience buzzed as an announcement came over the loudspeaker, ordering everyone to remain in their seats until they were instructed to leave.

The six posted gumshoes radioed for help, then converged on the death scene, calling for order in vain as the hysterical spectators pointed every which way and babbled about a filthy old man in an overcoat who'd jumped into the row behind them and then seemed to vanish.

The young boy who had been sitting alongside the old

man continued to stare at the woman on the trapeze as she executed a perfect quadruple.

Few saw her. There was no applause. The red-haired man in the clown costume attracted most of the crowd's attention by barking orders at the plainclothes agents and police.

Finally the audience was permitted to exit in single file, passing between two KGB men. Some were questioned, a few were searched. The old man was gone.

CHAPTER
TWO

The spacious Moscow office of the United States' Cultural Attaché was not the way Andrew Starcher remembered it. The American antiques and Wyeth landscapes with which Starcher had once surrounded himself had been replaced by massive and expensive pre-Revolutionary Russian pieces. The walls were dotted with a collection of gold and silver filigreed icons worthy of a czar.

Well, Starcher thought dryly, embassies always had money for office decorating. Congress only balked at frivolous expenditures, like saving the lives of intelligence personnel.

He took a cigar, an eight-inch Havana, from his jacket and lit it. The other man in the room, seated behind an imposing gold-trimmed mahogany desk, looked up briefly in disapproval but refrained from comment as Starcher blew a white halo of smoke toward him.

Richard Rand was a Californian who disliked smoking almost as much as he disliked Andrew Starcher. A big, handsome man with oversize, slightly myopic eyes tinted an impossible aquamarine blue by contact lenses, he had an air of my-body-is-my-temple physical righteousness about him. His shoulders were wide and square, the result of years of faithful attendance at exclusive health clubs. At his last posting, in Mexico City, Rand had quickly developed a reputation as the best tennis player on the diplomatic circuit. Clearly the man's pallor, mandatory for all permanent residents of Moscow at winter's end, did not suit him. Beneath Rand's smooth, regular features Starcher could see the desperation of a miserable creature who fantasized about waking up someday, tanned and whole, as if finally delivered from a nightmare.

No one would have been happier than Starcher to have that fantasy come true. As far as the old man was concerned, everyone would be better off if Rand were still triumphing at mixed doubles in Mexico. Rand was a diplomat, both by training and inclination, not an agent. Certainly not a network control, responsible for the lives of American operatives in the Soviet Union.

But then, the CIA's presence in Moscow had been greatly curtailed. Since the recent recall, expulsion, or death of virtually all its agents in Moscow, the Company was playing it safe by posting someone like Richard Rand as Head of Station. Rand would make no move without express orders from Langley, and Langley was not about to initiate any significant intelligence operations in Moscow at a time when there were no field operatives to carry them out.

The exception was Andrew Starcher, and that had been due more to Starcher's own persistence than to Company initiative. Starcher was still a respected operative at Langley, to whom almost everyone over the age of forty owed at least one favor. He had called in all those favors to get back to Moscow.

The mission wasn't much—a good first-year man might have handled it, if there were any first-year men in Moscow—but it was a chance for Starcher to go to work again, to get out of the sickroom on his family's estate where a battery of doctors and nurses shot him full of sedatives and tranquilizers in the hope that the old man would die with a minimum of suffering and a minimum of inconvenience to the rest of the Starcher clan. Compared with life on the estate, a little routine police work on the possible murders of some American nationals seemed as enticing to Starcher as a James Bond adventure. And when the head of Operations at Langley, also a man who owed Starcher a favor, tried to sour the soup by saying there was no way for Starcher to enter the Soviet Union legally, and that there would be no backup for him once he was there, it made him want to go all the more.

It had something to do with dying in bed, Starcher supposed. He had never wanted to die in bed.

"You said you wanted to talk about the murder at the State Circus last night," Rand said, finally acknowledging Starcher. Slowly he pushed aside some papers he had been working on. "You don't have any knowledge of that, do you?"

"Some," Starcher said blandly. "I was the murderer."

Rand inhaled sharply, his spine stiffening. His mouth opened slightly to protest, but his brain obviously couldn't deliver words of sufficient outrage. For someone like Rand, whose intelligence career had been spent pushing cookies at diplomatic receptions, Starcher's casual confession was beyond comment.

"He came at me with a wire," Starcher said, elaborating.

"Are you sure?"

Starcher took a deep breath and looked away.

"Isn't it possible that you made a mistake?" Rand asked testily.

"No."

"The police are in an uproar. There's a citywide manhunt for an old man with a foreign accent."

"I faked the accent," Starcher drawled, between puffs on the cigar. He blew a smoke ring and calmly watched it drift toward the room's high ceiling.

"You've been back in Russia three days, and already you've killed someone."

"Someone who was going to kill me."

"He was an *electrician,* for God's sake!"

Starcher expelled a raspy chuckle.

"What's so funny?" Rand asked softly.

"You. Your astounding capacity for swallowing bull-shit whole. The Soviets don't mount manhunts over dead electricians. Only dead KGB agents."

"I think your Russian paranoia has finally overreached itself," Rand said, rising.

"Tell that to the five Americans they've murdered."

"For the last time, Starcher, those people were not murdered by the KGB. If they had been, Langley would have sent over more than one agent."

And you wouldn't have been one of them, Rand thought. He walked from behind his desk to the far side of the room, withdrawing from the old man.

Andrew Starcher gave him chills. In his day, Starcher probably had been the best field agent the Company had ever produced. Even during Rand's training period with the CIA he had heard the stories about Starcher in West Berlin, in Czechoslovakia, in Indochina during the early years of Vietnam, as Moscow Head of Station during the brief reign of Premier Konstantin Kadar. Even now that his usefulness was over, the mention of the old man's name was still tantamount to a holy invocation in some CIA circles.

If it hadn't been for some crazy business of his two years ago in Cuba, Starcher would now be the grand old man of American intelligence, lecturing at Camp Pearson training school, regaling eager young men with stories about the good old days of spywork. But after being wounded in Cuba, the old fool had refused to be pensioned and had refused to become a CIA staff instructor. And now someone had felt sorry for him and sent him to Moscow on a wild-goose chase just to keep him out of the Agency's way.

The problem was that Starcher believed the assignment was for real, despite the fact that Washington had not provided any cover, any backup, or even any funds to fuel his windmill chasing.

"I was sent here because you can't keep any of your agents alive, and you know it."

"Oh, Starcher," Rand began with excruciating fatigue.

"The last time I left here, I had twenty-two legals and ten agents under deep cover, plus a string of trustworthy nationals and informers. They're all gone now, deported, missing, or victims of 'accidental' death."

"That was your own doing, Starcher. After your fiasco in Cuba—"

"Cuba was a black eye for the Russians, not us." Starcher's cigar ash fell to the carpet. For the first time his soft Southern drawl developed a hard edge. "Any damned fool would recognize that. Konstantin Kadar was deposed because of what we did in Cuba."

"It didn't help our relations with the Soviets much."

"Jesus, I can't believe what I'm hearing," Starcher said.

"They expelled almost every ranking diplomat we had in response to your shoot-'em-up down there."

Starcher chomped on his cigar and spoke between gritted teeth. "If I hadn't stopped them, the Russkies would've had someone like Kadar there right now, pointing an acre or two of missiles at us."

Rand closed his eyes, smiled wearily, shook his head. "Your self-aggrandizement is really nothing short of embarrassment," he said. "At best you're an embarrassment. At worst you're downright dangerous, and I think you've crossed the line this time. Don't think the Agency's not going to hear about your murderous little spree at the circus."

"Was the killing in the papers?"

"Of course. *Izvestia*. Front page."

"Very good," Starcher said. "Now, don't you think that's unusual, considering the Soviets almost never run stories about crime in their Utopian streets? They sure as hell haven't been publicizing the dead Americans." He spat out a piece of tobacco. "The man was KGB."

"Starcher, even my own people don't know you're here. You're an absolute illegal."

"That's why I don't understand the guy at the circus."

"What you don't understand," Rand said, coloring, "is that you murdered an innocent man."

"Then why isn't his body at the morgue?"

Rand sat up. "You went to the city morgue?" he asked in astonishment. "Starcher, you're in this country without cover of any kind. Don't you understand what would happen—"

"I had to see if I could place his face somewhere. But the body's been transferred. To Lubyanka, the attendant said."

Rand's face fell. "Lubyanka?"

"That's right. The Kremlin. Something's going on, and my guess is that it's got something to do with the murders of the Americans."

"Don't be ridiculous. There's no connection at all between those deaths and your episode last night. If the man was KGB, he might have recognized you from the old days. You probably blew your own cover."

Starcher leaned forward. "In three months five Americans have been killed—shot, stabbed, beaten to death—"

"Four. Routine muggings. It happens in every city in the world every day. The fifth death was purely accidental."

"Was it? He was *your assistant*, Rand. The number-two CIA operations man in Moscow."

"Cass died in a car wreck. He skidded off the Sadovo Ring Road. There was ice."

Starcher's gaze moved slowly to the window. "My last assistant in this job got lost in the woods and froze to death. *The New York Times* said so. When we finally got his body back, he had a bullet hole in the back of the head. Odd, the effects of freezing."

"Those days were different," Rand said. "Konstantin Kadar's anti-American sentiments were leading the Soviets straight to war with us. But times have changed. The new General Secretary is a young man. He doesn't have the kind of iron grip on the KGB that Kadar had. Pierlenko needs—and wants—a good relationship with the West. He wants to talk."

"I suppose he talked those five Americans to death," Starcher said.

"Damn it, he doesn't know what's going on any more than we do!"

Starcher hooted.

"That is to say, *if* anything's going on," Rand said, composing himself. "Which the Agency seriously doubts. It was only the unfortunate accident involving my assistant that prompted them to send you here at all."

"Just in case it wasn't an accident."

"Premier Pierlenko is aware that an incident resulting from these coincidental deaths could jeopardize the very fragile ties he's made with the United States since assuming office."

"Christ, you sound like you work for the Kremlin."

Rand walked back to his desk. "All I can say is thank God you're not sitting in this seat anymore."

"Amen to that," Starcher said. His years as the CIA Head of Station in Moscow had been the most boring of his career. Until the incident in Cuba. Cuba had made up for everything. Single-handedly he had squelched Kadar's plot to make the United States look as if it were provoking war with the Russians.

Almost single-handedly. He'd used an agent on the mission, one extraordinary agent who'd saved Starcher's hide more times than either of them could remember. As a result, the Premier of the Soviet Union had been ousted from office in disgrace and the entire KGB reorganized.

And the agent?

He'd disappeared then, almost as if he'd never existed. Starcher had looked for him, checked all his sources and contacts, but never could pick up a trail. The old man hadn't held much hope of finding him. When the Grandmaster wanted to leave, he left.

"What's that supposed to mean?"

Starcher blinked, surprised that he'd let his mind wander so completely.

" 'Amen to that?' " Rand reminded him.

"It means I don't feel like being murdered by a KGB agent while I'm kissing his ass," Starcher said.

"You've got a KGB fixation."

"Actually it's not a bad thing to have when you're surrounded by Russkies. You might remember that."

"I guess you've decided that the KGB is behind all these killings. That they've got some secret reason to be knocking off students, journalists, even tourists," Rand said sarcastically.

"What I've decided is that this is a slave state, Rand, and not a lot happens that the government doesn't want to happen. I'm just here to find out the details."

"Pierlenko swears the KGB isn't involved with the killings," Rand said quietly.

"And you believe him?"

"Yes, I do," the tall Californian snapped. "The Russians don't want war with us. Not over something like this."

Starcher puffed on his cigar. As much as he hated to admit it, Rand was right about that. The Soviets wouldn't incite outright war.

"Pierlenko's practically on his knees with the President," Rand said. "They're willing to do anything they can to help find out who's behind the American deaths. They even offered the use of some KGB resources."

"The Company's stupid sometimes," Starcher said, "but they're not so stupid that they're going to take the Russkies' word that their hands are clean."

"Stop calling them Russkies," Rand snapped. "How the hell did you ever get into this line of work?"

Starcher leaned back in his chair. "I'll tell you, son. I got into it back in the old days when America used to stand up for itself."

"Well, these days—" Rand cut himself off with an angry slash of his arm. "Forget it," he snapped. "I'm not going to get into a debate on international détente with some redneck fossil from Alabama."

"Virginia," Starcher corrected.

Rand looked at his watch. "If your cover's been blown, you'd better clear out before you drag the rest of us down," he said. "We can't risk having someone like you caught."

"I'm here on special assignment. You can't send me back without orders."

"I'll get orders, believe me," Rand said crisply. "There's no longer any place in international affairs for your kind of Wild West antics." He looked up, appearing paler than usual. "By the way, what were you doing at the circus in the first place?"

"I had to talk to an agent."

"What agent?"

"Someone I recruited myself."

"In three days?"

Starcher winked. "I work fast."

"Who is he?" Rand picked up a pencil.

The old man blew a lazy smoke ring to the ceiling. "You know, I don't believe I'm going to tell you that, boy."

"That's—that's absurd," Rand sputtered. "I'm Head of Station here."

"That's a fact. But if you're going to fire me, you sure as hell aren't going to get my agent."

Rand slammed the pencil on the desk. "My new assistant will be here by the end of the week. When he arrives, he'll have your orders of dismissal with him. *And* orders for you to turn over your operative to us."

Starcher stood up and ground the butt of his cigar into Rand's antique candy dish.

"A lot can happen in a week," he said.

CHAPTER THREE

Andrew Starcher walked briskly past the skaters in Gorky Park, pulling his hooded jacket tightly around him. The breath of the shouting and laughing ice skaters hung in a cloudlike haze, making an impressionistic blur of brightly colored clothing as the skaters moved about the rink to the strains of music from *Swan Lake*.

Passing a green bench with one wooden back slat missing, Starcher took a piece of blue chalk from his pocket and drew a long slash across its back. His action went unnoticed, and Starcher moved on without breaking stride.

Beyond the rink were the tables. Even in the early-morning cold the chess players gathered in a small crowd. They were old men, mostly, smoking and absently rubbing their gloved fingers for warmth between passes at a bottle of vodka, their rheumy eyes focused intently on the games before them.

Starcher stood for a while with a group of bystanders who stopped and stamped their feet for a few moments, watching a move or two. He then strolled casually toward a metal trash basket, wiped his shoe with a piece of blue paper he took from his pocket, and tossed the paper into the basket. A corner of it had been carefully folded before Starcher crumpled the paper into a ball. The number 3118 was written in the folded corner. The thirty-first of the month, tomorrow. Eighteen hundred hours. Six P.M. The blue paper signified the place, the Blue Mermaid Bar near Sokolniki Park in the northeast corner of the city. A crude way to arrange a meeting, but he had failed to make direct contact at the circus the previous night.

The blue paper was a rudimentary device, but the agent was young and inexperienced and Starcher didn't want to overwhelm a newcomer with the craft of the trade. Young agents with talent and nerve were hard to find.

But easy to destroy, he thought as he sat down at an empty table facing the wastebasket. He wondered why his first attempt at setting up a meeting hadn't worked. It might just be, he thought sadly, that his operative had been compromised.

He checked his watch. He would wait exactly one hour to see if anyone showed up to retrieve the message. Settling in, he took a shabby plastic chessboard from inside his wool jacket, set it up on the stone table, and weighted down the corners with four stones. Then he took the thirty-two chess pieces from a cloth folded inside his pocket and arranged them slowly on the board, giving himself the first-move advantage of white.

Not that it mattered. Starcher was such a mediocre player that anyone but the most uninspired *patzer* could beat him. Losing suited his purpose, though. If he were any better, the game might get interesting, and then he might take his eyes off the wastebasket.

As he arranged the pieces a young bearded man broke away from the group of onlookers and sat down opposite Starcher.

The young man wasn't a very good player, either, and the game absorbed little of Starcher's concentration. When the young man passed him a flask of vodka, Starcher refused it.

Within forty minutes he saw the girl. She was walking from the ice rink, her skates slung across her shoulder. A passerby called out a flirtatious greeting but otherwise she was left alone.

Remarkable, Starcher thought. When Sasha Kaminskaya traveled as the star of the Russian State Circus, she attracted the kind of crowds usually reserved for Western movie stars. But without makeup, her blond hair pulled into a sloppy ponytail, she resembled just another student or factory worker. Her cloth jacket was open, showing a bulky fisherman's sweater in need of a cleaning. On her feet were a pair of leather boots, worn to the point of shabbiness.

She's not vain, Starcher thought approvingly, and she's got some courage. A lot of new agents who were contemplating a first assignment might have skipped the rendezvous after the previous night's killing at the circus. But this one was different. While the fracas at the circus was going on, La Kaminskaya hadn't even flinched.

This one had real potential.

Sasha Kaminskaya stopped at the wastebasket, took a piece of chewing gum from her mouth, and stuck it onto the crumpled wad of blue paper she fished from the basket. As the bearded youth moved his king's knight in a dramatic but suicidal play, Starcher saw Sasha tear off the corner of the paper containing the time of their next meeting and roll it absently between her fingers.

Real potential. If she can live long enough to realize it.

Starcher looked back at the chessboard, then captured the young man's knight with his queen, simultaneously placing the man's king in check. The young man shook his head good-naturedly and rose to leave, then stood grinning as a young woman bounced quickly into the vacant seat opposite the old man.

Starcher was already putting the chess pieces away. "I'm sorry," he began in Russian, then noticed the blond ponytail. He scowled at her. Sasha's pale gray eyes registered nothing in response.

"I'm finished here," Starcher said curtly.

"Good," the young man with the beard said, and

smiled at Sasha. "Now you can go and have a vodka with me."

"Drinking in the daytime is frowned upon," she said sternly.

"What are you? The Commissar of Sobriety?" the man asked.

"Just someone who does not want to be pestered by you," Sasha said.

"I don't know," Starcher said vaguely. "A pretty girl like you must have many men following you." He looked sharply at her eyes.

"No one is following me," she said as she met Starcher's gaze. She reached forward and touched his hand. "Just one game," she said.

"Go on, old one," the young bearded man said. "Maybe you've met your match."

Starcher looked at him with disgust, then at the girl. At this point, he realized, he would draw more attention by leaving than by playing. "Do you even know how to play, little girl?" he asked rudely as he set the pieces up again.

He would talk with her later about the importance of discretion. But for now he would content himself with humiliating her.

He opened with the King's Gambit, quickly expanding it into a full-fledged Muzio Gambit and sacrificing his knight in a crushing attack. It was the only flashy opening Starcher knew, the one taught to him by the best chess player he'd ever seen, maybe the best who had ever lived. Starcher didn't know enough about the opening for it to have any effect against a really good opponent, but it usually sufficed to have beginners tripping over their own pieces.

He advanced his queen to a strong attacking position. Sasha smiled and moved a pawn. Starcher snapped his queen down onto the board, capturing one of her rooks.

"Through?" he asked rather arrogantly, beginning to rise. Then he saw Sasha's eyes lift from the board, cold gray eyes with a killer's certainty in them.

"Mate in five," she said.

There was a dim murmur from the few assembled spectators. Starcher was clearly confused, and the woman explained the next five moves.

"She's right," the bearded man shouted. The small crowd let out a chilly whoop.

Starcher stared at the pieces. Astonishing, he thought. A lucky find? A trick?

Or had he found another Grandmaster?

He swallowed his urge to blurt out a thousand questions. Where had she learned to play like this? Did she play in tournaments? Had she ever met . . . *him*?

"You keep the pieces," he said quietly, then got up and started away. The spectators cheered. No one followed him.

Another one.

Starcher felt as if he had just been thrust into a recurring nightmare. There had been another chess player once, a new agent like Sasha. Starcher had recruited the Grandmaster, trained him, used him . . . and then lost him.

During his brief time with the Company, legends had grown about the Grandmaster. He was unkillable, they said, almost superhuman. The Russians thought he was a demon straight from hell. And some actually believed he was the reincarnation of some Eastern mountain god. Starcher had heard all the stories. Alternately he had believed them all, or thought them all hogwash. To this day he still didn't know what he believed.

Not that it mattered anymore. The Grandmaster was gone now, probably long dead. He'd had demons inside him that only death could exorcise. A man like that never lived long. To take such a man as a son was to waste one's heart.

Still, Starcher had felt a recognition, a chilling sense of déjà vu when the girl raised her eyes in victory.

He turned up the collar of his coat. Foolishness, he decided. In his old age, Starcher was beginning to cling to his recruits as if they were the children he had never had time to sire in his youth.

It was a dangerous road, he knew. Controls couldn't afford to become too fond of their agents. The sense of loss when the young men and women died, as they often did, was just too great.

Forget it, he told himself. Just forget it. A lot of people played chess, after all, especially in Russia. And almost anyone who knew the game could flatten Starcher in twenty moves. Sasha's ability was just another talent among many—nothing more, nothing less. She would make a good agent. Maybe she would live long enough to retire and marry a rich banker in Switzerland or the United States.

Starcher exhaled a cloud of steam into the morning sunshine. He felt cold.

CHAPTER FOUR
ALEXANDER ZHARKOV

Bells.

Alexander Zharkov awakened slowly. The tinkling of the tiny bells came and went like half-formed memories. It seemed he had heard them before, in some fantastic, otherworldly place, a palace in the mountains. . . .

The image receded. It was replaced by a jumble of vague recollections, or murmuring voices and acrid smoke and the sensation of being moved when all he'd wanted to do was to rest and die. And always, the pain. It was constant and universal. The throbbing in his face was excruciating. The searing stabs in his hands, the ache in his legs, and the blistering heat in his back were all unbearable. It was all the same.

It had occurred to Zharkov more than once during brief moments of lucidity that he had indeed died and was now suffering the eternal torment of hell. Oddly, though, he felt no pain now. The ringing of the bells grew louder and more fixed. Yes, it was the present, and this was no dream.

He opened his eyes a crack. The room was dark, but even the small amount of moonlight that filtered through the slits in the stone-and-mud wall hurt them. He forced his eyes to work, and after the tears cleared, the bells came into focus.

Tiny silver bells, dozens of them, quivering against a bosom covered by a black apron. Below the bells was a wide, embroidered waistband of brilliant red; above them, a yoke of silver three inches wide, worked with elaborate designs and overlaid with thick ropes of silver.

The woman's face, flat and dark with the Mongol features of Central Asia, remained impassive as she worked, skillfully easing a blanket under Zharkov's naked body. Briefly her eyes met his. She stared in astonishment at seeing him awake and shouted something in a Chinese dialect.

Several other women adorned with equal richness rushed over, clasping their hands together or delicately covering their mouths while they exclaimed over him.

Alexander Zharkov's eyes slowly adjusted to consciousness. The room he was in was constructed of stone, with a roof of slats covered with dried gorse.

"*Chto . . . chto . . .*" he said, stammering. His voice rasped with the effort of speech. He swallowed, tasting the bitterness in his mouth. "What is this place? How long have I been here?" he asked in Russian.

The women chattered excitedly to each other but did not answer him. The oldest, the one who had been caring for him, signaled for him to wait. Brushing her hands on her apron, she snapped some sort of instructions to the others and hurried out of the hut. The remaining women, now noticeably subdued, glided efficiently around the hut, murmuring softly as they put the place in order.

The older woman returned, bowing at the squat doorway. The others did likewise, and Zharkov half sat up on his straw bed, peering through the darkness at the opening.

A man walked in, thin and very old, stooping slightly but with an air of authority about him. He was dressed entirely in black from his wrapped head to his cloth shoes. Wound around his waist was a silk rope from which hung a magnificently wrought sword with a blade as wide as the span of a man's hand.

The women in the hut bowed to him in silence. The old man flicked his wrist toward them, and they scurried out. He never spoke or looked at them. His gaze, respectful but intense, was trained on Zharkov.

Once the women were gone, he spoke, then waited for a reply. Zharkov shook his head, indicating he did not understand the man's language, but something about the words seemed familiar. It had not been the same tongue the women had been speaking. Zharkov looked up, puzzled.

"Do you require?" the old man repeated, and Zharkov understood. The man was speaking English.

Extraordinary, he thought. Wherever he was, it seemed far removed from the West. Why English here?

The old man said again, "Do you require?" and Zharkov answered in halting English.

"Water, please," he said.

The old man brought a ladle from a wooden bucket and held it to his lips. "The women will bring food when you are able to eat," he said. "Your body is not now accustomed to solid food."

"How long?" Zharkov croaked.

"You have been with us for two years."

Zharkov was stunned. "Two years," he said in Russian. The old man clearly did not understand him.

What had he been doing for two years?

"Where is this place?"

"Ghizou," the old man said. "You are in the valley of the Gi people."

"Ghizou? In China?" He strained to remember.

"You were brought here by the traveling ones, the Kazaks. They recognized you, Holy One. They saw your mark and brought you here. You have many followers in this village."

Zharkov blinked in incomprehension.

"Rest now, Patanjali. There is time for explanation when you are stronger."

"Patanjali," Zharkov whispered. It was a name he

knew. Not his name but another's, lost somewhere in the confusion of his long sickness, and the mere sound of it filled him with an inexplicable terror.

"Who is—" he began.

"Hail to Thee, O Wearer of the Blue Hat," the old man intoned.

Zharkov sat bolt upright.

His brain felt as if it were on fire. He coughed, and a cold sweat broke out over him. The old man was quick with his hands, gently pressing Zharkov back onto the straw.

"No more talk," he muttered. "You must rest now, Hallowed One. Rest."

Zharkov lay back, his eyes closing almost involuntarily.

When he awoke, it was nearing dawn. One woman remained in the hut with him, dozing on a stool propped against a stone wall.

He was thirsty and ravenous. He swung his legs over the side of the raised cot and sat crouched until his dizziness subsided. He was naked beneath his blankets, he noticed, and the straw on which he lay smelled foul.

Had it really been two years? Two years since his eyes had last opened to daylight? What had gone on before those two lost years?

He knew his own name. He was Alexander Zharkov. That was a start. And he was a soldier. A soldier, a Russian, an aristocrat of sorts. A man's face came to mind. His father, perhaps. His father had been an intelligent man, one respected by his peers. Then that face faded and was replaced by others, old and young and women, and one recurring face, too, that Zharkov tried to push from his mind. The face of a man with eyes like blue ice that looked up from over a chessboard . . .

Hail to Thee, O Wearer of the Blue Hat.

Zharkov clutched his head and rocked with the pain. No, he wouldn't think of the past now. There would be time later to sort the memories from the dreams.

He shivered with the cold. Wrapping a blanket around his shoulders, he stood and teetered toward a wooden water bucket in a corner. He was so weak that he had to hold the ladle with both hands. The water was cold and sweet. Zharkov drank, then spilled the rest over his face and chest.

The woman who was dozing against the wall cried out behind him. When he turned, she was kneeling with her forehead touching the floor.

Zharkov thought of how he must look, dripping wet and stark naked except for a filthy blanket wound like a cloak around him, holding a wooden ladle like a scepter. He burst out laughing.

Who do they think I am?

Hail to Thee . . .

He dropped the ladle. Stooping to pick it up, he noticed his arm for the first time. It was a mass of scars, white and shiny and twisted, like living serpents. The other was the same, as were his legs. There was no hair on them.

Burns, he thought. An image came to mind, of flames and rock as hot as metal, of falling, falling into fire, with blackened bodies all around him, stinking and sizzling in their own juices. A descent into hell, horrifying and painful. And then nothing . . .

Hail to Thee . . .

He shouted a curse, willing the pictures away.

Covering her mouth in alarm, the woman scrambled to her feet. Then she reached behind her for a black bundle, laid it at his feet, and backed out the door.

Zharkov examined the gift. It was clothing, a loose-fitting tunic, and a pair of trousers woven of coarse cloth. They were ludicrously small on him, but at least they were a step toward civilization.

He began to organize his thoughts. First he needed to find out exactly where he was. From there he would have to find his way back to Moscow. Somehow he knew that Moscow was home, although he had no idea what he had done there.

But that would come later. His mind was not impaired; he seemed to be able to remember most things if he concentrated. It was just the concentration that was difficult. Two years without disciplined thought was a long time.

A Russian word popped into his mind unbidden. *Nichevo.*

Nichevo, he thought. *Who cares?* What an odd thing to think of.

Nichevo.

It was on his lips when he slept.

The old villager with the kingly sword came every day for weeks as Zharkov's strength gradually returned. Often they did not speak at all. But always the man bowed in obeisance to Zharkov.

He came one morning carrying a small, cloth-wrapped package.

"Thank you for the clothing," Zharkov said, remembering to speak English.

"They are only the humble garments of the village. Your own were destroyed in the fire." He paused for a moment, watching the Russian's face, as if for a sign of remembrance. When there was none, he went on. "The Kazaks who brought you to us found nothing near you except for this." He unwrapped the bundle carefully and handed it to Zharkov.

Zharkov studied it for a moment, afraid to touch the gleaming thing buried in the folds of cloth. At last he picked it up. It was the silver hilt of a sword.

"I don't remember this," he said.

"Perhaps it is not yours. The Kazaks found it on the ground next to you, outside the burning wreckage of a building."

"Where? Where did they find me?"

"To the west," the old man said. "In the high mountains, far from the normal route of the Kazaks. They were searching for some missing animals and came across the blaze in an old abbey."

Zharkov walked outside and looked around him. The hut was perched on a small knoll above the rest of the village. Below, a cluster of gray-brown mud huts were separated by walkways of hand-cut stone. Beyond were the distant, misty peaks of the Himalayas.

He looked at the broken sword hilt in his hand.

And somewhere, deep in the recesses of his memory, a bell faintly tinkled.

Zharkov stood alone on the hill for a long time, clutching the hilt of the sword. He had no idea how he had obtained it. The events before the fire had been so bizarre that it did no good to remember them. It would be like remembering a dream. The recollection, no matter how vivid, would not make the dream real.

And yet so much of it had seemed real. There had been a woman in those mountains, powerful and ageless, who had shown him his destiny in the form of a man: a man born on the same hour of the same day of the same year as himself, a man with eyes like blue ice whose life was inextricably entwined with his own.

A man known as Grandmaster.

The Grandmaster was the reason he had been spared in the fire. The Grandmaster's death was the reason he lived. Zharkov had agreed long ago to kill the man with the ice-blue eyes, but his mission had been clear even before that. In the dim places of his soul, forged long before his birth or the birth of his father or grandfather, the Grandmaster had been waiting for him.

He *was* the Grandmaster, yet his opposite. There were two different bodies, two different minds, but one spirit between them.

He closed his eyes. Inside him he felt the first primal splitting of that spirit into two parts. Into one flowed the white light of creation; into the other, the darkness of chaos.

Zharkov felt the darkness enfold him like a cloak. He was no more evil than most men of power. He was a creature of reason. And yet the night flowed through him with his blood, urging him toward only one goal.

Kill the Grandmaster.

His reason fought back: To destroy half the spirit would destroy the whole. He, too, would die. But the ancient voices were stronger than his own, and the Grandmaster's scent haunted him like the blood of prey haunted a tiger.

The Grandmaster would die.

Zharkov dropped the silver sword hilt to the ground.

CHAPTER FIVE

On the night of the full moon the headman ordered a feast prepared in Zharkov's honor. It was held in the largest of the stone huts, crammed to bursting with the small brown men and women of the village, their faces all but obscured by their elaborate silver headdresses and collars.

By torchlight, the hut resembled the treasure room of an ancient king, the silver shimmering on the women's bosoms as they moved around him.

They served *zimeifan,* a platter of sticky white and yellow rice, and an aromatic, cooked salamander the size of a large dog, called *wawayu.* The salamander was served whole, and its face, round and smooth, resembled a human baby's. With his sword the old headman of the village hacked into the pulpy flesh at the neck, and the creature's juices flowed out of it in a stream.

The headman wiped the sword and replaced it in his silken belt, then handed Zharkov a cup of steaming tea on which floated a mound of yellow, melting grease.

"Yak butter," the old man said, pressing it on Zharkov. "Drink. It fortifies."

A woman slapped a slab of the salamander flesh into a bowl along with some of the rice and placed it in front of

Zharkov. His eyes slid toward the hacked carcass of the baby-faced animal.

"The *wawayu* is a rare delicacy," the headman said, watching him.

Zharkov picked up a morsel with his fingers and ate. It was delicious. The taste of meat almost made him feel drunk. He gorged himself while the old man looked on approvingly.

"That is the sign that you are well," the headman said. "Tomorrow we will make sacrifice to the gods for delivering you, Holy One."

Zharkov wiped the grease from his chin with the back of his hand. "Why do you call me that?" he snapped, suddenly angry.

"Because . . . you are. I meant no disrespect."

"And why do you speak to me in English?"

The noise in the room faded.

"But that is your tongue," the old man said, wide-eyed. "So we have been given to understand."

"What do you understand?"

The headman looked to the other villagers, then back at Zharkov. "That the living god, the reincarnation of Brahma, is a man from the West," he said in a whisper. "His title is Patanjali, and he bears the sign of the coiled snake."

With tentative fingers the old man reached across and touched the base of Zharkov's throat. "The Kazaks who found you did not know your face. But they saw the coiled snake and brought you to us." He smiled kindly. "Many from our village have followed the Patanjali in spirit. The holy men, they have often gone into the mountains to seek you. But it was you who came to us. For it *is* you, Holy One. You bear the sign."

Zharkov touched the spot where the old man's fingers had been, and the final pebble dropped into the sealed pool of his memory. Suddenly it overflowed and poured into the present. The coiled snake was a scar burned indelibly into the flesh of his throat long ago by the man these simple people had mistaken him for.

It had not been a dream, after all. It had never been a dream. There *was* a man called Patanjali, called Holy One, called Wearer of the Blue Hat, the incarnation of a god, a man with eyes like blue ice, whose destiny it was to die by Zharkov's hand. A man called Grandmaster.

At that moment Zharkov knew what he had to do. He waited through the evening until the last of the villagers had staggered drunkenly to their huts. Then he sat, along with the headman, and pieced together a rough map of the area extending from the village west to Katmandu.

"The city in the sky," the headman said. "The Kazaks speak of it. This Katmandu, then, is your home?"

Zharkov was too preoccupied to answer. There were plans to be made. And behind every movement, every thought, the image of the Grandmaster burned in Zharkov's mind like a fever.

"I will need guides and provisions," he said.

"I will take you to the city in the sky myself, Holy One. With four others and animals for travel. You will arrive safely."

"And money," Zharkov said.

The headman looked at him, puzzled.

"Silver. Two animals loaded with silver."

"But the silver is the treasure of the village," the headman protested. "It has been with us for a thousand years."

"Bring the silver," Zharkov snapped. "Patanjali demands it. You question the Wearer of the Blue Hat?"

The old man bowed to him.

They left the next morning. It took the six men eight days to reach the pass leading through the Himalayas to Katmandu. In the distance they could see the scattered thatched-roof houses of the hill tribes clustered along the shores of a mirror-still lake. Below stretched the carnival panorama of the city in the sky.

"We stop here," Zharkov said.

"But we have nearly—"

"Don't question me!"

The men made camp. Zharkov watched the headman's face as he helped gather the sticks and brush for the fire. The old man no longer smiled at Zharkov or even met his eyes. Ever since Zharkov had sold the silver for currency, the wrinkled old crone had gone about with a stooped and guilty air.

And why not? Zharkov reasoned. The fool had given up the only treasures of his village to appease some despotic deity. The great irony of it all was that the simpletons had chosen to worship the wrong man.

The sun was setting in a spectacular rainbow over the white peaks of the Himalayas. The headman carefully removed the sword from his belt and laid it beside him before curling up on his pallet to sleep.

Zharkov sat stock-still, eyes blinking slowly from time to time. The other men ate, then slept. Zharkov did not move.

The moon rose, full and white. The fire smoldered to nothing. Zharkov's eyes adjusted to the darkness. He rose and walked up to the headman.

"Idiot savage," he said softly. Then, striking like a snake, he smashed his heel into the old man's throat. The old man's eyes opened and fixed on him. The gnarled hands twitched, as if grasping some invisible and slippery object in the air. The feet thrashed, but by then Zharkov had already picked up the headman's sword and thrust it into the heart of one of the other men.

He moved swiftly, killing with smooth, long strokes. In the end there was no sound.

He left the sword with the bodies and walked toward Katmandu. Passing the lake, he knelt and drank deeply from its cool waters. The air was cold, but Zharkov was perspiring heavily. In the still blackness of the lake the moon shimmered like a pearl. He thrust his hands into the water and the pearl dissolved.

Back to the world of men, he thought. The prospect excited him, as the killing had. He was a soldier. Two years away from moving, real time had been too long. He hungered for his life.

And he hungered for something else. As he'd recovered, the face of the Grandmaster had crystallized in his mind until it was always there, behind every thought, hovering above every image his eyes took in. He was no longer afraid of his destiny. The voices inside him had welled up and spilled over until their song filled him.

He had only one reason to live now. He would find the Grandmaster. The time was coming.

The last drops of water trembled off his fingers, and the surface of the lake was still again. The moon returned, round and perfect.

Zharkov froze. There was something else in the lake, a sight so grotesque that he had to swallow the bile that rose in his throat.

"No," he whispered.

But he was a soldier, a Russian, a man of power, and he knew what was true. There was a gargoyle in the lake, and its face belonged to him.

He slowly moved his hands over his face. Ridges on ridges of scar tissue appeared in the water. The face he saw was disfigured beyond recognition.

Like the dream, the fire he remembered had been real. He could feel the flames again melting his flesh as the Grandmaster watched him burn.

"My God," he cried, covering his eyes so that he did not have to see the reflection of his monster's face.

Some wild dogs, attracted by the scent of blood, skittered into the brush, and the sound of his voice faded to nothing.

CHAPTER SIX
THE PREMIER

Sergei Ostrakov was a big man with the dull eyes of a beast. He had once been a military man, and his bulk had once been muscle. A civilian now, the muscle had softened to fat that spilled over the creaking wooden kitchen chair.

His wife, Svetlana, set a bowl of cabbage and boiled potatoes in front of him. Ostrakov was waiting, his fork clasped in his fist like a dagger, his vacant eyes staring down at a stain in the tattered tablecloth. He ate quickly and noisily, slurping the juice from the bottom of the bowl when he was finished.

There was a knock at the door, three sharp raps, officious and clear. Svetlana smoothed back her hair and opened the door. Two uniformed KGB officers stood at attention.

"Comrade Sergei Ostrakov," one of the men demanded without looking at her.

Ostrakov placed the towel on the table. "I am Comrade Ostrakov."

"We are instructed to escort you to the Kremlin. Please ready yourself."

Svetlana Ostrakov looked wildly from the two men to her husband. "Lubyanka?" she squealed, knowing "Kremlin" only as a euphemism for the prison attached to the nearby KGB headquarters. "But he has done nothing to warrant arrest."

"Shut up," Ostrakov said, and for a moment his military background showed. "I wish to know the purpose of this summons."

The military man straightened. "Your presence has been requested personally by Comrade Premier Nikolai Pierlenko, General Secretary of the Soviet Union," he said. "You are urged to come immediately."

Svetlana's mouth dropped open. "The Premier?" she whispered.

Ostrakov's hands trembled momentarily before he rushed into their small bedroom to dress.

The two KGB men led the bewildered Ostrakov through one of the unadorned side entrances to the Kremlin's Council of Ministers building and proceeded down a damp stairway into a section of white cinder blocks. It was not exactly a presidential welcome, Ostrakov noted, but neither was it the route prisoners followed when taken to Lubyanka. That was almost a mile away. While an underground passage connected the two buildings, prisoners were normally driven right up to the main entrance of Lubyanka.

They stopped in front of a white door with a wired glass window. Behind the door Ostrakov could make out rows of metal tables over which men and women dressed in operating scrubs hovered. There was no sign near the door, but as soon as it opened, Ostrakov knew from the smell that the room was a morgue. For a fleeting moment he had the terrible feeling that he had been brought here to be cut up in some bestial medical experiment.

One of his escorts pulled a paper from his coat and flashed it to an orderly, who shambled toward a bank of large metal drawers. He pulled one open and walked away without a word.

"Can you identify this person?" the KGB man asked.

Ostrakov blinked at the blue-white corpse. There were bruises at the throat, an expert blow expertly aimed.

"I—I think so," he stammered, his voice sounding his confusion.

"The name, please."

"Bulenski. Ivan Bulenski."

The KGB man scrutinized the papers in his hand.

"You are certain?"

Ostrakov swallowed. "Yes. He used to work under me."

With a snap the military man stuffed the paper back into his jacket. "You will follow, please."

They went out of the morgue and into what seemed like miles of corridors and stairways. The walls changed from cinder block to plaster to paneled mahogany lined with armed guards. At last they deposited him in a large carpeted anteroom, overseen by a steely middle-aged woman in uniform with whom they exchanged a few words.

"You will wait here," the KGB man said. "Good day, Comrade." The two of them inclined their heads briefly to him, then left.

The middle-aged woman did not acknowledge his presence for nearly an hour. Then a buzzer on her desk sounded and she approached him.

"Ostrakov?"

He nodded.

"The Premier will see you now."

He took a deep breath and rose, walking stiffly toward the huge carved door.

This was not the first time he had entered the Premier's office. During the previous administration Ostrakov had become, if not a confidant, at least an occasional visitor to the sanctum of Pierlenko's predecessor, Konstantin Kadar.

That association had cost him his career. At the end, his twenty-six years of service, his citations for military bravery, and his loyalty to the Party had meant nothing. On a mission in Cuba he had followed Kadar's orders.

When the failure of that mission toppled the Premier, everyone around him fell with him.

Kadar, of course, had escaped the Götterdämmerung intact, except for the disgrace of being ousted from the highest office in the land. He lived in exile in a large dacha on the Black Sea, along with his horses and the memoirs he would never be permitted to publish.

The fate of his staff had not been so tidy. There had been suicides, trials for treason, and exile to remote locales. There were a lot of men, like Ostrakov, who were simply dismissed from consciousness. He had been lucky; many had just disappeared.

On his return from Cuba two years before, Ostrakov had found his apartment locked and nailed shut. The price for reclaiming his family's clothing and personal possessions had been his signed confession for "conduct incompatible with the interests of the State" and a subsequent dishonorable discharge. His summer house and car had been confiscated, his son expelled from the university, his wife's shopping privileges revoked. At forty-eight, Ostrakov would never work again.

Such had been the price for entering the room behind the carved mahogany door.

CHAPTER SEVEN

Nikolai Pierlenko and Konstantin Kadar could not have been more different. Kadar exuded a kind of saturnine austerity; Pierlenko, on the other hand, was vigorous, well dressed, and physical. He smiled with ease as Ostrakov entered, and even rose to shake his hand.

"Welcome, Comrade. I am sorry to hear that things are not as well for you as they might be."

It occurred to Ostrakov that Pierlenko was directly responsible for his misery, but he said only, "Thank you, Comrade General Secretary. It is an honor to offer whatever service I may."

"Very good," Pierlenko said, touching the big man's shoulder. "Sit down, please. Cigarette?" He offered him an English Oval. Ostrakov accepted it as if the cigarette were made of gold. He could no longer afford cigarettes, and when his son bought him a pack, they were usually the cheap, strawlike Bulgarian *Shipkas*.

Pierlenko lit it for him and sat beside him on the leather sofa. He said nothing for a long moment but only looked, smiling, into Ostrakov's eyes.

Ostrakov squirmed in his seat. Unnerved by the closeness of the man, his only thought was that he should have washed before coming.

"So," Pierlenko said finally, "I fear that in their zeal to rid our government of corruption two years ago, the Russian people may have thrown out some good apples along with the bad. What do you think, Comrade?"

Ostrakov stubbed out the cigarette, although he had hardly smoked it. "I have always been loyal to my country, sir," he said. "I am . . . was . . . a soldier." He waffled. Words had never come easily to him. He couldn't think of any now to fill up the silence.

But despite the absence of a glib tongue, Ostrakov kept his wits. He noticed how smoothly Pierlenko had shifted the blame for Ostrakov's humiliation from himself to the uncomplaining shoulders of "the Russian people." That squared with what Ostrakov had heard about the Premier—that he was basically a soft man, too willing to compromise, too ready to deal with the West. For the last two years Ostrakov had been far from the seat of power, but he had heard that Pierlenko still had not gained firm control of the Politburo. Unless it was held in firm check, the twelve-member Soviet cabinet-parliament could thwart any Premier's will.

"Yes, I understand," Pierlenko said. "You have a good record. Spotless, except for . . ." The General Secretary smiled again. "Suppose you tell me yourself what happened in Cuba."

Ostrakov felt his face growing damp. "I only followed orders. . . ."

"Which were?"

Ostrakov looked around the room, a reflex. "We were assigned to back up . . . another group."

"Another branch of KGB?"

Ostrakov smiled at the floor. The pack of English Ovals came into his view. He knew there was no point in lying to this man. Pierlenko had already broken him. It would only be a matter of a telephone call, a memorandum, to destroy Ostrakov and his family completely. Without asking permission, he took a cigarette with hands shaking so badly, he could barely hold it. He said only one word.

"Nichevo."

"I beg your pardon?" the Premier said, looking mildly shocked. *Nichevo* was a slang expression that translated roughly into "What the hell" or "Who cares?"

"Nichevo was a personal organization of the Premier, sir."

"Which Premier?" Pierlenko asked, now wearing an expression of amused tolerance. "Kadar?"

"All of them, sir. All of them since Stalin. Stalin named it Nichevo, sir. As a joke. But this Nichevo is no joke."

"That's preposterous," Pierlenko said. He stood up. "How can there be an organization called Nichevo when no one's ever heard of it? *I've* never heard of it."

"It was a secret organization, sir," Ostrakov said.

"Obviously very secret," Pierlenko replied sarcastically.

"Yes, sir."

"If this Nichevo exists, why did you never mention it during testimony about the Cuban affair?"

"I was never tried, sir," Ostrakov said softly.

Pierlenko exhaled noisily. "You were questioned?" he said, more as a statement than a query.

"Yes. But no one asked about Nichevo, Comrade General Secretary."

"And you didn't volunteer any information?"

"I answered every question truthfully," Ostrakov said.

Pierlenko walked to one of the room's metal-meshed windows and looked out over the city. "What exactly did this Nichevo do?" he asked without turning.

Ostrakov spoke respectfully to his back. "Anything, sir, from what I understand. Anything the Premier wanted."

"How many members?"

"I don't know. Their identities were unknown."

"Come, now. Where are its records?"

"I never saw any records, sir."

Pierlenko turned back and smiled. "Forgive my bluntness, Comrade, but this all sounds like an old wives' tale to me."

Ostrakov could think of nothing to say in response. He smoked in silence.

"What makes you think this Nichevo was involved in Cuba?"

"It was explained to me by Premier Kadar," Ostrakov said.

"The Premier himself?"

"Yes, sir."

"Your rank at the time was general, was it not?"

"Yes, sir."

"Why you?" Pierlenko said as he returned to Ostrakov's side on the soft leather sofa.

"I knew the man at the head of Nichevo. His name was Alexander Zharkov. We served in the Army together."

"And where is this Comrade Zharkov now?"

Ostrakov shifted in his seat. "Reports were that he died in Cuba. His body was washed out to sea."

"Did you see the body?"

"No, sir. I don't believe it was ever recovered."

Pierlenko lifted his head, appraising the fat man. "Surely you weren't the only individual in Russia who knew this Zharkov."

"No, sir."

"Then why did Kadar choose you?"

Ostrakov was silent for a long time. At last he spoke, his voice cracking. "I believe, sir, that Comrade Kadar knew that I would obey orders."

Pierlenko nodded slowly. "Assuming this Nichevo ever existed," he said, "who runs it now?"

"I don't know, sir."

"Where are its records?"

"I told you, sir, I never saw any records."

"If it had any records, what kind might it have?" Pierlenko asked. Ostrakov looked blank, and Pierlenko clapped him on the shoulder. For a split second Ostrakov shrank away, afraid of being struck. "Come, Comrade General," Pierlenko said. "You may speak freely with me."

Ostrakov swallowed hard. "I only heard rumors, sir," he said.

"The rumors, then."

"I heard that Nichevo collected much information about many people, information that they would not want others to know. I believe such information was useful at times to the Premier when he needed support."

"Are you saying blackmail?"

Ostrakov nodded.

"Who besides Zharkov belonged to this organization?"

"I don't know, sir. Some clerks . . . there was an office once. . . ."

"Not the clerks. The operatives."

"I never saw any operatives alive. Several of them were killed in Cuba. None of them had had any previous experience with the military or the KGB."

"I understand you recognized the man in the morgue. Was he Nichevo too?"

Ostrakov blinked. "I don't . . ."

"What was his name?"

"Ivan Bulenski. He served under me in the KGB."

"He was also in Cuba, this Bulenski?"

"He was, yes, sir."

"And afterward?"

"I don't know. I thought he might have died in Cuba."

"He has been missing for two years. Where do you think he was?" Pierlenko asked.

"I have no idea, Comrade General Secretary. We were not in contact."

"He had no papers on him when he died," Pierlenko said. When Ostrakov didn't answer, he pressed him again. "Was he Nichevo?"

"I don't think so, sir."

"Why not?"

"Zharkov disliked the KGB," Ostrakov said. "I don't think he would have used Bulenski."

"Did Zharkov dislike you?"

"Me? Yes."

"Why?"

Ostrakov shrugged. "Perhaps he knew that Premier Kadar wanted me to kill him."

The General Secretary stiffened. "When?"

"It was to have taken place after the mission in Cuba. Bulenski, the dead man, was to assist me."

"But why?" Pierlenko asked. "If Nichevo belonged to Kadar . . ."

"Alexander Zharkov was an independent man, sir. His own thirst for personal power was beginning to threaten the Premier. General Secrētary Kadar apparently thought his potential danger outweighed his possible value. Of course, I cannot speak for Comrade Kadar."

"What do you suppose would have happened if you had succeeded in killing Zharkov?"

"I don't know, sir."

"Could you have taken over Nichevo? Would its personnel have followed you?"

"I did not speculate, sir."

Pierlenko's features softened. "You are a soldier, I see."

The fat man's beast-eyes shone. "Yes, sir. A good soldier. Always."

"I will be speaking with you again," the Premier said, escorting Ostrakov to the door. "Meanwhile I advise you not to discuss the details of this meeting."

"I understand, sir."

Pierlenko pressed the packet of English Ovals into his hand. "Take these," he said. "And tell your wife to have your uniform cleaned. You may need it again."

An involuntary gasp of hope escaped from Ostrakov's lips.

"We'll see, we'll see," the Premier said, smiling.

"Yes, sir," Ostrakov said hoarsely. He straightened his shoulders, tucked in his chin. Then, standing with his back ramrod-stiff, he saluted.

CHAPTER EIGHT

Pierlenko paced in his office, occasionally rubbing the moisture off his hands.

Nichevo!

So the secret brigade was not simply a legend. The buffoon named Ostrakov confirmed everything. Konstantin Kadar had used it, then allowed the group to disappear when he fell from power.

The fool. Nichevo was the most important tool any head of state could possess. It was almost unthinkable: a small band of nameless, faceless men who knew all the secrets of everyone in power; a group that worked exclusively for the General Secretary of the Soviet Union and was entirely outside the influence of the Politburo, the Central Committee, the KGB, the military, the police, and international law. Astonishing.

The question was, where was Nichevo now? Its members, unknown to anyone except Alexander Zharkov, had vanished. The secret brigade had disappeared like mist in sunlight.

Or had it?

Pierlenko reconsidered. Konstantin Kadar was no fool. He had headed the KGB for nearly three decades before ascending to the highest office in the country. During his years there, the Soviet intelligence apparatus grew by more than half a million operatives, becoming the largest intelligence organization in the world.

Once in power as General Secretary, Kadar had used the KGB as if it were his personal property. With it he had ruled the Soviet Union with a despotic strength unknown since the days of Stalin.

As it was, despite his humiliating removal and exile, the common people still referred to Kadar as *Vozhd*, or "great leader," a title formerly reserved only for Lenin. Even among the elite at KGB headquarters, the nickname still frequently slipped out in conversation. Such lapses should have been censured, but since they occurred so often, the offender simply excused himself, as if he had belched at the dinner table, and the others kept quiet about it. Everyone knew that Konstantin Kadar would always be the *Vozhd*, regardless of who happened to be the Premier at the moment.

Pierlenko knew this and understood that there was nothing he could do to stop it. The knowledge made the questions even more puzzling. How could such a man have allowed something as priceless as Nichevo to slip through his fingers? Did it still exist? Did Kadar still control it? Was that dead man in the morgue one of its operatives?

And what of Alexander Zharkov? Pierlenko had heard of the man and of his father. The Zharkovs were an old, aristocratic family whose influence in government had begun before the reign of Peter the Great. It was one of the very few noble families to have survived the Revolution, and perhaps the only one in all of Russia to have retained its power, thanks to the remarkable intellect of Zharkov's father.

Vassily Vassilovitch Zharkov started Nichevo during the Stalin years and managed to maintain the organization's autonomy because of Stalin's paranoia. Stalin loved secrets; he doubtless found the existence of a secret army irresistible.

The elder Zharkov's own sense of secrecy was just as great. While he lived, he trained his son, Alexander, to take over Nichevo, so that no outsiders could know the real workings of the organization.

Alexander's brilliance outshone even his father's. A chess prodigy, he became the youngest man ever to attain the rank of colonel in the army during peacetime. When his father died, Zharkov was ready. Nichevo continued to operate seamlessly.

According to every report Pierlenko could gather on Zharkov, Nichevo was the central focus of his life. There was nothing else. Under these circumstances, would Zharkov have made absolutely no contingency plans in the event of his death?

There was only one answer Pierlenko could accept. Nichevo still existed.

Nikolai Pierlenko needed the organization now. For two years the Politburo had blocked all his attempts to breathe life into the Russian economy. Didn't these ossified cretins know that the economy was the engine that provided power for everything else? For the military, for foreign policy? Without a strong economy, a country would always be second-rate. Marx himself had said it.

But the Politburo had blocked him at every turn. They even tried to interfere with his attempts to warm up the uneasy relations with the West. Pierlenko had tried to convince the Politburo that closer contact with the West meant greater access to the West's technological secrets and was in Russia's best interests. Still they had fought the idea.

Nevertheless, Pierlenko had drawn closer to the United States. Now someone was endangering all his plans by killing Americans.

So Nichevo was a blackmail organization? Fine. He needed it. First to get those idiots in the Politburo in line, and second, to find out who was killing the Americans.

Alexander Zharkov was dead. All right, but Pierlenko could not believe that the Nichevo had just simply shriveled away. That was for textbooks in Marxist theory. Organizations in Russia never shriveled up and vanished. They endured forever in one form or another.

The man who had been killed the night before in the circus constituted another piece of evidence. He was a KGB man who had agreed to kill Alexander Zharkov for Kadar. When Bulenski was found the previous night, a killing wire was in his hands. And he had been missing ever since Kadar had fallen from power. Too many coincidences. Pierlenko did not believe in coincidences.

Nichevo must still be functioning.

And one man must know something about it.

Pierlenko pressed the buzzer on his telephone. "Get Sterlitz. Have him come over at once."

Konstantin Kadar should never have been permitted to live. Even in exile, under constant guard, he was a dangerous man. But now he was the only possible link to Nichevo. And he would tell what he knew.

Less than ten minutes later the intercom buzzed, and Maxim Sterlitz, the Director of the KGB, was announced.

"Send him in," Pierlenko said.

A tall, lank man, Hollywood handsome but possessing the cold, flat eyes of his profession, entered. Pierlenko did not greet him. "Bring former General Secretary Kadar here for questioning," he commanded. "I wish to see him alone first."

The tall man looked down at his hands.

"Well?"

"Comrade Premier, there has been some difficulty. Just this morning, actually no more than two hours ago . . ."

"He's not dead, is he?"

The KGB director steeled himself. "That is doubtful, sir. During the routine check this morning it was found . . . some things were not in order. The servants believed him to be asleep—"

"Where is Kadar?" the Premier snapped.

Sterlitz's skin was mottled with red blotches. He spoke as if he were ticking off items on an agenda. "The former Secretary is gone from his home, sir. There were tracks of horses near the cellar entrance. He could not have been alone at the time of his escape. Our men are actively seeking him at this time. Kidnapping has not been ruled out and—"

"You've lost him," Pierlenko hissed. He remained utterly motionless while he spoke.

The KGB Director had once been in the hills of Turkey on a hunting expedition. While climbing, he happened across a vulture sitting on a crag, chewing on the haunch of a small, dead animal, its foot dangling from the bird's mouth. Now, looking at the leader of the Soviet Union, he experienced exactly the same impression he'd had when he'd looked into the eyes of the vulture.

"Sir, it is only a matter of time," Sterlitz offered lamely.

"It is only a matter of time before he eludes you completely. You have held your post for two years. Kadar held it for thirty. Who do you think has the advantage?"

"With all due respect, sir, Comrade Kadar is an old man. And we have the necessary manpower—"

Pierlenko shoved him bodily. When he spoke again, his voice was barely audible. "Find him. Find him and bring him to me. Do you understand?"

"Yes, Comrade General Secretary," Sterlitz said, blanching, his hand already on the knob of the carved mahogany door.

After he left, Pierlenko thumped the wood with the heel of his hand. "Kadar," he muttered.

Kadar was the key. One way or another, Kadar would lead him to Nichevo.

CHAPTER NINE

A pair of screeching loons settled on the mirror-like surface of the lake. Zharkov rose unsteadily. His knees were muddied and cold, and he was hungry. By mid-morning someone would come across the bodies of the guides from Ghizou.

He shook himself like a dog. He had to get his bearings. The lake was the main landmark and he remembered it, but the configuration of the mud huts around it had changed with time. Years before, when he had set up the emergency station here on his way into the mountains, the area had not been so populated. *Bharral,* the Himalayan blue sheep of the region, had placidly grazed beside the fields of barley and wheat. The house with the two willow trees in front had stood like a beacon in the center of a ring of sloping mud huts. Now it was hidden somewhere among clusters of crude buildings.

For a moment Zharkov was seized with panic. What if the house was gone? A lot of time had passed, nearly twenty years. The climate here was not gentle. What if the family who owned the house had moved?

With aching legs he staggered toward the dwellings. There was a greater fear. What if his face was seen? No one would ever forget it. He shuddered, remembering the horrible visage staring up at him from the lake, the gargoyle head that belonged to him.

The first cluster of houses yielded nothing. At the next group he saw them, two willow trees growing so closely together that each was green on only one side.

After what seemed like hours of pounding, the door creaked open. A slatternly woman dressed in a filthy shift faced him. Her features were Mongolian, and her face was puffy with sleep. At the sight of him her eyes widened, and the corners of her mouth twitched with revulsion.

Zharkov said only one word. "Nichevo."

The woman's breath caught. Her hand fidgeted with the door, as if she were about to slam it in his face, but instead she opened it to him with sullen, downcast eyes.

Without a word she walked through the dirt-floored main room of the house to a smaller room in the rear, littered with junk of every variety: old Western-style chairs sprouting rusted springs, pieces of abandoned cars, a broken bamboo birdhouse, books, papers, even rocks. Methodically she began to clear away the debris from the center of the small room, revealing an old rug, threadbare but with the look of fine Indian weaving. This she pulled aside with a jerk, filling the room with dust.

When it settled, Zharkov could see, beneath the thick filth, the outline of a trapdoor. The woman wedged her fingers into the crack and pulled it up, revealing a stairway below. Not meeting Zharkov's eyes, she wiped her hands on the garments she wore and shambled away.

Zharkov felt his way along the slime-covered walls and down the cement stairs. The chatter of rats punctuated the silence as he groped for the table at the bottom. It was there, where his men had left it, along with a kerosene lamp and a box of matches in a rubber cylinder. He lit the lamp. Its light spread to a large metal box.

Zharkov felt his heart pounding as he lifted the case from the radio. It was still here! He pulled over a three-legged stool and sat in front of the machine, studying it.

It was not the same radio. But, of course, he thought,

it wouldn't be. Signals from a twenty-year-old system would be too easy to intercept. Nichevo took care of details like that without being told. Even in an emergency outpost like this one, in the middle of nowhere, the equipment was kept in perfect order. It was one of the reasons why Nichevo continued to exist, though heads of state disappeared into obscurity, and national policies changed with the wind. Nichevo worked because it was perfect.

Konstantin Kadar had once angrily told Zharkov that he was running the "Czar's secret army," and Zharkov had accepted the description. Nichevo had been started by Stalin, and that despot had been nothing if not a Czar. The idea of a secret army helped foster the legend of Nichevo.

How surprised Kadar would have been if he had known that Nichevo was never more than a dozen men, and of these, only six had been of the first rank. But each of those six controlled many; each had access to organizations and personnel, but none in those organizations knew that they worked for an agency called Nichevo. They were drones and asked no questions. The only ones who needed to know anything were the top half dozen men of Nichevo, the best and the brightest that Zharkov could find anywhere in Russia or its satellite states. Each of those six shared all Nichevo's secrets. Others of the top dozen knew of Nichevo, knew of Zharkov, but they did not know all the organization's plans. That would come when and if they were promoted to the first rank, to fill vacancies caused by death. There were no retirements from Nichevo.

Zharkov had been absent for two years, but he had no doubt that Nichevo still existed, lying dormant, still awaiting his return. Each man had been hand-picked by Zharkov. Even in their leader's absence, each was able to live from secret funds that Zharkov had deposited in Western banks. They existed, and they waited for his return. He knew that. Had he died, they would secretly have continued to receive funds until their own deaths. Then, and only then, would Nichevo cease to exist.

The radio was equipped for ultra-shortwave and would send a blast of less than one second's duration that would show up merely as a screech on any intercepting machine. Even if a radio intercepting the message happened to be listening for such a screech, taped it, and slowed the frequency down to the point where separate sounds could be discerned, the interceptors would be left with no more than a sequence of numbers distilled from a one-time-only code.

Zharkov sat for a long moment, making sure he remembered the code, for Nichevo would not respond to an imperfectly transmitted message.

Then he began: "Nichevo. Double willows. Require Kolodny and apparatus, also entry to Moscow. Zharkov."

He turned off the set. There was no need to wait for confirmation. Nichevo received the message and would understand it. "Double willows" was the location of his transmission. Kolodny was the plastic surgeon in Minsk who would put his face back together. Moscow was where he had to return, to reassemble his life before he could again face the Grandmaster.

He found the woman sitting cross-legged on one of the dusty mats in the main room, her hands rubbing her arms for warmth. There was no fire and no wood near the stove.

"I'm hungry," Zharkov said in Russian. She did not reply. He repeated the statement. Finally he took some coins out of the bag given him in exchange for the silver ornaments and threw them at her. She scrambled after them like a crab.

"Food!" he shouted, thumping his belly.

She brought him a drink made from yogurt called *lassi* and a half-eaten loaf of round bread gone green with mold at the edges. Zharkov wolfed them down ravenously. When he was finished, he leaned against the wall, ready for sleep.

The woman nudged him. She held out her empty hand, palm up.

"What do you want?"

She showed him one of the coins he had thrown at her, then thrust out her hand again.

"More? Why on earth should I give you more money? I've already paid a thousand times what that foul bread was worth."

She grunted, compelling him with her eyes to look at her. Her legs were spread, and she began rubbing her crotch.

Her fingers reached out to stroke him through his clothing. Zharkov's mind reeled in disgust at the sight of the filthy creature, but he did not stop her. He could not. It had been too long since he had known the touch of a woman, and even if she was a gross caricature of femininity, his body responded.

She touched him expertly, bringing him to hardness, then mounted him. He let her ride, smelling her musk, pressing her deeply onto him. What difference did it make if she was ugly and sluttish? No one but a whore would bare herself before that mask of a face he wore. He should be grateful, he thought bitterly. And so he pleasured himself with her like a beast in rut, crying out, using her wet darkness until he poured himself into her.

Sleep came upon him almost instantly. As he dozed, he felt a pressure on his shoulder. It was the woman, curling up in his arm for warmth in a parody of romantic love.

"Get away," he said, kicking her. As an afterthought, he threw two more coins at her and turned on his side to sleep.

CHAPTER TEN

For eleven days the woman brought him food during the day and lay beside him at night. He never left the house with the double willow trees.

On the twelfth day, after dark, there was a caller. As soon as the knock came at the door, Zharkov sprang behind the woman, pressing a knife against her throat.

She said something in her own language.

The response from outside was "Nichevo."

Zharkov pushed the woman aside and opened the door to a lean, youthful-looking Asian, who was carrying a roll of burlap. If the man was shocked by Zharkov's appearance, his face betrayed nothing of it.

"It is good to see you again, Comrade Zharkov," he said in flawless Russian, depositing the burlap on the floor. "I have come in response to your message."

Zharkov felt a flood of relief wash over him. "I remember you, Mr. Lin."

Lin was half Russian and half Chinese. Zharkov had first seen him in Yakutsk, during a weapons exhibition. Lin was an expert with firearms, but his prowess with a knife was extraordinary. And he possessed other qualities that were even more valuable: intelligence, discretion, obedience, and, best of all, the ability to kill with absolute indifference. Zharkov had made him a member of Nichevo more than ten years before. When one of the older members of the six-man inner circle of the organization died, Zharkov had replaced him with Lin.

Lin shrugged lightly in response to Zharkov's greeting. "Nichevo," he said with the hint of a smile.

He stepped into the room and turned to the woman. "*Namaste,*" he said, bowing and pressing the palms of his hands together.

The woman repeated the gesture. "*Namaste.*"

"It means 'I salute the god within you,' " Lin explained. "The usual greeting here."

Smiling, the woman turned toward the small kitchen area in the back of the house. From his goatskin vest Lin took a Chinese throwing knife. It was ten inches long and reed-thin, with a forked bamboo handle. Without seeming to aim at all, he cupped it behind his ear, the handles resting between his fingers, then set it loose in front of him, his fingers pointing toward the woman. It struck her at the base of the skull.

Zharkov stared at her for a moment, then at her killer.

"It was necessary," the Asian said, unrolling the length of burlap.

Lin worked quickly, rolling the body into the cloth and tying it expertly. "She was the last of the family. You will recall it was quite a large one," Lin said. "A few years after we installed the first radio, the old man—her father, I believe—was found trying to sell the apparatus on the black market. He was eliminated, naturally. Still, the family apparently did not learn its lesson, despite a generous stipend for their discretion. Two years ago, after your disappearance, I replaced the radio with a new model. Given your circumstances, I thought it possible that you might turn up in this area. But the family tried to sell that radio too."

"So they were all killed?"

"Oh, yes. It was made to look like a mountaineering accident. There were no traces, sir. However, I had to keep one member of the family alive in the event of your return. I suggest that after we leave this place it be destroyed."

"Agreed," Zharkov said. "Are you alone?"

"Certainly not," Lin said. "If I were, I could have been here within a day. You requested Dr. Kolodny. I had to travel to Minsk for him."

Lin carried the body of the dead woman outside and returned with another tied burlap bundle. He deposited it on one of the rattan mats and cut the cords. Inside the burlap was a man in his early sixties, gagged and unconscious.

Lin went out twice more to the truck parked between the double willow trees and the house. It was a battered vehicle, a tinker's truck loaded with gewgaws and secondhand junk. He returned with two large crates and a box of canned goods.

"He'll come to before daybreak," Lin said. "And then he'll need another six hours or so before he can begin. Will you sleep till then, Comrade Colonel?"

Zharkov blinked. The nightmare was over. Nichevo was in charge again. "Yes, yes. I'll do that. And tomorrow, many questions."

For the first time since he'd awakened from that terrible long sleep of death in the hills of China, Zharkov was able to rest. He slept long that night, without dreams and without fear.

Zharkov woke long before Dr. Kolodny. The room had been transformed. There were tables, cots for the three of them, enough high-intensity lamps to equip a photographer's studio, a hospital sterilizer, boxes of medicines, and stacks of medical instruments carefully wrapped in cloth. A gasoline generator purred busily in the corner, providing electric power.

On the wall Lin already had arranged more than thirty photographs of Zharkov's former face, taken from every angle, as well as computer diagrams of every feature.

"I didn't know so many pictures of me existed," Zharkov said, rubbing the sleep from his eyes.

"Neither does the KGB," Lin said. "They will be destroyed after the procedure."

Zharkov looked for a long moment at the imperturbable Mr. Lin. "Does my appearance surprise you?"

Lin returned his gaze levelly. "Nothing surprises me," he said.

"What of Kadar?" Zharkov asked.

"He has been deposed," Lin said easily.

"Deposed? Not dead?"

"He lives in exile. There was the usual pogrom after the unsuccessful mission in Cuba."

Zharkov smiled slowly. "I didn't think it would be so easy to remove the *Vozhd* without me."

"He has been succeeded by Nikolai Pierlenko. The new General Secretary is a younger man. . . ."

"Yes, yes, I remember him. A politician. He lacks Kadar's instincts."

"I do not believe he was a favorite of the former Premier's," Lin said. "Kadar would not have told him about Nichevo."

"Good," Zharkov said. He looked away, then asked, "And what of the Grandmaster?"

"There has been no word," Lin said. "We think he must have perished."

"He will die only when I do," Zharkov said softly, as if to himself. He brought his attention back to Lin. "He's not with the CIA? No sign of him?"

"None, sir, although we have learned that the man who ran him, Andrew Starcher—"

"Starcher is dead. I killed him in Cuba."

Lin hesitated. "I'm afraid not, sir. Our information shows that as of last week, the man is living in the United States."

"Impossible," Zharkov said. "I killed him. I saw him go down."

"He lived through it, then. Our sources are good. Starcher is alive in Virginia."

Zharkov's scarred face cracked into a smile. "Andrew Starcher, alive," he said. He felt his pulse quicken.

"Do you want him found?" Lin asked.

Zharkov shook his head. "No. Not yet. Who has replaced Starcher in Moscow?"

"A man named Rand, a weakling."

Zharkov breathed deeply. "There are so many things I need to know."

The doctor groaned as he came to, fumbling for his eyeglasses. Lin handed them to him. "There will be time," he said gently to Zharkov.

"This is outrageous," Dr. Kolodny said, complaining. "I have no X-rays of this face, no proper equipment, no nursing care, no facility. The skin grafts themselves would take months. I cannot undertake such a complex series of operations in a mud hut in the middle of winter."

"But you will, Doctor," Lin said softly, pulling out the fork-handled knife.

Kolodny did not question him again.

Two days after his arrival, the doctor stood over Zharkov as he lay on a metal operating table inside the house with the double willow trees. An old-fashioned gauze ether cup covered Zharkov's nose and mouth as the doctor dribbled anesthetic onto it.

"Count backward from one hundred," he said.

Zharkov obeyed. "One hundred . . . ninety-nine, ninety-eight . . ."

Hail to Thee, O Wearer of the Blue Hat.

"Ninety-seven . . . ninety-six . . ."

As he sank into a spinning unconsciousness a series of bizarre images came to him: two boys, playing chess in a hall decades ago . . . a young monk in a mountain monastery . . .

"Ninety-five . . . ninety-four . . . eighty-nine . . ."

A man buried alive, then risen from the dead, his eyes like blue ice . . .

"Eighty-five . . . eighty-two . . . eighty-one . . ."

A silver sword, useless against him, the one with eyes like blue ice, the one called Patanjali, reincarnation of Brahma, Grandmaster . . .

CHAPTER ELEVEN

THE GRANDMASTER

The man who swept the floor in the abandoned monastery looked nothing like a spy. He was forty-two years old with a shaved head and wore the saffron-colored robes of the order of monks that had once dwelled there. His skin was nut-brown from long hours in the sun and the cold mountain air, and his hands were as tough and hard as planks of oak. He was an American, but except for his height and his ice-blue eyes, he would not be taken for a Westerner.

Justin Gilead moved through the great gilt-covered hall like a whisper, soundless, barely stirring the air. He felt at home here at Rashimpur, in the vast, empty fortress cut into the sheer rock face of a mountain. Its sole inhabitant for the last two years, he had begun to develop an almost fussy proprietariness about the place. Each day he swept and cleaned and repaired. He lit a small fire in the kitchen every morning and cooked his daily portion of tea and gruel. Outside, in warmer weather, he tended a small garden, which in the fall would yield a few baskets of pungent white turnips, and these he would pickle in brine for the winter.

Through each day, a hundred times or more, he would pray for the souls of the dead. Sometimes, in the coming darkness of evening, he could see them again in the Great Hall, the bodies of the monks slain here years before.

Justin had been a young man then. So had the man who ordered their massacre, Alexander Zharkov.

He could again hear the terrible silence of their deaths, smell their fresh blood. No matter that the attackers had paid for their crime. Through the lonely years the one thing Justin had learned was that death was not made less painful by revenge.

He eschewed the altars and prayer wheels that the monks had used for devotions when they had been alive. Formal prayer seemed unnecessary for a hermit living alone in a cleft of rock. Instead he prayed at the Tree.

The Tree had grown in the center of the Great Hall ever since Justin could remember. It had been old when he was still a child. In the legends of the old monks of Rashimpur, the Tree of the Thousand Wisdoms had been planted by Brahma himself at the beginning of time and could therefore never be destroyed. It grew miraculously, without light, and its leaves were possessed with the power of healing.

The monks who had once lived here believed that Patanjali, the teacher who founded Yoga, had been the first incarnation of the creator god Brahma. Their legend was that Patanjali had first appeared in the Tree of the Thousand Wisdoms in the form of a golden snake. Through a hundred generations the throne of the Patanjali was never vacant, filled always by a man who was believed to be the newest reincarnation of Brahma, and each of those who occupied the throne wore a gold amulet depicting a coiled snake inside a circle.

Justin Gilead wore such an amulet around his neck as he swept the stone floor with a twig broom.

He had not been born into the life of the monks. He was a Westerner, a chess prodigy from America, but as a child he was taken by the monks of Rashimpur to be raised as their leader. Here he learned the secrets of the holy men, their reverence for life. Here he was installed as the Patanjali, true incarnation of Brahma.

Here he first dreamed of the Prince of Death, coming for him out of the ancient mists of time. And here he met the man he recognized from those dreams.

When Justin was a young man, Alexander Zharkov came with his soldiers and their rifles and the smell of death on them. At Zharkov's command the soldiers destroyed Rashimpur and killed every one of the monks. Justin's teacher, Tagore, was singled out for special punishment.

Only Justin himself had survived. At the moment he saw the carnage done to Brahma's sacred place, Justin Gilead exchanged his own soul for revenge upon the man named Zharkov, the one he knew to be the Prince of Death.

Justin left the monastery to follow Zharkov into his own world. For fifteen years he sought the Prince, killing whenever it was necessary to move a step closer to the man. Life meant nothing to Justin, not others', and especially not his own.

He craved death. During those fifteen years he had embraced it again and again, death the lover, coming toward him with outstretched arms.

But he did not die. Instead, with each day of life, the face of Alexander Zharkov became more deeply etched in his memory. The need to destroy him grew into an obsession that devoured everything else in Justin's heart.

In the end his spirit was as empty as the bloodstained hall of Rashimpur. He was born to be a perfect man, but in seeking Zharkov's death, Justin Gilead had become as base as Zharkov himself. But that had been his bargain: his soul for Zharkov's death.

He found Zharkov and fought him, and vanquished the Prince of Death in flames.

For nothing. Alexander Zharkov, Justin knew in his heart, was still alive. The Patanjali had sacrificed his soul for nothing.

In the two years since his return to the ruined monastery, Gilead had tried to atone for his affronts to his god. He rebuilt Rashimpur with his own hands, restoring the wreckage, cleaning the blood of the monks left after the massacre so many years before. And he prayed constantly at the Tree for forgiveness, for the souls of the dead, for the monks' misplaced hopes for him.

There was never any answer to his prayers.

Justin accepted the god's indifference. There was nothing for him to do now except to tend the monastery and wait for death. Perhaps it would come for him again soon, its arms outstretched in welcome. Perhaps Brahma would let him die now, for Justin was no longer the Patanjali, he knew. Brahma would never use such a corrupted vessel to hold his precious wine.

Perhaps death would have him now.

Suddenly the broom halted. Justin jerked his head right and left. He sniffed the air like an animal of the woods.

There were men near. He could sense them.

Rashimpur stood in a fissure of red rock near the top of the sacred mountain of Amne Xachim. Inside the fissure spread a plateau holding a lake ringed with rhododendron bushes. Below it, on another, wider plateau, was an identical lake. There sixteen men waited.

They were dressed as Justin was, in saffron-colored robes covered with blankets and yak skins for warmth against the snow that had begun to fall. They built no fire and made no attempt to approach the monastery on the next level of the mountain.

When Justin appeared, they knelt and bowed toward him, their foreheads touching the snow-covered ground. They remained there like statues.

Justin walked down the steep path reluctantly. These men from the world of the living were intruding on a shrine for the dead.

"What do you want here?" he asked, standing before them.

One of the monks rose and approached him. He was a very old man, with the withered, pale skin of age and no hair at all. The most striking thing about him was his eyes, or the lack of them. Beneath the bald ridge where his brows should have been were two twisted, blackened knots of scar tissue. His face was ugly and fearsome, and if he had not been a holy man, Justin would have turned away in revulsion.

"We have come from a far place to petition the Patanjali," he said.

"Then you have wasted your journey."

"You are the one we seek," the monk insisted. "Do you not wear the amulet of Brahma around your neck?"

Startled, Justin's hand went to his chest, resting on a medallion carved with the image of a coiled snake.

The monk's ugly face softened. "One does not need eyes to see such a thing."

Justin took a step back. Someone must have told the vile old creature what to expect, he thought. "I wear it only for safekeeping," Justin said. "I cannot help you, and no one else is here. Go back to your own place." He turned away.

"We are hungry," the thin, old voice called after him, "and one of our brothers is sick."

Justin turned back and saw that the blind man was telling the truth. One of the monks, a young man, was as emaciated as a skeleton. His limbs shook as he crouched on his knees, making his obeisance. Justin lifted him up and saw the fever in his eyes and the sweat that poured off his face. "Come inside," Justin said curtly, picking up the sick man in his arms.

In the kitchen he prepared a poultice for the monk, who lay on a pallet near the hearth.

"Your herbs will not help him," a raspy voice said from behind him.

Justin whirled around. "I did not hear you come in."

"Then you were not listening. Did you hear, at least, what I said?"

Justin swallowed his annoyance at the remark. This was a simple monk, he reasoned, blind and old and probably treated with respect by the others simply because of his age and infirmity.

"The man has fever. He must have something to clear his lungs."

"That is not enough. He is dying," the old monk said.

The sick monk lay writhing in a delirium by the fire. His skin was the gray color of a beggar's rags. His eyes bulged from the dry, hacking coughs that racked his body. He had the look of the wasting sickness about him. The old monk was right. Death was not far away. Justin looked at the gauze-wrapped poultice in his hand. "It is all I can do," he said.

He felt the monk's gnarled old fingers on his arm. "Bring him to the Tree," he whispered. "All know of the healing magic of the Tree of the Thousand Wisdoms."

"The Tree does not always heal," Justin answered, remembering. The Tree's legendary dark leaves had not helped the slaughtered monks of Rashimpur when Zharkov and his men came to kill. They had not stopped the spilled blood that had once covered the walls of the Great Hall. The Tree could not save the great teacher Tagore, who had been crucified and burned on it.

"If the Patanjali wills it—"

"It will not heal," Justin snapped.

The blind man said nothing. He remained still, the vulture-claw of his hand gripping Justin's arm.

"I will carry him to the Tree," Justin said finally.

He lay the sick monk gently beneath the dark branches of the tree that grew without light. The monks gathered around, kneeling and chanting their prayers.

"Heal him," the old monk called aloud.

Justin looked up in panic. "I am not a healer," he said awkwardly. "I only agreed—"

"Hail to Thee," the monks chanted.

"The will of Patanjali can bring life back to him," the blind man said softly, and in his cracked, broken voice was something desperately seductive to Justin.

If I could . . . If the spirit were somehow still within me . . .

Hesitantly he placed his hands on the dying monk. He felt the man's bony ribs, his labored breath.

"Hail to Thee . . ."

"Bring the power of Brahma out of yourself," the old monk commanded him. "Bring life out of the perfect karma of the Patanjali and into this diseased body."

Perfect karma.

"I am not . . ." Justin began, feeling his sweat running down his back.

"Hail to Thee, O Wearer of the Blue Hat."

"Remember who you are," the blind one said.

Perfect . . .

"*Stop!*" he shouted.

The monks looked up in sudden silence.

Justin rose, holding his hands up in front of him. "Did you expect to find them glowing like halos?" he snarled.

His arms dropped, and he turned to face the blind man. "You tell me to remember who I am." His voice quieted. "What I am is a killer. I am not fit to utter the name of the god, let alone heal in His name. I have no power."

He ran out into the cold.

He remained outdoors all night, unable to face the monks who had prayed for a miracle and had received in its place only a cheap fraud.

He walked over the mountain, oblivious to the wind and snow that swirled around him. Physical hardship no longer affected him. During his life he had endured enough pain to inure him. It was the pain inside that Justin could not bear.

At dawn he saw the monks walking in a procession down the far side of the mountain, carrying the body of their dead brother to a blazing funeral pyre.

"You should never have come here," he whispered.

"Are you speaking to us or to yourself?"

Justin started. It was the blind monk, again seeming to materialize from nowhere. "How did you know where I was?"

"One does not always need eyes to see," the old man said. "All it takes is practice." He smiled. "And a little patience."

Justin looked back to the flames. In the howling of the wind he heard snatches of their keening. "Shouldn't you be with them?"

"It is more important that I be with you now."

"Why? To shame me? I told you I could not heal the man. I told you I was not the Patanjali."

"What one *says*, if one is an honest man, reflects only what he believes. It is not necessarily what is."

The corners of Justin's mouth turned down bitterly. "Don't be a fool, old one. It is true I was to have been the Patanjali. But I have desecrated myself. There is none of Brahma's spirit left in me now."

"My son—"

"Leave this place. You have made your petition, and I have failed you, as I knew I would. There is nothing more for you here."

The blind man laughed gently. "I have not even told you of our request yet."

Justin's eyes flickered back to the funeral pyre. "But the young monk. Was he not—"

"He will return blessed in his next life for dying here," he said simply, patting Justin's hand. He breathed deeply, and Justin saw the ruined face grow almost beautiful with an inner peace. "This place is filled with beauty, your magic mountain."

"I . . . I suppose so," Justin said. He looked around him. The mountain *was* beautiful. It had been years since he'd even noticed. Amne Xachim, home of the god of creation, was surrounded by legend. Even the brilliant blue sky was said to be a part of the Patanjali, the "blue hat" of the first human incarnation of Brahma. At his feet a white rabbit twitched its nose and hopped toward a cave covered with hanging snow.

"Its family is inside," the blind man said. "I have been exploring."

"You heard the rabbit?"

"Of course. It was within an arm span."

"Who are you?" Justin asked slowly.

"A name is meaningless. If you must have a word for me, call me Eyeless."

Justin winced. The name was too descriptive to be comfortable. But the old monk only walked ahead, picking his way delicately over the slippery, rock-strewn path.

"Where are you from?" Justin asked, following him.

"We come from the lamasery at Laskaya."

"Laskaya? Under the Saskya Lama?" The Lama, known as Manjusri, was perhaps the most learned man in the religion of Brahma. "Is he still alive?"

"Barely," Eyeless replied. "He is an old man now."

"I remember seeing him at my investiture. I was a boy then. My teacher, Tagore, pointed him out to me. He wore a green silk robe and stood alone. Manjusri, the Bodisat of Knowledge, Tagore called him. The line of Manjusri led the religious lives in these mountains since the time of Kublai Khan, you know."

"He is only an old man," Eyeless said.

Out of respect for the blind man, Justin tried to keep silent but could not. "He is revered as the wisest of all holy men. Your rudeness does not become your calling."

Eyeless shrugged. "Manjusri does not require my adoration to be Manjusri," he said.

Justin bristled. "How dare you speak with such disrespect," he said. "You denigrate such a man as Manjusri while you bow your head to me."

"Why should I not? You are the Patanjali."

"And you are an even bigger fool than I thought you were."

He scrambled off the path, running down the slope of Amne Xachim toward Rashimpur. When he neared the monastery, he looked up to find the old blind monk still on the path above him, walking gracefully toward the sun. And behind the sung prayers of the monks below, he heard the old man's laughter.

CHAPTER TWELVE

Toward evening, Justin walked to the dying embers of the funeral pyre. The monks had long since finished their prayers and returned to their self-appointed tasks in the monastery. All that remained of the young man who died was a heap of ashes on the glowing circle of charred wood.

He touched his fingers to the ash. "I wish I could have been the one you expected," he said. "I might have helped you once, long ago." He wiped his hand across his eyes. "Too long ago."

The warmth of the embers made him realize how tired and cold he was. The wind had stopped, and the sky was beginning to take on the bright cobalt hue of twilight. Justin closed his eyes and let the heat from the smoky remnant of the fire wash over him. In a moment he was asleep, with the ash of the dead monk's body still on his fingertips.

He awoke cold. The fire was out. In the full moonlight he could see the eyes of the monks, sitting around the fire in a circle, seemingly oblivious to the snow on the ground.

"What are you doing here?" he growled.

Eyeless stood up. "We have made our intention clear from the beginning, O Patanjali."

"For the last time, I am *not* the Patanjali. You have seen that for yourselves. I am nothing. Go home where you belong."

"We will remain here," the old man said stubbornly, "until our request is heard."

"Then you will wait until the day you die." Justin got to his feet, shivering.

"Don't run away," Eyeless said. "You have nothing to fear from us."

"You do not frighten me," Justin said sharply. "You annoy me. I have nothing to say to you."

"Good, because I did not ask you to speak. Only to listen." The old man walked around the circle to him. The others followed, gathering behind him. "I offer you a bargain."

Justin glared at him. "What sort of bargain?"

"It is fair, I believe. I wish for you to help us. You wish to be left alone."

"I cannot help you," Justin began in exasperation, but Eyeless held up his hand for silence. "Let me finish," the old man continued. "I have arrived at a solution. We will fight."

Justin stood in silence for a moment, unable to believe what he had heard. "We will what?" he asked at last.

"I will fight you. I alone, you alone, without weapons. If you win, I will take my brothers and leave you in peace. If I win, you will make every effort to grant my request, whatever it may be."

Justin tried to suppress a smile.

"Will you insult us by refusing even to answer?" Eyeless demanded.

"I will not fight a blind and feeble old man. That is my answer." He turned and walked away.

Suddenly a blow like a hammer struck him on the side of the head. He fell sprawling on the ground.

Above him stood Eyeless, his gown still billowing from the movement.

Without a word Justin raised himself back to a standing position, but in the next instant the old man's foot shot out, kicking Justin behind his knees. He smashed to the ground again, groaning.

"One other condition," the old monk said. "If you do not fight me, I will kill you." He slammed Justin under his chin.

"All right," Justin said, anger exploding inside him. "You will die for this, old one."

He spun off the ground, kicking as he rose, his instep aimed at the blind man's withered neck. But when he drew close, his foot struck at empty air. Eyeless was gone, already moving behind Justin.

Enraged, Justin lashed out with his hands. The old man stopped them in the air, his fingers curled around Justin's wrists. He held them for a moment, standing as rigid as a temple carving. Justin coiled his legs beneath him. Surprisingly the old man's grip never loosened, and Justin hung suspended in space, his face level with Eyeless's.

Taking his breath deep within him, Justin forced his legs out, his feet calculated to burst the old man's rib cage. But they met no more resistance than a whisper against the monk's cotton garment.

Justin heard a soft slap and felt an almost imperceptible change in the powerful grip around his wrists. That was all. But the old man was gone.

A whimper of confusion rushed out of Justin before he heard the soft words behind him: "It is you who are blind, my son."

Before Justin could respond, his wrists suddenly fell free. At the same time he felt a slight pressure on the outside of his thigh, but the blow had been so perfectly placed that his whole body swung upside down, then cartwheeled through the air like a child's paper toy. He seemed to float, weightless and insubstantial, as in a dream. He lost all sense of time during that fall, as if he had been falling in just that way—turning, drifting, and bodiless—for an eternity.

It was not until the breath whooshed out of him that he felt the pain of his fall. He had landed on his back, and the jolt rattled every bone in his body. Justin's legs swung up reflexively, then crashed down again. It was several minutes before he could bring himself to sit up and assess his injuries.

There were none. Even in that, the old monk with no eyes had been perfect. Justin felt foolish and shamed by the holy man, who was clearly his superior.

He raised his eyes to apologize, but the blind man was gone. The other monks stood around him, their faces intent.

"Where is he?" Justin asked weakly.

One of the monks helped him to his feet. "Manjusri awaits you inside," he said.

Justin felt a cold rush of air fill his lungs. "Manjusri?" he whispered.

The monk nodded. "He is the one you know as Eyeless."

The old man was in front of the Tree of the Thousand Wisdoms. Justin knelt beside him.

"Forgive me," he said quietly. "I am just an ordinary man, not the god you believe me to be. But I will do my best to give what you ask of me."

Manjusri smiled. "That will be enough," he said.

While the other monks slept, Manjusri and Justin spoke into the night.

"It began seventeen years ago, with a woman," Manjusri said. "Or what passed for a woman. The Abbess Varja, who called herself goddess."

Justin knew the name well. "It was Varja who directed the Russian soldiers to Rashimpur."

The monk nodded. "During those days many holy places were burned or turned into Soviet outposts to monitor Russia's border wars. The monasteries at Labrang and Pemiogchi were obliterated, their ancient relics turned over to Varja's treasury. Then Rashimpur was taken, although it was never used by the Russians."

"There were no survivors among them," Justin said.

Except one. But Manjusri did not need to share the burden of Justin's memories of the Prince of Death. "Go on," Justin said.

"After the massacre here, Varja took a consort, a lover, by whom she bore a child." The blind man sighed. "She called him Siraj, meaning Black Star in the tongue of the ancients. The boy was imbued with all of Varja's evil. He was raised in the ways of devil worship, schooled in secrets of Varja's cult. But he had always been an exceptional child, possessed of an extraordinary gift."

"Like you?" Justin asked. "With your special sight and strength?"

Manjusri shook his head. "My poor talents are as nothing compared with the boy's. Anyone can learn to see without eyes or to fight a man who needs eyes to see. But Siraj can pierce a man's very heart with his mind. He can make others believe what he wishes. He can convince them to see what is not present, to feel what does not exist."

"A hypnotist."

"There is not a name for him or his killing gift," Manjusri said sadly. "He is only Siraj, the Black Star."

Justin shifted uneasily. "How do you know him?"

"One of Varja's slaves escaped several years ago and found his way to our lamasery. Siraj had caused the slave to bite off his own fingers for criticizing him in some trifling matter. By the time he reached us, the man was stiff with infection. He died shortly afterward, but not before telling us about the child.

"He said he had overheard the ritual of the boy's initiation into the mysteries of Varja's cult when Siraj was thirteen years of age. She had charged her son then with the task of obliterating the name of Brahma from the earth.

"After burning the slave's body I set off to Varja's palace with a few of the monks from Laskaya."

"To kill the boy?"

"You know that we are forbidden to kill." He took Justin's hand. "When I threatened you with death, it was only a ruse to make you fight me. But I could never kill a child, even the devil-spawn of Varja. I planned only to rescue Siraj from his mother and raise him in the ways of Brahma, so that he might one day understand the evil of Varja's teachings.

"We took the boy, although at great cost, for he had already learned his magic. One of our monks set himself afire. Another punctured his own eardrums. A third we lost on the route home. When we found him, he had been disemboweled by wild dogs.

"The journey back to Laskaya was long and arduous, and the boy nearly died, but even then we dared not set him free among us. Eventually we reached the lamasery and gradually released his constraints. He studied with us for almost a year and appeared to accept us. But Siraj was sly beyond his years. He bided his time while his powers grew with his body, knowing his mother would devise a plan.

"We learned of it soon enough. Varja sent a troop of Russian soldiers to Laskaya, telling them there was treasure there beyond counting. They came like birds of prey, killing us for sport and setting fire to every chamber in the lamasery after the looting was done.

"Siraj let loose the killing gift then. He looked at me with the glow of pure hatred in his eyes. Eyes of ice blue, hooded like a reptile's . . ."

The old man swallowed. "Those eyes were the last things I ever saw. Without a thought I picked up two burning coals from the blaze in the lamasery and set them on my own eyes."

As he spoke, Manjusri squeezed Justin's hand, reliving the pain. "I do not remember what happened after that. One of the brothers who rescued me from the fire told me that the boy eventually turned on the soldiers. In a frenzy, the Russians killed one another, and themselves, and those of us who were still whole.

"At last, when the sky was black with the smoke of a thousand burning bodies, Siraj left with a few of the soldiers.

"Where they went, I do not know. Most of us who were left were near death. Only those of us now at Rashimpur survived."

"When was this?" Justin asked softly.

"Over two years ago. Afterward we prevailed on another monastery to accept us. But we had no peace, knowing that the boy was free to carry out his mother's command. Even when we heard of Varja's destruction, we knew that her evil did not end with her but grew as her son grew. We did not know where to turn, what to do. We prayed for two years without ceasing. And then, some weeks ago, Brahma sent us a sign."

He touched a white bundle of rags on the floor beside him. "In the lore of our faith," he said, "the enemies of Brahma forged a sword of pure silver to fight the first Patanjali. The sword was given to the evil shamans when Patanjali was an old man. With it the shamans cut off Patanjali's hand."

"I know the legend," Justin said. "His hand was restored miraculously."

The blind man lifted the bundle into his lap. Unwrapping it carefully, he reached inside and pulled out the silver hilt of a sword.

Justin gasped. He had seen the sword before . . . in the hand of Alexander Zharkov. "Where did you get this?" he asked, picking it up tentatively.

"Word reached me that the headman of my home village of Ghizou had died. I had known him since he was a boy, so I made a pilgrimage to bless his ashes. Though he had been dead for many weeks, the villagers had only recently retrieved his remains. He and five others had been murdered in a faraway place. All the silver treasure of the village had been stolen. At least they know now that it was stolen. At the time they believed they had given it to you."

"To me?" Justin asked, bewildered.

"A man with a horribly scarred face had been brought to them by nomads. The people of Ghizou thought the man was the Patanjali because of a mark on his neck. An unmistakable mark, they said."

Justin closed his eyes. "Of a coiled snake within a circle," he said. He understood now. He had given Alexander Zharkov that scar himself. "What happened with him?"

"When his eyes finally opened, he told the headman to give him all the silver of Ghizou and to lead him to the City in the Sky. He demanded these things as the Patanjali's due."

"And the sword?"

"It was found near him, at the ruins of the temple. The place was, of course, Varja's palace. The villagers did not recognize it as the magic sword of the ancient shamans. But I have touched it. I know. It was the sign that we were to find you."

Justin ran his fingers over the silver hilt.

"Take it to the Tree," the old man said.

Justin obeyed, placing the sword handle against the tree's massive black trunk. The silver hilt seemed to glow. A light emanated from it that softened its outlines. Before Justin's eyes, the object melted into a shimmering and shuddering puddle and then reformed itself slowly, until it took the form of a coiled snake. It swayed back and forth hypnotically, then opened its mouth and flashed toward him.

Justin started back from the snake. Its bared fangs struck the hard rock of the floor, then slowly vaporized.

It was gone. There was no snake in front of the great tree, no sword hilt. There was nothing.

"It . . . it has vanished," Justin whispered.

"Such a relic could not exist here, in Brahma's home," the monk said calmly. "The forces of the god are too strong now. But if the boy comes back fully grown, as he will be now, and in command of all his powers, Brahma will weaken and die."

Justin stood up, still awestruck by the miracle that had taken place in front of him. "I don't understand," he said. "The god cannot die."

"He lives on earth only through the Patanjali," Manjusri said. "But the prophecy of the Patanjali says only that the throne of Rashimpur will be taken by a boy with eyes of blue ice, who plays the game of Shah Mat. Siraj, like you, understands chess, the game of Shah Mat. And his eyes are the color of your own."

The air seemed to deaden.

"There are many monasteries in this region, many shrines," the blind man said. "But Rashimpur is the most sacred among them, for the mountain of Amne Xachim is the resting place of Brahma. He who serves as High Priest here guards the very soul of the Creator. Siraj will destroy that soul. It was the purpose to which he was born. If he is permitted to grow strong enough, he will come back to these mountains, to Amne Xachim, and turn its magic to his own use. Others will help him. But there is only one true Patanjali. Whether or not you believe yourself capable, you must stop him. And you must stop him alone."

Justin stood in silence for a long time. "And Zharkov?" he asked at last. "The one with the mark of the coiled snake on him . . . what has he to do with the boy?"

Manjusri smiled. "Do you not yet understand?" He bowed his head. "He is the boy's father."

Justin felt himself trembling.

"It is time," the old man said.

It is time.

Tagore had spoken those same words to Justin once, spoken to him somehow from beyond death.

It is time.

He always knew that Alexander Zharkov was his destiny. Now the god was giving him leave to fulfill it.

"Where is he?"

"The men from Ghizou were slain near Katmandu, the City in the Sky. Where you find the man, the boy will be also."

It is time.

"I will go," Justin said quietly. "But there is something I must learn from you first."

"Name the thing, my son."

Justin raised the blind man to his feet. "Teach me to see without eyes."

CHAPTER THIRTEEN

The next morning Manjusri and his followers faced Justin Gilead on the side of the mountain. The monks carried long sticks of bamboo.

"These are our weapons, carried with us from the lamasery at Laskaya. I want you to see them before we begin, so that your disadvantage will not be too great."

The monks held the batons over their heads. They were about four feet long, worn smooth with use.

"Are they going to hit me with them?" Justin asked.

"They are going to throw them," Manjusri answered, tying a blindfold over Justin's eyes. "Just prepare yourself. Expect the unexpected."

From his earliest years his teacher, Tagore, had taught Justin speed and skill and resourcefulness. As a boy, Justin swam the lakes of Rashimpur while weighted with stones. He had climbed boulders made slippery with ice. His hands were as strong as iron. He could endure anything.

"I am ready," he said quietly.

At a signal from the blind man the monks let fly their sticks. Justin batted them away with his arms as if they were a swarm of offending, annoying insects.

"Very good," Manjusri said. "Tagore taught you well.

You have potential." Then, without warning, his foot
lashed out and kicked the still blindfolded Justin in the
chest. He fell unceremoniously, the wind knocked out of
him.

"Alas, it is only potential," Manjusri said. "I warned
you to expect the unexpected." He removed the blindfold
and dismissed all the monks but one.

Justin struggled to speak, but Manjusri held up a hand.

"Spare yourself the effort. I know it is unfair. But
when a man is fighting for his life, he does not always
obey the rules."

"I didn't ask to fight," Justin said, wheezing. "Only to
see."

"Ah, that is wise." Manjusri laid a finger on the side of
his nose. "Because if we had been fighting, you would be
long dead. There were fifteen men here. I counted twenty-
two blows against your body. Many of the sticks struck
you on both ends."

"Struck my arms and legs," Justin corrected. "That
was all."

"And if those sticks had been fists, or feet, or bullets?" The aged monk helped Justin to his feet. "You
will have to fight, my son," he said softly. "You may
have to kill."

"Again," Justin said.

Manjusri took his arm. "Come with me."

He led Justin to a cave on the other side of the monastery. One other monk followed them silently.

"Do you know this place?" Manjusri asked.

"Yes," Justin said, touching the round rock by its
entrance. "Tagore once sealed me inside to test my patience. I failed."

Manjusri smiled. "Then perhaps you have learned something. Come inside."

The cave was absolutely dark except for the small area
of light at the opening. Justin was surprised to see that
there was food inside and a bucket of water. "We will
stay here for a while," the old man said, and instructed
the other monk to roll the stone over the opening. As he

did, the faint light diminished to nothing. Justin lost all concept of space and direction. When Manjusri finally spoke, his voice came from someplace Justin had never expected. "Now you are in my world," the old man said. Justin felt the man move beside him, although the blind man had made no sound.

"What do you hear?" Manjusri whispered.

"Nothing."

"What a pity," he said with a sigh. "You are missing so much."

Justin felt his annoyance rising. "What do *you* hear?"

"I hear what is. The wind is singing from the back of this cave. The sound is not as sharp as it would be if the air were whistling through a crack, but soft. There is another opening to this place."

"No, there isn't. I spent weeks here."

"And you never noticed?" He clucked in dismay. "No matter. I will show you in time. That is only one of a thousand sounds. A millipede is crawling over some pebbles near my feet. Here." He reached down and picked something off the ground, then handed it to Justin. It was moving on legs as fine as baby's hair.

"Ah, my brother is returning to the monastery. He is walking above us now."

"You *can't* know that. You must—"

"Listen!" Manjusri snapped. "Listen with your whole body, not just your ears. Do not rely so much on your reason, for your thoughts miss everything that cannot be put into words. Put your energy outside yourself and feel with it. You know how. Trust yourself."

Justin quieted himself in the way the yogis of his sect had taught him since he was a boy. He willed every muscle in his body to relax. He wiped his mind clear of thought.

"Now. Turn your energy outward."

At the command Justin felt his life force flowing outward. It prickled his skin; it seemed to surround him like an aura. From that aura it grew, extending beyond him, into the air, through the darkness and the rock. And there, at the limit of its farthest tendrils, it brought back to him the faint throb of a man walking.

"Yes . . . I think . . ." But it was gone. Whatever had emanated from him to make contact with the monk's movement through the rock had shrunk back and withered inside his skin. "I'm sorry," he said.

"Next time, do not think. What is this?" Manjusri slipped something smooth and round into Justin's hand.

"It's a stone," Justin said, puzzled.

"What does it smell like?"

"Smell?" He sniffed it obligingly. "Like the cave, I suppose."

"You see?" Manjusri said shrilly. "That is your mind talking again. You smelled nothing. You only assumed. You cannot trust yourself even to smell what is in front of your nose." His voice softened. "Trust yourself."

Justin tried again. He let his mind empty of thought and became still to the core of his being. In the silence of his body the tendrils of his energy grew outside him again, reaching toward the smooth, round pebble in his hands. A thousand sensations washed over him: the stalactites of the cave, endlessly seeping water from the rock above; the rock itself, wearing away over centuries into nothing; the underground streams, flowing warm beneath the frozen, snow-covered earth of Amne Xachim; lime and iron and silver, picked up by the moving water as it rushed through the mountain and fed into the perfect lakes of Rashimpur. He felt it seeping into the roots of the rhododendron bushes, bringing them to flower in spring, felt it rise into the air during summer. He fell with the water as it moved in the clouds overhead, racing with the wind, then falling on a green meadow half a world away, to begin the process again. The stone was the stuff of oceans and stars, forever changing, as much a part of Justin as his own blood or sinew. He could taste its life.

"Yes, my son, yes," Manjusri said, folding his hand over Justin's own. "Remember. Trust yourself. It is the only way."

"I will remember," Justin said.

The two stayed together in the great cave, heedless of time. Later he was surprised to find that three days and nights had passed in what had seemed to be no more than an hour. With Manjusri he explored every inch of the cavern's smooth, damp walls. There was another cavern beyond the first, as the old man had said, with a trickling waterfall and a passage through the rock leading to the outside.

Justin walked with bare feet over the pebbled floor, and when the blind man asked how many stones he had walked over, Justin could answer with certainty. He had not counted them, but he knew. The life force inside him had begun to embrace the world as part of himself.

"Now," Manjusri said, "go beyond."

"Beyond? But I have gone beyond myself. Beyond the cave. Even beyond the earth."

"Go farther."

"How?"

The old man touched Justin's clenched fists. "Trust yourself," he said. "There is no other way."

Justin opened his hands. The energy poured out of them like smoke, curling into the corners of the cave, reaching past the rock of the Earth, beyond the sky. And Justin flew with it into the airless blackness of space, through the planets, the red, parched dust of Mars, the frozen kaleidoscope of Saturn's rings. He found the moons of Jupiter and Uranus, worlds of their own, emitting their own energies, and past them, to other globes and moons not yet seen by the men and machines of science because they could see only with their eyes. He moved past them, toward a distant sun in the center of a far galaxy, dotted with blue light and the detritus of a hundred billion years, flying faster, past ancient, unformed gases and then the pure blackness curving, involuting, pushing him toward chaos, his energy crackling, violently dispersing, shattering finally in a burst of pure white light and soundless music and the perfect stillness of the Beginning.

And there he stood, waiting as the world grew beneath

him, as the Mountain of Amne Xachim formed out of the Earth's torment, as the first snows fell, as the seed of the Tree of the Thousand Wisdoms sprouted, green and promising on the cliff side. And he saw his body inside the cave, waiting, too, its hands outstretched for him.

This poor, fragile body.

He touched the warm hands, trembling with its tiny life, and passed inside them.

Tears were streaming down Justin Gilead's face.

Manjusri stood quietly and left through the inner chamber. Behind him he had left a strip of silk.

Justin tied it over his eyes. It was time, he knew, for him to leave the cave.

The rock rolled away from the opening. Outside were the songs of birds and the scent of coming spring. The cold air rushed in, tasting of salt from the sea and spices from the desert lands.

He walked outside. From within himself he felt the air in front of him parting sharply. He smelled tension. He allowed himself to move automatically, without thought, without reason.

One, two, three . . . The batons clicked in his hands. Not one touched him. Not one fell.

Manjusri removed the blindfold. Spread out in front of Justin were fifteen bamboo sticks, each tipped with a razor-sharp arrow point.

The blind man smiled. "Now you are ready, Patanjali."

BOOK TWO
OPENING GAMBIT

CHAPTER ONE

Andrew Starcher sat in the back of the Blue Mermaid, slowly drinking a glass of warm beer. He wore the ill-fitting rough clothes of a Russian peasant and kept a cap pulled down over his forehead.

His meeting was scheduled for six P.M., but he had arrived before five, just to watch the crowd, to see if there was anyone who seemed too interested in the people around him.

If there had been, Starcher would have finished his drink, walked casually outside, and made a blue chalk mark on the sidewalk in front of the tavern, canceling the meeting with Sasha. But he saw no KGB shoes, no red-haired agent this time. He ordered another beer.

She arrived at 5:45 P.M., obviously with the same idea in mind. She had her long blond hair pulled up under a knitted skullcap and wore no makeup. Her soft gray eyes were hidden behind a pair of glasses with the sort of cheap black frames issued to factory employees who could prove they did close work.

Once more Starcher was impressed, not so much by Sasha's homely disguise but because she had come early. In an untrained agent that showed good instincts. Starcher had been in the business long enough to know that he would trade all the training in the world for somebody who had innate common sense.

Without seeming to, she looked over all the people in the small tavern as she walked into the room. When she spotted Starcher, she opened her lips in a grin that revealed two blackened-out front teeth.

"God Almighty," Starcher grumbled.

"Uncle Vanya," she said, loud enough to be heard by the men in the bar to whom a young woman's presence was a novelty in itself, and walked back toward Starcher's booth. Those who had seen her toothless smile turned away.

She leaned over the small table and kissed Starcher on the forehead, then sat on the bench opposite him.

"I am happy to see you again," she said.

"You should be so happy to see a dentist," he grunted. They exchanged meaningless small talk until the bartender took Sasha's order and returned with it and Starcher's beer. When the man was safely back behind the bar, Starcher leaned across the table so that his face almost touched Sasha's.

"It was reckless to play chess with me yesterday," he said.

"Why? I won, didn't I?"

"Don't be pert. It gets on my nerves. We shouldn't be seen together any more than we have to be." He spoke in Russian, as he always did with Sasha, using the broad rural accent of the Caucasus.

"Nobody would recognize us looking like this," she protested. "Especially you. Your disguises are always—"

"Sasha!"

She quieted to a whisper. "I'm sorry. I guess I'm just excited about seeing you again. I didn't expect to."

"I've been back less than a week. I tried to contact you."

"I know. I got your messages, but I couldn't get free last Monday. A benefit performance. Then when you came to the circus and ruined my act, I remembered our old plan for Gorky Park."

"How did you know it was me at the circus?"

She shrugged. "The talk there is that a smelly old man murdered a KGB agent during my quadruple. You're the only smelly old murderer I know."

"They say he was KGB?"

Sasha nodded, lighting a stubby brown cigarette. "Part of some elite group that even the Premier doesn't know about. But who knows? It makes a better story if the man was KGB. It could just be talk."

"It may not be," Starcher said. "Sasha, are you still willing to work for me? I can't pay you much."

"I've told you how I feel." Her jaw clenched. "And I make more money than I can use as it is."

"All right," he said. "Five Americans have been killed in Moscow lately. Murdered. Have you heard about them?"

"Of course not. In our newspapers, Americans are never victims. Have you been gone so long that you've forgotten?"

"They don't seem like political executions, but my government has sent me over here to make sure."

"Why you? When you left the last time, I thought you were retiring."

"I volunteered. We don't have enough men in Moscow for the essentials, and this may lead to nothing. Besides, there may be a leak. That guy at the circus tried to kill me first."

Sasha's face took on a pained look. "Andrew, don't risk your life for something like this. You're not young anymore."

"That's right, kiddo," he said acidly. "I'm long past the age where I need a twenty-year-old bubble-gummer to mother me."

"I'm twenty-four," she said sullenly.

"And I'm sixty-eight. That makes me the senior partner in this dog-and-pony act. Now, are you with me or not?"

Her gray eyes flickered with anger. "You're so stubborn, I could kill you myself."

"You will, if you keep making a spectacle of us in a public park. Where did you learn to play chess like that, anyway?"

She smiled. "Pretty good for a bubble-gummer, no?"

"I've seen worse."

"My father taught me. I've been staying in practice so that I can play him when I see him and my mother again. It would please them."

Starcher looked down at the table.

"There's a boy at the circus I play with. If you think I'm good, you should see him. Brilliant."

"How well do you know him?" Starcher asked, alarmed.

"Oh, Andrew, he's only a teenager."

"That's not what I'm talking about. Does he know you've come here?"

"No," she said firmly. "Don't worry, all right? He's far too young to be a KGB agent." She rolled her eyes. "You see? You ought to retire. You've become—how do you say it—jittery," she said in English.

That was what Rand had been saying, he thought. Maybe he *was* turning into a demented old paranoid, if even the girl noticed. . . .

Sasha saw the hurt on his face and patted his gnarled knuckles with her own callused, strong hands. Starcher withdrew them from her. "I was only teasing," she explained.

"You've got paws like a gorilla," he said, grousing. "And a smile that would scare John Dillinger."

"Well, no wonder you're so crazy about me."

He shook his head. "You're a piece of work, Sasha."

"Just the dog in our dog-and-pony act," she said gently.

His eyes met hers and softened.

"What do you want me to do?"

"Not much for now. Just keep your ears open. Take advantage of who you are. Go to every party you're invited to."

She made a face. "I hate parties."

"I hate parties," he mimicked. "Look, it beats a sharp stick in the eye, doesn't it? You'll go. And if you hear anything about the murder of any of those Americans, any tip, any rumor, anything about a leak in the American embassy or the CIA, let me know immediately."

"How will I reach you?"

Starcher gave her an address just off Ulyanovskaya Street near the freight yards. "Top floor, rear apartment. It's safe there. Knock four times, groups of two. Do you have it memorized?"

She nodded.

"Keep it to yourself. I wouldn't even give my embassy that address." He glanced at his wristwatch. "Are you performing tonight?"

"Same as always. Every night except Monday, twice on Saturdays and Sundays."

"Still working without a net?"

Her nostrils flared. "La Kaminskaya does not need a net. She flies on Lenin's spirit."

They both laughed, remembering the solemn-voiced ringmaster who used those very words at each performance to announce her act.

He stood to leave. "Do me a favor, will you?"

"No net."

They left the café and walked to the corner. "It would be in my best interest to keep you alive for a while."

"I'll stay alive," Sasha said. "At least long enough to see my parents again."

Starcher felt a flood of shame wash over him.

When will I tell her?

"And afterward?" he asked.

"Afterward I don't care."

A bus came by. Starcher stepped into line and got on.

Starcher had first met Sasha Kaminskaya in Italy eight years before, when she was still a child. His sister had invited him to spend six weeks with her in a rented villa north of Rome. The purpose of the trip, she repeatedly told him, was for Starcher to recuperate from the bullet wound in his lung he had received in Berlin.

At first Starcher was eager to escape the constant stream

of visitors at Ellingwood, the family estate in Virginia, where his sister had made Southern hospitality into a full-time career.

Of course, Amelia Starcher made sure to have an equal number of callers from among her European friends at the villa, plus a host of arm-waving, jibber-jabbering Italian doctors and nurses who not only never gave Starcher a moment's rest but presumed to confiscate all his cigars too. After two days he escaped into Rome, prowling around the bars and smoking for all he was worth.

Sasha was in one particularly seedy-looking place. When he walked in, he burst out laughing. For one thing, the loud clientele at this bar seemed to consist mostly of dwarfs and leaping acrobats. There was also a monstrously fat woman, a person of indeterminate gender with an enormous snake wound around his or her neck, several young men of stunning musculature, and a young girl who couldn't have tipped the scales at more than a hundred pounds. She was fighting a sweaty, bearded hulk of a man and winning. The fracas ended when the hulk flew past Starcher and landed on the sidewalk outside.

Sasha had grown up tough, in the trailer lots of circuses traveling around Europe. Her parents were Russian émigrés to France who'd never bothered to renounce their Soviet citizenship. They were trapeze artists, too, although neither ever reached the level Sasha had. They had not begun early enough. But from the time she could walk, they trained their daughter with weights, trampolines, and, at the age of eight, on the moving bar. By the time she was fifteen, Sasha Kaminskaya was already a minor star in France, England, Holland, Germany, Italy, and Spain and felt at home in all the Western European capitals. Her parents, too, achieved a certain celebrity through her. In the *London Times* her father was quoted as saying there was nothing like freedom to spur talent to its limit.

Then her parents went home to Leningrad to visit her dying grandmother, and the gates closed behind them. Her father was arrested on a false morals charge and was carted off to a "rehabilitation center" from which he never emerged. His wife was not told the location of the camp. When she began to make a nuisance of herself, the authorities committed her to an insane asylum.

Sasha was cloistered in the Russian State Circus. Under the care of a wardress and the enforced tutelage of the best gymnasts and trapeze artists in Moscow, she blossomed into the most accomplished flyer the circus had ever seen. The Soviet press adored her, calling the slight young beauty "Little Bird" before according her the title of La Kaminskaya.

For three years she cooperated, politely answering any questions asked, hoping to hear something about her parents. But there was no information about them. No letters, no messages, not even a report saying they were still alive. It was as if two people had somehow vaporized, ceased to exist altogether.

On her first European trip after returning to Russia she tried to escape. The wardress caught up with her in the hotel lobby, slapped her across the face, and sent her back to her room.

A week later she had met Starcher in the Rome restaurant.

"They will send me back now," the young girl lamented drunkenly. "There will be no more tours, no more chances."

"Why? Because of *him*?" Starcher gestured to the spot where the loser of the fight had made his exit. "God, girl, you've got a right to defend yourself, haven't you?"

She laughed bitterly. "No. That is, he was not a lover. He was a chaperon."

"Ah."

"Who wanted to be lover." She raised her glass of vodka and drank it in one draft.

Starcher then promised to visit her if ever he came to Moscow.

He did, as soon as he had been assigned to the embassy. He knew her for a potential operative even then, and he began to meet with her—not often, once every month or so, backstage at first, then for coffee in some out-of-the-way café. It wouldn't take much to turn her, he knew. She had not cooperated with the authorities since she'd gotten back from that first and last tour. She refused to compete in the 1984 Olympics, though she was a qualified gymnast. Even though the Russians later boycotted the Games, Sasha was not permitted to leave the country again. All word of her achievements was banned from the press. She was denied access to the elite stores on Granovsky Street. Whatever scant files had ever existed on her parents were conveniently lost.

Still, she fought back. She accepted no pupils. She never spoke to any government official on any pretext.

"One day I'll find my mother and father," she confided to Starcher one evening years earlier. "I'll find them and take them out of this country. And then I'll come back and kill every KGB agent I can find before they shoot me."

"Now don't get dramatic on me," Starcher had said, but something inside his head clicked in place as he watched her narrowed eyes and determined jaw. He would use her one day, he knew.

And so he had pulled every string at his disposal, every agent, every file clerk at Langley, to locate Sasha's parents.

I should have told her then, he thought. *I should tell her now.*

But he had to run Sasha. The truth would have to wait.

CHAPTER TWO

The main room in the house of the double willows was absolutely dark. Zharkov sat up woozily, smelling the reek of his own body, instantly reminded of the throbbing headache that pounded constantly now behind his eyes.

He had lived in a faint twilight world for months. As winter had melted into spring, the pace inside the walls of the jerry-built infirmary seemed to grind to a halt.

Dr. Kolodny had worked without rest. The short man, rotund at the time of his capture, was now scrawny and pinched-looking, his wire-framed eyeglasses sliding off the bridge of his nose, which was constantly shiny with sweat. It was hot in the room and the windows were never open. The gasoline fumes from the electric generator hung heavy in the air, but Kolodny was never permitted outside. Only Zharkov's subordinate, Lin, was at liberty to leave the premises.

With his Mongol features, Lin could walk unnoticed through the dense streets of Katmandu. He had adopted the dress of the region, wearing a long, sleeveless tunic and *suebas,* woolen boots soled with yak leather. In such costume he performed the shopping and all the menial tasks of the household uncomplainingly, his bland face as impassive as always.

Lin had also found ways to keep Zharkov supplied with drugs. The doctor's supplies of Demerol and of laudanum were depleted within a few weeks. To lessen Zharkov's pain, Lin procured a steady supply of black opium, and day after day Zharkov sat on his pallet, unbathed and uncaring, smoking from a long hookah, the fever of pain close to the surface of his eyes.

Zharkov, too, had grown pale and thin. As the weeks and months had progressed, he and the doctor had begun to take on an almost symbiotic relationship. Each morning Zharkov would present himself, dream-filled and stinking, to the doctor. Kolodny examined him, selected his instruments, and began to cut, using ether and novocaine sparingly, and only on the most sensitive areas. For most of the work he relied on opium. Grafts were taken from Zharkov's thighs, back, and inner arms. After only two weeks his body had resembled a patchwork quilt, until there was no more skin to take and Kolodny had to use the epidermis of pig embryos to finish the operations.

The three men rarely spoke to one another. Zharkov lived in his own dream; Lin, if he had thoughts of anything besides his household chores, did not reveal them. In the evenings, while Zharkov dozed in an opium haze and Kolodny slept the rock-hard sleep of the exhausted, Lin remained awake, watching the two of them, his master and his prisoner, listening for sounds at the door, waiting.

As time progressed, Kolodny had become feverish about his work. The reconstruction of Zharkov's face was by far the most challenging task he had ever faced. Even if the operations were performed under crude circumstances, he could see the artistry of his work emerging each time the bandages were removed from Zharkov's face.

Never was Kolodny tempted to make the face more attractive than it had been originally. His goal was to create a perfect reproduction of the pictures on his wall, now marked with notations and measurements, each plane and curve memorized. He reconstructed the thin, hooded eyelids of this man, blue-veined and sensitive, the right slightly lower than the left, the aquiline nose with its high bridge, the peaked upper lip. It was a handsome enough face, Kolodny noted more than once, although women would not have said so, since it was the sort of face that had never looked young.

He sculpted and cut, transplanting each hair of each eyebrow, each fold of ear. It was his greatest creation, a work of art in its way; a living, breathing testimonial to the genius of Kolodny's hands.

In time the doctor nearly forgot about his family and practice in Minsk. There was no time, there were no separate days. There was only work and sleep. And both were filled with only one image: the face of Alexander Zharkov.

Only one thing bothered him. It was the scar at the base of Zharkov's throat. Stanislas Kolodny was the best plastic surgeon in Minsk, perhaps the best in the entire Soviet Union. He could remake the human wreckage from motorcycle accidents and transform the simian features of a Premier's daughter into those of a refined beauty. But never, never had he seen a scar such as the coiled snake.

"Was this done originally for ornamentation?" he had once asked, fascinated by the red, twisting welt that always seemed as fresh as if it had just been created.

Zharkov stared at him through his bandages, a stare so cold and threatening that Kolodny suddenly remembered he was not in charge here. "Just remove it," Zharkov hissed.

And he had tried, first with Zharkov's own flesh and then with the smooth skin of an unborn pig. But each time the scar had been too prominent to cover. Finally Kolodny used the skin of an adult pig's belly to cover the entire area, after abrading it down to raw muscle tissue.

"There will be a slight discoloration," he announced in despair. The patch at the bottom of the throat was the only flaw in an otherwise perfect face.

"That is of no importance," the Chinese answered.

Kolodny knew better than to discuss the procedure

further with these men. Whoever they were, they were not common criminals. Obviously, the Russian was a man of importance despite his stuporous condition. In fact, Kolodny could not imagine how Zharkov withstood the pain of almost three months of facial surgery with only opium and ether. Whoever this Zharkov was, he was a man unafraid of pain.

Kolodny could determine nothing about the Asian. Although he was subordinate to Zharkov, Lin himself was articulate and intelligent. He had the cold eyes of a scholar and the bearing of a nobleman. Yet, Kolodny thought, he seemed to harbor no resentment toward Zharkov. Rather he watched over him like a servant over an ailing master.

Or so it seemed. Kolodny had seen enough Oriental faces to know that it was next to impossible to read emotion on them. Even now, on the day when the last of the bandages were to be removed, Lin sat back impassively, appraising the thin, half-naked form of Zharkov, weaving on the edge of the metal table.

"Done?" Zharkov asked, his voice phlegmy.

"Nearly," Kolodny answered, cutting the gauze and unwrapping it expertly. "The skin will still be tender and somewhat discolored, of course, but those should be temporary conditions. Keep still, please."

None of the men spoke, but Zharkov could see by the light in Kolodny's eyes that the plastic surgeon was pleased with his work. Still expressionless, Lin went to the wall, removed all the photographs of Zharkov, and threw them into the open fireplace, then lit them with a match. "We are finished here," he said softly.

"I think I have a mirror," the doctor said, eager to show off his masterwork. From the array of implements laid out on his instrument table he took a small hand mirror and gave it to Zharkov. "As you can see, there are no major scars, even on the throat." He touched the thickened area where the pigskin covered the mark Justin Gilead had once burned in Zharkov's neck. "The skin here may become slightly darker with time, but . . ." He withdrew his hand with a gasp. "It can't be," he whispered.

Zharkov felt himself shaking, first the mirror in his hand, then the trembling of his entire body as, before his eyes, the smooth skin at the base of his throat inexorably darkened and twisted, the reddening flesh changing into the shape of the coiled snake.

"This is impossible," the doctor said haltingly, his eyes fixed on the scar, which had reappeared so suddenly.

"Get out!" Zharkov screamed. He threw the mirror at the wall, where it shattered into a rain of glittering glass shards. Dr. Kolodny ducked, protecting his glasses with his cupped hands, then stumbled to the door and flung it open, running at full speed toward the lake.

A peasant passing by the house carrying water on a pole across his shoulders stopped and stared at the white man's terrified face as he rushed by. In his panic Kolodny bumped into one of the buckets and sent the peasant falling to the ground in a cascade of water. The man sat up, stunned, watching the small doctor running toward the lake. Turning around, he saw the open doorway and the elaborate infirmary where a tall Chinese stood near a half-naked white man with a strange scar on his neck.

Inside, Lin slammed the door, his black eyes registering a brief instant of panic. He stood to run after the doctor, then turned around as Zharkov grabbed a handful of instruments from the surgical tray.

"I'll take the damned thing off!" Zharkov shrieked.

Lin held his arm, shaking with the strain of Zharkov's inhuman strength. Lin was not a powerfully built man, but his hands were strong from constant practice with his knives.

Using two steely fingers he pressed hard into Zharkov's wrist until the instruments clattered to the floor. Then, in a movement as graceful as an acrobat's, the Asian took off his shirt while still grasping Zharkov's arm. He tore the fabric with his teeth and bound his superior's wrists together.

"Forgive me, Comrade Colonel," he said.

Zharkov's arms went limp. "The drugs. It has been too long. I must have no more." He closed his eyes. "Now kill the doctor," he said softly. "His work is done."

Lin nodded, expressionless.

Dr. Kolodny squinted against the sunlight. It was his first time outside in more than three months. He had never seen the exterior of the house of the double willows before.

Ahead of him stretched a large lake, its shore wide and muddy from the early spring rain. On his left, far in the distance, was a cluster of small stone and thatch houses. He knew, from overhearing Lin speak to Zharkov, that they were near the city of Katmandu.

He smelled his own fear. It had never occurred to the doctor that he would need to escape. The work had been so engrossing that he had thought of nothing else since the operations had started.

What an idiot! Of course they'd kill him. The Chinese had even taken the precaution of burning the model photographs the moment the final procedure was complete. They would never allow anyone who knew so much about the man named Zharkov to tell his story.

He ran, shambling on legs unused to exercise, toward the cluster of houses on the far side of the lake. And what a story it was, he thought. The facial burns were unimportant, except for Kolodny's work on them. But what would fascinate the medical world was the mark of the coiled snake on Zharkov's neck. How did it reappear so quickly from beneath the layers of skin? Could it be an example of stigmata? Was this medicine or miracle? And why *that* shape, the sign of Lucifer? And why that man, with his power and his secrets and his personal Chinese assassin?

Kolodny slipped twice on the slick mud of the embankment. Sweat was streaking into his eyes, and his chest felt as if it were filled with molten lead. The day was getting brighter. Kolodny guessed the time to be about nine A.M. Someone would see him.

After all, the peasant had been around. He should have stopped the man, he realized, and asked him to get help, but at the time Kolodny hadn't thought of anything except getting away. The man would still be around somewhere.

He looked around him feverishly. There was no one in sight. The peasant's buckets were still lying in front of the house, but the man had fled.

Kolodny turned away and ran. Someone would come. Someone would help him get to Katmandu, where he would telephone for help and escape the man whose face he had made from nothing, and the expressionless Oriental with the eyes of a bird of prey.

His breath came in ragged gasps now, his steps faltering on the mud, but he refused to look back. If they were following him, he did not want to know.

His heart thumped. The peasant he had bumped into was coming around the back of the cluster of houses. He was still soaking wet, his hair plastered to his head.

"*Pazhahlsta!*" the doctor shouted, waving his arms overhead. "Stop. Please."

The man looked up, saw him, hesitated for a moment, then loped toward him at a trot.

"Help me," Kolodny called out, nearly weeping with relief. Even though the breath in his lungs felt like a spear, he pumped his legs faster. "You must . . ."

The peasant stopped suddenly, staring at some point behind the doctor. His eyes widening, he turned back, running wildly toward the cluster of houses.

"No, come back!" Kolodny cried in despair.

The man ignored him. He had almost made it back behind the houses when a shot rang out, sending the peasant sprawling to the ground, his back exploding in a bright blossom of red flesh.

"Oh, God, no," the doctor whispered. Then he felt a second shot himself, in the back of his neck.

The impact of the bullet knocked him into the mud of the embankment. He heard the gun's report just before his face slammed into a rock, splintering his nose with a soft crack and shattering his eyeglasses. His mouth filled with blood, and he suddenly felt very cold and alone. He spat, surprised that he could move his facial muscles, and tried to make a fist. Weakly he picked up a stone and drew a mark in the mud before his vision failed him and the last wormlike threads of life crawled out of him.

"Are you well enough to travel?" Lin asked curtly as he closed the door behind him. Without waiting for an answer he began to gather the doctor's medical instruments and other things that could not be left behind.

Zharkov lowered himself off the table with an effort, digging his thumb knuckles into his eye sockets.

"Hurry," the Asian said, wrapping a blanket around him and half carrying him outside. "You can change into other clothes in the truck."

While Zharkov waited, Lin took two cans of gasoline into the house. A short while later he emerged, hesitating in the doorway for a moment before getting into the truck just as the house of the double willows exploded into flames. The roof crashed in as they drove away, flames shooting upward like a crown.

A hundred yards away, the body of Dr. Kolodny lay in the mud as his final message was dried into permanence by the slow, rolling heat of the fire.

Lin's truck looked like a dilapidated heap, but its engine was as sophisticated as a race car's. The six-hundred-mile trip to the Russian border took a full day, including a stop to bury Kolodny's instruments. From there, Zharkov knew, the remaining seven hundred miles to Moscow would be easy.

His withdrawal from the opium was painful. There were times, sitting in the truck with Lin, when only the force of reason convinced Zharkov that his body was not being attacked by crawling insects. Once he asked Lin to tie his wrists together to keep him from clawing at his own writhing, itching flesh. But such was the level of his discipline that he never requested more of the drug, or lost his civility toward Lin.

By the time they were near Minsk, Zharkov knew he would live, even while examining himself and realizing that he had lost a drastic amount of weight and that his skin was so pale, each of Dr. Kolodny's sutures showed a bright pink. But his mind was sure again. The drugs were out of his system. Again in control, he drifted off to sleep.

When he awoke from his nap, Zharkov said, "I don't want to enter Moscow under my own name. Not until I see what kind of reception we might get."

"Of course," Lin said. "I have papers for you."

"Which papers, please?" He held out his hand.

Lin looked over at him briefly, then pulled a large white envelope from his breast pocket. It was filled with official documents, many of which included Zharkov's photograph.

"Domestic passport, workbook, institutional pass, *kharakterstika,* and a residential permit," Lin said. "All the important ones under the name Ivan Petrov. We thought it a common enough name to go unnoticed. There's also a letter addressed to Petrov from a commune in Kazakhstan."

Zharkov examined the passport. "This is very good work. Forged?"

"Absolutely authentic. The real Petrov even bore a slight resemblance to you."

"He's dead, I assume."

"He was caught under some heavy machinery during a freak accident near the Siberian border," Lin said. "His features were obliterated, his hands smashed beyond recognition. He was never identified."

"Thorough as usual," Zharkov said. He put the papers away. "Thank you."

"My pleasure, Comrade Colonel."

He drove on, and Zharkov stared ahead, trying to will the miles away. He was going home at last.

CHAPTER THREE

TWO KGB agents, intercepting the news through a tap on the main switchboard in Katmandu's police station, arrived on the scene of Dr. Kolodny's murder even earlier than the police officers. The chief Russian investigator, a man named Boris Galanin, had photographs taken from every angle of the bombing site, the dead doctor, and the strange mark left in the mud.

The Nepalese officers were no help, arriving more out of formality than curiosity. These hill people had ways of their own and shunned intruders from the city, especially police. Even now the locals stayed shut up in their houses, reluctant even to be seen.

Besides, they reasoned, the dead man was obviously a foreigner. Let the Russians handle it. Any interference with the KGB would only result in someone else getting killed. The police from Katmandu duly recorded what facts were readily available, then left with the body. Their indifference was fine with Galanin. He didn't want any interference on this one.

"Sir, there's some blood over here," the young man with the camera said, pointing at the spot where the peasant had fallen.

"Probably dragged himself from there," Galanin mumbled, glad for once of his assistant's inexperience. Kolodny could not have moved from the site of the blood spots to the place where his body was found. His tracks all went in the opposite direction. The blood belonged to someone else.

Keeping the photographer busy at the site of the explosion, where Galanin knew nothing of value would be retrieved, he followed the trail of blood leading from the empty spot. It stopped in some recently trampled grass near a cluster of houses on the west shore of the lake.

A local had been hit, he guessed, and the neighbors had come out to help. They hadn't bothered with Kolodny, naturally. Galanin had been posted in Nepal for two years—since Nikolai Pierlenko took office—and the one thing he had learned since coming to this backward hellhole was that these people didn't want anything to do with foreigners.

He walked to the row of silent houses, where he saw a smear of blood on the side of a doorway and knocked. Getting no answer, Galanin drew his gun and opened the door with his shoulder.

Inside, a woman covered her face in fear. Beside her lay a young man on a straw pallet, his torso bound with crude bandages. He was lying on his stomach, and as he craned his neck to look up at the stranger, the wound on his back oozed blood.

"Don't be afraid," Galanin said in the local dialect. He put away his gun. "I only want to ask you some questions."

The woman wailed, but the man on the pallet waved her away, and she grew silent. They knew the intruder was KGB; it was better to give him what he wanted than to try at some pretense of innocence.

"Bullet?" Galanin asked.

The man nodded.

"Did you see him?"

"There were three. . . . One was running. I tried to help him. He was afraid, he was screaming for help. . . ."

"What about the other two?"

"One was Chinese," the man said with an effort. It

took him a few seconds to catch his breath. "The other was a white man. Another white man."

"Describe him. The white man."

The wounded man lay down his head, too weary to continue. Galanin pulled him up by his hair, but the man only groaned.

"He is hurt, can't you see that?" the woman shrieked.

Galanin let go. The man's face already had the gray cast of the dead, and his breathing was beginning to take on a heavy, rattling quality. Boris Galanin knew the peasant wouldn't last more than a few minutes.

"All right, then. I just want you to look at a picture for me. Can you do that?"

The man didn't answer, but his eyes opened. Galanin took a worn, faded photograph from his billfold. It was a grainy blowup from a group picture of Russian officers taken more than twenty years earlier. The face he showed the dying man was young, but the features had remained the same over the years: the light hair; the deep-set, hooded eyes; the humorless mouth. It was the face of Alexander Zharkov.

"Was this one of the men you saw?" Galanin asked.

The man stared at it, trying to focus. Then, slowly, he nodded his head.

"Thank you," Galanin said. He put the photograph away carefully. Then, still kneeling beside the wounded man, he took out his revolver, spun a silencer onto the barrel, and held it to the woman's forehead. "Don't make a sound," he said.

The woman complied, quaking.

Galanin pulled the trigger, spattering her brains on the far wall.

The wounded man moaned in protest and tried to squirm upright, but his arms failed him. He flattened onto the mattress, his eyes rolling. The Russian held the gun to his temple and fired.

"We've got enough," he said to the young photographer outside. "Give me the film."

*   *   *

Later that afternoon, Galanin developed the pictures himself. He put all the photographs of the exploded house, along with their negatives, in the envelope that contained his report to his superiors in Moscow. The body of a man resembling the descriptions of Dr. Stanislas Kolodny, missing since January, was recovered in a hillside settlement near Katmandu, Nepal, his report summarized. Apparently the doctor had been fleeing a residential building that had exploded. There was a wound on the back of the dead man's neck, possibly caused by flying debris from the blast. The cause of the explosion was unknown, but the victim appeared to have been living in the building alone and may have triggered the accident himself, he concluded.

He then put the other photographs into a separate envelope. These he placed in his attaché case and took to his car.

Galanin drove for three days and nights, stopping only when he could not drive without falling asleep. He rested in his car for no longer than twenty minutes at a time, ate while driving, and relieved himself along the side of the bumpy roads. On the fourth day he passed through Moscow and headed southwest. He arrived at a dense wood, where he parked his car and walked, briefcase in hand, past several men with rifles leveled at him from behind the trees.

He finally reached a metal door, which opened silently before him. Inside, Galanin opened his briefcase, removed the envelope with the photographs, and handed them to a figure half hidden in the darkness of the room.

The shadowy man clicked on a small high-intensity lamp that shone only on the photographs. He looked them over carefully, slowly.

"You've talked to a witness, you say?" he asked softly.

"I have," Galanin answered. "Alexander Zharkov is alive."

CHAPTER FOUR

Justin Gilead arrived in Katmandu two days after Zharkov and Lin left. In the squalid bustle of Dhurma Square, where legless children peddled maggot-covered meat pies before the shrines of goddesses, the murder of one foreigner was not even remembered by the townspeople.

After an afternoon of useless questioning, Justin found his way to a crumbling doorway in a stone-terraced side street of the city.

At first glance the building seemed deserted. The wooden stairway had fallen away in places. Rats scuttled to avoid his footsteps. As he reached the first landing Justin heard the faint sound of voices and smelled the sickly-sweet aroma of burning opium.

Manjusri had told him of this place. The owner was a man who had once come to his lamasery in flight from the police, and Manjusri had given him shelter. The proprietor, a Chinese named Tu-Yen, owed Manjusri the favor of his life.

Justin mounted the last set of stairs, hearing a bell ring as he trod on one step. At the top, a blotchy-faced woman waited for him. Behind her was a small room, empty except for a few divans stinking of urine.

"I am here to see Tu-Yen," he said in the local dialect.

"There is no one here by that name," the woman answered automatically, beginning to close the door.

Justin stopped her. "Tell him I come from Manjusri of the lamasery at Laskaya," he said.

The woman's eyes held no recognition. She closed the door. Justin heard her soft footsteps, followed the creak of another door opening.

A few minutes later the door was opened again, this time by an elderly man bearing features too Asiatic even for the hill peoples around Nepal. "Come with me," he said softly, motioning for Justin to enter.

He led him through the second door, into a room lit only by candlelight. The sweet smoke curled thickly in the dense air of the room, where a dozen people lay on pillows and long divans while pipes filled with black resin were brought to them. Tu-Yen found a corner in this room and gestured for Justin to sit down across from him.

"What news have you of Manjusri?" he asked softly.

"He is at the monastery at Rashimpur," Justin said, bringing out a piece of paper imprinted with the chop mark of his new teacher. Tu-Yen opened it and read it near a flickering candle.

"He says my debt to him will be repaid if I help you." He held the paper over the candle's flame until it turned to ash. Then he raised his eyes to Justin. "What is it you require?"

"Only information," Justin said. "I seek a man. A Russian. On his neck is a scar in the shape of this symbol." He held his amulet near the flame. In the flickering light the coiled snake seemed to writhe with life.

The old man stared at it, then searched Justin's face. "There is only one who may wear that amulet," he said.

"Yes. I am he."

Tu-Yen looked into his face again, then dropped to his knees. "Hail to Thee, O Patanjali." He remained kneeling, head down, until Justin touched his back and bade him rise. Finally the Chinese said, "There is a white house three doors to the south of here. Knock twice at the door, then wait and knock once more. My manservant will answer. Wait for me there. I will bring you what I can."

By nightfall, Tu-Yen appeared. He was carrying a lantern. "Come with me," he said.

They were driven to the lakeshore on the outskirts of the city, where the mountain tribesmen kept their houses. When they parked, Justin could smell the charred scent of the pile of burned rubble that had once been a house.

"A foreigner lived here for several months," Tu-Yen said. Justin forced his heart to stop pounding while he listened. "But he was not the man you seek. He was a Chinese. He bought opium. Not in quantity, just a personal supply."

"If you know I have no interest in this man, why bring me here?"

"Before he came, a woman lived in this house. Her body was found in a ravine shortly after this man's arrival."

"Did the police arrest him?"

Tu-Yen made a clicking noise. "She was never identified. The people here do not trust the authorities. But it was the woman who had lived here.

"A few years before, the same man came. He killed the woman's family in the hills."

Justin shifted his weight impatiently. "An evil man, perhaps. But not the man I seek."

"He left the day before yesterday . . . with another man. Before they set fire to this home, he shot two others. One was a villager, a neighbor, who survived the shooting. The other did not live. He was a round-eye."

Justin's jaw clenched.

"The dead foreigner did not wear the mark. But he was a famous man, a Russian doctor who had been missing for many months."

"What about the other man who left?"

"No one ever saw his face."

"Can you take me to the villager who was shot?" Justin asked. "He may have seen something."

"He is dead now," Tu-Yen said. "An officer of the Soviet secret police broke into his home. The bodies of the man and his wife were found with bullets in their heads. No one understands why the KGB would be interested enough to kill here. And they took thousands of pictures."

"Of what?"

Tu-Yen gestured with his lantern. "The dead foreigner drew this in the mud before he died."

The old man lowered the lantern to the cracked soil. In the dim yellow light Justin could read clearly the message Dr. Kolodny had left: a crude circle enclosing a coiled snake.

CHAPTER FIVE

The performance had ended and the circus was closed. Only the sideshows and cheap amusements alongside the main building were still operating. The painted wagons that housed them stood in stark contrast to the imposing brick structure of the State Circus, where internationally known stars performed to the lush strains of a live orchestra. Here, the tinny, recorded music was barely audible above the noise of the nearby subway, the lights from dim yellow bulbs hardly illuminating the darkness of an April night.

Sasha milled around the sparse crowd that had idly gathered around a wagon bearing the printed sign: LEARN THE SECRETS OF THE PHARAOHS.

She wore a plain knit beret on her head, a pair of glasses with out-of-style frames, and smoked a cigarette. Again no one recognized her. Perhaps it was because Muscovites were unused to having celebrities walk among them. In this ostensibly classless society, members of the privileged orders almost never associated with commoners. They shopped at different stores, ate at different restaurants, and attended different functions. If Sasha Kaminskaya were to announce her identity to the idlers around the sideshow, no one would have believed her.

When the crowd had swelled to as large a size as it would ever be, a scowling middle-aged man appeared from the side of the wagon. His appearence was utterly bizarre, from the stained "Egyptian" headdress around his painted, sagging face to the ragged Russian overcoat covering his naked chest.

His name was Dmitri Kraskovich, a Ukrainian whose decades with the circus had been based exclusively on his expertise in the black market. Whatever the bureaucrats who ran the circus wanted—liquor, girls, imported clothes for their women—Kraskovich could supply, as long as no questions were asked. In exchange he was issued a permit for his show every year, despite its lack of educational value and the fact that the good Kraskovich used an unregistered alien minor as an assistant.

"Forty kopecks," he said, deftly passing a box around the crowd. He paused at Sasha, giving her a particularly sour look as he shoved the box in front of her.

His breath smelled of liquor. She dropped in some change and blew a cloud of cigarette smoke in his face before stubbing out the butt on the ground.

Kraskovich walked away. Like all professional parasites, he knew when to swallow his pride. But he didn't have to like the meddlesome yellow-haired bitch. The boy in his act, the foreigner, cozied up to her, although he had no idea what interest a grown woman would have in a sullen brat with no endearing characteristics. Who knew? Maybe she was a pervert.

God knows, they were always sitting around over a chessboard. Who knew what their hands were doing under the table. Once Kraskovich had even caught the boy in La Kaminskaya's private dressing room.

He'd punished him then. Oh, yes. And with good reason. His kind didn't belong with the stars of the State Circus. The girl should have been grateful instead of having Kraskovich arrested and charged with assault.

The circus officials had cleared things up then, but not without a humiliating reprimand and a threat to look into the death of the boy's predecessor, who was found beaten and in a coma in a Moscow alley. Since then, Kraskovich had made sure not to mark the boy's face or hands. If the bitch wanted to charge him with striking the boy below the waist, she would have to admit how she'd seen the evidence.

He smirked as he got back into the trailer and stashed the money in a strongbox.

"Ready?" he asked the boy. The boy didn't answer. He never did. Kraskovich took off his coat, threw down another swig of vodka against the cold, and raised the side of the wagon.

Sasha shifted from one foot to the other, stifling a yawn as Kraskovich began his incantations to the ancient gods of Egypt. After all her years around the old phony, she was still surprised that anyone bothered to pay to see his drivel. He practiced the cheapest, most transparent illusions imaginable. Even a child could see through Kraskovich's sloppy tricks, pulling rubber snakes from the boy's mouth or pretending to cut him in two.

She felt sorry for the boy. Everyone knew that Kraskovich had killed his last assistant in one of his drunken rages, and he'd been big for his age. This one was small, with a good mind for chess, which meant he could think. Thinking was unhealthy for anyone around Kraskovich.

"God knows whose ass the little *zopocnik* was sticking his tongue in before I took him on," was how Kraskovich introduced his new protégé. But the boy hadn't complained, not so much as a whimper, even after the beatings, which had been heard by everyone in the circus. He seemed to accept all things with the patience of a stranger who knows he has no rights.

Kraskovich, in his ridiculous costume, raised his arms in triumph as he pretended to saw through a box where the boy lay, rubber feet dangling improbably from the far end. There was mild and scattered applause, but most of the onlookers were busy gossiping with each other, paying little attention to the forty-kopeck spectacle. Scanning the crowd, the boy's tan face was blank until he spotted

Sasha, then broke into a restrained smile. Sasha smiled back.

Some of the audience wandered away, disappointed in the predictable finale in which Kraskovich would reassemble the box, and the boy would step out. Someone flicked a cigarette butt at the magician. Kraskovich swore and made a lewd gesture at the perpetrator while he chanted the magic "Egyptian" words. Some of the spectators laughed.

But the boy kept his eyes on Sasha, and she nodded encouragement to him. Finally Kraskovich removed the lid to the box.

"Rise and walk, young Pharaoh," he commanded.

The boy did not move.

"You are whole again. Rise!" Kraskovich shot a dirty look into the casketlike box, but still the boy did nothing but gaze at Sasha, his stare now glassy and unfocused. A titter rose from the sparse crowd.

"Maybe you'd better goose him," someone yelled. Kraskovich maintained an air of arrogant dignity but surreptitiously prodded inside the casket with his wooden scepter. The boy didn't respond, not even with a blink of his transfixed eyes.

The laughter of the crowd dissipated, replaced by restless silence. Sasha pushed her way toward the front, alarmed, and looked into the box.

Her breath caught in her throat. Her face drained of color. Something was happening there inside that box, something so inexplicable that even Kraskovich stood gaping. The boy's face had turned to the audience. He was staring through them as if they were made of smoke.

Then he rose from the coffin.

Not with his arms or legs, not with wires or pulleys or an invisible platform beneath him. He simply floated, higher, higher, until his prone body hovered a foot above the top edge of the box. It remained there, suspended in midair for a full ten seconds before beginning its descent.

Through it all no one spoke; no one even seemed to breathe. It wasn't until the boy sat up, grinning at Sasha for her approval, that Kraskovich flourished his scepter and flicked the switch that turned the tinny music on again.

The crowd shouted cheers. Kraskovich bowed theatrically. The boy flushed, his rail-thin arms shivering with cold. Only Sasha remained immobile, her brow creased by two deep lines, as the side of the wagon came down.

She stood there for some time while the crowd stumbled away, all of them chattering excitedly about the magnificent feat of the strange young boy in the sideshow.

How did he do it?

Sasha lit another cigarette and walked around the circus grounds, breathing the acrid, familiar circus scent of animals, sawdust, and cheap junk food. The trick had been none of Kraskovich's doing—of that she was sure. The old drunk didn't have the skill for such a sophisticated illusion.

The question was, had it been an *illusion*?

Sasha Kaminskaya was not a gullible young girl. Nor was she susceptible to tricks. She had been raised in circuses, among people who used trickery for a living. During her short life she had seen magicians of every variety, from mind readers to men who ostensibly could make buildings disappear. But she had never seen a levitation as convincing as the boy's.

What made it even more strange was that it wasn't the first time she had wondered about the boy. There had been another, eerier incident. A couple of months before, she had miscalculated her timing at the very beginning of her act and released the trapeze bar too early. She had panicked in the split second it took to realize that she wouldn't make the catcher's grip. Since Sasha never worked with a net, a miss could mean death. She stretched in as far as she could. Her catcher, too, pulled himself to the limit, but it was not enough. Time froze. She felt the sickening sensation of dropping. The audience saw it, too, rising to its feet in shock and concern. But then, just as the nausea began to rise in her throat and the figure of the catcher seemed to grow perceptibly smaller, she inexplicably felt herself propelled upward.

When she connected with her catcher, the audience cheered as it had never cheered before. Still, she had been so shaken that she barely made it through the rest of the act and had canceled her trademark quadruple somersault. When she walked off, perspiring so heavily that she could scarcely see, she spotted the boy standing near the exit curtain. He had smiled at her then, but she was too upset to acknowledge him.

She had tried not to think of that incident again, because she hadn't wanted the memory to shake her confidence. But now, again, she wondered. How could a person fall *up*?

She had to ask him. Tonight, before she left. She knew he had the kind of crush on her that every lonely young man feels for an older woman who has shown him friendship, but had he saved her life? *With his mind?*

She checked her watch. He ought to be alone by now. Quickly she walked back to the old trailer.

The sideshow had closed. The boxy wagons stood abandoned in the darkness, the crowds gone. But Kraskovich was still there. She could hear his gravelly voice berating the boy behind the trailer.

"Why couldn't you do that for the owners?" he shouted. His words were slurred. Sasha could tell he'd been drinking. "For them you're a nothing, a parasite."

She heard the crack of flesh against flesh and winced. The boy's face was probably the target.

"I could have a place in the main building. Money, the newspapers, everything. We'd be famous. Power to do whatever we wanted. But you are too lazy. Now, tonight, with no one but bums watching, you do this act for a handful of kopecks. Idiot!"

There was another thud. The wagon shook.

"Why did you pick tonight? It was *her,* wasn't it? It was because she was watching, the tramp on the trapeze. Is she giving you some? Is that why you're so lazy and worthless that you can't be bothered to make an effort unless she's there to make you hot? *Igrat' v volokite?*"

Sasha heard a low moan, like an animal's growl, then Kraskovich's strangled cry and the crash of glass. She ran around to the back of the trailer.

Kraskovich's eyes fluttered on her for the briefest second. He was standing a few feet away from the boy. His left hand was rubbing his neck. There was the jagged neck of a vodka bottle in his right.

"He attacked me," he said to Sasha. "He deserves what he's going to get. And you'd better clear out if you don't want to see it."

The boy never looked at her.

"Stop it!" she shouted. "Leave him alone or I'll call the police."

"Try it and you'll be next," Kraskovich said, raising the broken bottle.

Sasha started to run toward him, but the magician suddenly convulsed, screamed and turned away.

"*Cort voz'mej,*" he muttered, gasping out the curse as the bottle shook violently in his hand. He panted like a crazed animal, eyes glaring at his arm as if it belonged to someone else when it drew the sharp edges of the broken bottle closer to his face. Then, with a sob, his whole body arched, and he dashed the jagged glass against his own throat.

As Kraskovich dropped, his lips still moving in a pink froth, a fountain of blood shot out of his neck. It splashed Sasha's face. She staggered backward and fell to the ground, stunned.

The boy remained motionless, his hands hanging at his sides. He turned his head in a jerky motion toward Sasha. For a moment her eyes met his—ice-blue, large, and staring—and the only thought that came into her mind struck her as absurdly stupid afterward: *This is all a part of things*. And she felt a strange peace with that benediction.

Then the boy blinked, and whatever thread had connected them for that moment snapped.

"You have to get out of here," she said. "Come with me."

The boy shook his head no.

"It's not safe for you. The police may not understand. He did business with some of them."

"They won't harm me," he said. "I will go when I'm ready. But not with you. I have a place." He turned away from her.

Sasha got to her feet, rubbed the blood off her face with the palms of her hands, and ran.

CHAPTER SIX

Richard Rand's new assistant at the embassy was a young Harvard man named Mark Cole. Rand liked him. Tall, intelligent, well connected, he fit the diplomatic profile of the new CIA perfectly. He also provided a target other than Rand, himself, for the maniacs who were killing Americans in Moscow at random.

They had discussed the killings in Rand's office immediately after Cole had arrived that afternoon. The younger man obviously appreciated Rand's choice of furnishings, handling objects with the respect they deserved instead of treating everything as an ashtray for a smelly cigar.

"Did they tell you at Langley that Andy Starcher is here?"

"Yes, sir," Cole said, suddenly looking uncomfortable.

Rand's face fell. "I take it his dismissal wasn't approved."

"No, Mr. Rand. Langley got your request, but the people in Covert want to give him a little more time."

"Damn it. Can't they see that the old fool could undermine everything the Ambassador's trying to do with the Russians? He's already killed a civilian."

Cole shrugged. "Covert trusts him. In all fairness, sir, the man does have a good record."

"He's a hundred years old, for God's sake. His mind's wilting with delusions of the Red Peril. I'll tell you how bad his paranoia is. Just last night he told me he thinks the man he murdered is part of some secret KGB squad."

Cole smiled. "Are you serious?"

"I wish I weren't. According to Starcher, this maniacal fraternity of homicidal agents is so secret, even the Premier doesn't know about it. Only Starcher, the avenging Russkie-buster."

The younger man laughed out loud. "Incredible. Simply incredible. How on earth did he get an idea like that?"

"An agent he's running told him, he says. Obviously someone who likes a joke."

"An agent? I thought Starcher was working alone."

"Oh, that's another thing. This is someone he recruited himself."

"Has this guy been cleared through Langley, at least?"

"Who knows?" Rand said hotly. "Starcher won't even give me his name."

Cole blinked in disbelief. "You don't know who he's using for an operative?"

"That's right. You see, Starcher doesn't trust me. As far as he's concerned, I'm probably a Russian agent too." He sat back heavily in his seat. "And Langley wants to keep him here."

"Is there any chance he might be right? About the KGB squad, I mean."

Rand shot him a disgusted look.

"No, I suppose not," Cole admitted.

Rand sipped at a cup of tea. "Well, we don't make the decisions. We just have to live with them. Maybe you can make more sense out of the old beanbag than I can."

"I'll certainly try, sir," Cole said, flashing Rand an orthodontically flawless smile.

*　　　*　　　*

That night Cole was introduced to the other embassy personnel at a small reception.

"We're all glad to have you aboard, Mark," Rand said as he shook the young man's hand. "I'm afraid Mrs. Rand and I have to leave for a party the French Ambassador's giving, so you're in charge here."

"Yes, sir," Cole said brightly, standing very erect.

Rand consciously straightened his posture. Even after the fourteen hours of connecting flights from the States with no sleep, followed by one of the dreariest cocktail parties on record, Cole's handsome face was as fresh and poised as if he were posing for an ad in *Gentleman's Quarterly*. With more than a twinge of envy Rand saw himself in that face, or a version of himself that had existed before the nightmare of living in Moscow. Rand had once been one of the bright young men of the diplomatic set, with endless energy and firm ambition.

Well, let Cole run with the ball, he thought wearily as he helped his wife on with her coat, so that they could make an appearance at a party at the French embassy. Eighteen more months in this chamber of horrors and he would be on his way to Vienna. Civilization. A language that made some sense. And no more cowboy spies.

His driver snapped to attention as the Rands approached the big ZIL limo waiting outside. Jesus, it wasn't even Russian spies he worried about, Rand thought. It was the Company's own field men. If it weren't for crazy spooks like Starcher murdering everybody who looked at him sideways, détente might have a chance to work.

His wife's taffeta dress rustled as he settled in next to her. The chauffeur started the engine and pulled away from the curb.

Rand's training was in diplomacy and intelligence, not espionage. He had never liked the glory-boy agents with their Genghis Khan mentality. As far as he was concerned, they weren't just wrong; they were dangerous. The way to achieve peace wasn't through armed confrontation. Compromise was the key. Compromise, discussion, give-and-take.

After Starcher's debacle in Cuba, the Agency was willing to give peace a chance through Rand's appointment as Head of Station in Moscow, even though the damage to relations had already been done. But who'd been sent in as soon as there was a little problem? Starcher. There was just no way to win.

He sighed deeply, thinking thoughts of Vienna in summer, as the limousine sped through the starless night.

"What's that up ahead, dear?"

Rand looked up. Ahead were two sawhorses with blinking lights. He tapped the driver on the shoulder. "Roadblock?" he asked in Russian.

The driver shrugged. "Probably a police search."

Disgusted, Rand took out his diplomatic passport. "This had better not take long," he said. "I'm exhausted."

But the man in charge of the lights wasn't a policeman. He was an ordinary-looking, well-conditioned, middle-aged man in work-clothes. As he neared the car's headlights Rand's driver stepped out hurriedly.

"They're all yours," he said in Russian to the approaching man.

Rand's wife gasped. "What is this, Richard? What is he—"

Her words became a scream as the man pulled a gun with a silencer out of his jacket and leveled it at the driver, who could only stare disbelievingly.

"But you said—"

The bullet took him expertly in the middle of the forehead, with no blood.

Rand reached for the door, but by that time, the man had reached inside the car with his weapon and popped three rounds into Mrs. Rand's chest.

Her head snapped back violently. Blood shot out of her mouth and hit the gray flannel ceiling of the car, then dripped back onto her dress.

"Oh, God, no," Rand whispered, reaching a tentative hand toward her.

He never felt the first bullet, nor the second, nor third.

In fact, one of the sources of confusion about the murder after the bodies were found was why the killer had shot Richard Rand twenty-seven times.

Every part of his body had been struck by bullets. A madman, the newspapers would say. A terrorist gang. Perhaps, they would hint, the killings had even been orchestrated by the American CIA to push forward a confrontation between the world's superpowers. The Soviet journalists would not mention that now seven Americans had been killed on the streets of Moscow.

Neither would they mention that one part of Richard Rand's body had been spared the bullet. His neck had been left clean, reserved for a particular mutilation.

On it was burned the mark of the coiled snake.

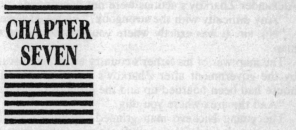

CHAPTER SEVEN

Zharkov looked at himself in the mirror. The facial scars had almost completely healed. Only the red welt on his neck stood out in perfect bas-relief. He regarded it with horrible fascination until a knock came at the door. Covering the scar with the high collar he always wore, he opened the door.

A big Scandinavian-looking Russian named Malenadze entered with a metal strongbox. Like the man's boots, it had been wiped off but not washed clean of earth. The aide's fingernails, too, still bore the grime of digging.

Zharkov examined the box, found that the locks hadn't been tampered with, then nodded for the aide to set it in a corner of the room.

The small apartment in the unfashionable district off Leningrad Road near the old Dynamo Stadium had recently been converted into temporary headquarters for Nichevo. Zharkov lived simply. A cot against the wall and a small hot plate were the only amenities he needed. Those and a chessboard on which the pieces were placed in exactly the same positions they had held during a game played years before with an opponent long vanished. The rest of the place was filled with desks, hard chairs, and communications equipment.

The Nichevo men, as they appeared at Zharkov's bidding, asked no questions about their leader. He was back; he was in charge again. That was enough. No one asked why Nichevo was no longer working for the Premier—or, seemingly, for anyone. It didn't matter. Alexander Zharkov's actions were not questioned.

"Any difficulty with the strongbox?" he asked tersely.

"No, sir. It was exactly where you showed me on the map."

The map was of his father's country estate, confiscated by the government after Zharkov's disappearance. The house had been boarded up and the grounds neglected.

"And the area where you dug?"

The young Nichevo man grinned. "I buried another box in its place. I filled it with old magazines from the early days of the Revolution. If anyone finds it, they'll think your father was saving Stalin's speeches."

Zharkov stared at him for a moment. The man's grin waffled. Then Zharkov permitted himself a chuckle that grew into a hearty laugh and rumpled Malenadze's hair. The aide, astonished at such a show of affection from a man who was famous for his disdain of physical contact, felt a wobbly smile return to his face.

"Very good, Malenadze. Very clever. You were not seen?"

"No, sir. I was done before dawn. I've been driving since then."

Zharkov was silent for some time, appraising the young man. He was the youngest of the six men remaining in the Nichevo inner circle.

Only six of us left, Zharkov thought.

The secret of Nichevo's perfection had always been its size. There had never been more than a dozen men in the core of the operation. Excellent men, to be sure, each one superior in his field, but still only a dozen. Zharkov's father had determined during Nichevo's first years that twelve was the maximum number possible in an enterprise in which there could be no weakness, no question of loyalty, and no mistakes.

But the numbers had changed. Zharkov lost five men in Cuba to Starcher and Justin Gilead. Afterward, during his two-year absence, another member had died of heart failure. Of the original twelve, only five men remained, plus Zharkov.

These five he summoned to Moscow from around the world. He would need them all to fight Justin Gilead again.

Lin had expressed concern over embarking on a mission with so few men. He counseled delay, advising Zharkov to wait until some new members had been recruited, but Nichevo was no democracy. Zharkov would have no delay. Six men would have to do.

"Malenadze," he said finally, "it may be that we will have to go on a journey, all of us. You will, of course, come along."

The young man's face flushed with pride. "It will be my honor, Comrade Colonel. Where will we go?"

"*If* we go, we will go to the Himalayas. We will be searching for one man. When we find him, we must kill him."

"Only one man, sir?"

"One man. But he will not be easy to kill."

"A soldier, then," the young man ventured.

"No. A priest."

Another knock sounded at the door.

Lin entered without being asked. His expressionless eyes looked levelly at Zharkov, then at Malenadze.

"You may leave now," Zharkov said quietly. The young man walked from the room, locking the door behind him.

"There has been another murder," Lin said without preamble. "The American cultural attaché, Richard Rand."

"The CIA Head of Station?" Zharkov said, almost amused.

Lin nodded. "We intercepted a call to the militsia. I got there before the police and saw the body."

"And?"

"Rand was shot three times, but when the KGB arrived, a few minutes after the police, they unloaded four automatic handguns into the body. They used American guns."

"American? Are you certain?"

"Yes, sir. I was well hidden but near enough to see. The police took the weapons as evidence later."

Understanding smoothed the lines from Zharkov's brow. "So that the CIA will be blamed for the murder of their own man, I suppose."

"Evidently," Lin said. "Rather a heavy-handed solution, but it may save the Soviet administration from some immediate retaliation by the Americans. From what I understand, there have been several murders of Americans in Moscow over the past three months. Rand's death is bound to cause serious repercussions in the West."

Zharkov arched an eyebrow. "If that's the case, it's unlikely that the KGB murdered Rand to begin with."

"Most unlikely, given Premier Pierlenko's efforts toward peace with the United States." Lin lowered his voice, although the two of them were alone in the room. "Sir, there is something else you should know about the dead man."

"Yes?"

"His body was marked, Colonel. The neck. Someone branded him with the emblem of a coiled snake in a circle."

Zharkov came crashing forward.

"It is identical to your own."

Zharkov sat in stunned silence for a long moment, his breathing shallow, the muscles of his throat stretched taut. Finally he noticed that Lin was still waiting at attention.

"Go," he said quietly.

Lin saluted and went out.

Zharkov's mouth was dry. He opened the box Malenadze had brought and took out a folder. The rest of the box was filled with letters. In the folder was a photograph of a man with a golden amulet around his neck. An amulet of a coiled snake inside a circle.

He had to sort out his thoughts. He might be wrong, after all. He couldn't allow himself the luxury of believing something simply because he wanted it to be true.

The killing wasn't KGB. Too risky, too blatant—not their style anymore. Premier Pierlenko's fear of a confrontation with the West was well known. Now, if Konstantin Kadar were still in power, he thought, there would have been no question in his mind about Rand's killers. The Vozhd would have wanted to provoke America into war while the Soviets were still ahead in the arms race. But Pierlenko was different, and these days the KGB was different too.

The Americans?

No. The CIA would not kill Rand under any circumstances, even if the man were a proven traitor. The Americans didn't operate that way.

There was only one answer: Rand's murderer was the same man whose face looked up from the old photograph. He was here, in Moscow. And the killing, Zharkov was sure, was a message.

The Grandmaster was calling a challenge to him.

Zharkov touched the face on the photograph as if it were living flesh, then set a match to it and watched it burn.

CHAPTER EIGHT

The second time Sergei Ostrakov was summoned before the Premier, he took time to wash. He appeared in full uniform, buttons shining, battle decorations displayed proudly despite the fact that it was four o'clock in the morning.

"You cut a fine figure," Pierlenko said, smiling at the former general. Ostrakov still had no commission in the Army. The ostentatious show of military splendor was obviously a ploy to get one.

In time, the Premier thought. *But first you work for those eggs on your epaulets.*

There was another man, handsome and bored-looking, sitting in a chair in the corner of the Premier's office.

"Excuse me, Comrade Ostrakov. This is Comrade Sterlitz, who heads the Committee. You may talk freely in front of him."

Ostrakov nodded glumly. It was one thing to talk to the Premier but something else entirely to spill what he knew to the Director of the KGB. Words spoken in front of such a man had a way of coming back to haunt a person. Ostrakov suddenly had the thought that instead of being returned to duty status, he might have just become an expendable man.

"Let me come to the point," Pierlenko said brusquely. Ostrakov snapped even more rigidly to attention. "When last we spoke, you mentioned an Alexander Zharkov. How many people knew of his existence?"

Ostrokov looked puzzled. "Why, I don't really know, sir. The Gen—the former General Secretary, of course . . . " He floundered. "There was a Nichevo staff also—"

Pierlenko cut him off with a sharp gesture. "There's no record of anyone—repeat, *anyone*—who ever worked for this so-called Nichevo."

Ostrakov blinked. "But I don't—"

"And there is no mention of this Zharkov. Not a word, not a photograph. Not in any section, any computer. Nothing to prove he ever existed."

"But you know he did! You knew his father."

"Of course. The point is, the *records* have somehow been blanked out of the master computer files. Is Nichevo capable of such a thing?"

Ostrakov toyed with his hands. "Nichevo is capable of anything, sir. That is why Comrade Kadar permitted their existence. Nichevo was useful to him."

"Would Nichevo operate without Zharkov?"

"No, sir. Nichevo only reported to Colonel Zharkov."

"I thought they worked for the Premier," Pierlenko said.

"Only through Zharkov, sir."

"But he's been missing for over two years," the KGB Director snapped. "Or isn't he missing? What do you know about that?"

Ostrakov stared at his shoes. "I don't . . . that is . . ."

"Never mind," Pierlenko said. "Come with me." He led the fat man out of the room, Sterlitz following. The guards in the corridor snapped to attention, as did every guard they passed, until they again reached the basement morgue.

The attendant there was noisily eating a sausage when the three men walked in. Choking, he drew his hands first across his mouth, then across the front of his lab coat, as he fumbled upright.

"Sir."

"Show us the body, please," Pierlenko said.

The attendant scurried away. He did not have to be told which body. There was only one corpse presently in the morgue that warranted the attention of the General Secretary himself.

He came back wheeling a gurney that held the naked, sheet-covered body of the American cultural attaché.

"Here is the report of the examination, sir," he said, holding out a fluttering sheet of paper. "No other recent scars, no sign of torture or forced captivity . . ."

Pierlenko waved him away. The attendant seemed to melt out the door.

When the two officials were alone with Ostrakov, Sterlitz pulled the sheet down to Rand's chest and shoved the corpse's head backward.

Ostrakov gasped.

"What do you know about this?"

"It . . . it is the same mark Colonel Zharkov carried," Ostrakov said incredulously. "In the same place."

"Is it the symbol of Nichevo?" Pierlenko asked.

The fat man squeezed his eyes shut, trying desperately to organize, to remember. "I don't think so," he said. "There was another man once . . . Zharkov hated him. And in Cuba, I saw him . . . I'm sure I did, only everything happened so fast then. . . ."

"Did he have the same scar?" Pierlenko asked impatiently.

"Not a scar. A necklace of some kind. But with the same mark: the coiled snake."

"And the man's name?"

"An American. A CIA operative. But I had heard that he, too, died in Cuba. I heard—"

"Dammit, his *name,*" the KGB man barked.

"Gideon, Gillian . . ." He looked at Pierlenko helplessly. "I'm sorry, Comrade General Secretary."

"Think!" Pierlenko snapped.

Ostrakov sweated. *Govno,* he should have paid more

attention. The American was the reason Zharkov went to Cuba in the first place.

And he was sure the American was the reason Zharkov disappeared then too. But it was all so long ago, ages ago, before he'd ever dreamed his life could disintegrate in the way it had. . . .

"Gilead," he said triumphantly, his head suddenly clear. "The man's name was Justin Gilead. They called him the Grandmaster."

Later, alone in his office, Nikolai Pierlenko tried to sort it all out. First, the man who had been killed at the circus was a former KGB man who had been in Cuba at the same time Zharkov had been there. Possibility: He had worked with Zharkov, even if Ostrakov had said that the man's mission was to kill Zharkov.

Item: All references to Zharkov and Nichevo had been wiped out of the computers and written, hard-copy files. Ostrakov had said that Nichevo was capable of such a thing.

Possibility: Nichevo was still functioning.

Item: Ostrakov had said Nichevo worked only for Zharkov.

Possibility: Zharkov was still alive.

Item: Ostrakov had said that there was bad blood between former Premier Kadar and Zharkov.

Possibility: This was just a ruse to cover the trail of their collusion with each other.

Item: Somebody was killing Americans and imperiling Pierlenko's hold on the Party apparatus.

Possibility: Kadar and Zharkov were working together, with Nichevo, to try to drive Pierlenko from office.

So many possibilities. They could all be answered if only he had Kadar. And that fool Sterlitz had allowed the man to slip away. Where was he? There had been no sign of him. Was it possible that Sterlitz, too, was working with Kadar?

And who was Justin Gilead? Something was going on that Pierlenko didn't understand.

They called him the Grandmaster. . . .
Pierlenko reached for the telephone.

"Mr. Cole?"

"Yes?" the young man answered sleepily, groping for
the alarm clock beside the bed. It was five A.M. Outside, the first light of dawn shone through the frost on
the window.

"American embassy calling, Ambassador Downing on
the line. Go ahead, please."

"Yes, sir," Cole said, suddenly wide-awake as he heard
the operator switch off.

"I'm afraid I've got some bad news for all of us." The
Ambassador's smooth voice held a hint of panic. "Rich-
ard Rand and his wife were found dead a few hours ago.
They were murdered."

"Oh, my God. Who—"

"Unfortunately the killer or killers have not yet been
apprehended." There was a slight pause as Downing
sipped a drink. "The bodies are being held at the Kremlin. I've notified the authorities that we'll be coming to
claim them."

"I'll take care of it right away, sir."

"Thank you," Downing said wearily.

"Sir?" Cole could picture the Ambassador reluctantly
putting the phone back to his ear. "Has the President—"

"All appropriate authorities have been notified," the
smooth voice said sharply. "We are to consider ourselves
on alert."

The KGB Director walked back into Nikolai Pierlenko's
office carrying a computer printout, which he laid on the
Premier's desk.

Pierlenko looked down.

GILEAD. GILEAD, JUSTIN. GELIAD. GILIAD.
GILDEA. JUSTIN. JUSTINE, JUST. The list of spell-
ing variants covered two separate sheets of paper. Next
to each entry was the same response: NO FILE.

Pierlenko snapped, *"Cort voz'mej.* Damn it, your success in finding this Justin Gilead is equal only to your brilliance in finding Konstantin Kadar."

The KGB Director looked pained. "I am still trying, sir. I am awaiting a phone—"

The telephone rang. Pierlenko nodded to Sterlitz.

"Yes," the Director said, nodding. "What do you know of a man named Justin Gilead?" He made notes as he listened. Finally he said, "Very good. Thank you."

He looked pleased with himself as he hung up the telephone and met Pierlenko's quizzical eyes.

"That was my man in charge of security for the national chess team. When I heard that Justin Gilead was known as the Grandmaster, I thought he might be known to our chess—"

"Get on with it, man. Who is Justin Gilead?"

Sterlitz looked at his notes and cleared his throat. "Justin Gilead is an American grandmaster. My man says that he is possibly the greatest of all chess players. There is no doubt that he was an American spy. It seemed that there was some kind of enmity between him and Colonel Zharkov and that the failure of the Cuban fiasco was probably the work of this Justin Gilead. According to my man, he used his chess ranking as a cover for his work for the CIA. He played infrequently in international tournaments, but whenever he did, we lost personnel or . . . more," he said, finishing discreetly.

"Where is he now?" Pierlenko asked.

"My man does not know. Gilead dropped from sight after Cuba. There were rumors that he was dead. My man said that his contact here was with Andrew Starcher, the former head of the CIA in Moscow."

"Former? Where is he now?"

"He has retired. He lives in Virginia in the United States," Sterlitz said. He smiled thinly.

The idiot expects praise, Pierlenko thought. "Find Kadar," he muttered.

"I beg your pardon, sir?"

The Premier looked up at him with a glance that threatened personal violence. "I said find Kadar," he hissed past clenched teeth. "I don't care if it's through this chess player or through your ass, but don't come back here without him."

Sterlitz nodded, glassy-eyed. "Yes, sir."

"*Zopa s ruckoj*," Pierlenko sighed.

Two hours later Justin Gilead stood in front of the ornate entrance to Moscow's subway on Tchaikovsky Square, watching. In the early-morning sunshine, a river of people with passive and unfamiliar faces poured out of the station, shoving past him. The flood soon diminished to a trickle and then vanished as the people made their way to separate destinations. Justin moved on.

He didn't know where or how to look for one face in a city of six million people. For a boy he had never seen before.

If Andrew Starcher was still working in Moscow for the CIA, that would have been his answer. But he had not seen Starcher for two years, since Cuba, and the old man had been wounded then. By now Starcher was retired and living back in Virginia. Or dead.

Justin had grown gaunt since the beginning of his journey from Katmandu. Much of the trip had been on foot. He lived on the generosity of farm families he met along the way, and on what he could scavenge from the fields. There were no fields in this gray city of oversize stone, and Justin was hungry.

His feet were uncomfortable in the lumpy *suebas* he'd brought before leaving the mountains. The cloth jacket he wore hung loosely on him like rags on a scarecrow. For the first time since leaving Rashimpur almost twenty years earlier, he felt afraid.

Before, he had feared only the great abstractions: hunger, loneliness, injury; the noble things that drive youth to adventure. Now, at forty-two, he no longer feared even death. What ate away at him was a fear deeper than death. It was the fear that he would never find Alexander Zharkov again.

If Manjusri was right, the Russian was more dangerous

now than ever. And the boy. How would he ever find *him*? Justin had never even seen his face. What was more, what could he do if he did find them? He was just an ordinary man, no matter what Manjusri and his monks chose to believe.

Trust yourself. There is no other way.

So be it, he thought. If it was Brahma's will that he confront the Prince of Death and die by his hand, Justin could accept that. There were worse things than death, he knew. He had lived through most of them.

He caught a glimpse of his own face in the reflection of a store window. It was a face he had not seen in many years: a hard face, no longer beautiful in the way it had been in his youth. What he saw was the reflection of a man who had led a difficult life.

Just then he saw another reflection, a vision that stopped the blood in his veins. In the glass he recognized the cruel mouth, the aristocratic nose, the hooded eyes. Zharkov's face, thirty years younger but with one other difference: The eyes of the boy were as blue as ice.

He whirled around. Down the street, a slender back disappeared into a crowd congregated near the Tchaikovsky Music Hall. Justin ran to catch him, bursting into the center of the group, searching every face for the haunting image he had seen in the window. But the boy was gone.

A man with bright red hair walked through the forest where Boris Galanin had brought his message from Nepal. Again the rifles in the trees were leveled but did not fire. Again a man sitting in the half shadows of a darkened room waited and listened.

"Someone was digging on Zharkov's estate this morning," the red-haired man said. "He removed a box and replaced it with another. One of our men followed him when he left. Another dug up the box."

The man sitting in darkness flicked on a small tensor lamp so that its light shone into the eyes of the red-haired man. "What was inside?"

"Nothing of consequence, but we kept it just the same.

The fellow who put it there was careful about not being followed. We had to change cars and drivers five times to keep him from becoming more suspicious than he already was."

The voice behind the bright glare of the bulb said, "He was trained to be careful. But you stayed with him despite his precautions, I presume."

"We did. He entered a building near the Dynamo Stadium. When he came out, he didn't have the box with him."

"Did you kill him?"

"No, sir."

"Good."

There was a long silence. Then the tensor lamp clicked off, and the red-haired man knew it was time to leave.

CHAPTER NINE

Starcher met the acting Head of Station at the embassy. It was a risk for him to return, but it was also easier than letting Cole come to him. The green-gilled Harvard boy probably wouldn't even know if he was being followed. So Starcher donned a black toupee, added some padding around his stomach, and blended in with a group of American tourists entering the building. From then on things were easy.

The entire floor housing the cultural attaché's office seemed to be on the verge of hysteria. But Starcher had to admit that Mark Cole seemed to have himself under control.

"Hell of a welcome to Moscow," Starcher said.

"That's the truth. I was here less than twelve hours when Rand was murdered and mutilated. Ambassador Downing woke me with the news." He extended his hand. "Sorry for running on like this. I guess I'm still a little shaky. Thanks for coming so quickly, Mr. Starcher."

Starcher shook his hand. "How was Rand mutilated?"

Cole sighed and picked up some photographs, thrusting them at Starcher. "The bodies are at a local funeral home, being prepared for transit back to the States. Hideous, isn't it?"

Starcher leafed through the pictures of Rand's body. "I've seen worse," he said. "This looks like a plain old-fashioned gangland massacre."

"In more ways than one. All but three bullets in him were of American make."

"The other three Russian?"

Cole nodded.

"Russkie bullshit," Starcher said as he tossed the photos back onto the desk without looking at the entire stack.

"What do you mean?"

Starcher gestured toward the pictures. "What makes this murder different from the others? You do know about the others, don't you?"

"Of course. They're the reason Langley sent you."

"Then you know that none of the other victims were blasted into pieces of Swiss cheese. My guess is that the Russian bullets did the job, and our friends at the Committee for State Security came in later with a bunch of Stateside weapons to confuse the issue. It'll all come out in the lab."

"Then why do it this way?" Cole asked. "I mean, doesn't it seem like the long way around? If the KGB killed him, it seems they would have used American bullets from the beginning."

Starcher considered. "On the face of it, the method doesn't make sense, I'll admit. Pierlenko's talking détente and friendship with America. This'll cut the legs right out from under him. On the other hand, maybe the entire KGB isn't involved."

Cole templed his fingers. "Rand told me you had an idea about some rogue group running wild. Frankly that sounds like grasping at straws."

"A straw's better than nothing," Starcher said. "It's sure as hell not as farfetched as the theory that Rand and the rest were killed by other Americans, which is what the Russians want us to believe."

"Yes, yes, Mr. Starcher," the young man said placatingly. "Everyone, including the Premier and the President, is just trying to find the truth. The Soviets are being very cooperative. They supplied these photographs. Maybe you should look through the rest of them."

Starcher picked them up and skimmed quickly through them. "When you said he was mutilated, I thought it would be worse than this."

"Keep going."

More of the same. Then he turned to the last photograph and froze. It was a close-up of Richard Rand's neck.

"Mr. Starcher," Cole said as he came around the desk and sat in a chair next to the old agent. Cole spoke to him with the respect of a student for a favorite teacher. "I made a study of you at Langley, sir," he said. "You're among the great men of history there, you know." He smiled but got no response. Starcher was still staring at the photograph. "I managed to find out everything I could about you. Justin Gilead's name came up more than once. I recognized the symbol when the photos arrived."

Starcher seemed to shrink into himself. "He'd have no reason to do something like this," he said. "Even if he were alive, which I doubt. No one's seen Justin Gilead for two years."

Cole studied him silently.

"He's not working for me, kid," Starcher said acidly.

"Yesterday Rand said that you were running an agent on your own."

"I *said* it wasn't Gilead."

"Who is he, then?"

Starcher's lips hardened into two thin lines.

"All right," Cole said. "Nobody's going to torture you into revealing his name. Not till you get back to Langley." He said it lightly, but Starcher noted the threat.

"Anyway, I've been thinking about Gilead ever since I saw that photograph. Maybe he's not your agent but someone else's."

Starcher bristled. "What are you saying, boy?"

"I'm saying that the agency had its suspicions about

this operative called Grandmaster from the beginning, and you took him on, anyway. He's a maverick, from all reports. A loner."

"He's all that," Starcher admitted. "He was also the best goddamn agent we ever had."

"I'm not saying he wasn't special. The business in Cuba was brilliant. But the fact is, Gilead never checked out. No records to speak of, no background, nothing, except for some bizarre story about being raised by monks somewhere in the Himalayas."

"He did his job," Starcher said stubbornly. "He was clean."

"Maybe *was* is the operative word," Cole said. He leaned forward. "Mr. Starcher, as far as we know, Gilead had no allegiance with any country, including our own. A report in your own words said Gilead only agreed to work with you in order to get close to some Russian."

"But he was—" Starcher stopped. There was no point in explaining what the Grandmaster was. What he *wasn't*, was an agent in any ordinary sense of the word. Or even a man in any ordinary sense, either. Starcher had seen Justin Gilead remain under water for more than twenty minutes without taking a breath. He had seen him break through a steel door with nothing but the power of his two hands. But despite Gilead's powerful skills, there had been an innocence about him, a simple desire, to see the good guys win, that Gilead had never lost. Starcher loved him for that, loved him like the son he had never had. Could such a man kill so brutally?

Then Starcher remembered the other face of the Grandmaster. The man who could kill silently, efficiently, and without remorse. That was why Starcher grieved so now. Could Justin Gilead kill like this?

The answer was yes.

"Face it, Mr. Starcher. The scar on Rand was made by that medallion the Grandmaster always wore."

Starcher looked at him, then nodded slowly. "Maybe the KGB knows that too. Maybe there is a killing squad the Premier doesn't know about and they're responsible for all these deaths. And maybe they're just trying to shift the blame onto an American."

"Good try, Mr. Starcher," Cole said, shaking his head. "But that doesn't hold water. If some rogue group from the committee was behind these killings, trying to weaken Pierlenko, they wouldn't have had any reason to blame the deaths on an American agent. I'm afraid that doesn't work."

"No, it doesn't seem to," Starcher agreed slowly. "But I can't really believe that Justin Gilead is alive. And I can't imagine him being in Moscow. He's never been here before as far as I know. He doesn't know anything about the city."

"It looks like he learned something. Chances are he's responsible for these deaths. All of them."

Starcher didn't answer. He just sat on his chair, hands folded over the photographs on his lap.

"Do you want to look for him? Or should I tell Pierlenko?" Cole asked.

"If it is Justin Gilead, the KGB wouldn't find him if they looked till hell froze over," Starcher replied dully.

"You have any ideas?"

"Yes," Starcher said.

There was a long, empty silence.

"Well?"

"Not right now, Cole. Let me see what I can find out first."

"I'll sit tight until Langley tells me otherwise," Cole said. "I've got to tell them what's going on, you know."

"I understand," Starcher said. "I'll start looking in the meantime."

"Do you need anything? Money? A place to stay? Anything?" Cole asked.

"No," Starcher said as he rose from his chair, dropped the photographs on the cultural attaché's desk, and walked slowly from the office.

Cole watched him go, then returned to his desk and started to make notes on a large yellow pad.

*　　*　　*

Starcher walked slowly through the winding, narrow streets of Moscow's old Zarechie district, not wanting to believe but afraid not to.

Justin Gilead had always been something of a mystery, even when he worked under Starcher's control. Gilead had agreed to work with the CIA in exchange for the promise that Starcher would someday, when he asked, tell Justin where he could find Alexander Zharkov.

That day had come two years ago in Cuba. Gilead had upended a Soviet plot to kill Fidel Castro and blame it on the United States. No matter what the revisionists now thought, it had been a wonderful day for American foreign policy. The Russian government and its dangerously anti-American Premier had been toppled, and Soviet influence in the Caribbean had been cut sharply.

Few had known about Justin Gilead. Starcher doubted that even the KGB would have had much in the way of records about the amulet he wore around his neck. Still, the evidence was strong. The mark on Rand's neck was pretty good proof that Justin was alive, back in Moscow, and perhaps killing Americans.

Walking with his head down, Starcher bumped into a pedestrian and swore at him in Russian.

Unless . . . he thought. There was one Russian, the object of Gilead's obsession from the beginning: Nichevo's head, Alexander Zharkov. Zharkov knew about the coiled-snake medallion.

Starcher did not think that Zharkov had survived Cuba. But suppose he had? And suppose Nichevo, his secret organization, was still running under his command? Killing Americans in Moscow would be the kind of thing they might dream up.

Was it possible?

Starcher stopped at a corner, waiting for a traffic light. He glanced idly up at the traffic pole. A poster proclaimed:

CITYWIDE SPEED CHESS TOURNAMENT
9 A.M. SATURDAY, HOTEL VLAD

Starcher read the sign, then reread it. Suddenly he knew what to do. If Gilead or Zharkov were alive and in Moscow, there was a way to flush them both out.

He hurried to a building on Japoski Street. It was in the worst section of Zarechie, in a row of dilapidated pre-Revolutionary houses near the train yards, but it was home for the time being. No one but Starcher and Sasha knew of its location, not even Starcher's superiors at the embassy.

As he mounted the crumbling steps to the three-story wood-frame tenement, Starcher thought that Mark Cole did not seem to be cut from the same cloth as Richard Rand. At least he had entertained the idea that the killings might be a KGB act. Rand had even disregarded Starcher's firsthand report that the man who had tried to kill him at the circus was KGB. Maybe Mark Cole was part of a new wave of CIA men from Langley. Maybe the CIA was finally coming around to the harsh realities of intelligence gathering, forsaking lawn-party diplomat agents.

Starcher walked up three flights of wooden steps to the top-floor apartment. The hallway window overlooked streets where the cracked pavement was buckling under the heavy truck traffic to and from the nearby railroad yards.

He had sublet the apartment illegally, from a woman with four children who had returned to the Ukraine for a prolonged visit with her family after the death of her husband. Had she notified the housing authorities of her trip, she would have found the apartment rented to someone else. Starcher's offer of cash had seemed a sensible alternative to the shrewd woman.

There was a faint odor of curry in the hallway. The door to the apartment, originally painted an institutional green, was now almost black with fingerprints and grime. Inside was worse. Filthy walls surrounded a few cheap pieces of furniture upholstered in torn plastic. A broken light fixture hung from the ceiling. Whatever else the woman from the Ukraine might have been, Starcher thought, she was a slob.

The place served his purposes, though. He took off his black wig and rubbed his sweat-matted white hair with a dirty rag, then removed the pillow he had used to pad his waistband.

Finally he sat down at the kitchen table that rocked on uneven legs and began to hand-letter a sign.

Mark Cole stretched his hands out over the beautiful gold-trimmed desk that was now his.

American and Soviet diplomats were already in constant contact. The President was worried. Nikolai Pierlenko's credibility as a man of peace was swiftly eroding. Military bases all over the world were being mobilized, their missiles directed at the United States and the Soviet Union. The two most powerful nations on earth were in a state of chaos, all because one weak-kneed ass in the CIA had been the last victim in a string of murders.

Cole had been directed to have all his available agents aid Starcher in finding Rand's killer, but that was virtually impossible. The Company had only a handful of agents in Moscow these days, and Rand hadn't lived long enough to brief Cole on their identities.

But Andrew Starcher would find Justin Gilead. The old man was a lot smarter than idiots like Rand thought. Too smart, perhaps, but that would be taken care of after the Grandmaster surfaced.

Everything was going like clockwork.

CHAPTER
TEN

Sasha drove past the railroad yard, then parked on a side street off Japoski. It was after midnight, and the usually busy street was quiet. If she was stopped now by police, she would simply tell them she had been out for a drive, taken a wrong turn, and gotten lost. She was La Kaminskaya. There would be no trouble.

She walked a block to the rear of the safe house, where some three-story buildings stood, their windows dark. A broken stub of a ladder hung from the metal fire escape over her head. Soundlessly Sasha leapt into the air and caught the ladder's lowest rung. She raised her body until her hands were at hip level, then softly stepped up onto the fire escape platform. Once she was sure of her footing, she looked up and down the street. It was empty. Quietly she climbed the three flights of metal steps and slipped onto the roof.

From the rear of the building Sasha could see the safe house across a spotty dirt yard. While the yard was only thirty feet wide, the distance was too far for her to jump from one roof to another. She looked around and saw a clothes pole below her, but there was no clothesline. Russian women kept their clotheslines inside most of the year to prevent them from freezing.

Sasha lowered herself from the building roof to the clothes pole, caught it between her strong legs, then shinnied down to the yard. She then ran alongside a fence to the back of Starcher's building. There was an identical wooden clothes pole at the corner of his building, and she clambered up it, balanced herself precariously on top of it for a moment, then leapt up and grabbed the edge of the roof. She pulled herself up easily.

Sasha looked through a skylight on the roof that opened onto the third-floor hallway. It was locked from the inside, but the lock was a simple one. Using her car key, she was able to force the lock. With a faint squeak the skylight opened, just enough for her to slide her body through. Then she hung from a piece of wooden molding while she slowly lowered the skylight closed with her free hand.

She dropped softly to the hallway floor, bending her knees to cushion her fall and muffle any sound she might make.

As she stood erect, she turned in a circle, smiled, and bowed to an imaginary audience.

Starcher woke. There was a sound near the door. As he waited, he reached under his pillow for the .38-caliber revolver he kept in defiance of agency rules, which required agents to use 9-mm automatics with clips.

He was fully dressed as he walked quietly to the door. There was a faint knocking, hardly more than the brushing of fingers over the door panel.

Two scrapes, a pause, two more. The pattern was repeated after a few seconds. Starcher opened the door, then locked it again as Sasha slipped by.

"What a disgusting place," she said. "I thought you people had expense accounts."

"How the hell'd you get in here?" Starcher muttered. "I gave up on you after two A.M."

"I was at one of the parties you love me to attend. I only now got free."

"Well? Did you find out anything?"

"Not much, except that the murdered diplomat everyone's referring to as the Archduke Ferdinand of World War III was probably an American spy. But I guessed as much, anyway."

Starcher nodded. "He was my boss. Did you hear anything about who might have killed him?"

"Nothing."

"Then why did you break in here?" he said loudly.

"How else could I get in?" She strolled over to the kitchen table and sat down in front of the stack of handbills. "You really ought to fix your roof, Andrew. Many of the tiles are missing. The beams have probably rotted through in places."

"You came over the *roof*? That was the first thing I checked when I moved in here. Nobody could get here over the roof without equipment."

"My equipment," Sasha said, spreading her arms. "Why did you contact me?"

"I need to have some handbills distributed. Purely legitimate, but naturally you or I can't do it. Can you find a kid to nail them up?"

Her face was puzzled. "What handbills?"

"Those," he said, gesturing to a small stack of hand-printed flyers.

Sasha read aloud, "Citywide speed chess tournament. Featuring the return to competition of Alexander Zharkov. Who is he?"

"Look, you're only the dog. I'm the pony, all right? Just see that they get posted around the Hotel Vlad."

"Whatever you say, boss." She picked up the stack of flyers and rolled it into a tube that she stuck under the belt of her jeans.

"There's something else too," Starcher said. "I'm going to enter the tournament."

"You?" She snickered. "You're a terrible chess player."

"But you're not. You're going to play. I'm just going to move the pieces."

She rubbed her chin. "It's very difficult to cheat at chess."

"Damn it, you figured out how to crawl into this house like a cat burglar. Now find a way to keep me in the freaking tournament for a few days."

"That will take a lot of cheating," Sasha said.

"Get the hell out of here."

He stood in the doorway and watched Sasha hop lightly up on top of the rickety wooden rail alongside the stairwell. She leapt up and grabbed the molding under the skylight with one hand, while with the other she reached far overhead and pushed the skylight open.

He marveled at her strength. Most trained male athletes could never accomplish the things that came to her so easily. She pulled herself smoothly through the skylight opening, then looked back down and blew him a silent kiss before disappearing into the night.

Through the dirty glass Starcher snapped a salute in return.

CHAPTER ELEVEN

Kraskovich's funeral was a small one, attended only by the few circus performers and officials who were willing to stand in the rain and pretend to pay their respects to a man who had been universally disliked. The assistant director of the circus said a few words about the magician's dedication to children everywhere, while the performers exchanged glances of undisguised disgust.

The boy was there, standing apart from the group. He was not paying attention to the casket, nor to the speaker, nor to the other mourners. It was as if he were suspended in time, waiting for something only he knew would be coming.

No one had volunteered to look after the boy. He was practically grown now and had never been the sort of lovable youngster who brings out tenderness in others. He had come to the circus a stranger and would leave as one. The officials had decided to send him to a state orphanage as soon as the paperwork could be arranged.

When the brief ceremony was over, Sasha went to his side. Although he was sixteen and at his full height, Sasha was still taller than he was.

"Come back with me," she said as the mourners were returning to the circus. She took him in her own car. At the gate she put her arm around his shoulders and walked with him past the guard through the performers' doors of the main building.

"Where are you going now?" she asked gently, now inside her dressing room.

He looked at her and smiled lightly with his mouth, but none of the smile reached his pale blue eyes.

"I will be fine," he said. "I have other friends besides you."

She reached for his hand. "One last favor, then, for an old friend. Take these and put them up near the Hotel Vlad," she said, thrusting the handbills at the boy.

The boy took them and read one silently. The strange blue eyes looked up at her. This time they were smiling.

"Hurry up!" She lit a cigarette impatiently and sat down at her makeup mirror. "I just want to get this over with."

After the boy left, she stared at her own reflection until the features of her face seemed to change before her eyes. The innocent young girl—who had dared the quadruple when no man had had the courage or skill—was gone, replaced by a person she no longer cared to know.

She picked up a ceramic rouge pot on the vanity and threw it at the mirror. The face there disintegrated into a thousand sparkling shards.

It was after midnight. Zharkov lay asleep on the cot in the small apartment that served as Nichevo's headquarters. The Oriental, Lin, was dozing on a chair. At the sound of a knock on the door the two men were on their feet, plastered against the wall, their weapons drawn.

The knock came again. It was soft, not the imperious rap of the KGB. A mistake, Zharkov thought. A wrong address. He nodded to Lin, who went and opened the door.

Malenadze, the other Nichevo man, stood in the doorway, holding on to the collar of a young boy.

Not roughly, he steered the small boy into the room ahead of him, and Zharkov quickly closed the door.

"What is it?" he said.

Malenadze handed him one of the handprinted flyers about the chess match.

"I found him putting these up on the street, Comrade Colonel," Malenadze said.

Zharkov looked at the flyer, frowning when he read his own name.

He looked at the boy for the first time. He was a slender lad with brown skin and blue eyes that made Zharkov shudder.

They were almost Justin Gilead's eyes, only more cruel. And, like Gilead's, they possessed something special. They possessed power.

Alexander Zharkov understood power. Not the ordinary power of money or position—anyone could acquire that kind of power. And anyone could lose it by a stroke of fate. What Zharkov recognized here was real power, a ring of force unassailable by ordinary men, a legacy from the gods. Justin Gilead had possessed that power. Zharkov had felt it when the amulet of Rashimpur had been burned into his flesh. And he felt it again now in the presence of this thin, underfed, sullen-faced boy. It was unmistakable.

"Who are you?" he asked.

The boy met his eyes coldly. "I am Siraj," he said.

"Where did you get these?" Zharkov said, holding the piece of white paper in his hand.

The boy seemed to choose his words carefully. "A man gave them to me. He asked me to put them up. He gave me two rubles."

"What man?" Zharkov said.

The boy shook his head. "I do not know his name."

"What did he look like?"

"Like a man," the boy said. Malenadze cuffed the boy lightly on the back of the head. The boy seemed not to notice. "Except . . ." he said.

"Except what?" Zharkov snapped.

"Except he wore a medal around his neck."

Zharkov sipped air between his lips. "What kind of medal?" he said slowly.

"Gold. Of a coiled snake inside a ring."

Zharkov jumped forward and grabbed Siraj by the shoulders, but the boy's eyes seemed to penetrate him like weapons. Zharkov released his grip.

"This man? Do you know where we can find him?"

The boy nodded. "I can take you to him," he said. "Come with me." The boy turned and opened the door. Zharkov nodded and followed him. The other two men walked behind. Malenadze's face was a mask of incredulity. Lin's was, as usual, devoid of expression. But the Asian knew the stories of the amulet and the Patanjali of the high mountains, and in his eyes now shone the glint of fear.

The place where he took them was an hour outside of Moscow by car. Malenadze drove, while the boy pointed out directions. He did not speak, and when the men tried to talk to him, he would not answer.

Not for a moment did Zharkov believe the boy's story that he had been accosted on the street by a man with an amulet. He might have believed, if it had not been for the boy's eyes. Eyes like that did not belong to ordinary people.

Zharkov thought it amazing. So the Grandmaster, instrument of the ancient gods, was not unique in the world, after all. There were two—a son, perhaps?

The boy held up a hand for Malenadze to stop.

The Nichevo man parked the car by the side of the road.

"We walk now," the boy said.

As they got out of the car Lin said to Zharkov, "This is probably a trap, Comrade Colonel."

Zharkov answered only, "We will follow the boy."

Siraj had already set off across the field on foot. He showed no sign of trying to escape. The men followed a few paces behind.

They crossed the field and as they entered a deep wood near a small stream, the boy turned to face them. All three men stopped in their tracks as the boy fixed on them a strange, otherworldly glare that seemed to pierce through all of them at once.

Malenadze looked reflexively behind him. "What's he looking at?" he grumbled.

The boy spoke. "Only you may proceed from this point, Colonel Zharkov."

"How do you know my name?"

"I know many things," the boy said. "You come with me."

"Not in your lifetime," Malenadze said. "We go with the colonel."

"You will stay," the boy said, and his voice was as cold as death. Malenadze groaned softly. As the others watched, the big man fell to his knees, clutching his stomach. He looked up helplessly at Zharkov, his terrified eyes rolling like a wild boar's at the moment of the kill. Blood trickled from his mouth.

Zharkov stepped back in horror. There was one powerful convulsion, a thick jet of blood and vomit, and then Malenadze lay still, his fingers still digging into his belly.

Lin moved instantly. He reached behind him, pulling a double-handled knife from inside his belt. His movements were like a cat's, swift and economical. In two strides he was behind the boy, the knife arcing expertly toward the slender throat. The boy never moved.

But the blade missed. It whistled downward, then up again, gaining momentum as it passed the boy's face and struck deep into Lin's left eye.

The Asian made no sound whatever. With the hilt of the knife protruding obscenely, its point lodged somewhere inside his brain, he weaved on his feet for a few horrifying seconds, then fell.

Zharkov felt sweat running cold down his back, but he kept his gaze focused on the boy, careful not to move so much as a finger.

The vacant look passed from the boy's eyes. He blinked

as if he'd just awakened. Zharkov saw his hands tremble momentarily. Then he turned and resumed walking, oblivious to Zharkov and the two bodies beside him.

The Russian knew better than to run. There was no way to escape the boy. He concentrated instead on one salient fact: If the Grandmaster had wanted the boy to kill him, he surely would have done that by now.

But what would he do when he finally saw the Grandmaster again? Gilead's power had obviously taken a bizarre turn. He had killed before, but Gilead had never been a *killer* in the way this boy was. And the power itself was never so manifest. Compared with this Siraj, Justin Gilead had been nothing, a cop on a beat, a fly to be swatted away in annoyance. The boy possessed magic, magic unlike anything Zharkov had seen since that time—so long ago, it was—when he had felt the magic of the gods in himself.

Siraj knelt in some heavy undergrowth, ignoring the thorns and brambles that cut his smooth skin, and crawled through a cleft in a huge boulder. Zharkov followed, feeling his way with his hands along the dirt path in the darkness.

Ahead of him, a square of light shone on the ground. The boy beckoned to Zharkov. Inside the square of light was a long cinder-block stairway.

Zharkov descended with Siraj behind him. At the bottom two men carrying automatic rifles and Sten guns stepped out of the shadows. Their clothing, Zharkov noticed, was civilian and of Russian manufacture. He stopped abruptly in front of them, but they made no move. The boy passed him and nodded, signaling him to come ahead.

They went together through a low tunnel, lit by steel mesh-covered light bulbs, the sort used in mines. More men were stationed along the walls, all heavily armed, all civilians, all half shrouded in shadow.

But why did the Grandmaster have them here? He had always worked alone. Even when he was involved with American intelligence, Gilead had not commanded men or even been part of a team. What he had here was tantamount to a small army.

At the end of the tunnel was a wall of solid steel. Siraj gestured to the last of the armed men, and together they pulled it open. Beyond it lay what looked like ordinary living quarters. From the doorway the boy pointed for Zharkov to enter alone.

The room was large but sparsely furnished. All four walls were lined with books. In the dim light it seemed to be empty, until Zharkov saw the tall figure move slowly out of the shadows in the corner.

Zharkov gasped. He had been prepared for anything, for the boy's killing magic, for Gilead's own hocus-pocus, even for death. But not for this.

"Konstantin Kadar," he whispered as the steel door closed behind him.

CHAPTER TWELVE

"**C**olonel Zharkov," Kadar said with a flourish of his hand. Even this small gesture seemed to disturb the stillness of the room.

Kadar seemed not to have aged a day. His posture was still ramrod-straight, his large frame a monolith of athletic strength. The silver hair along his temples framed the great bald dome of his head, and a pair of dark, round, sharklike eyes stared benignly at Zharkov from behind steel-rimmed glasses.

Zharkov lifted his chin a fraction. "Why have you brought me here?"

Kadar spread his immaculate hands. "In the fullness of time, my dear fellow. Drink?" He proffered a decanter of brandy which, Zharkov knew, Kadar himself never touched.

"All this politeness is not necessary," Zharkov said brusquely. "Obviously you have sought me out for a reason. I wish to know what it is."

"Perhaps it was merely the desire of an old man to chat with you, *priyatel*."

"Don't call me friend. We were never friends."

Kadar shrugged. "As you like. I understand you have not offered Nichevo's services to the new Premier.

"That is not your concern."

"Ah, you're right," he said mildly. "I'm no more than a private citizen now, a broken man living in exile. . . ."

"In hiding, apparently. It's unlikely that even this soft administration would permit you to live in an underground fortress with an armed guard."

"Ordinary precautions," he said with the hint of a smile. "Premier Pierlenko was about to have me arrested."

Zharkov raised an eyebrow.

"I see the prospect amuses you, Colonel. As it should, I suppose."

"Why am I here?" Zharkov said.

Kadar shrugged again, then took something from his pocket and tossed it across the room.

Zharkov caught it and examined it. It was a reproduction of the coiled-snake amulet of Rashimpur, made of base metal and blistered on the surface that had been exposed to heat.

"So Rand's killer was you," Zharkov said disinterestedly. "How did you make this? The boy?"

"It suffices that I had it made, does it not?"

Zharkov tossed the fake onto a small table, trying not to show his disappointment. So the Grandmaster was not here. Lin had been right. Zharkov had walked into a trap, after all, and had lost two good men in the process.

Kadar walked around to him and picked the medallion up. "Ingenious, don't you think? Just the thing to flush Alexander Zharkov out of the walls." He looked from the amulet to Zharkov. "Do you really want the Grandmaster so badly?"

Zharkov was silent.

"Gilead is near," Kadar said.

"How do you know that?" Zharkov heard the catch in his own voice.

Kadar nodded toward the door, indicating that Siraj waited outside.

"Who is he? The boy. *What* is he?" Zharkov asked.

"He works for me. That is all you need to know

and—perhaps for your own safety—all you should want to know."

"That is not enough," Zharkov snapped. "He killed two of my men, seemingly by nothing more than the force of his will. How did you develop that?"

The Vozhd laughed. "Now, Zharkov, if I were responsible for Siraj's extraordinary ability, I certainly wouldn't tell someone of your brilliance how I got him that way. Alas, I had no part in it. He's simply a wild card, a mental mutant of some kind. We chanced upon each other."

He sat down in a heavy wing chair, which shaded his face even further. From the shadows he spoke.

"While I was still in the Kremlin, the boy came to Moscow with a few soldiers returning from patrol in some remote outpost. Most of their platoon had perished in a riot of some kind. It was difficult to get all the details, since the starving and frostbitten survivors were close to delirium when they were picked up. They died shortly afterward, by the way."

"Naturally," Zharkov said with irony. The Vozhd would not have permitted common soliders to live with the knowledge of anything as remarkable as Siraj's gift.

"Oddly, the boy showed almost no ill effects from the journey, or so the medical personnel told me. On the contrary, he could perform amazing feats—levitation, they said. Telekinesis. The scientists were very interested in studying him, but when I met him, I knew I could put his talents to better use."

"How did you hide him?" Zharkov asked.

"In the circus, of course. What better place to store a diamond than in a bin filled with costume jewelry?"

Zharkov sniffed. "If he's as unusual as he seems, you should have used him in Cuba."

"At the time I did not believe the affair in Cuba would have such disastrous results. I used *you* in Cuba." The gaze from Kadar's doll eyes pierced the darkness and settled on Zharkov.

"And tried to have me killed as part of the operation. *Priyatel.*"

"I did not want to sacrifice you, Colonel. Had you died, it would have grieved me greatly."

"Ah, yes. As you no doubt grieved over the deaths of the scientists who found out about the boy. They *are* dead, aren't they?"

Kadar raised his open palms. "I'm glad we understand each other," he said softly, "because I would not expect you to help me out of friendship alone."

"Help you?" Zharkov almost laughed aloud. "Ever since I can remember, you've done everything you could to destroy Nichevo and my family. And now you expect me to help you?"

"Yes. For a price."

"I have no price."

"No?" Kadar flicked on the tensor light. Beneath its beam he placed the replica of the coiled-snake medallion. "I can get you Justin Gilead."

Zharkov felt his heart begin to thump in his chest.

"What I'm asking in return is small, very small, but it is something only you can do. There will be no risk to your life, or to Nichevo. Afterward you will be free to do with Gilead whatever you wish."

"What do you want?" Zharkov whispered.

Kadar walked over and stood face-to-face with Zharkov. "Help me become Premier again."

Zharkov stared at him for a moment, then turned away. "You must be mad."

"Listen to me!" Kadar hissed, grabbing the colonel's arm. "The people will agree to it. The *nomenclatura,* the military. They see where the soft policies of that fool Pierlenko are leading the Soviet Union. His infatuation with the West will destroy us all. Unless we show the Americans force, they will crush us in the name of peace."

The colonel walked slowly around the room. "Even so, it would be impossible for you to become General Secretary by armed coup. Not in this day and age, and

certainly not through Nichevo. The organization is far
too small—"

"An armed coup will not be necessary." Kadar's eyes
were shining. "Not if the Politburo is behind me."

"The Politburo arranged to have you removed from
office," Zharkov reminded him.

"The Politburo can be influenced!" He smoothed the
front of his vest, as if physically calming himself. "No
one knows that better than you. And your father before
you," he added quietly.

Zharkov pretended to examine a stone sculpture before answering. "If you're talking about the so-called
Nichevo file . . ."

"I am. You know it exists. Your father and I had many
differences of opinion, but I never doubted his intelligence. Keeping detailed accounts of the private misdeeds
of everyone in government assured him of a lifetime
position."

"And a lifetime," Zharkov added dryly.

Kadar forced a small smile. "Come now, Colonel. The
KGB was not so brutal as the rumors would have you
believe."

"Nichevo does not operate on rumor," Zharkov said
hotly. "The KGB under your direction was the most
murderous pack of thugs since Beria's secret police."

"Perhaps that was true of a few individuals. But one
makes concessions for loyalty." He was staring past
Zharkov at the steel door behind him.

Suddenly Zharkov understood. "My God," he said.
"You've *kept* them. You've still got the KGB in your
pocket."

"Only some. After the Politburo made the disastrous
error of forcing me to leave office, they proved their
stupidity by depriving the best internal KGB agents of
their jobs. Those men did not deserve to be humiliated
as they were, stripped of their livelihood, unable to care
for their families, often exiled, even tortured. Instead
some chose to work for me. Others managed to keep
their positions in the organization but will never trust

Pierlenko again. They know I will come back, so they have continued to watch out for my interests."

"Then it wasn't just Rand," Zharkov said, almost to himself. "Of course. You killed all the Americans. They were murdered at random, weren't they, just to turn the United States against Nikolai Pierlenko."

"That was necessary," Kadar said dismissively. "If Rand had been the only one, Pierlenko and his diplomats might have passed it off as a random killing by some madman. Now the Premier has nowhere to turn. His newly forged links with America are disintegrating. His weakness toward our enemies has already cost him his credibility at home. The Politburo—that pit of spineless worms—is ready to turn on him. It would take only a small reminder of each of their pasts for them to reinstate me after Pierlenko's death."

"A reminder provided by the Nichevo file."

"That is all I need from you, Comrade Colonel."

"And afterward?"

"You'll have your Grandmaster. I give you my word."

"How?"

Kadar folded his hands in front of him. "Allow me some autonomy, Zharkov."

"Gilead first. Then the Nichevo file."

"Done," Kadar said.

Zharkov turned toward the steel door. "Done."

"I'm afraid you will be staying with me for a while," Kadar said to his back.

Zharkov turned around, his hooded eyes narrow with indignation. "How dare you attempt to hold me prisoner here!"

"Now, now," Kadar said placatingly. "You know perfectly well that if you were free to contact Nichevo, my life would be worthless as soon as I produced my half of the bargain. But *prisoner* is too harsh a word and not at all true. Prisoners are not treated as you will be. Rather consider yourself my guest." He pressed a button and bowed to Zharkov as if he were still a head of state acknowledging an equal. The huge steel doors opened, and Kadar beckoned the boy inside.

"Siraj will show you to your quarters," Kadar said. "I'm sure that you will find him a most interesting companion."

"One question, Kadar."

"What is that?"

"You had the boy bring me here. Why did you bother to take the risk of passing around that ridiculous flyer announcing that I was going to play chess? Isn't that risky?"

"Ahhh, that's an interesting point," Kadar said, with the faint hint of a smile on his face. "I didn't do that. I had nothing to do with it."

"Then, who . . . ?"

"Obviously someone looking to bring you out into the open. Perhaps even Justin Gilead himself." He retreated into the shadows of the room.

Zharkov!

Kadar paced, almost unable to keep himself from shouting out loud. The years of waiting and planning had finally paid off. Zharkov was his. And the office of General Secretary was waiting for him.

Who would have thought that the invincible Alexander Zharkov had a weakness, a weakness so profound that he would give up his life for it? For the information he possessed on the Politburo—and Kadar, himself, for that matter—was his lifeline. Without it, Zharkov was dispensable.

As to Nichevo, Kadar would not need the organization. He had his own secret army of former KGB agents who had remained loyal to him. No one in his new administration would know of their existence. They would be his eyes and ears, his hands moving in the shadows, the silent fist that he would need to crush the West.

And all in exchange for one misfit American.

The boy led Zharkov to another wing. The compound

was much larger than it appeared and expertly designed. Except for the absence of windows, there was no indication that the place was below ground. The ventilation shafts had been worked neatly into the layout of the compound, looking like tall panels of venetian blinds.

The boy said nothing as he escorted Zharkov through a labyrinth of corridors. Finally he showed him to a small, nondescript room decorated with only a photograph of a horse.

"Thank you," Zharkov said automatically, starting to close the door, but Siraj stood in his way.

"I must speak to you," the boy said.

"About what?"

"I come from the mountains of the Patanjali," Siraj said softly.

A shiver ran down Zharkov's neck. Even Kadar did not know Justin Gilead by that name.

"You once served another there, who is no longer of living flesh. My mother, the goddess Varja."

"Varja . . ." Zharkov searched the young face. He had not bothered to study it before, but now the resemblance was unmistakable. Yet there was something else in it too. . . .

"She chose you as her prince. Now I choose you as mine. Follow me and you will possess power greater than anything you have ever imagined."

He's insane, Zharkov thought. "Please go," he said. "I'm very tired."

"You doubt me now, even after what you have seen? But I warn you, and I warn you only once. Underestimate me at your peril, Zharkov." He fixed his eyes on him. "At your peril."

Siraj raised one finger. On its tip was a spark the color of flame. As Zharkov watched, it seemed to grow as if fed by the boy's own energy until it was a glowing, whirling sphere of light the size of a grapefruit. Then, with a flick of his hand, he sent it shooting toward Zharkov.

Zharkov gasped as he caught it in both hands and felt its searing heat. Before he could drop it, the globe exploded into a spray of light that fell over him like mist, the fine particles changing color from yellow to green to indigo and then vanishing.

He looked at his palms. They were still red from its touch.

"All the power of the goddess Varja is invested in me," he said. "Though I was not present, I saw her death. In the moment of her final agony I felt her power come into me, completing me. I am ready now to take her place."

The Russian swallowed. "Why are you here?" he asked.

"For you, and for the Patanjali. In Kadar we have found a catalyst to bring us all together. When we leave, the Patanjali will be dead. I will kill him for you."

"Gilead is mine," Zharkov said. "I must be the one."

"You are not strong enough to fight him."

"That doesn't matter. If I die, he will also. It is our destiny to die together," he said bitterly. "But I will not die for nothing."

"You will not die at all if you are with me," the boy said. "I can break the chain of karma, change your destiny. Through me you will no longer be tied to the Patanjali. I will wear the amulet of Rashimpur, and you will still live to serve as my disciple."

It took Zharkov several minutes to find his voice. *He would live.* Gilead would die but he would live. At last he would be free. "Why . . . why would you do this for me?" he asked shakily.

The boy reached up with a soft, slender hand, as if to touch Zharkov's cheek. Instead he ripped open the colonel's high collar to reveal the scar of the coiled snake. "Because you are my father," he answered.

A low moan escaped from Zharkov's lips.

"We are of the same flesh, Zharkov," the boy said softly. "I own you. I always have." He stepped back from the colonel. "Kneel."

Zharkov did not move.

"You are too proud. I told you to kneel to me. For

your life, Zharkov. It is a small price to pay." Mockingly, he added, "Father."

Alexander Zharkov was a man of reason. What did it matter that he was a descendant of royalty, that he had never bent his knee before any man or god or power? It was a meaningless gesture, signifying nothing. *He would live.*

He knelt.

"Lower," the boy commanded.

Zharkov touched his head to the floor in a kowtow.

When he looked up, the boy was smiling. Without a word Siraj left the room.

Zharkov remained on his knees, like a dog, and felt sick. Now he knew what he had seen in the face of the boy. He had seen it before, in a reflection on a lake in Nepal, and had screamed at the sight. It had been the face of a monster. He had seen himself.

BOOK THREE
THE ATTACK

CHAPTER
ONE

CITYWIDE SPEED CHESS TOURNAMENT
ALL WELCOME

One of the surprises of the tournament's first day session was an unknown, unranked old man who trounced three opponents before lunch, despite looking as if he had never played chess before. The man's hands shook. When he lifted a piece, he seemed never to have seen one like it before. It took him so long to put the piece back on the board that it appeared he had forgotten where he wanted to move it.

Still, Comrade Krylenko, so old that he looked as if he had grown like moss over the chair he was occupying, had played Yuri Zhenevsky, a fairly well-known Moscow player with a master's rating. To everyone's amazement the old man had won.

The two of them had drawn a crowd from among players waiting for their next games to begin. Those who knew chess had trouble believing the reserves of memory that the shabby Krylenko seemed to possess.

Speed chess is a bastard by-product of the normal game. On average, players have less than thirty seconds to consider each of their moves. The game puts a high premium on memory—if a player can remember a thematic position from a famous game and also remember how the position was played, he can move immediately and hoard the remaining time on his clock for use later in the game.

Comrade Krylenko had a vast memory of famous chess games. His repertoire seemed to encompass the best plays of the best players in history, from Paul Morphy to Anatoly Karpov.

At one point one of the spectators, evidently believing that Krylenko was deaf, said aloud, "Why hasn't anyone seen this old *perdun* before?"

Krylenko pulled away his chair and stood up, his clock still running. He lit a cigar, narrowed his eyes in the smoke, and said from behind a shaggy, overgrown mustache, "Maybe because this old fart has more important things to do than play chess." He poked the embarrassed spectator in the chest. "Be advised to keep your papers in order, Comrade."

"KGB," the crowd whispered as the old man went into the men's room. The talker made a hurried exit and others followed. Zhenevsky, himself, looked up from the board in dismay and loosened his tie.

Meanwhile, in the men's room, the old man applied a dot of spirit gum to the underside of his mustache. It was driving him crazy, and his unconscious movements to remove the irritant were loosening the thing.

Starcher checked his watch. Nearly two o'clock and still no Grandmaster.

In a way it was a relief. Oh, he would still have to hunt down Justin Gilead, but he would be hard to find. And maybe in time Justin would find out that the Company was on to him and leave Moscow. . . .

Starcher winced. He was thinking like a fool. Sparing Justin Gilead would do nothing but salve Starcher's paternal feelings toward him. But Justin wasn't his protégé anymore. He was either an insane killer or working for one. He had to be caught. He had to be questioned. And most likely he would have to be killed.

Starcher left the men's room and passed Sasha, who was pretending to be absorbed in a game at another table. She was better than he thought, that one. The signals she was sending him by touching various parts of her body might not pass muster in the big international tournaments, but no one was going to catch on here. Especially since no one paid her much attention. She had worn a homely costume and completed her disguise with missing front teeth.

The code they had worked out several nights before had been simple. Parts of her body represented various pieces, and her face was divided into a rough grid that would indicate the number of the square to move to.

When Starcher sat back down, he saw Sasha's right hand resting on her right thigh. When she was sure he had seen it, she touched a spot under her left eye.

King's rook to rook four. Starcher sat down, hunched up his shoulders, and moved the piece.

Zhenevsky, his opponent, looked puzzled. Obviously he didn't know what "Krylenko" was doing. And neither did Starcher, who looked desperately to Sasha for help.

While she focused all her attention on the players at the table next to her, she spread five fingers over her hip.

"Mate in five?" Starcher said dubiously.

Zhenevsky stared at the board. Then his brow smoothed in good-humored resignation. "Ah, yes," he said, laying his king on its side. "I almost missed that. Very subtle, Comrade." He rose and extended his hand. "A pleasure."

"The pleasure was mine," Starcher said, wanting fervently to wipe the sweat off his upper lip, beneath the mustache.

As Zhenevsky left the hotel, he was so engrossed in mentally replaying the extraordinary game he had just lost that he didn't notice the man in the ill-fitting clothes reading the poster on the building's facade. But the doorman did.

"You. Get going. We don't want any bums hanging around this place."

Justin Gilead didn't hear him. This was the place. He had been wandering the streets for an hour looking for this hotel, ever since he had noticed the crudely drawn flyer on a utility pole, advertising the tournament and the fact that Alexander Zharkov was going to play.

He had trouble believing that anyone with Zharkov's mania for secrecy would consent to have his name advertised on a public poster.

"Didn't you hear me?" The doorman shoved him.

Unless it was a trap. But who was the prey? Not himself, surely. Of the few people who ever knew he had even existed, none would suspect that now. Except for Zharkov, himself. . . .

"I said, get out of here." The doorman snarled.

It might be Zharkov. Manjusri had said that he would find Zharkov and the boy together, and he had seen the boy. Or someone he thought was the boy.

The doorman grabbed Justin by the shoulders. "Get your drunken ass out of here now!"

Justin plucked the man's hands off his jacket as if he were picking off lint. The fabric tore where the man's fingers still clutched it.

"I'm going in," Justin said without animosity. "I'm a chess player."

The doorman dropped the two strips of cloth and stared after the ragged stranger for a moment before running after him.

The registration clerk at the door to the main ballroom also noticed Justin's appearance. "I'm sorry. We're not accepting any new registrations today. It's too late." He sniffed disdainfully as Justin signed the register.

The doorman appeared with two security guards.

"Well, it's about time," the clerk shrilled. "What's the idea letting someone like this in here in the first place?"

"He forced his way past me," the doorman said. The clerk crooked an imperious finger toward the security men as he snatched away the registry. The guards lumbered forward.

"Wait, wait," the clerk said, looking up from his book.

"Justin Gilead?" He searched the stranger's face. "Good heavens, it *is* you, isn't it?"

"May I play now?"

"Of course, Comrade Gilead. This was just a mistake. A terrible mistake." He rapped on the table and shooed the guards and the doorman away. "I hope you'll accept my personal apologies, Comrade Gilead."

Justin scanned the room. Zharkov was not there. But someone else he knew was. Starcher's eyes met his but not before Justin had noticed a girl who immediately moved away from two players she was observing and strolled slowly toward the registration desk.

Justin was instantly on guard. Starcher was a professional. The flicker of a glance was enough. The girl belonged to him.

Still, Justin didn't like the way she moved. Two quick for a greeting, too wary for an exit, too smooth. Too something.

As she approached, he took two steps toward her, heading her off, and before she could respond, he clapped his hand around her wrist.

Outrage flared in the girl's eyes, but Starcher intervened with a discreet nod. The girl dropped her arms. Justin still held her fast.

"Comrade Gilead?" the clerk said, trying hard not to be alarmed by the strange dance between the international grand master and the homely young hanger-on. "You'll be playing against Comrade Krylenko, the elderly gentleman over there. He's not rated, but so far he's beaten every opponent he's played. I believe you might find him an interesting challenge. By the way, I must tell you I had the pleasure of following your games in the journals, Comrade Gilead. It has been a long time."

Justin continued to look for Zharkov, oblivious to the woman whose arm he was still gripping tightly.

"Yes, too long a time," the clerk chattered on lamely. He pressed his fingertips together. "Er . . . would you like me to call security?"

"Where is Alexander Zharkov?"

The clerk blinked. "Well, he hasn't appeared yet," he said aplogetically. "Actually he hasn't been registered in the tournament, but I understand his name has been on some posters."

He turned the registration book so that the most illustrious player in the tournament could see for himself, but Justin walked away toward Starcher's table, dragging the girl behind him. Sasha squealed in protest. Justin looked at her, as if surprised to see her attached to him, and released her.

"I hear he's an eccentric man," the clerk whispered to her. "Just look at the way he's dressed."

Justin sat down. "Hello, Starcher," he said softly in English.

The old man's eyes devoured him, taking in every small change in Justin's face. It was harder now, leaner. The face of a murderer?

There had been so much to say before. For two years Starcher wondered how he would greet this man, closer than a son to him, if he ever found him alive. And now, when it had finally happened, instead he had to plan how to dispose of the man's body.

"Let's play chess," he croaked, moving the king's pawn. "And it's not Starcher. It's Comrade Krylenko. Can't you tell by my mustache?" Starcher said.

"Krylenko," Justin said softly. "A fine historic name in Soviet chess."

"Oh?"

"Yes. He was an epileptic degenerate who made Russian chess part of a worldwide spying operation. I thought you'd know that."

"I'm a chess player, not a spy," Starcher said.

Justin moved his own king's pawn, and Starcher responded quickly by moving his queen's pawn forward two squares. It was the start of a gambit opening in which the player of the white pieces sacrifices a pawn or more in hope of gaining an attacking position. While gambits had a long tradition, they had almost vanished from modern chess, and no one played them against a grand master of Justin Gilead's class.

Justin captured the gambit pawn, and Starcher countered with a stunning flurry of pawn moves, offering up sacrifice after sacrifice.

"You've improved," Justin said, "from when you thought this was a checkerboard."

Justin captured all the gambit pawns, moving immediately without hesitation. He realized he had not touched a chess piece in more than two years. At lower levels of skill that could seriously harm a man's game, but in Justin's case it meant only that he would be a little slower than usual.

Starcher again responded with a surprising attacking move and then, after Justin answered, another. The amusement left Justin's face. This was not an exercise against an amateur, but a game that was turning into guts and glory against a ferocious intelligence. And when Starcher sacrificed a knight to try to force a checkmate against Justin, the Grandmaster knew that the intelligence was not Starcher's.

The ice-blue eyes looked up from the board. "Excuse me," he said, and got up to walk around the room.

Very few players were left, and none of them was playing with any real skill. Then he saw the girl again, positioned two tables behind his own. She touched her hip, then her eyebrow, looked at Starcher, and touched her hip and eyebrow again.

Justin smiled. So the honorable old Southern gentleman had resorted to a simple scam in order to finally win at chess.

Well, he supposed it didn't do any harm at this level. But the girl intrigued him. She had a good mind, even if she did look like the cleaning lady in a boardinghouse. In fact, she was almost *too* unattractive.

He stared hard at her. Take off the silly skullcap, the librarian glasses, straighten her posture, remove her lumpy clothing, do something about those god-awful teeth, and she would be a beauty. Maybe.

So why was Starcher going through this elaborate double charade? For Zharkov? Justin's pulse quickened. Is that what he was doing, waiting here, as Justin was, for the Prince of Death? Or had he reached out for Justin himself?

He forced himself to go back to the table and resume play. When Zharkov came, he would be ready for him. But soon, even the prospect of seeing the Russian faded into the background of the magnificent interchange between himself and his silent opponent. The sixty-four squares of the board were her battleground, and she was a warrior. He attacked hard; she countered with an attack of her own, from a secure position a lesser player never would have violated.

"Marshall," Justin said, referring to the champion who had been famous for such attacks.

"What?" Starcher said.

"Never mind, Comrade," Justin said.

Sasha was fearless. She played like an artist, bold and free, sacrificing the safe move for the big kill.

Both players were running short of time on their clocks. Under the rigid rules of this speed tournament, each player had to make forty moves in twenty-five minutes or less. Any player who failed to make his moves in the stipulated time lost by forfeit. If both players fulfilled the time requirements, then the position would be judged by a tournament official who would declare a draw, or a win for the player with an obviously superior position.

Starcher moved his queen into the middle of Justin's camp. Gilead responded immediately as did Starcher, as quickly as he could get the signals from Sasha. Neither had time to think through their moves now; each move was made on instinct, on judgment, on a special chess sense of seeing, as chess players called it, "something there."

Justin moved for the fortieth time and captured a pawn with his knight just as his clock ran out.

There was a short exclamation behind him. He turned around. The girl coughed into her hand, but her face was flushed with excitement.

Theirs was the last game of the tournament's daytime session. Already several of the players who would compete that evening had come into the hall. The registration clerk was sitting primly at his desk, wearing his overcoat and galoshes, obviously waiting for his relief to come.

Starcher smiled across the chessboard and stood up. "Better luck next time," he told Justin, obviously believing he would have the winning position in the view of the judges.

Justin smiled back. "Sorry, Comrade Krylenko, but you've been checkmated," he said. He reached over and lay Starcher's king on its side.

Starcher stared at the board, then growled in Russian at Justin, "Keep this up, Gilead. You might have a future at this game." He saw people standing around the table and said, "Let's go. I want you to meet my niece. The beautiful one." When they were reasonably out of earshot, Starcher introduced them.

She was still flushed with the excitement of the game. Justin could feel her pulse as he shook her hand. When their eyes met, a universe passed between them. He *knew* her, as intimately as a lover; she had walked inside his mind and understood it. For a moment Justin felt an almost overwhelming desire to make love to her, that moment, there on the floor, and knew she would have consented.

He pulled away from her. The registration clerk was shooting evil glances at all three of them. As he had them sign the scorecard for the game, he asked Justin, "Will we see you again tomorrow?"

Justin nodded.

"Please try to come earlier. There should be many interesting players for you. Maybe even Comrade Zharkov."

"Somehow I don't think Comrade Zharkov will be coming," Justin said, glancing at Starcher.

They started through the lobby for the hotel's front door before Starcher said, "We're parked out back. Let's use the rear exit."

"What are you worried about, Comrade Krylenko?" Justin said with a faint smile.

"I'm not worried about anything," Starcher said gruffly.

Outside, Justin turned to the girl. "You played very well," he said. "Where did you learn?"

"My father taught me the moves. But a boy in the circus taught me to play well," she said, obviously flattered.

"I didn't think I could fool you for long," Starcher said. "Anyway, there's time for all that. And other things. We've got a lot to talk about, son." A cloud passed over his face, but he dispelled it with a grin. "Think you could use a little food? Never mind. I know the answer just looking at you. The car's right here." He clapped Justin on the shoulder and, at the same time, nodded to Sasha, who had positioned herself behind Justin.

At the signal she took a hypodermic from her purse and plunged it swiftly and expertly into the back of Justin's neck.

He slumped forward. Starcher caught him in his arms and dragged him into the automobile.

It took the old man a few moments to see through the windshield. He just sat, his hands gripping the wheel.

"Are you all right?" Sasha asked. "This drug won't last long."

"I'm fine," Starcher said hoarsely. He blew his nose and started the car.

CHAPTER
TWO

When Justin regained consciousness in the safe house, Starcher was ashamed to look at him. He had already seen enough.

The Grandmaster had once been an extraordinarily handsome man, with coal-black hair and ivory skin and the physique of an athlete. Now he was barely recognizable as the man who had saved Starcher's life so many times. Age had begun to gray Gilead's hair and roughen his face, and his extreme thinness had dug deep hollows into his cheeks. The ropes around his wrists and ankles seemed like an obscenity; this man, bound and trussed so carefully, was no danger to anyone.

Only his eyes were the same. Cold and wise, they had looked a thousand years old when Justin was little more than a boy. Those same ancient eyes opened now, and their infinite sadness made Starcher turn away.

I'm too old for this, Starcher thought. There was a reason the Company didn't keep agents in the field very long. It wasn't that they lost their ambition or even their skill. They lost their single-mindedness, just as Starcher was losing his. They began to think about the world in shades of gray. They looked at their enemies and saw men instead. They saw their own leaders and ideals as no longer infallible. And then they lost their nerve and died.

Why do I have to be the one to betray him?

"Why have you done this to me?" Gilead asked thickly.

The old man didn't move. Sasha took a step backward, the .38 in her hand poised to fire.

"Answer me, Starcher!"

Starcher whirled around, picked up a day-old copy of the *International Herald Tribune,* and thrust it in Justin's face.

The headline read:

> U.S. DIPLOMAT, WIFE MURDERED.
> TWO DEATHS MAKE TOTAL OF 7 AMERICANS KILLED IN MOSCOW.

"Look familiar?" Starcher growled.

Justin squinted to focus while he read. "Should it?"

"You'd know better than anyone." Starcher threw the paper on the floor.

Justin shook his head slowly, a bitter smile playing on his lips. "You never change. In the beginning you risked my life for a test to see if you could trust me. You should have saved yourself the effort."

"I didn't want to believe this about you," Starcher said softly.

"I see. That's why you're about to execute me, no doubt."

"Damn it, there's evidence against you. Strong evidence." Starcher ran his fingers through his thick white hair. "All right, who owns you now?"

"*Owns?*"

"Is it Pierlenko? Did that scum-sucker hire you, or was it someone else? The Bulgarians? Castro, maybe?"

"Hire me for what? To kill seven people?"

"Seven of your own people. But then, that wouldn't matter to you, would it? You don't owe your country anything. Isn't that right?"

"Go to hell."

Starcher turned to the girl. "Kill him," he said.

Sasha looked up in surprise.

"Do it. He's not going to talk. I should have known that."

She aimed, double-armed, straight at Justin's face, but her eyes wavered. Justin saw that black plugs had been removed from her teeth, and long blond hair splashed about her face. He'd been right. She was beautiful.

"The man's a professional, Sasha," Starcher said patiently. "He knows what to expect."

"But it might be a mistake," she said squeakily, her hands trembling.

"And it might not be. We'll see if the killings stop."

"How can you . . . ?" She lowered the gun and threw her head back as if she were in physical pain.

Starcher snatched the gun away from her. "Get out of here," he said.

"Andrew . . ."

"I said, leave. I'll handle this myself."

The girl walked swiftly to the door.

"Come back when you've got a stomach for this work," he called after her. She slammed the door behind her.

Starcher's eyes never left Justin's as he reached inside the torn upholstery of the chair and took out a silencer.

"Was it worth the ego trip to leave your calling card on Richard Rand?" he asked, screwing the long metal tube onto the barrel.

"Just shoot," Justin said with disgust.

Starcher pressed the gun against Justin's temple.

"Talk, God damn you."

Justin said nothing.

"Fine by me." Starcher pulled the trigger. The gun clicked—empty. The old man sighed and tossed it onto a chair.

"Did you know it wasn't loaded?"

Justin swung his legs over the couch. The ropes around his wrists and ankles fell free. They had been torn into pieces, broken by sheer strength. He stood up. "No," he answered.

"Jesus. When did you do that to the ropes?"

"When you started in on me."

Starcher bit off the end of a cigar and spat it out. "I suppose you figured I'm such a senile old fool that I wouldn't have the nerve to kill you."

Justin shook his head. "No. I'm just tired, Starcher." He spoke to the bare wall, his hands on his hips. "You would have been doing me a favor."

Starcher puffed his cigar thoughtfully. "Why are you in Moscow?"

The Grandmaster shrugged. "Running, I suppose. Again. I thought there was someone here."

"Who?" Watching Justin, the thought dawned on him. "Not Zharkov," he said.

Justin didn't answer. Starcher let the silence envelop them while he smoked, waiting.

"Zharkov," Justin said finally. "It's like a disease. I knew Zharkov before I ever met him. I saw him . . . in dreams. . . .'" He rolled his head back. "I'm sorry, Starcher. I'm talking like a crazy man."

"Zharkov's dead," Starcher said. "I saw him die myself, son. So did you. This obsession of yours has got to end."

"He wasn't dead. I saw him again."

"Where? In a dream?"

Justin pinched his eyes between two fingers. "Maybe it was. I don't know anymore. I've tried to forget it, forget him, but I can't. It's as if some force outside of me is pulling me toward him. I don't understand it, I never have, but I can't stop it, either. And I'm going to find him here. I know that. I can sense him."

"Hell, you're not talking like a crazy man," Starcher said. "You're talking like a damned pervert. Listen to you. What would you do with him if you found him, anyway?"

Justin looked at the floor. "I don't know. Maybe I'd find some peace."

Starcher flushed. "Is that what you were doing when you murdered Richard Rand? Looking for peace?"

"I didn't murder anyone," Justin said calmly. "You know that. I don't even know who Richard Rand was."

"Come on," Starcher shouted. "No one else on earth would leave that mark on him."

"What mark?"

Starcher poked the cigar in the direction of Justin's chest. "That. The snake necklace. It was burned into Rand's neck."

"What?"

"I know you've done it before. Zharkov used to have a scar just like it. Was it some kind of ritual murder? Did you see Rand in a dream too?"

"I was right," Justin whispered. "Zharkov's here."

Starcher waved him away. "There is no Zharkov, I tell you. The poster at the tournament was for you."

Justin was quiet for a moment. "So was Rand's scar," he said.

She should report it, Sasha thought as she drove back toward the circus building. They wanted Justin Gilead? Well, she would give them Justin Gilead. But Starcher would have to go free. That would be the deal.

She thought about it for a long time as she moved expertly through the gathering evening traffic, then shook her head. She didn't trust anyone to keep their promises, and there was no way she could guarantee Starcher's safety.

She loved the old man. He had been kinder to her than anyone since her father. Why didn't he just go back to the United States and leave things alone? He was too old, and this game was too dangerous.

Justin Gilead was different. He was younger. He knew what he was letting himself in for. What happened to him was his problem, no one else's.

She felt her body tingle as she thought for a moment about the game of chess they had played that afternoon. In chess, as in few other activities, nothing was hidden. One looked right into the mind for one's opponent, and for a few brief moments she and Justin Gilead had shared each other's minds. His was a special mind, quick and all-encompassing. While she had explored it through the game she'd felt privy to a tremendous intelligence.

She knew Starcher would never kill Gilead without finding out what he needed to know. She had played her part well enough, but it was Starcher who would get the man to talk.

And what would he find? Nothing. Gilead was innocent. Another innocent man about to die.

She touched the brake, thinking for a moment about going back and telling Starcher the truth. It wasn't too late. He could get out of the country and take his friend with him.

Tears welled up in her eyes. Who was she kidding? she thought. It was too late. It was too late from the moment she'd struck her bargain with Konstantin Kadar for her parents: her services for their lives. Year after year she'd kept them alive with her small, shameful favors to him, but after this, they would go free. The *Vozhd* would arrange it. One last payment, and she would see her father and mother again.

Remember them, Sasha told herself. She stepped angrily on the gas pedal. Nothing else matters.

Starcher supposed he had known it from the beginning. Justin Gilead had denied his accusation of murder, and Starcher had believed him. What was this hold Gilead had over him that Starcher would ignore hard evidence in favor of the man's unsupported word?

"I must be an ass for trusting you," he said aloud.

"I trusted you," Justin reminded him. "You could have shot me before I got free."

"No, I couldn't. Not once I saw you again." He shook his head. "It's a bitch, getting old. You get to thinking too much about living."

"Who's the girl?"

"Sasha's my agent."

"What does she do at the circus?"

"Hold on. Who said she was with the circus?"

"She said that's where she learned to play chess. From a boy at the circus."

"That doesn't mean she's *with* the circus," Starcher said stubbornly.

Justin smiled. "Maybe not," he conceded. "But after she stuck that needle in me she caught me as I was going under. And in my fog I sort of remembered her carrying me up some steps to get here. Women her size don't do that unless they're athletes."

"Okay, Sherlock," Starcher mumbled as he lit another cigar. "She's an aerialist. The best trapeze flyer in the world. Her name's Sasha Kaminskaya."

Justin looked around at the small, shabby apartment. "The two of you work out of here?"

"Pretty much." Starcher sighed. "She's the only operative I've got at the moment." He sat down heavily.

"I guess you *have* fallen on hard times, haven't you?"

Starcher growled. "Ahhh, when I left here the last time, before we went to Cuba, I had the best roster of field agents that we ever had in Russia. Then the whole goddamn thing fell into the hands of the live-and-let-livers. Every operative got handed up, every single one. It was as if the CIA were being run by the *Boston Globe*. A nightmare."

"How'd the girl survive it?" Gilead asked.

"I hadn't used her for anything. Too young. When I got back, though, she was all I had, so I had to call her out. I just don't want to get her killed."

The cigar traveled from one side of his mouth to the other. "I could use another man," he said quietly. "Just until I get a handle on who's killing the Americans."

"You mean, besides me?"

"Don't get smart, boy," Starcher said.

"Do you have a clue?" Justin asked.

"Not much. I only got here a few days ago, and somebody's already tried to kill me. At the circus. I don't know if Sasha's compromised or not."

"Who tried to kill you?"

Starcher shrugged. "No ID. He used a wire. The job

seemed like KGB to me, but that doesn't make sense, since the killings are hurting Pierlenko, the new Premier. Maybe some renegades. Sasha said she heard rumors about some secret KGB killing squad. I don't know."

"What's your embassy say?"

Starcher coughed. "You're fooling, I take it. Rand's successor is sure it's you. I was supposed to track you down and neutralize you."

"Neutralize," Justin said with scorn. "You people have a hundred words for murder."

"All right, all right. Anyway, I can't tell them you're here. If they thought I had you working with me, they'd have us both . . ."

"Neutralized," Justin said, finishing for him.

"Sanctioned," Starcher said with a smile. "Well, now that I've made you such an enticing offer, will you work with me?"

"How could I refuse?" Justin said. "I'll do the outside work for you. For a while, anyway. But if I find Zharkov . . ."

"I understand. I'll even help you look for him if I can. Are you sure he's here?"

Justin fingered the golden snake amulet around his neck. "I'm not sure of anything," he said.

Sasha returned to the safe house that night to see what Starcher had done with the chess player.

Again she went over the rooftop, into the yard, climbed the clothes pole, and went quietly through the skylight. She waited outside the door to Starcher's flat, listening for voices, but there was only silence inside. She was about to knock when suddenly the door was pulled open and a hand grabbed her wrist, yanking her into the dark apartment. The door swung shut behind her. As she opened her mouth to scream, a strong hand clamped down over it.

Then she was spun around. In the faintest glimmer of light from a streetlight outside, she saw Justin Gilead standing before her.

"Oh, it's you," he said, releasing her wrist.

She rubbed the ache away. "Where's Andrew?" she said.

"He went out," Gilead said. He saw the fear in her eyes. "Relax. He's fine. And you're safe with me."

Justin looked at her carefully in the dark, then reached up and took the knitted cap off her head. Her blond wavy hair fell down around her shoulders. "You look a lot better than you did when I first saw you today," he said.

"Forget that. How did you know I was here?"

"I heard you."

"I was quiet," she said.

"I heard you, anyway."

Her eyes were growing used to the darkness now. In the faint light she could see Justin smile. It was a tentative smile, almost as if he were afraid of her.

"I'm glad he didn't shoot you," she said.

"No more than I am," Justin replied. He turned away, but Sasha reached out and grabbed his arm. When he looked back, she placed a hand behind his head and pulled his face down to her lips. Her arms circled around him as she kissed him. Justin felt as if he were falling into a pool of mountain water, shocking yet comforting. Her body pressed against his, and as he felt himself respond, he pulled back.

The young woman looked up at him. Her eyes twinkled in the faint light from the windows. "Are you like him?" she asked.

"Like Starcher? How?"

"Nothing matters to him except his work. Not even his life. He's too old and he should be back in America, but he won't hear of it. Everything is for his precious Agency. Is that how you are?"

"Not for the Agency," Justin said. "But each of us has something he lives for. Why does it matter to you?"

"Because you just pulled away from me," Sasha said. "Because I don't want to like you too much if there's no response."

"If it makes you feel better, there's a response," Justin said. "It's just—" He stopped.

She reached out, took his hand, and held it. "Just what?" she said.

"Just that I don't live . . . the way most people do."

"Oh? Where do you live? On the moon?"

"You're closer than you know."

"Welcome to Planet Earth," Sasha said. She pressed her weight against him and steered him backward toward the bedroom. He let himself be pushed down onto the bed, even as he told himself that it was wrong, all wrong.

There had been only one woman in his life, and she and Justin had been little more than children. She was gone now. Justin had known no women since. There were no women at Rashimpur; Justin used his mind for meditation, and his body only for labor. He had come to think that the lure of the flesh was behind him, beneath him, beyond him somehow, but now, under the peeling paint of the shabby little room's ceiling, he found in Sasha's touch an exhilaration so old, he had forgotten it.

She undressed him slowly, her long fingers playing slowly over his buttons, then tracing delicately over his bare skin. She paused to touch the many scars that mottled his body, each of them a memory of a lesson learned, a mission accomplished.

When he was naked, she rose and said, "Your body is beautiful."

Naked, he felt somehow embarrassed, as if his body were wrong and what he was doing was wrong, and he did not answer.

He watched as Sasha stood before him in the room's soft light and began to undress. He wondered again if this was the right thing for him to do, but no voice from years past whispered into his mind. Then she was in bed with him. She curled up alongside him and rested her head on his flat stomach. Her long blond hair splashed across his chest; tendrils tickled his nipples. Her fingers lightly touched the fine hairs on the insides of his thighs.

He felt the tip of her tongue brush against his stomach

as her fingers teased him, touched him, lightly stroked him. All was right, he thought. Life was right, and this was part of life. Sasha lowered her mouth to him, and he remembered another time, when he was but a boy, that such an act had shocked him, but now there was no shock. There was only a warm glow of contentment and a feeling that this was how it should be.

He reached down after a while, cupped her head in his hand, and pulled her up alongside him. He felt again the strength in her arms as she drew close and guided him inside her.

Sasha's legs wrapped around his hips, and she pulled his face down to hers. He kissed her, then kissed her again as she explored his mouth with her tongue. Beneath him, he felt her body moving sinuously, and he put his lips close to her ear.

"I . . ." he began.

"No," Sasha said. "Don't say anything. Don't speak a word. Let your body speak for you."

He closed his eyes until all his senses diffused. It was as if neither of them existed, as if they were nothing but sexual parts that had come together to be as one. Justin no longer felt the blood coursing through him, no longer felt himself growing inside her. Time ceased to pass—it might have been seconds or hours—and then he felt her body moving faster under him, grinding against him. Her breath came shallow and quick, and he felt her shudder as her powerful legs tightened around him and pulled him deep into her. She moaned, and Justin felt himself exploding into her, driving deeper until he could go no deeper. They both lay locked in an embrace, their bodies molded together as one.

It was long minutes before Justin was aware of the weight of his body bearing down on the young woman, and he rolled onto his back. She placed her head in the crook of his arm but she did not speak. Turning her head toward his in the dim light, he saw her strong white teeth flash in a smile.

She put her left arm around him and pulled herself

closer to his body. The room was silent but for the sound of their breathing. There were no traffic sounds from the street below, no noise that spoke of life in the rest of the building.

Finally Sasha said, "You're not just a regular spook, are you?"

Justin smiled. "A spook?"

"That's what Andrew calls spies. He never says 'spies.' But he called you a professional. That means spook, I think. Like me."

"No, I guess I'm not a regular spook," Justin said. "But I'll be working with you for a while."

"Good." She wrapped her leg around his. "And then?" Her soft gray eyes looked up at him, and Justin said, "I don't belong here."

She exhaled her disappointment in a sigh. "Where do you belong? Where do you live?"

"On a mountain," he said.

"And there are no women on that mountain?" she asked.

"No," Justin said, but then was silent.

"My father always wanted to have a house in the mountains," she said. "He was born in Siberia."

"It's funny," she went on. "He loved the circus life, moving from place to place, but whenever he got drunk, he always talked about settling down in his homeland. I think that's why it was so important for him to come back to Russia when my grandmother was dying. He wanted to see the mountains again. I can't imagine anyone wanting to see Siberia, but he did."

She tossed around in the bed, then grew still. "That was a big mistake he made. The KGB came after him. They took him to a rehabilitation camp. When my mother fought them, they took her too."

She was staring up at the ceiling. "My parents are still imprisoned."

He kissed her softly. "That's why you're working with Starcher."

"I love that old man," she said, "but I would work with the devil himself to free my parents."

"Let's hope you don't have to," Justin said.

She looked at him as if he were staring straight into her soul. "Sometimes it can't be helped," she said softly. "There are demons inside all of us. They push us ahead, they keep us alive. And they must be satisfied, even if that requires sacrifice. Do you understand me?"

Justin thought of Manjusri's charge to him. He saw Alexander Zharkov's eyes again and, behind them, those of the unknown boy, ice-blue eyes like his own, setting their gaze on the throne of Rashimpur.

"You're cold," Sasha said. She placed her hand on both sides of his face and kissed him.

He held her tightly, not wanting to let go. But he would have to, he knew. He had his own demons to satisfy.

"I understand," he said.

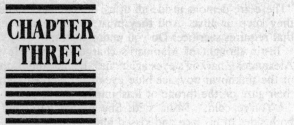

CHAPTER
THREE

In the morning, when Starcher returned, Sasha donned her disguise as Comrade Krylenko's granddaughter in preparation for the tournament.

"How do I look?" she asked, putting the finishing touches on her blacked-out teeth.

"Gruesome," Starcher said. "You make me shudder."

"Dear, sweet Grandpapa," she said, batting her eyelashes.

Starcher groaned, went into the bedroom, and came out with a pair of well-worn Russian boots. "As for you," he said, pointing at Justin, "see if these fit. You look like a goddamn Tibetan yak driver."

Justin put them on. They fit moderately well, although in combination with Justin's ripped, quilted Nepalese jacket, he resembled a refugee from a displaced persons camp.

"Look at us," Starcher said, his fists on his hips. His long overcoat dragged almost to the floor. "What a pitiful crew." He jerked his head toward the door. "Let's go."

The tournament room was packed with so many people that it was hard to breathe. "Comrade Krylenko" grandly informed the tournament director that he had resigned. Sasha was permitted to fill the vacancy.

"The other players have already begun," the tournament director said. He was the same prissy little man from the day before.

"That's all right," Justin said. "I will play the lady." They pushed their way to a vacant table at the end of the room while Starcher stood watch near the door.

The clock and chessboard were already set up. Justin looked across the table at Sasha, who grinned at him, showing her blacked-out top front teeth. Justin laughed.

"Shhhh," a man barked from the chessboard next to them.

Justin leaned over the table and whispered to Sasha, "I rarely have a chance to play against someone so fetching."

She crossed her eyes, and Justin laughed again.

"Shhhh," came the voice again.

Justin opened with the Ruy Lopez, and both players moved through the first dozen moves in less than two minutes. Then Sasha slid off into an unusual defensive variation.

Justin studied the board and said, "I suppose you have some idea what you're doing."

"That's for me to know and you to find out," she said.

"Shhhh," came the voice near them.

Justin studied the board, then leaned across the table and whispered again. "You're an animal," he said. "This is my own game. I played this in Warsaw."

"Aha," she said softly. "In time, light penetrates even the thickest skull. Are you ready to resign?"

"Not yet," Justin said.

"Why not? When you played this, it was a forced win."

"Yes," he said, "but I wasn't playing me." He smiled and moved.

"You are an arrogant dog," she said. "You'll pay for that."

"Shhhh," the man's voice hissed.

"How old are you?" Justin asked her suddenly.

"Old enough. Didn't you find that out last night?"

"Touché," he said. "When did you study my games?"

She sighed. "Okay, it's on your clock. It was the boy in the circus. He had a book with some of your games in it."

Justin moved and hit his clock. She moved a pawn, then made a face. "You see? All your talk made me make a stupid move."

"Who was the boy?" Justin asked.

She shrugged. "Just a circus urchin. We pick them up sometimes. But he was a strange one. For a long time I thought he was a mute, but he could talk when he wanted to. And his eyes . . ."

"What did you say?"

"His *eyes*." She looked up at Justin and blinked. "Why, he has eyes just like yours."

The player at the next table slammed his fist on his board and glared at them.

"We're sorry," Sasha said.

"This is outrageous!" the man said, bristling. "You've destroyed my game. I'm reporting the both of you." He rose in a huff and pushed his way imperiously through the crowd that had gathered around.

"Look. We have an audience," Sasha whispered.

But Justin didn't notice. He was thinking about the boy she'd described. "What was his name?"

"Who? The boy in the circus? Siraj. I think he might have been Indian or something."

A loud murmur rose from the crowd, and all heads faced toward the entrance doors to the ballroom. Above the din of voices could be heard the banging and scuffling of a fight. One of the tables crashed against a wall. There were some shouts and moans, but most of the people spoke in whispers as the crowd swarmed around itself like bees inside a hive with no means of escape.

"KGB," Justin heard someone say.

"But what did he do? He's such an old man. . . ."

"Starcher," Justin said, and jumped up from the table. The crowd was so thick around them that he could barely move his chair away. The movement knocked over the chess pieces and sent them spilling onto the floor where they were crushed underfoot.

Justin viciously pushed his way through the sea of bodies, Sasha following, but by the time they reached the main door, Starcher was already gone.

While people poured out around him, Justin caught a glimpse of four men dragging Starcher outside. The old man's false mustache was dangling from his lip, and the left side of his head was covered with blood.

When he reached the door, the men were pulling Starcher into a waiting car. It sped off even before its doors closed.

"Get back, Justin!" Sasha screamed. "It's a trap!"

A man with hair the color of fresh rust grabbed her around the neck and pressed a gun to her head. While Justin watched helplessly, he pushed her into the back of a small enclosed truck.

"You next," said a voice behind Justin. Two men with Sten guns trained on him began moving slowly toward him. "Don't try it," the red-haired man said. "Those weapons fire twenty rounds a second. Go for one of us, and the other fires into the crowd. And, of course, the girl dies too."

Justin submitted. As soon as he got into the truck, he felt something heavy smash him on the back of the head. He slumped over onto Sasha's lap.

"God forgive me," she whispered.

CHAPTER FOUR

He awoke in utter darkness with the scent of earth around him. His right ankle throbbed, and he felt a heavy weight on his back.

It took Justin a moment to realize he was lying face-down, his legs pressed up behind him. He was unbound but unable to get up. His back was warm.

Slowly he extended his arms until they touched the other wall, less than a yard from his face. The place he was in was no more than six feet wide.

He shifted slowly, steeling himself against the ache in his ankle. The thing on top of him stirred, and Justin felt the contours of bony limbs and hair brush against his face. Justin touched the hair. Beneath it was a mass of coagulated blood.

"Starcher."

The old man moaned softly. Justin rearranged himself so that he cradled Starcher's head in his lap.

"Justin," the old man said weakly.

"I'm here."

"Four men. One of them was KGB. I recognized him from the circus. Red hair." He felt the slimy wall. "Where's the girl?"

"I don't know."

Starcher struggled to pull himself upright, but he was too weak. Justin could already feel fever on him, and he remembered that Starcher had a bad heart.

"Don't move for a while," he said. "You've been hit pretty hard."

Starcher slumped down. "Wish to Christ I had a cigar," he said. He felt for his mustache; it was gone. "I guess my disguise was easier to see through than I thought," he said. "Those goons made me right away. I didn't even get a chance to fight." He sniffed. "Where in hell are we, anyway? Smells like some dungeon. Jesus, I suppose this is the KGB's idea of prison reform."

Justin clapped a hand over the other man's mouth. He heard the soft *whoosh* of a door opening.

A *door?* Here?

Of course, he thought. He should have known it as soon as he was conscious. This hole, inexplicably, was *indoors*.

There were other smells in this place besides those of earth and human bodies and Starcher's blood. From above came the scents of stale tobacco and food, of paper and machine oil and metal. Manjusri had taught him how to use the darkness, but he had forgotten.

Now he focused his senses, as he had in the cave on Amne Xachim, and once again he was able to reach beyond his boundaries. He heard the soft whir of machinery, felt wisps of moving air. Inching his hand slowly up the wall, he felt the earth become drier and harder, and he knew that the air in this place, wherever it was, was artificially cleaned. A sealed place. But it was more than that. The bottom few inches of wall and the floor he was sitting on were not earth at all but solid rock covered with fallen dirt that had been packed down. Bedrock. It was underground, and this oubliette was a level below that.

Starcher gasped at the sudden appearance of a blinding light overhead. The fluorescent light revealed a wire grate at the top of the deep cylinder holding them.

Footsteps approached, the measured, easy pace of someone who knew his way. Then the tips of a pair of men's shoes stopped on top of the grate. Above them, far above, a face appeared. Starcher squinted to try to make out its darkened features.

Justin didn't have to. To him the face was as clear as it had been the last time he saw it, lit by flames, with the spark of divine evil shining in its reptilian eyes.

Zharkov.

The Prince of Death had come for Justin.

CHAPTER FIVE

"**I**'ve kept my end of the bargain," Kadar said. "You have your precious Grandmaster."

Zharkov nodded. The *Vozhd* was surrounded by shadow, as he had been every time Zharkov saw him in the underground fortress. It was as if Kadar had himself become a creature of the darkness, pale and blind.

"Now," Kadar said, "the Nichevo file."

"Allow me to leave and I will get it for you."

"No need." From behind his desk Kadar lifted the metal strongbox and set it in front of Zharkov. Its lock had been smashed open. "All the details have been taken care of."

Zharkov's hands clenched into fists. "What did you do with my men?" he demanded.

"There, there, Colonel. Nichevo is safe. My people went in just after you left with Siraj. The place was empty." He patted Zharkov's shoulder. "No harm done, eh?"

"No harm . . ." Zharkov brushed Kadar's hand away angrily, checking an impulse to strike the man. "Very well," he said. "You have the file. I'll take Gilead and leave now."

"Droll," Kadar said, chuckling. "My dear friend, if all

I needed was the file, I wouldn't have gone to the trouble of getting Gilead for you in the first place, would I?" He pulled a handful of papers out of the strongbox. "Letters," he said. "Love letters from Vassily Zharkov to your mother. How sentimental of you to guard them so jealously." He fanned them in front of his chest. "If I know anything about your late father, I know that the best cryptographers in the country couldn't decode these letters."

He was right. When Zharkov was still a boy, his father had taken a full year to teach him an extremely complex code designed to be used only by the two of them. The code was based on family references, using nicknames, the birthdates of servants, and hundreds of other personal facts that no outsider could understand.

Vassily Zharkov had begun it as a game, and the child loved sharing the elaborate secret with his formidable father. But by the time he was twelve years old, Alexander knew the exact purpose of the code.

"Keep this in your memory," his father had said. "One day your life may depend on it."

Soon after Konstantin Kadar had become Director of the KGB, he threatened to destroy Nichevo because of its closeness to the Premier. In order to protect the organization he had carefully put together, Vassily Zharkov had begun to write letters encoding the Nichevo files, which he mailed to his wife during a long stay in the Urals. Alexander's mother had read them lovingly, then stored them away among her private things. On Vassily's death, she'd passed them on to her son.

"These are for you," she'd said. "Read them carefully. Remember all your father taught you."

The file had been a revelation to Alexander. It provided, he knew, a way to stay alive despite Kadar's efforts.

Zharkov kept the file up to date in the same manner as before, writing letters ostensibly from his father and periodically placing them into the strongbox buried on his family's estate. Later, when Kadar became General Secretary of the Soviet Union, the immediate danger to Zharkov lessened, since Nichevo always functioned as a tool of the Premier in power, but the letters remained buried.

Now Kadar possessed the Nichevo file and cursed himself for not having had them translated when he'd had the chance.

"Please translate them," the Vozhd said courteously, gesturing for Zharkov to use the desk. He turned the small lamp so that it illuminated the letters.

Zharkov sat down and began to write.

When he finished, hours later, he stood up wearily and handed the sheets of paper to Kadar. "That's all of it. I'll go now."

"Not quite yet," Kadar said. "I'm afraid I'll have to impose on you for one more favor before I can permit you to leave."

Zharkov raised his face, feeling the first wisps of betrayal.

"Give me the names and locations of all the Nichevo operatives."

"You must be joking."

From the shadows of the doorway leading to the rest of the compound, Siraj's slender figure emerged. The malicious eyes shone bright blue, even in the dim light.

"Am I?" Kadar asked.

Zharkov brushed past the boy to go to his room, but he heard Siraj's soft voice behind him in the corridor.

"Give him what he wants. Those people are of no use to you now. Tell Kadar who they are."

"I certainly will not," Zharkov said, walking on in contempt.

"Do not turn your back on me. Ever."

The threat in the boy's voice stopped the colonel in his tracks. In his anger he had forgotten that this was no gangling teenager to be dismissed at will. He turned back, his jaw set.

"Do not make a pretense of your pride now, Father. You have already touched your face to the ground before me."

"You cannot expect—"

"I am your High Priest, and I expect you to obey me," Siraj said. "You must not place the lives of mortal men above me. If I were to tell you to kill them with your own hands, you should willingly do so." His voice sweetened. "I am the center of your life. You are to have no other loyalties. Give the names of the men to Kadar. It will be a new beginning for you, free of earthly encumbrances."

"That is asking too much."

"I am not asking, Father." The blue eyes were dancing with amusement.

"Get away from me," Zharkov said, pushing the boy to the floor.

Siraj sat up, his face knotted with rage, as Zharkov marched down the hallway.

"You have defiled me with your touch," he said, stretching out two fingers toward the retreating figure.

Zharkov felt an obstruction in his windpipe. He tried to cough it out, but nothing moved. His chest heaved; saliva dripped off his lips. He felt his eyes bulging. His hands grasped at his throat.

"I ought to let you die here, on your belly like a worm," Siraj said.

Zharkov dropped to his knees, pleading with one outstretched arm.

"Beg my forgiveness. My mercy. Beg for it, Father."

Zharkov clasped his hands together. They were trembling, their knuckles white. Then, with an immense effort, he forced out a guttural, growling sound. "Please," he said. "I . . . beg you."

The boy nodded, and Zharkov felt the air whoosh back into his lungs. He remained on the floor, his senses reeling, tasting his sweat as it trickled between his lips.

The boy took a small cloth bag from his trousers pocket. From it he pulled out two flattish red items.

"Here's a souvenir for you," he said, throwing them at Zharkov as if he were tossing scraps at a starving beast.

Zharkov picked one up. Its red color came off on his hands. It was blood. The article was a human ear.

"They're both right sides," the boy said, smiling. "There were two men at your apartment today."

Zharkov cast the ear away in horror.

"You see? I can find them without you. I was just giving you a test of your allegiance to me."

A deep, protracted groan came from the colonel's throat.

"You failed, Father," the boy said softly. He laughed, and the laughter rang in Zharkov's ears long after he had crawled back into his room and sat crouched by the door.

He sat on the floor like a terrified animal, his hands digging into his face.

How had he let this happen?

Nichevo was gone. The creation of his father, a force that had shaped the world, was finished. Only one operative besides Zharkov now survived. That operative would soon be dead. No one could fight Siraj and win. Not even the Grandmaster.

He had seen Justin Gilead as he had never seen him before, battered, humiliated, sunk in a fifteen-foot hole. It was not the Grandmaster who had filled his obsessive dreams, the giant who had evolved for a score of centuries to do final battle with Zharkov. Just a broken wretch without a chance, a beast in an abattoir marked for slaughter.

But Zharkov would live. He would live as the slave of a psychotic boy with a freak gift.

The thought suddenly struck him as obscenely funny. Alexander Zharkov, the man of reason, had spent his whole life guarding his freedom in a society where freedom was not permitted; now he had thrown it away in exchange for an endless servitude.

Father. The word nauseated him. He was no more a father to that devil-spawn than the water of a lake was to the slime that clung to its shore. Siraj belonged with Kadar. It was not blood, but their perverted venality, that made them kin.

There was such a thing as greatness among men. Zharkov's father had possessed it. Vassily Zharkov would not have betrayed everything dear to him because of the fear of death. And Justin Gilead, dying by inches with no hope of escape, possessed it too.

But Konstantin Kadar and Siraj would never understand greatness. They were vermin, directing other vermin to spread their filth. Such would be the inheritors of the earth.

Unconsciously his back straightened. It did not have to be this way. It would not. He was Alexander Zharkov, descendant of princes, not some dancing puppet who allowed his strings to be manipulated by one maniac and then snipped at will by another. He would not permit it. Not for himself, and not for the only man on earth who was his equal.

The Grandmaster belonged to him. No one else. And when the time came, they would die together, unafraid.

The first thing he had to do was to find a means of escape. The ventilation shafts were too small for a man to fit through, but he knew that Kadar must have a way.

Kadar was not in his office. Zharkov scanned the room carefully. There were no cameras. That was one thing in his favor.

Three walls of the study were lined with books. Zharkov ran his hand carefully over each leather binding. At last he found what he was looking for: a solid line running down the spines of a column of false books. He pulled on it, and the shelving slid away noiselessly. Like everything else in Kadar's hideaway, the folding door was simple and efficient. The hidden panel was no more elaborate than a folding closet door covered over by books. Behind it was the expected shaft into which a small aluminum ladder had been bolted.

Zharkov climbed up. At the top was a small hook below a metal plate. He tried it, pushed the plate open a crack. Daylight streamed in, hurting his eyes. Before now, he had never been so acutely aware of the difference between natural and artificial light.

Not far away, he could hear a steady beat of footfalls on the dried leaves. They walked a short distance, turned around, and walked the same distance in the other direction, then turned around again.

Zharkov closed the plate. A guard obviously, and probably more than one. He would wait for night, when it wouldn't be so easy to be spotted.

He climbed back down and eased the panel of books into place.

"What are you doing here?"

Zharkov spun around. It was the boy, standing in the doorway.

"Just looking for something to read," he said, forcing a smile. "I was going to ask Comrade Kadar's permission, but he wasn't here."

"You looked as if you were trying to escape." The boy smiled coldly. "That would be a grave mistake, you know. The guards outside would shoot you on sight. As it is, you're only being kept alive because of me."

"Kadar . . ."

"He doesn't need your Nichevo. He'd like to eliminate the ones who are left, but they don't pose much of a threat to him. The *Vozhd* has hundreds of men who will fight for him."

"Even you call him *Vozhd*," Zharkov said.

"Why not? It is a straw title, easily transferred to another. But Siraj is the Black Star forever. While Konstantin Kadar is Premier, that star will rise over the largest nation on earth, and his successors will not be able to block its light."

His eyes shone, and Zharkov felt the boy's power as if it were a palpable entity that filled the room.

Zharkov hastily snatched a book from the shelves and retreated. He had found the escape route; now he would have to rely on the Grandmaster to lead them through it.

In the corridor he saw a woman slipping into the door of Kadar's sleeping quarters. She was wearing something sheer and long, with feathered slippers on her feet. He approached the door slowly and waited outside for a moment. He could smell her expensive perfume.

CHAPTER SIX

"Thirsty. I'm just thirsty," Starcher said, opening and closing his eyes slowly. "Can't understand it. Are you there? Are you there, son?"

"I'm here," Justin Gilead said.

They had been in the pit only a few hours, but Starcher had been drifting in and out of consciousness, and Justin was worried about him. The old man was—what, seventy years old?—and had a bad heart. The knock on the head he had taken when being captured might have fractured his skull.

"Was I out?" Starcher asked for the fourth time.

"It's all right," Justin said. "We don't have much else to do but rest."

"I wonder what they've done with Sasha," Starcher said raspily.

"I don't know. Don't talk." Justin put Starcher's feet firmly on the ground and propped him against the wall. Then he slid his own hands into the mud of the wall and tried to climb. The wet earth loosened and fell onto his face and shoulders.

"It's not going to work, Justin," Starcher said. "Save your strength."

"I don't know what else to do." Justin felt like screaming. The pain had gone from his right ankle, but for the first time since he was a child, he felt helpless.

Zharkov had looked in on them, said nothing, and then left. He had not come back. Was that his plan? To let Gilead and Starcher rot here in this hole until they died? Was there nothing more to Justin and Zharkov's destiny than this slow and insignificant death?

"I've got to try, Starcher," Justin said.

And he tried, hour after hour, until his fingers were bloodied raw and the loose clumps of earth and mud had clustered around their ankles.

Suddenly Justin stopped. "Someone's coming," he said.

The overhead light came on, and a small face appeared over the grate. It was the face Justin had seen in the reflection of the store window.

"Can . . . can you help us?" Starcher asked.

The boy looked down at them innocently.

"My friend's hurt," Justin said. "Some water. That's all we want. Can you bring us some?"

The boy's mouth spread into a slow grin. "Thirsty?" he asked.

"Yes," Starcher began. "We just—"

Justin clapped a hand over the old man's arm.

"Don't," he whispered.

"What?"

"He's dangerous," Justin said.

"Don't be—"

"So you know me, Patanjali?" the boy called.

"What'd he call you?"

Justin ignored Starcher.

"You are Siraj."

"Your executioner," the boy said.

"My friend has no knowledge of our lives. Let him go."

Siraj shrugged. "Why should I?"

"Whatever you want with me . . ."

"All I want is to kill you. I just have to decide how." The boy's face grew cold. "Do you remember my mother?"

"The abbess Varja was—"

"The *goddess* Varja. She could only be destroyed by magic. You used it on her."

"I have no magic," Justin said softly.

There was a long silence before the boy answered him. "I do."

Justin heard a hissing sound at his feet. Water had begun to gush through the bottom of the hole.

With a cry, Starcher fell on his hands and knees, scooping up the crystal water.

"Don't drink it," Justin commanded him. "It's a trick, an illusion. That's how he works. There's no water here. You'd be drinking nothing but mud."

Starcher looked up, his eyes pleading, but he understood the Grandmaster well enough not to doubt his word. He let the precious liquid run through his hands. He hung his head.

"Illusion or not, it will drown you," the boy said. "Your minds will accommodate the vision."

"Stop it!" Justin shouted.

"Fight me. Varja's magic was not strong enough to kill you. Mine is."

Starcher hobbled to his feet again and plastered himself against the wall as the water, now muddy and swirling, inched up his torso to his chest.

"Not enough?" the boy teased. He pointed a finger directly at Starcher's eyes.

The old man screamed and banged his head against the wall of mud, his arms splashing uncontrollably in the neck-high water. Justin grabbed for him.

Siraj smiled. "I don't believe I'll kill you yet," he said. "The old man amuses me. Perhaps I'll wait until his fear kills him. Then you will be left alone with his body while the maggots devour it. How would you like that, Patanjali?" His fingers curled over the grate. "You will beg for death then. And I will find a very special way to accommodate you."

He got up and walked away softly. The light clicked off.

Justin and Starcher leaned against the mud wall, each

absorbed in his own thoughts. In time Kadar's servant opened the grate and lowered a bucket of water to them, and they drank.

"In a few minutes I'm going to wake up from this," Starcher said. "I almost got killed, drowned, and *nothing was there*. That boy . . ."

"He's real. He comes from . . . where I do," Justin said.

"*Jesus*. Can you . . . ?" He turned little circles in the air with his hand.

"No. It's a freak ability he has. The killing gift," Justin said.

"Jesus," Starcher repeated.

"You never should have gotten mixed up with me again, Starcher."

Kadar lay nude on the bed with Vassily Zharkov's letters and their translations strewn around him. He was reading one and taking notes on a small stenographer's pad. He laughed out loud.

"This is wonderful," he said. "Badushenko—the one on the Central Committee—used to beg his secretary to shit on him. Can you imagine? And he has his eye set on the General Secretary's office. And this one, Teratznovich." He picked up another letter and dropped it gleefully to the bed. "A homosexual. Notorious, apparently. There's so much information on him, it's embarrassing."

Across the room Sasha forced a smile, unconsciously covering her breasts with her arms. "I thought he was dead," she said.

"Long dead. But a . . . protégé, shall we say, of his is now in the Politburo. Denis Novasharadzne, the handsome one married to the ballerina. Everyone knows Teratznovich arranged that wedding, but here it is on paper, with full references by number to corroborating documents. Hah! Zharkov, you were a genius."

He scooped up the letters and kissed them. "What I can do with these, eh?" He placed them on the nightstand and patted the bed beside him. "Come here, little one. I am in good spirits tonight. I have the energy of a bull."

The woman walked forward hesitantly. Kadar grabbed her by her wrist, pulled her down, crushed her in his fleshy arms, and kissed her neck.

She felt a thick stream of drool trickle onto her breast. "You wore my perfume this time," he whispered.

"I was grateful for the gift," she said. "For all your gifts."

He pushed her away from him with both hands on her upper arms. "You have a strange way of showing it," he said curtly. "My men said you tried to warn Gilead when they took him at the chess tournament."

"That was because of Andrew. The old man. You promised he wouldn't be hurt. When I saw the blood on his face—"

He squeezed her close to him. She could smell his staleness. "Sasha, *dochka*," he murmured. "That was necessary. And a head wound always looks worse than it really is."

"But you said you wouldn't take him."

"He will be released the moment it is safe to do so. Meanwhile he is quite comfortable here."

"Where is he? I would like to see him, just to know he's all right."

Kadar held her away and looked frankly into her eyes. "Sasha, do you think this American spy would like to see *you* again after what has happened?"

She hung her head. "I suppose not," she said. "When will you be able to let him go? He knows nothing. He's very old and not strong anymore."

"It will be soon, little bird, very soon. My time has come. The Nichevo file was my last obstacle. I will be named General Secretary by May Day."

Sasha stared at the wall. "Then my father and mother . . ."

"I will see to everything," he said.

His fingers had left red marks on her arms. "Ah, I've

hurt you, *dochka*," he said. "I forgot how fragile you are, how like a child still."

He buried his face in her hair. "The clothes suit you," he said, his short fingers untying the silken strings of her gown. He reached in past the transparent lace of her bodice and pulled out her breasts. "You should always be like this." He stroked her nipples, his eyes half closed. "I like you as a woman, although I miss the little girl you once were."

She tipped her head back so that he could not see her tears. "I will never forget what you have done in keeping my family alive," she said.

"Nonsense," Kadar whispered in her ear. "You did it with me because you loved it. You loved it, didn't you?" His hands tensed on her arms.

Sasha swallowed. "Yes, *Vozhd*."

She thought, *One day I will kill you. Vozhd*.

It was pitch black in the mud oubliette when the faint creak of the door opening in the furnace room overhead woke Justin. He waited for the light to click on, but the footsteps approached in the darkness.

His stomach turned. What did Siraj have planned for them now? Starcher was too weak from hunger and thirst to stand much more violence. Being awakened out of his sleep by one of the boy's spectacles might kill him.

"Starcher," he said, shaking him gently. "Andy, wake up."

"What . . ." The old man sat up with a start. "Is the little son of a bitch back?"

"Quiet," the voice above them whispered.

Justin put his arm across Starcher's shoulder for support as the grate rattled above them. A shower of rust fell. Then, with a grunt, the steel-ringed mesh lifted and thudded onto the cement floor.

"What the hell's going on?" Starcher said.

Something was moving toward them from above. "It's a bucket," Justin whispered, grasping the object. "On a rope." He squinted through the darkness toward the opening. "Who's there?"

"Sasha?" Starcher called hoarsely.

There was no answer.

"Have it your way," Justin said, tugging on the rope. "We're coming up." He lifted Starcher and was about to tie the rope around the old man's waist when the room was suddenly flooded with light.

In the brightness Justin saw Alexander Zharkov's astonished face looking toward the door.

Zharkov?

Why would Zharkov help him to escape? That was clearly what the Russian had been doing, because now Justin could hear the shuffling of other feet in the doorway above him.

"I thought you might try something like this," Konstantin Kadar said. Flanking him were two men with submachine guns leveled at Zharkov. Kadar jerked his head. The gunmen closed in.

Zharkov tried to fight them, but the men overpowered him. One of them shoved the butt of his weapon into the back of Zharkov's head. When he lay still, Kadar pulled up the rope and handed it to one of the guards. Once the rope was clear, Kadar kicked the unconscious Zharkov into the pit.

Justin and Starcher stared mutely at Zharkov as another set of footsteps sounded in the room above them. A woman's voice said sleepily, "What's the matter? I heard so much noise. . . ."

"Sasha," Starcher called hoarsely. "Here. We're here."

She ran over to the pit, looked down, and screamed.

"Get her out of here," Kadar ordered the guards.

"Bastard!" she shouted as the men muscled her away.

Then the door closed with a soft *snick,* and the place was utterly quiet again.

"That voice," Starcher said. "Whoever's up there with Sasha. I've heard it before. . . ."

"He's still here," Justin said.

"Very perceptive, Grandmaster," the smooth voice

above them said. "I hope you will be able to tolerate the inconvenience of close quarters for a short time. Your friend Colonel Zharkov has decided to spend his last hours with you."

"Jesus Christ, it's the *Vozhd*," Starcher said.

"I'm flattered that you recognized me," Kadar said.

"Why are we being kept here?" Justin demanded.

There was a short silence before Kadar answered, "Not a reason in the world any longer, gentlemen."

His footsteps receded. In a few minutes the two guards came back to replace the metal grate. They kept the light on when they left.

Zharkov came to slowly, rubbing the back of his head. He blinked when he saw the legs of the two men with him. Then his gaze traveled upward and met Justin's eyes. The two men stared at each other for what seemed like an eternity to Starcher. Then Zharkov laughed, softly and bitterly.

"It was not supposed to end this way for us, was it?" he said, leaning against the mud wall.

Justin touched him, as if trying to ascertain that the colonel was real. "Why did you come for us?"

Zharkov took a deep breath. "I don't think it makes much difference anymore," he said. From his pocket he took a cigarette and offered it to Starcher. "Let me tell you a story."

CHAPTER SEVEN

The telephone by his bed rang four times before Premier Pierlenko was able to pull himself from sleep to answer it.

"Yes?"

"I am sorry to disturb you, Comrade Secretary," came the voice of Maxim Sterlitz. "But I think we may know where Kadar is."

"Where?"

"In an underground headquarters about sixty miles outside the city," the KGB Director answered.

Pierlenko sat up in bed. "How did you learn this?"

Sterlitz hesitated for a moment. "A woman called. She told me about it."

"What woman?" Pierlenko said.

"She would not reveal her identity," Sterlitz said.

"What makes you think she is telling the truth?"

"She knew a great deal about Kadar," Sterlitz said. "It was not a crank call. I have already sent men."

"All right," Pierlenko said. "Now do one more thing."

"Yes, sir."

"Get dressed and go yourself. And this time, if you don't get Kadar, don't bother coming back."

* * *

In the pit, Zharkov told them everything, about the seven American murders and why Kadar had engineered them, about the scar on Richard Rand's neck, about the army of ex-KGB agents and Kadar's spies throughout the Soviet government, about the Nichevo file. "He's going to blackmail the Politburo members into reinstating him in the Kremlin," he said.

"And deposing Pierlenko?" Starcher croaked, rubbing his throat. He was so thirsty, he could barely speak, but his professional instincts were stronger than his discomfort. "On what grounds?"

Zharkov shrugged. "Using the KGB to kill Rand and the others, perhaps. It won't matter what lie Kadar gives them. Pierlenko's denials will be rejected. That is, if it comes to that."

"What do you mean, *if*?"

"Konstantin Kadar knows firsthand what a deposed ruler is capable of doing. I doubt if Pierlenko will live long enough to face a trial, even a spurious one."

Painfully Starcher tried to swallow. "Then I suppose things will go back to the way they used to be here." He stopped himself from adding: "Except now there's practically no CIA presence in Russia."

"Much worse than that," Zharkov said. "The United States still trails the Soviet Union in the production of weaponry. Kadar wants war before that balance shifts." He looked up at the circle of light visible through the mesh grate. "Perhaps it is better that we die now."

They sat in silence for a long time. Despite the tension, Starcher forced himself to sleep. At last Justin spoke softly, so as not to awaken the old man. "Will Siraj kill you too?" he asked Zharkov.

"Yes." It was the response of a soldier, completely without emotion.

"It is said the boy is your own son."

"All the same, he will kill me. I have betrayed him." He lifted his chin. "And willingly."

"What did he want from you?"

Zharkov looked into Justin's eyes with a spark of his

old hatred. "I promised him your death," he said. "In exchange for my life."

Justin stared at him. "Can he do that? Change—"

"He can."

"And yet you tried to free me."

Zharkov didn't answer.

The metal grate moved again.

Justin woke to see Sasha's face, tense with concentration as she lifted the heavy steel cap. Her muscles straining, she set it down without a sound. Then she tied one end of the rope with the bucket to a pipe and lowered the other end into the pit.

Zharkov recognized her as the woman he had seen going into Kadar's room. He was about to speak, but a muffled burst of machine-gun fire suddenly broke the silence in the bunker.

Sasha looked over her shoulder at the sound of running footsteps in the corridor. "Hurry," she said. "There isn't much time."

Justin nudged Zharkov to climb up first. Starcher was getting to his feet groggily. Before he could object, Justin hoisted the old man onto his back and took hold of the rope.

"I'm not a damn monkey," Starcher whispered. He was embarrassed to be carried like a child in front of Sasha, but he knew he was too weak to climb himself.

"Where's the boy?" Zharkov asked.

"He's gone," Sasha said. "We have to move fast."

There was another burst of fire, this time followed by answering weapons, fire and shouting.

"Who's that, the cavalry?" Starcher asked, rolling off Justin onto the cement floor.

"There's no time to explain," Sasha said. She stuffed some dried apples into Starcher's shirt pocket. "Eat when you can. Follow me."

They ran down the corridor toward Kadar's office. The shouting was coming closer. A voice barked, "KGB. Surrender peacefully and you will be in no danger."

Shots rang out from inside the office. When they entered, Kadar was standing near the opened bookcase. In front of him a uniformed KGB officer hung by one arm to the narrow stepladder leading to the outside. The side of the KGB man's jaw had been blown off, and blood poured onto the blue shoulder board of his uniform. His rifle lay on the floor. Kadar fired again, straight into the man's face.

Sasha pushed the others out of the room before Kadar saw them.

"How else do you get out of this place?" Starcher whispered when they were almost at the furnace room again.

Zharkov closed his eyes. "That was the only way."

Outside, the din of machine-gun fire was growing heavier. There were more shots from Kadar's office.

Justin put his hand tentatively to one of the ventilation shafts protruding from the wall. "This," he said.

"Fine, if we had a blowtorch," Sasha said, casting about frantically. But Starcher and Zharkov only looked at Justin. They had seen before what the Grandmaster could do.

"Get the rope," Justin said quietly, placing his fingertips along the welded seams of the shaft.

As Zharkov ran back into the furnace room, Justin directed his strength into his arms and began a steady, mounting pressure on the seam. The metal buckled and broke through. Justin withdrew his fingers and waited for a moment, focusing his energy again. Then, in a movement so fast that it appeared to be no more than a blur, he thrust his hands into the shaft again and peeled away the metal as if it were paper.

By the time Zharkov arrived with the rope, the hole in the side of the ventilation shaft was big enough for a man to enter. Justin took the rope and wound it quickly around his waist.

"I'll go up first and take care of any obstructions at the top," he said to Zharkov and Sasha. "When I yank on the rope, tie Starcher in and follow him closely so he doesn't fall. You can get a foothold inside."

He had one leg already inside the shaft when a bullet pinged off the metal, near his face. They turned to see Kadar in the corridor, an automatic in his hand.

"You'll take me with you, or I'll kill you where you stand," he said.

Sasha moved first. She rolled into Kadar below waist level, locking his knees and toppling him. With her elbow she caught him in the groin, then flipped upright onto the back of his wrist and took his gun.

"Go, now," she said to Justin, stepping back from Kadar, the gun trained on him. "I'll keep him here."

Justin hesitated.

"Leave her," Zharkov hissed.

The machine-gun fire drew nearer.

"I said get out of here, damn you!" Sasha screamed. "I know what I'm doing."

Justin climbed into the shaft.

Moving on his hands and feet like a crab, he inched his way up the shaft until he reached a vented metal plate at the top. The plate was bolted onto the shaft. Justin took up some of the dangling rope, wound it over his hands, and shot his fists through the plate.

In one swift motion he grasped the edge of the plate and hurled it at an advancing KGB guard, neatly severing the man's head.

On the ground nearby he could see the bodies of two other men. The regular guard, Justin thought. They must have been shot.

He looked around. No other bodies, though. He could hear the sound of the steel door being battered down some distance away. He crawled up out of the shaftway, attached the end of the rope that had been wound around him to a tall tree, and signaled for the others.

Starcher came up first, half seated on Zharkov's shoulder. Justin took the Russian's hand to pull him up.

At his touch, Zharkov looked down at their entwined hands, as if surprised at the warmth in the Grandmaster's flesh, then broke away. A thousand unspoken words flew between them, but there was no time now. They both knew they would have to meet again, to finish what they had started.

"We'd better separate," Justin said. "It will be difficult for them to catch us both."

Zharkov nodded. In a moment he was gone, running through the deep woods.

Justin set off in the opposite direction, supporting Starcher as they walked. There was water nearby. Through the sharp odor of spent ammunition, he could smell it. Soon he heard it, too, a small running stream twisted among the big trees. He led Starcher to the stream and brought water in his cupped hands to the old man's lips. "Drink this," he said.

Starcher obeyed. Then, reviving, he turned onto his belly to drink with Justin from the stream.

"This is as far as you go," a soft young voice behind them said.

The two men whirled around, their hands still dripping water. The boy had approached so quietly that even Justin had not heard him.

"Give me the amulet of Rashimpur," he said.

"I cannot. Its power is for me alone. Others have taken it before. . . ."

"I am not *others!*" the boy shouted. "It is mine by the right of my mother's prophecy. It is mine."

Justin made a move toward him. He felt as if he were repelled by an invisible wall.

"You dare to challenge me?" the boy said. "You who have wasted every opportunity for greatness? Did you never know the power of the amulet? With it you could have ruled the world. But you are not Patanjali. You are a fraud, a nothing. You do not deserve to do battle with me."

The boy raised his arms. His light blue eyes glinted in the dying moonlight as he glared at Justin.

"Kneel before your High Priest," he commanded.

Justin felt his throat closing. *What does he have?* he

wondered. It was the killing gift. Its legacy had come down through generations of evil to this young boy, its final keeper. Against his will, Justin dropped to his knees.

His heart was fibrillating, pulsing wildly before slowing, then stopping altogether as Justin felt numbness begin to settle over him like a blanket of snow.

The boy stood as rigid as a statue, his entire attention focused on Justin, his arms extended like a sorcerer's. Starcher crawled to the body of the dead guard and picked up his rifle. Slowly, concentrating what was left of his strength on operating the weapon, he brought it up to his shoulder and aimed.

The boy spun around. In a split second the rifle skidded away, and Starcher's hand felt as if it were on fire. At the same time he writhed from four terrible, invisible blows to his stomach.

Justin sucked in the air that rushed to his lungs. He rose and staggered toward the crumpled Starcher.

"Take it!" he screamed. He reached under his shirt for the amulet on its gold chain and ripped it off. "Take it. Just leave him alone."

A gleam of triumph danced in the boy's eyes as the three of them stopped, suspended in space, the golden amulet dangling from Justin's hand.

The boy lunged forward and snatched the medallion. With a shriek of pain he flung it away. The hand that had touched it was burned.

"Magic!" he screamed.

Justin looked at the ground, puzzled. Then he saw it, the ancient golden amulet of Rashimpur. It lay in the grass in two pieces, cleft up the middle, the color of lead.

"You used magic to hurt me!"

Justin picked up the pieces. So it's gone now, he thought. He had tried to give away the relic of the ages, entrusted to him for safekeeping, and in response it had destroyed itself.

"I have no magic," he said softly.

He felt a terrible pain in his chest. The pieces of the

medallion fell from his hand as he looked at the boy in astonishment.

"Die," said Siraj. The hatred in his eyes was so strong that it seemed a palpable thing, an entity of its own.

Justin's heart constricted again. His fingers clutched at a clump of grass. Blood bubbled up over his lips.

The boy's mouth curled bitterly. "I came here to fight a king and found only a sniveling dog. Die a dog's death, then." He turned and walked away.

The Grandmaster lay still.

Starcher knelt beside him. "Oh, son," he said. He wiped Justin's bloody lips with his shirt. "Why'd you have to come back?" He closed Justin's eyes and rocked the body in his arms.

On the other side of the woods, the gunfire had stopped. An eerie silence that hung in the air was suddenly broken by a man's shrill scream, quickly followed by a new burst of gunfire. Other weapons joined in.

Starcher kept rocking, oblivious to the noise and the danger. He was there a long time before he was aware of someone standing over him. Zharkov.

The Russian looked down at the Grandmaster.

So I did not die with you after all, he thought.

The mystics of the ancient world had foretold the coming of two men who shared one spirit. All their lives, Justin Gilead and Alexander Zharkov had been trained to believe that they were those two men. Their destinies forever intertwined, they were to have fought the battle of the gods against each other and died together.

Was that prophecy no more than a fairy story for children? Had everything in both their lives been for nothing?

At Justin's feet, Zharkov picked up the two gray pieces of the amulet. They were cold.

"You'd better go," Zharkov told Starcher briskly. "The KGB is everywhere. If you want, let them capture you. They'll make a trade for you. But do it away from here."

"What about you? The secret police aren't crazy about you, either."

"Get away before I kill you myself," Zharkov snapped.

The old man stood up, took a last look at Justin Gilead's body, and limped away.

Zharkov carried Justin's body to a mound of moss-covered earth nearby. He quickly dug a shallow grave with his hands, then placed Justin's body inside. Over the Grandmaster's heart he laid the two pieces of the broken amulet.

"Farewell, then," he said, scooping a handful of loose earth and leaves into the grave.

Hearing the sounds of men approaching, Zharkov got to his feet and ran to the creek. Sloshing upstream, he moved away from the voices until they receded. He looked over his shoulder a last time, but the KGB men were no longer behind him.

"Hold it," someone called. A uniformed agent stood directly in his path. "KGB. Surrender quietly and you will be in no danger."

Zharkov raised his hands in the air, thinking, What did it matter now? He had nowhere else to go.

CHAPTER EIGHT

Amne Xachim, magic mountain of Brahma.

He saw it rising around Him in the gathering mists, its perfect twin lakes ringed by flowers, its silent white peaks, its inaccessible cliff of red rock. And at its center, growing without light in the cave that was to become the shrine of Rashimpur, appeared, fully grown, the Tree of the Thousand Wisdoms.

"This shall be my home," whispered the voice of Brahma.

The voice was His own, speaking without language, without sound. When it stilled, it did not speak again for ten thousand years.

He awoke as a snake, living and golden, entwined in the Tree. His movements were the first stirrings of the god on earth. He took His strength from the Tree, from its bark and from its healing leaves. And there Brahma waited, while the mists of time rose and fell and rose again, while men appeared on the earth and took as their leaders the prophets, seers, and magicians.

Varja, Goddess of Time, Daughter of Darkness, sent her vassals out in legions to conquer Brahma's creation and destroy it. Through her evil the earth grew sick and weary. The mists that enfolded Amne Xachim were heavy with Brahma's tears.

It was time for the golden snake to sleep and awaken again as a man.

His name was Patanjali, first human incarnation of Brahma. He awoke, fully grown, in the cave of Rashimpur. There he lived, and there his followers built the monastery in the cleft of red rock. There was forged an amulet, a coiled snake created from the mountain's gold, and the ancient memory of Brahma.

Life follows life: Brahma would live long after the vessel of His flesh withered and was no more. And so Patanjali, Wearer of the Blue Hat, named for the skies over Rashimpur, grew old and died, and the mists covered the sacred mountain again. But at the moment of His death the Patanjali's spirit came to life inside the newborn body of a baby.

Brahma suffered the pain of death, felt the last of His breath, His final heartbeat, then rose, breathing life again with renewed will and hope and purpose. The monks of Rashimpur found the reborn Patanjali and offered the babe the golden amulet of the coiled snake. None but the true incarnation of Brahma could accept its power.

The child took it, unharmed, and the circle of karma spun once more. The mists of Amne Xachim rose again.

With each life He lived, the followers of Varja lessened in number and power and the earth renewed itself.

They called Him Jesus. They called Him Buddha and Muhammad. He was the first son of kings and the last child of beggars. He was all colors, male and female, savage and scholar, and within Him spun the circle of karma, the certainty of eternal life, the preservation of Good, the spirit of creation.

But Varja, Goddess of Time, knew that the way of men was not to follow the difficult path of good. The easy road of destruction and chaos was their way. So at the exact moment of the birth of the new Patanjali, she caused another to be born, to weaken Brahma's power.

From that moment until their deaths, Varja's creation and the Patanjali would play out a strange and terrible game for the gods. For one lifetime, good and evil would merge, repel, and connect again within two men. It was a game played with lives.

One man was the Prince of Death.
The other was known as the Grandmaster.

CHAPTER
NINE

The mists closed around Brahma once more. He wept for the burst heart inside the man who had kept his spirit. He did not wish to leave this life. The Patanjali's work was unfinished, his destiny yet unfulfilled. If the Circle of Karma were allowed to be broken, another Patanjali would never rise again.

So, making His will known through the mountain winds, Brahma blew the mists away from Amne Xachim. He infused his spirit once again into the pain-filled body of the Patanjali. He felt once again the suffering of mortality. The earth, His own beautiful earth, was choking Him, pressing down on Him like the weight of ages, and His heart was beating again, constricting, willing Him back to life and its sorrows. The mists of Amne Xachim faded and took the sacred mountain with it. For Patanjali was a man again, and the dreams of Brahma vanished. In its place was the smell of fallen leaves, the sound of a running stream nearby, and the tickle of a newt's spongy feet as it scurried across his face.

And this, too, was beautiful.

Dirt was swept from his eyes. Sunlight streamed in thin rays from the trees above him. Then he saw a woman's hands, their fingernails blackened, their skin raw and covered with cuts, and heard her sobs and felt her tears.

"Justin!" It was almost a scream. Then she bowed her head and prayed to whatever god she knew.

Two spots of light dappled his chest, over his heart, and he thought they were from the sun, too, but they grew brighter and brighter, and he touched them with his hands and they glowed with blinding white light, and the warmth of them spread through his body like the growing roots of a tree.

He pulled himself up, and the woman—oh, Sasha, more lovely than a queen with her blackened nails and tear-streaked face—was staring at the glowing spots on his chest, her hands over her mouth, her eyes unbelieving.

But they dimmed, and the two halves of the amulet of Rashimpur fell to his lap like two gray slugs.

The coiled snake of Patanjali had performed its last miracle.

Justin held the broken pieces in his hand for a moment, as if they were two small dead birds, then slipped them into his pocket.

"What is that thing?" Sasha asked, nearly hysterical.

"It's nothing anymore," Justin said quietly.

She held him tight, stroking her own tears off the back of his neck.

"I don't understand any of this. Who are you?"

He looked up at her. "It doesn't matter now," he said, and his eyes held such helpless pain that Sasha kissed them closed.

Her lips found his mouth. And there, in the copse in the wood, she undressed him and made love to him as if her body would salve the hurt inside him.

He responded, slowly at first, and then with all the passion of a burning need. For whatever else he might have been, in those dim memories of the magic mountain, he was a man now, flesh and earth and tears, and he gloried in the beauty of life.

*   *   *

The afternoon sun warmed Sasha's face as she nestled in the crook of Justin's arm. There would be time later, she thought, to face herself and all the people she had betrayed. First Andrew, then Justin, then her own family. Her parents were surely dead, now that Kadar was free to arrange their executions. He had many soldiers among the guards in the prison camps. Through Kadar those guards had kept her mother and father alive all these years. At his command they would die like sacrificial goats. He had warned her.

Her own life was forfeit. She was ready to join them. But she would not give in yet, not until the two men she loved were safe from Kadar and the killer with him. Then she would go gladly to whatever hell was reserved for people like her.

For now, though, she had to live.

"Where's Starcher?" Justin asked softly.

She pulled herself out of her thoughts. "I don't know. I've been searching these woods for hours. At least I haven't found his body, and I know he wasn't caught." She touched his shoulder. "Justin, lie back. You're not strong."

He struggled upright. "Was it bad for you there?"

"Easier for me than it would have been for you or Andrew."

"I'm sorry. . . ."

She touched her fingertips to his lips. "It was the only way. The KGB would have killed Andrew if he had been caught, and he couldn't have gotten out of the bunker without you. I knew the interrogators wouldn't give me any trouble. I'm a celebrity, remember?" She batted her eyelashes. "So it's forgotten."

Justin smiled. "Not by me." He brushed the leaves and dirt off his clothing. "Did anyone mention Starcher or Zharkov?"

"They captured Zharkov. No one said anything about Andrew, and I didn't tell them about either of you."

"And Kadar?"

"He escaped. I saw the bodies of the agents who'd

been holding him. It was horrible. They were torn to pieces.''

''Then the boy is with him.'' He took her hand. ''We've got to get back to Moscow.''

''Justin, we can't.'' She bit her lip. ''Kadar has already killed . . . too many people.''

My parents among them, she thought. *When I pointed that gun at Kadar, I threw their lives away.* Tears spilled over her face. ''I won't let you and Andrew die too. We can all leave this country,'' she said feverishly. ''There are ways. The three of us can run from him, maybe go to America. . . .''

''I can't run from Siraj,'' Justin said. ''Wherever I go, he'll find me. If I can get hold of Starcher, maybe he'll take you— ''

''No,'' she said, drying her eyes. ''If you stay, I'll stay with you. But Andrew must leave. It's too dangerous for him now. I'll look for him in Moscow. You mustn't do anything until you're well. Promise me that much.''

He squeezed her hand. ''Let's go,'' he said.

''You owe me a favor for rescuing you.''

''I thought you said it was forgotten.''

Sasha smiled. ''Not by you, remember?''

CHAPTER TEN

When Pierlenko came to work in the morning, Maxim Sterlitz was waiting for him in the outer office. Pierlenko gave him a brief, surly glance, then flicked his hand for the KGB Director to follow him inside.

"You have him?" he asked gruffly.

Sterlitz hesitated a beat before answering, and Pierlenko knew immediately that Kadar had escaped again.

"*Zadnica*. You idiot, can't you do anything right?"

"We had him, I swear to you," Sterlitz said. "Six of our men took him to the wagon. All six were found dead, horribly mutilated, and Kadar gone." He wiped a line of perspiration from his upper lip with his handkerchief. "However, we did capture Alexander Zharkov."

The Premier's face changed. "Where is he?"

"In Lubyanka."

Pierlenko had gone to the window to look out. He spun around. "Are your bully boys questioning him?"

"Yes. They are trying to find out where Kadar is," Sterlitz answered.

Pierlenko shook his head. "*Govno*. Everywhere I turn, I am surrounded by stupidity. Call your men and tell them to leave Zharkov alone so I can talk to him and not his corpse."

*   *   *

"Where are you keeping Konstantin Kadar?"

The interrogator slapped Zharkov across the face with the back of his hand, leaving a gash across Zharkov's cheekbone with his large gold ring.

Zharkov's mouth was swollen and he wasn't sure of anything anymore, except that he was in Lubyanka prison. The looming spires of the Kremlin were the last things he'd seen before being dragged into the enormous subterranean world peopled with "enemies of the State."

Most of those enemies were politicians, high military or government officials from previous regimes. Some were artists—the writers, poets, and musicians whose worst transgression was nonconformity. Few were of the stature of Alexander Zharkov, and in a place notorious for its secret and inventive punishments, the most creative means of penance were reserved for him.

His keepers seemed to be in a hurry, Zharkov decided. With most prisoners the interrogations and beatings came once a day. The prisoner began to adjust to the routine, and then the interrogators would change it, beating a prisoner in his sleep or coming during his lone meal of the day.

But with him, Zharkov noted, they seemed frantic—beating him continuously and without relief. He suspected that Kadar's escape had compromised some high official, because the questions came furiously.

Where is Kadar? What was your relationship to him? What crimes were you planning against the State? Who else was involved? Vague questions that Zharkov didn't even bother to answer. He knew they were just beginning.

Then they beat his arm with a metal chain, and the questions became more specific. What was Kadar's plan? Who among security officials was privy to the plan?

His arm quickly blackened, and his wrist swelled to the size of a melon. They handcuffed his wrists and ankles and administered electric shock to his genitals. They clamped his palms to a table, then cut the skin between his fingers with razor blades. He fainted, woke up, and the beatings resumed. Only this time the questions were different. What is your name? What have you done with Kadar? Who is Justin Gilead? How old are you? What is Kadar planning? What is your name?

He did not answer; he never answered. He had interrogated people before. He had not used the tactics of the KGB specialists at extracting information—he regarded them as dumb brutes—but he knew that one answering word signaled defeat. It didn't matter whether he knew what they wanted or not. One lapse, one moment of weakness, one piece of information offered in exchange for the cessation of pain, and he was a dead man.

"What is your name?"

They threw him in a small cell with no toilet, where he had to lie in the filth and vomit of the prisoners who had preceded him. The pain from his arm racked his body with every breath he took. The Grandmaster suffered this, he thought as the fever dimmed his senses. Was Justin Gilead here now? Of course not; he was dead. It was important not to lose one's reason. The KGB would not kill him as long as he was actively withholding information, but he had to keep a clear mind. Anything could happen if he became incoherent. He had seen men tortured to the point where they could no longer think. They were useless then, and had to be destroyed like diseased cattle.

Still, he could sense the Grandmaster near him, curling around him like mist, could almost see the bright gold of the coiled snake entwining around the two of them, melding them together into one being as the mist closed around them.

So I will die with you, as the prophets foretold, he thought numbly. *The boy has killed us both.*

He felt his life ebbing, oozing out of his body like pus from a wound.

"What is your name?"

His name? *He is called Patanjali, the Wearer of the Blue Hat. I am the Prince of Darkness, sent by the Old Spirits and the woman-god Varja. But we are the same*

*now, and my body lies shimmering below, still warm in
the heat of life around it. We have played our game long
enough, Justin Gilead and I. And not as kings but as
pawns . . . pawns of a new High Priest.*

"What is your name?"

There was a blinding flash of golden light as the mists
blew away. He was left cold, shivering, as the world
suddenly rolled in on itself and he was staring out at it
from the body of a man racked with pain. Then the billy
club cracked against his arm and Zharkov screamed.

"What is your name?"

"I am . . ." He dug his fist into his mouth, bit into it
until it bled. He was Alexander Zharkov. He would not
speak with these dogs.

He heard a telephone ring.

A moment later he was unconscious.

The first thing he saw was the cage. It was made of
diamond-patterned steel wire, and it surrounded his bed.
The lights were bright. They stung his eyes, and the smell
of disinfectant hung heavy in the air. The only sounds
were the creaking of bedsprings and the occasional squeak
of rubber-soled shoes on linoleum. He tried to move,
then noticed the bandages on his arm.

Beyond the cage, Zharkov could see the nurse's station, where three men in white uniforms sat in a row,
silently doing paperwork. Behind them hung a portrait of
Lenin, with a small vase of wilted flowers on a shelf
below it.

One of the men in white looked up, saw him stirring,
and picked up the phone. After saying a few words he
came over, pulling a round, wrist-sized key ring from his
pocket, and unlocked the door to the cage. He examined
Zharkov cursorily, lifting one eyelid, peering beneath a
bandage on his head. The nurse's face was fleshy and
gruff, the face of a grave digger. He was clean-shaven,
but the beginnings of a heavy black beard showed just
below the surface of the skin.

"Where am I?" Zharkov rasped. He tongued his swollen jaw. He had lost a tooth in the beatings.

"Lubyanka." The nurse lowered the rigging on Zharkov's cast. Another male nurse brought over a wheelchair, taking care to lock the door to the cage after entering.

"Are they here?" the first nurse asked the other.

"Right outside." Together they lifted Zharkov from the bed and placed him in the wheelchair.

"Where are you taking me?"

"The guards outside will take you. We had orders to notify the Premier's office as soon as you came around." The big man smiled with some warmth. "Looks like you've got friends in high places."

He met Pierlenko in a small lounge near the infirmary. It struck Zharkov as odd to see the General Secretary of the Soviet Union sitting on a chair with a plastic-covered cushion, a coffeepot on a hot plate at his back. The guards had handcuffed Zharkov's good arm to the wheelchair and now waited outside the door.

Pierlenko brushed some crumbs off the table in front of him. "First of all, I'm truly sorry about the treatment you've received," he said quietly. "As soon as I heard about it, I had you moved to the hospital here. It was not my intention to have you tortured."

"Whose intention was it, then?" Zharkov asked thickly, feeling the broken stub of tooth in his mouth.

Pierlenko sighed. "Colonel Zharkov, let me come to the point. I understand there is an organization, an organization you head, that has traditionally operated under orders from the office of the General Secretary. For some reason you have chosen not—"

Zharkov laughed. It was a thin, sad sound. Tears welled up inside his eyes and coursed down his face until he wiped them away.

"Of course," he said. "You want Nichevo. Kadar means nothing to you." He coughed and spoke with difficulty. "The burns, the beatings, the electric shocks . . . they were for nothing, weren't they?" He squeezed his eyes shut.

"Comrade Colonel, I'm sure—"

"I was almost beaten to death just to prepare me for this conversation with you," Zharkov shouted.

"You're delirious," Pierlenko said as he rose.

"Did you think I would be so grateful to you for sparing my life that I would offer you my undivided loyalty for life? Is that what you thought?"

Pierlenko pressed his lips together. His face reddened. "You gave it to Konstantin Kadar!"

Zharkov rested his head on the back of the wheelchair. "Is that what someone told you? Konstantin Kadar?" He spat the name out as if the taste of it were foul in his mouth. "The man is insane. Even *your* gorillas should know that. I was held there as a prisoner."

"Then why did you give him Nichevo?"

"Don't be a fool, Pierlenko. He doesn't have Nichevo."

The Premier's eyes flashed. No one talked to him that way, not even a man in Zharkov's condition.

Zharkov coughed. "And neither will you. Now kill me and get it over with."

Why not? Zharkov thought. *Why not be dead? Nichevo is dead. All but two of its members gone, and my turn next. It's just a matter of time, anyway, so why not now?*

Pierlenko took a few moments to compose himself. "Why won't you work under this administration?" he asked reasonably. "You, the rest of Nichevo. You can all have a good life. Why become a rogue elephant, only to die?"

"We all have to die," Zharkov answered. "Even the General Secretary himself."

Pierlenko's nostrils flared. "Is that a threat?"

"It is a guess," Zharkov said.

"Who?" the Premier demanded. "Who is going to . . . to try to kill me?"

"Someone you won't be able to stop," Zharkov said.

Pierlenko narrowed his eyes. "Ah, I see. But *you* can

stop it, can't you? You've told me this to make a deal with me."

Zharkov smiled bitterly. "Don't waste your shrewd little hopes. Konstantin Kadar is a thorough man. He had the Americans killed to weaken your ties with the West. Once you're out of the way, he intends to regain the office of Premier."

"Don't be absurd."

"He'll do it too. I can assure you," Zharkov said. "With me or without me, you won't live out the week, Comrade."

Pierlenko stood up. "Liar."

Zharkov shrugged.

"If you are not trying to deal, why are you telling me this?"

Zharkov sat back in the wheelchair and closed his eyes. "Because I have nothing left to lose."

Pierlenko snapped, "You know that you can be executed anytime for conspiring to murder a head of state."

Zharkov said nothing. The game was over. Death was the only natural ending. Checkmate. Shah Mat. The King is dead.

With a controlled effort Pierlenko's features softened. He bent over the wheelchair so that he was on a level with Zharkov. "I understand that you have been under considerable stress, Colonel Zharkov," he said, trying to convey his good intention by staring into Zharkov's eyes. "Tell me where Nichevo is and I will arrange personally to have you freed."

Zharkov shook his head. "Nichevo is dead," he said. "As I will be soon." He swallowed the thin spittle in his mouth. His voice was beginning to tire. "And you, too, I'm afraid."

Pierlenko backed away as if he had touched a leper. He was about to speak again but didn't. There was nothing to say to a man who was certain of his own death.

The Premier pulled open the door and to the guards outside said quietly, "Take him back."

It was finally over, Zharkov thought. An odd sense of relief passed through him. He was done. Nichevo was done. There was only one member left in Russia besides himself, and he would never be able to free Zharkov from Lubyanka. No one could.

He looked forward to death as a blessing.

"Execute him," Maxim Sterlitz said. "His loyalty has already been compromised. You could never trust him."

"You ass," Pierlenko growled. "Without Zharkov, Nichevo will vanish like dust in the wind."

The Director stared at his polished nails. "In all deference, sir, there is no hard evidence that this so-called organization even exists. Zharkov himself insists that it no longer does. Besides, the greatest security force in the world is at your disposal." He held his head up with pride.

"Headed by you? The greatest security force in the world could not even manage to hang on to one doddering old man."

"Comrade General Secretary," the Director said, "Kadar is an extraordinary individual. You said yourself—"

"I said you were an ass, and never have I spoken more from the heart. Kadar was the one killing those Americans. We are on the brink of war with the United States because of him. And you let him escape."

"Six of our men had him surrounded," Sterlitz whined.

"Spare me that song," the Premier said dryly. "I have heard it before."

"But, sir, he must have killed them all single-handedly. Six of our best men."

Pierlenko filled his soft, fleshy cheeks, then expelled a puff of air. "Do you really believe that?" he asked.

"Why . . ." the Director began, then fell silent.

In a way it was a relief for Pierlenko to be able to discuss Nichevo with someone other than that bemedaled old fool, Sergei Ostrakov. Although Sterlitz wasn't much less of a fool, and while he didn't know it, he was even more expendable right now than Ostrakov was. After

Sterlitz's poor showing over the past few weeks, the position of Director of the KGB would soon be vacant, Sterlitz eliminated. Pierlenko could say anything he wanted to him now.

"It was Nichevo," Pierlenko said. "*They* rescued him."

"But why, sir, would they rescue Kadar, not Zharkov? Zharkov is their leader."

"They no doubt had orders to give Kadar their first priority. The men of this organization obviously take their orders seriously, unlike the waffle-headed imbeciles you employ. Nichevo was told to free Kadar, and it did."

I must have it, Pierlenko thought. All the strength of the KGB, all its personnel and power, could not give him the protection that the invisible men of Nichevo had given Kadar.

"But what of their loyalty?"

"They have no loyalty," Pierlenko shouted. "They are machines that function on Alexander Zharkov's orders. Do you think Zharkov will order them to serve me, after what you've done to him?"

"We tried to get him to talk," the Director said with dignity.

"You nearly had him killed and you know it." He stood up. "Idiot. As it is, he doesn't know half of what he's saying."

"But," the Director ventured, "if this Nichevo came for Kadar, wouldn't it stand to reason that they'd also try to break out Zharkov?"

Pierlenko's head snapped toward Sterlitz. "Yes. It's very possible," he said slowly. "But not in Lubyanka. Even Nichevo couldn't penetrate it. I'll have him transferred . . . to a camp, perhaps. . . ."

"You *want* Nichevo to break him out?" Sterlitz asked in astonishment.

"I want them to try. We catch the operatives in the attempt, then get them to talk. They can't all be as hard—or as far gone—as Zharkov. Once we get a handle on Nichevo through the members of the organization itself, we won't need Zharkov. He's too dangerous to keep alive, anyway."

Pierlenko paused, running the possibilities through his mind. Why keep Zharkov when Zharkov's organization was all he wanted, anyway? When he had Nichevo, he would eliminate Zharkov. The American killings would stop and . . .

"The only problem would be getting Zharkov's men to find out where we are keeping him," Sterlitz said. "I could have word leaked out through the press, I suppose."

"The press," Pierlenko mused.

"I could arrange a meeting with the new editor of *Izvestia* this afternoon."

"Not just *Izvestia*," Pierlenko said. A smile spread on his face. "I want the international press."

Sterlitz blinked. "Won't that be a bit obvious?"

"Not at all. I'll announce that the killer of seven American citizens in Moscow has been caught—thanks to the superb work of the KGB—and is being detained in a work camp until a fair trial can be arranged. It will satisfy everyone. Even the Americans will be pleased." He thought for a moment. "The Peace Killer, we'll call him. I think that has a nice ring, don't you?"

"The Peace Killer," Sterlitz repeated, smiling in admiration. "Wonderful, sir. Inspired. The whole world will know Nikolai Pierlenko as a man of his word, willing to cut out a cancer in his own society in order to further the cause of peace."

Pierlenko drummed his fingers on his desk. *And I will own Nichevo.*

CHAPTER
ELEVEN

Starcher waited at a table at the Blue Mermaid Café. He wore an old beaver hat pulled over his ears to cover the bandage on his head.

The old woman who had taken him in near Kadar's underground fortress outside Moscow had given him the hat when he left. Starcher had taken a chance with her, telling her he'd been beaten and robbed by a man to whom he owed money, but he had read her for the sort who didn't turn easily to the police.

The woman bandaged his head and gave him tea. She lived on a small private farm. For years she had managed, with her husband, to keep the two-acre plot away from the authorities, but her husband had died six months earlier and she was waiting for the state to seize her land. There was an icon in her house. Starcher had guessed well. She had looked after him as if he had been the last member of her family.

She wanted him to stay, warning him that head injuries could be dangerous, but Starcher had to move as fast as his tired old body could take him back to Moscow. He'd kissed her when he left, on the cheek, but she'd turned and pressed her mouth on him.

It had been so long since he'd kissed anyone that

Starcher had forgotten his own age. The woman, whom he'd considered an old crone, was possibly a year or two younger than he was. Embarrassed, he stripped his wristwatch from his arm and gave it to her. She'd refused. He'd insisted, and in the end, she took it but gave him a five-ruble note in case he was stopped by the militia, so that he could prove he wasn't a vagrant.

Starcher looked around the café. It was late afternoon, and the room was filled with mostly young people. But young people could be KGB too. Starcher knew he was taking a chance coming to a public place, but he had to risk it. Justin Gilead was dead. If his death was to have any meaning at all, it was important that Konstantin Kadar be stopped. Not that Starcher considered Nikolai Pierlenko much of an improvement over Kadar; but at least Pierlenko was talking peace. Kadar was planning to drop a bomb on somebody. Starcher had to report it, and in Moscow, public places were the safest locations for spies to meet.

He glanced at his wrist, but his watch was not there. He noted the time on the clock over the bar and told himself he would give Mark Cole exactly five more minutes.

The new CIA Chief in Moscow arrived at four, obviously agitated about something. Starcher thought he would have to keep this meeting short, if he didn't want his cover blown completely. Cole had the kind of look on his face that would prompt any part-time informer to call the police and report a man acting strangely.

"What do you want?" Cole asked, sitting down abruptly beside him.

"I don't have a lot of time, so I'll make it quick. Konstantin Kadar's behind the killings of the Americans. Rand's too. I think he wants to make them look like some kind of anti-Western ground swell. He's got something going against Pierlenko. An assassination, I think. The guy's nuttier than a squirrel but loaded. He's got his own private army."

Cole looked as if someone had just hit him on the head. "How . . . how do you know all this?"

"Long story and I don't want to take the time here with it, but I ended up a prisoner in his underground fortress. There was a raid. I got away and I think he did too."

Cole was staring at him, glassy-eyed.

"Jesus, will you stop looking like a drug pusher? Somebody'll call the cops. Try to look like we're talking about the weather."

"I don't know what to say." The young man glanced around, then leaned closer to Starcher. "I got a call from Pierlenko this afternoon. He said he's got the killer in custody. Somebody named Zharkov. Apparently he's some kind of a one-man terror squad. Pierlenko's called a press conference about it."

Starcher's wrinkles deepened. "Nothing about Kadar?"

"Not a word to me. Why would he lie?"

"Russians always lie," Starcher said. "He needs somebody to pin it on, I suppose. Did he mention anything to you about any other prisoners? A boy, for instance?"

"A boy?"

"About sixteen years old. Or a young woman?" Starcher asked.

Again a blank look from Cole.

Starcher said, "Never mind. What did Pierlenko say about Zharkov?"

"The usual," Cole said. He looked as if he were trying to pull his thoughts together. "Petty thief, unemployed."

"What about Nichevo?"

"Nichevo?" Cole asked. "What's that supposed to mean?" He looked around nervously. "I can't be seen here with you." He started to get up.

"Wait a minute," Starcher hissed. "For your ears only. They've got the wrong man. That background's a phony. Zharkov didn't have anything to do with those murders. It was Kadar, I tell you."

"What the hell do we care who it was?" Cole asked irritably. "The Russians have got somebody to blame now. That's what matters. Kadar or his hired killer, or whoever it was, is going to pack away his guns now."

"I can't believe I'm hearing this," Starcher said.

"Look. There's no point in playing the Lone Ranger here, Mr. Starcher. Rand and the others are dead. Our muddying the diplomatic waters isn't going to bring any of them back. Let them frame Zharkov, if that's what they're doing, for the sake of international relations. We've got to get along with these people, and they've got to get along with us. The sooner this thing is patched up, the better."

"What about Kadar?" Starcher said, raising his voice. He lowered it again. "The man's a walking nuclear bomb. He hates everyone west of Leningrad and right of Joe Stalin, and that includes the Premier of this country. He's probably going to try to assassinate Pierlenko. And then he's going to bomb us."

"Oh, come on."

"I'm dead serious, Cole. If he gets back in power, we've got World War Three."

"Starcher," the young man said evenly, "I think you've become too involved in all of this. I mean, listen to what you're saying! This is *Russia*, remember? A deposed leader here has about as much chance of coming into power as a street cleaner does. Kadar's a nonperson. They're probably not even interested in catching him."

Starcher looked up. "You hear something? Do you think he got away?"

"Well, it's pretty obvious, isn't it? Either that or the KGB's deliberately letting him off the hook for the sake of propaganda. It really wouldn't do to expose the former Premier as a mad-dog killer." He smiled, stared at Starcher for a long time, and the smile faded. "*If* what you're telling me is true."

"*If!* Why, you green little punk! That maniac had me in a hole, a goddamned *hole* . . ."

A waiter finally came to the table. Cole waved him off, then sat drumming his fingertips together.

"Listen . . ."

"No, you listen, Mr. Starcher." There was nothing unprofessional about Mark Cole now. Starcher recalled seeing him before in the embassy office. Now, as then, he had the sensation of a mask falling away from the young man's face. The ingenuous, youthful eyes were suddenly steely and resolute. They were the eyes, Starcher thought, of a rifle marksman. "I've tried to reason with you long enough. It's clear to me that you've lost your perspective in this matter. And perhaps in other matters," Cole said.

Starcher sputtered. Cole let him. When the old man was done, he continued in the same even tone, as if chatting to a dinner companion. "Now, you've had an enviable career, and all the bright young men at Langley will remember your name for time immemorial. But the fact is, this case is closed. Whether that was accomplished by you or the KGB is immaterial. I will, of course, give you all the credit in my report. But as far as I'm concerned, your job here is over."

There was a long silence. Starcher gripped the edge of the table as if it were keeping him from sliding off his chair.

"You can't fire me," he said finally.

"Go out gracefully, Andy." Cole's face resumed its harmless, college-kid look.

"I don't work for you. I'll get off this when Langley says to get off it," Starcher said coldly.

"Maybe that can be arranged," Cole answered.

"Dammit, man, I thought we were on the same side."

Cole smiled and shook his head. "Don't be paranoid. Of course we're on the same side. I only think you've been working too hard for a man your age. I can see it in your judgment."

"There's nothing wrong with my judgment," Starcher said stubbornly. "Not on this score. This Kadar business isn't over."

Cole shrugged. "Maybe not. But you don't seem to understand that it doesn't matter. There's no right or wrong in this business anymore. Pierlenko's going to announce he's got the killer. Count on it. That means the killings stop and our countries can get back to trying to make peace. That's the way it is, and anyone who doesn't know that isn't just out-of-date, he's dangerous. Rand knew that. You should. That old style of vigilante justice simply doesn't work here anymore, and the sooner you face it, the better."

He stood up and patted Starcher on the shoulder. The old man's head bobbed on his neck. "You can have a nice retirement, Andy. Your family's got a lot of money. You won't have a care in the world."

Starcher brushed Cole's hand away.

"I'm not leaving until Langley pulls me out."

"Okay," Cole said agreeably. "I'll talk to Langley right away and I'll meet you tonight. Gorky Park under the covered bridge. Say midnight. We'll see what Langley says to do." He smiled again, his Harvard undergrad smile, and pulled out some Russian bills. "Now I've got to go. Here's some money to tide you over for a while." He tried another unanswered smile. "This will all work out fine, you'll see," he said affably. "Pierlenko's even invited the Ambassador to attend the circus with him tonight, to show that the threat is over. I'm going along too."

"The last time I went to the circus, one of Kadar's men slipped a wire around my throat," Starcher said.

Cole sighed in exasperation. "That isn't going to happen to me," he said.

"Or the Premier?"

Cole looked at him but didn't bother to answer. After he left, Starcher sat for a long time in the café, his hands gripping the edge of the table.

CHAPTER
TWELVE

It was spring, and evening was approaching. Starcher thought that he had never been anyplace where spring was finer than in Moscow. In Virginia, his home, it was beautiful, but Virginia's weather was mild and beautiful all the time. Russia, after the ferocious, bone-cracking cold of winter, spring was something extra, something special, the gods' visible proof of renewal.

The gods. Forget the gods.

Starcher had had enough of gods, enough of mysticism, enough of magic. Justin Gilead had been a man, nothing more, and the proof of that was that he was now dead. He was a special man but only a man, after all. And the boy? He was some kind of hypnotist; he made you think you were hurt when you weren't hurt at all. It was a trick, and for all the talk of Justin and Zharkov and the boy about gods and goddesses and mountain temples, it was all nonsense, all some dream they had smoked up together on an opium pipe.

He told himself that and he knew he did not believe it, but he pretended to because it made everything simpler.

Starcher shambled along the Kalinin Prospekt with its big stores and wide boulevards. He had no particular place to go until his late-night meeting with Cole. He had no friends at the American embassy, and it was too risky to try the safe house. By now the KGB would have learned of it from Sasha.

Sasha. What had the KGB done with her? She was not a professional. She would break if they knew how to question her, and the KGB knew all the tricks.

For all he knew, Sasha was on her way to a prison camp now. Even there, he thought, she would be looking for her parents, trying to find a way to free them.

Christ, why had they left her back in the bunker? She could have killed Kadar on the spot and come with them.

But then, he realized, Kadar would not have been available for questioning. Amateur or not, Sasha had been smart enough to understand the necessity of keeping the *Vozhd* alive for the authorities.

Not that any of it amounted to a hill of beans now. Kadar was free, Justin Gilead was dead, and Sasha . . . What had happened to the sweet kid who used to black out her front teeth for him?

He tried to steer his mind away from her. Some questions were better left unanswered.

He stopped and lit a cheap Stewardess cigarette and checked the streets behind him. If Kadar was on the loose, it was possible that his men, too, had a tail on Starcher. The old man didn't *feel* a tail, but then, he considered ruefully, his reflexes were probably on the wane, along with his judgment.

Well, he wasn't going to make it easy for them. There wouldn't be a bullet in his head while he lay sleeping in the safe house.

If there was a tail, they'd have to kill him right in the open, in the middle of Moscow. The eighth American dead. See how Cole would explain *that* one to the liberals in Congress.

He smiled at his own resentment. There was nothing more ridiculous than a bitter old spook. He'd seen them all his life, the timeworn field men who refused to retire, as if the only thing they lived for was fear. But he understood it. Fear became a kind of aphrodisiac after a while. It put you on the edge of the razor, and when you ran on that blade, you made your best time. Living with fear, controlling it, working with it, was a high that nothing else could match.

And when the fear passed, you got worried because when you weren't running on the blade, your life had no more meaning than a deflated balloon. Field agents didn't have friends. They didn't play sports or have hobbies or own a house to fix up. They didn't have families to go home to. Oh, some of them had wives, but those marriages were a sham. If you can't tell your wife what you've been doing every day and night for most of your life, you really haven't got much to talk about.

In the end, you wind up living for nothing more than the next run across the blade. And one time you don't make it all the way across and you end up with a bullet in the back of your head and a John Doe tag on your big toe. Or like Sasha, being tortured by the KGB butchers.

Starcher had accepted that, all of it, forty-four years ago when he'd started running for the OSS. He didn't even mind dying anymore, if a bullet was to be the way.

But it wouldn't be the way. The day after tomorrow, he'd be in a house in Virginia, an old man with a bad heart. And the folks there would strain their charming Southern smiles and refer to the stranger in their midst as Uncle Andy while they sloshed mint juleps down his throat and figured out how to get him into a nursing home.

Hell, he should have gone to bed with the old bat out in the country while he'd had the chance.

Suddenly he stopped short in the middle of the sidewalk.

There was a blue chalk mark on the corner of the building beside him. If someone had asked him how he noticed it, he wouldn't have been able to explain, since he hadn't even been aware where he was walking. But there are some things spooks never miss. The blue chalk mark was Sasha's.

Starcher looked down the street, then hailed a public bus with a Gorky Park legend in the top window.

He tried not to run into the park. People running in Moscow were always suspect to the police. But he walked quickly, and he saw her by the chess tables. She ran into his arms.

"Thank God," Starcher said. "How did you get free?"

"The KGB questioned me all night at Dzerzhinsky Square. But don't worry. I didn't mention you. I don't think they know you exist."

"What'd you tell them?"

"That Kadar's men kidnapped me from the circus and brought me to him for some hanky-panky. Apparently the circus officials reported me missing right from the beginning, so the interrogators weren't very hard on me. They know the *Vozhd*'s got strange habits. The idea that he'd molest a trapeze artist didn't seem to surprise them much."

Starcher looked dismayed. "Did he?"

"I'm a big girl, Andrew." She didn't meet his eyes. "I can handle it." She shook her head impatiently. "Anyway, that's not important. They've got Zharkov. I don't think he's told them about you, either. But Kadar got away. He was planning—"

"I know. I've already told my . . . boss." He said the word with distaste.

"Your boss?" She looked puzzled. "I thought Richard Rand was your boss."

"This one's new. His name's Mark Cole."

"What does he plan to do about Kadar?"

"Nothing," Starcher said. He thrust his hands into his pockets. "Not a damned thing."

"What? But this . . . this . . ."

"He doesn't believe me," Starcher said. He laughed bitterly. "We've got enough information to stop World War Three, and I can't find anybody who'll even listen to it."

Sasha leaned against a tree. "What happens now? Will you go home?"

"I don't seem to have much choice. Cole thinks everything's hunky-dory with the Russians these days. He's going to the damn circus tonight with Pierlenko and the U.S. Ambassador. Will you be working?"

She nodded.

"Good. Maybe you can drop a water balloon on them." He grinned sheepishly.

"I wish I could have done more to help you, Andrew. And less to hurt you."

He ruffled her hair. "You were the best, kid. Just promise me you'll stay out of this business from now on. Marry one of those rich politicos who are always drooling over you. Who knows, you might get to like diamonds."

"Maybe," Sasha said.

Starcher shifted his feet. "There's another thing," he said. "It's bad news. Justin . . . he didn't make it."

Watching his grief, Sasha wanted to comfort him with the truth, but she knew that together, Justin and Starcher would both die trying to fight an enemy they could never vanquish.

"I'm sorry," she said.

"I am too."

She embraced him when they parted. Soon, she thought, Andrew Starcher would be leaving for good, to live out the old age he deserved. And Justin, too, would have to leave, whether he wanted to or not. Staying in Russia after Kadar took over would mean death for them all.

She was going to be the only one to stay. That was how it would have to be.

But how could she ever bring herself to say good-bye to Justin Gilead?

Mark Cole waited in the embassy's communications room while the clerk sent his coded message to Langley:

KGB HAS CAPTURED KILLER OF AMERICANS. PERPETRATOR IS A RUSSIAN NATIONAL. PIERLENKO DESIRES PEACE UTMOST BUT NEGOTIATIONS ENDANGERED BY PRESENCE OF ANDREW STARCHER. STARCHER UNSTABLE AND HOSTILE TOWARD U.S.–SOVIET PEACE EFFORTS. REQUEST RECALL STARCHER IMMEDIATELY.

The message from Langley arrived within the hour:

STARCHER WITHOUT COVER. MAY NOT RETURN THROUGH LEGAL CHANNELS. IF CAUGHT, ALL KNOWLEDGE WILL BE DISAVOWED.

Cole laughed out loud. So the Agency had never intended to bring the old man back alive.

That was perfect, he thought. He picked up the telephone and reserved a seat on Aeroflot for Andrew Starcher, nationality American.

Let the KGB take care of him, Cole said to himself. He went home and dressed for the circus.

Justin was waiting for Sasha in her apartment. She put her arms around him, thinking as she held him that it might be for the last time.

"You're trembling," he said. "Are you cold?"

She shook her head. "I'm afraid."

"Then don't go up tonight."

She looked at him, bewildered.

"It's been more than a week, and you haven't had much practice since you've been back."

Her lips parted. "The *trapeze*? You think I'm worried about flying?"

"Isn't that what you were afraid of?"

She laughed. "Oh, Justin," she said, kissing him. "Make love to me."

"Now?"

"Right now. In case . . ."

"In case what?"

He stroked her hair. "Sasha, there's nothing for you to worry about."

"Please. I need you."

She pulled him into the bedroom. The radio was playing, but she did not hear it. She tore off her own clothes, then reached for Justin's, but he pushed her hands away and held her back onto the bed.

She bit back a scream as his lips touched her breasts.

Justin caught both her thin wrists in one hand and held her still as he trailed his mouth up and down her body.

"Please, please," she said. "Please. Now."

But Justin's lips again fixed to her hardened nipples, and finally she stopped writhing and lay back submissively, her eyes closed.

As he made love to her with his tongue and lips, Justin released her wrists and slowly removed his own clothing. She was as still as a sleeping baby as he moved between her legs and their flesh united, but when he was inside her, she exploded again, devouring him in a frenzy, crying out, scratching him until she was sated and lay panting and quiet beside him, listening to the soft music on the radio.

She was the first to speak. "Where is the mountain?" she asked, looking at the ceiling. She turned to him, and the fire had gone out of her eyes. She looked like a hurt little girl. "The place where you live."

"A world away," he said.

"I wish I could go there with you." She drew circles in the air. "Sometimes I let myself dream. In my dreams I am an old woman, and you are an old man, like Andrew. And we have a son who looks like you."

He lowered his head. How could he tell her that for him simple desire was as unattainable as the stars? He would never lead a normal life with a normal woman. That had been decided for him long ago. So he said only, "If it were possible, I'd want that more than anything."

The radio crackled. An announcer interrupted the music with a bulletin.

"Premier Pierlenko, General Secretary of the Union of Soviet Socialist Republics, announced tonight that State police have captured the man responsible for the Moscow killings of seven Americans since last October, including last week's murder of the American embassy's cultural attaché, Richard Rand. The suspect, known to authorities as the Peace Killer, was identified as Alexander Zharkov."

"They've pinned the blame on Zharkov," Justin said.

"Because they can't catch Kadar." Sasha sat up. Her face was flushed with anger. "Don't you see? With Siraj, Kadar is invincible. He will kill us all." She clutched his arm. "Justin, leave while the boy still believes you're dead. You can't fight him and win."

Justin thought of the broken amulet of Rashimpur. "That is not for me to decide."

"It is!" Two deep lines formed on either side of her mouth. "There's nothing more any of us can do, except save our own lives. Andrew's going. He knows it's lost. That's why I didn't tell him you were . . ." She turned away.

Justin pulled her around to face him. "Tell him what?"

She didn't answer. He did it for her. "That I'm still alive?"

She stood up defiantly.

"He doesn't know, does he?" Justin said, his voice accusing.

Sasha walked into the small bathroom to dress for her show and shut the door.

CHAPTER THIRTEEN

Clad shoulder to toe in a blue sequined cape, Sasha stepped into the spotlight. The crowd cheered as if she were a missing child come home.

They got to their feet as she strutted toward the trapeze, her gold hair splashing around her shoulders. She dropped the cape onto the sawdust-covered floor. When she began her climb up the ladder, the audience quieted itself in reverence to La Kaminskaya.

On the other trapeze, sixty feet away, her catcher swung lazily back and forth. As she reached the small platform atop the ladder, Sasha was helped up by the other flyer, a young blond man also dressed in blue sequins.

"Did you check the rigging?" she asked.

"Don't be insulting."

"I'm sorry, Anatoly. I guess I'm nervous because the Premier's coming. Is he here yet?"

"No," the young man said. He nodded toward the ring floor below. "They're saving three seats for him. He's coming with the American Ambassador and some cultural aide or something."

What was his name? Mark Cole, Sasha remembered as

she looked down at the vacant seats at the side of the ring. She powdered her hands on a rosin bag.

Justin doesn't trust me now, she thought. *He'll get to Andrew and convince him to stay. And then they'll both die, because of me.*

Anatoly was passing his hand in front of her face.

"What?" she asked, irritated by the intrusion on her thoughts.

"What planet are you on? The bar's come by three times. Ivan's pissed."

She looked over to the catcher. He was scowling as he sat patiently on his swinging bar.

"I hope to God you can pull your concentration together for the quadruple."

"Get stuffed," she said.

Sasha pushed off and began to swing out gently, building her momentum and synchronizing her rhythm with that of her veteran catcher. He had now locked his legs around the bar of the trapeze and was dangling, head downward, watching Sasha's smooth movements through the air.

He clapped his hands together to indicate the timing was now correct.

Anatoly, a competent workman who didn't mind being a backdrop to Sasha, watched for her first somersault, then pushed off, matched it, and exchanged places with her in the air. Then Sasha began to fly, spinning between the two men, seeming to defy gravity.

Seventy-five feet below was the hard, wood-covered cement floor of the ring.

It was going right. Every move, every placement was perfect. Even Ivan the catcher winked at her after a straight-legged double requiring such speed that no one had performed it since the legendary Jean Saint Pierre in the last century.

And then it was time for the quadruple somersault.

The audience waited for it, expected it, and when the ringmaster made the announcement and the drums rolled and the lights began to dim, no one dared move.

At that moment a phalanx of guards pushed into the back of the auditorium. They marched down the aisle of the amphitheater, leading two men.

Sasha was ready, holding on to the trapeze bar, feeling it all, the tension in her muscles, visualizing the swing, the layout, the perfect release that would carry her across the air like a dancer with no need of the earth.

She waited only for the spotlight to focus on her. But suddenly the announcer's voice spoke again.

"Ladies and gentlemen, Comrade General Secretary and Premier of the Soviet Union, Nikolai Pierlenko," he announced.

The houselights brightened for a moment, and the Premier turned and waved to the crowd, a light smile on his fleshy face.

Sasha dared not look over and break her concentration. Before the lights dimmed and the spotlight illuminated her alone, she glanced over at Ivan. The catcher was ready and she launched. She swung back and forth in great, lazy arcs. At the top of one of them she tossed her head so her hair streamed out behind her. Her eyes shifted focus for just a second, and she saw the Premier in his specially reserved seat. Next to him was a gray-haired man she recognized as the American Ambassador, and beside him . . .

Mark Cole?

She came down from her swing. It couldn't be. That couldn't be Mark Cole. Ivan clapped. At the top of her forward swing she released.

No, no. That couldn't be Mark Cole.

She missed.

She was far too high coming out of the somersault and crashed against Ivan's midsection, missing his hands. She hit him and slipped, but her reflexes worked like lightning. She grabbed the right-hand rope of his trapeze and hung on with one arm.

The crowd stood up, screaming, while she dangled from the rope. Ivan reached up and helped her to stand up on the trapeze bar, straddling his body, and then the two worked in unison to swing the out-of-rhythm device back toward the safety of the platform.

When she reached it safely, the crowd stood and cheered, but Sasha did not even acknowledge them. Instead she clambered down the narrow ladder toward the ring floor and ran out of the auditorium.

CHAPTER FOURTEEN

Starcher waited beneath the covered bridge. It was 11:48 and raining. There was no moon, and the air carried the clammy, oppressive chill left over from winter.

It was just as well that he would be leaving soon, Starcher thought. Another Moscow winter would be something he would not miss. He was in good shape, considering the wounds he'd taken and the fact that he had suffered a heart attack two years before. But time was beginning to tell on him, especially in winter. His hips hurt when he walked, and his fingers slowed to a standstill in the cold.

He hadn't brought a gun. He had his revolver back at the safe house. While Sasha had not told the KGB about the apartment, Kadar's people might still have found it, and he was reluctant to go there.

The soft patter of footsteps approaching pulled him out of his thoughts of Sasha. Cole was coming, and it would soon be over. Starcher would go back to America, and Sasha would go back to concentrating on the circus. It was her passport to fame, and the young woman handled fame the way most people treated relatives: accepting but never letting it get the best of her. He wondered what it would be like to be famous. That had always been the last thing he wanted. Even as a child he'd kept to himself, which wasn't easy in a family the size of his. But he'd believed that solitude gave a person strength.

Maybe that was why he'd taken so easily to poor Justin Gilead. And why Justin had seemed to feel that abnormal kinship with Zharkov.

Lonely men all, reaching out to each other for some shred of companionship and never finding it.

He would probably be gone tomorrow. Justin was dead. And Zharkov? Zharkov would surely die at the hands of the KGB. In an appliance-store window Starcher had watched Pierlenko on television, blaming the murders of the seven Americans on Alexander Zharkov. He could never be set free now.

Only Sasha would go on, flying, smiling to the applause.

"Langley's recalling you," Cole said brusquely as he stepped into the darkness under the bridge. "You're expected back Thursday morning." He handed an airline ticket forward.

Starcher took it. "They want me to fly back on Aeroflot?" he asked. "I'm as illegal as you can get. No papers—"

"They've taken care of everything," Cole said genially. "You won't have any problems." He smiled. "One last thing. I believe you have an operative here. Rand told me about it but I didn't know much."

"I wanted to keep the name to myself until the threat of the killings was over," Starcher said.

"Ah, yes," Cole said softly. "You were protecting Rand."

Starcher swallowed the insult. There was no time left for squabbles now. "If you give me a time and place, I'll tell her to meet you, but I don't think she'll work for you."

"She?" Cole said.

"Her name's Sasha Kaminskaya. She's a trapeze artist at the Russian State Circus."

"I saw her tonight," Cole said. "Does Langley know?"

"No. I recruited her myself years ago. This time around,

I picked her up on the fly. I'll tell them when I get back."

"You have other agents? What about Justin Gilead?"

"No other agents," Starcher said. "And Gilead is dead."

"I see." Cole nodded. "By the way, I've got something else for you."

He reached into the pocket of his jacket just as some small stones plopped into the rain puddles beyond the south end of the covered bridge. Crouching and turning as smoothly as a cat, Cole brought out a gun and aimed it at the south entrance to the bridge.

There was silence. Starcher slowly lowered himself to the ground as Cole soundlessly crept toward the entrance. He stopped, listening.

Nothing.

Then, with the speed of a cannonball, two legs shot in from the opposite end of the bridge. The figure somersaulted in the small space of the covered bridge, then landed flat on both feet. Cole fired. Dirt sprayed up from the damp ground, but the figure was rolling. Before Cole could fire again, two small hands reached up and yanked the CIA man's feet out from under him.

It was then that Starcher recognized the intruder. Her blond hair spilled out from under the cap she was wearing.

"What the hell are you—" Starcher began as Sasha sprang upright and kicked the gun from Cole's hand. Cole reached for it, but the girl was too fast.

She had a wire wound over the knuckles of one fist. Expertly she unrolled it and pulled it taut, even as she was moving toward the fallen man. Then, as Cole was struggling to pull himself upright, she slipped the wire around his neck and jerked it. The bone snapped cleanly with a small pop as the wire broke the skin.

Starcher watched in horror as Cole's blood covered his chest like an apron. He ran to the young man and knelt beside him, checking futilely for a pulse. He was dead, of course. The wire always worked.

"Don't waste your pity on him," Sasha said, discarding the weapon.

"My God, girl. Do you know what you've done?"

"I had to, Andrew. He was going to kill you."

Starcher looked down at the palms of his hands. They were sweating. His heart was thudding painfully, and he could still feel the hairs on the back of his neck standing on end. And he realized that he had been in this state of fear since before Sasha had arrived.

He had feared Cole. No, not Cole, exactly: He had feared death. From the moment Cole reached into his pocket, Starcher had sensed the familiar presence of something dark and nameless. His instinct had warned him. But this time he hadn't listened to his instinct. Mark Cole was his superior, his control. This time Starcher's instinct had gone haywire.

Hadn't it?

"Do you know who this is?" he demanded.

"His name is Yevgeny Sumonov. He has been an officer of the KGB for fifteen years."

"This is Mark Cole. . . ."

Sasha shook her head. "No. When I saw this man at the circus with the Premier, I knew a trap had been set for you. I have seen him before, but not as Mark Cole. As Sumonov. He works for Kadar."

Starcher's eyes squinted, as if he were unable to believe what he was hearing. "And you?"

"I work for Kadar too," she said simply.

He dropped the man's arm and exhaled as if the air were whistling out of his lungs for the last time.

"Are you going to kill me now?" Sasha asked.

"Would you let me?"

Sasha's shoulders were shaking. "It was never supposed to go so far," she whispered. "My parents had been gone for six years. I tried everything I could to find out where they were, to get them released somehow. I wrote dozens of letters to the Kremlin, to every official I could think of, but they were never answered. Then, when Kadar took office, suddenly there seemed to be hope. I was called in to see him. The Premier! He sent a car for me, a limousine. Kadar told me that he had seen me fly and that he was shocked to learn that such a terrible thing had happened to my family."

She brushed the tears from her face. "Shocked," she said bitterly. "I thought they would be free soon. But that was just the beginning of the lie. The next time Kadar sent for me, he said that my parents had been convicted of treason and that it would be difficult even for him to help them. But he promised to keep them alive. He said he would prevent their executions if . . ." Her voice trailed away. Starcher said nothing. "If I would do things for him." Her hand moved in a hopeless gesture. "Sexual things."

Starcher nodded. "Go on."

She turned away to face the wall. "I agreed. I did everything he wanted me to. I became what he wanted me to be. Then Kadar was removed from office."

"But that didn't stop you from being his mistress," Starcher said cynically.

"I couldn't stop!" she screamed. The sound echoed in the damp tunnel of the covered bridge. "He told me that if I left him, he would arrange to have my parents' throats slit while they slept."

Starcher lit a cigar. "That would have been an impressive feat, considering he was under house arrest and constant guard at the time."

Sasha shook her head. "It would have been nothing for him to have them killed. Even in exile he was a powerful man. You, of all people, should know how powerful. From the dacha where he was kept under house arrest he controlled vast numbers of followers. Influential people. Half the KGB was still loyal to him. Even some of the house guards were his men. They were the ones who smuggled me in to see him. They helped him escape."

"He didn't escape for two years, from my understanding."

"He needed the time to reorganize. Konstantin Kadar is a thorough man. He didn't want to risk capture or betrayal. Pierlenko's government would have found out about his secret army and destroyed it. He had to wait for the right moment."

"Which was?"

"Which was when the man you call Mark Cole came to see him."

Starcher coughed. "When was that?"

"Nearly six months ago."

"Cole didn't arrive in Moscow until the day Richard Rand died."

"It was the same man," Sasha said stubbornly. "I was with Kadar that night. I saw Cole. He was treated with great respect by the KGB men who got him in to see Kadar. They talked for several hours."

"About what?"

"I wasn't permitted to be with them," she said. "But shortly afterward the murders of the Americans began."

Starcher was silent for some time. "Then you knew about that. From the beginning. And you told Kadar about me."

She wouldn't look at him.

"Where'd you learn to use a wire like that?" he asked softly.

"Kadar arranged to have me trained in some things," she said in a small voice. "After a while the sex was not enough for him. He thought that my profession would put me in a position to meet people who might be useful to him."

"Meet them and kill them," Starcher said through a cloud of smoke. "So it was you who told him I was back in Moscow."

"I didn't know he would try to have you killed," she said. "He told me that his men were just going to use you to make some kind of deal with the Americans. He promised me they wouldn't hurt you."

Starcher ground out his cigar on the wall and stuffed the remains into his pocket. "Aren't you the innocent one," he said, his eyes hard. "You knew all about the man who tried to wire my neck at the circus."

"I didn't, I swear it!"

"And afterward?" he shouted. "After you knew Kadar had tried to have me killed? After I'd taken you in with me?" He stared at her for a long moment. Finally he turned away in disgust.

"I am giving you my life now," she called after him. "And my parents'. Do you think Kadar will let them live after he learns what happened here tonight? Do you think he will keep me alive?" She shook her head wildly, like a child. It stuck to her wet face. "Yes, Andrew, I was once willing to do anything for the slimmest chance of seeing my mother and father again. I would have sacrificed you. I hated myself for that, but I would have seen you die to keep them alive." Her voice cracked. "Until I saw you in that—that hole. You and Justin Gilead. I knew then I had to make a choice. You or my family. I chose you."

She sobbed into her hands.

"Sasha—"

"My parents are both dead now. I've killed them." She threw her head back, sobbing. "Isn't that enough for you?"

Inside the covered bridge there was no sound except for Sasha's weeping and the patter of rain.

"Your parents were already dead," Starcher said softly.

She looked up, making a choking sound.

"Your father died of cholera less than a year after his arrest. Your mother . . ."

The rain stopped, and there was no sound at all.

"What about my mother?" she whispered.

Starcher forced himself to look at the girl while he spoke. "They put her in an asylum for the criminally insane. After three months she took her own life."

Sasha's face narrowed to a pinched mask. "That can't be true."

"It is. I've checked."

"Then Kadar . . ."

"He was lying to you all along."

She made a sound as if she had been struck. "How long have you known?" she asked.

"From the beginning."

"You didn't tell me."

"No."

They both stood facing each other as the rain started again. Sasha backed away toward the opening of the bridge. "Then we've betrayed each other. For nothing."

"Have you told Kadar about the safe house?"

She shook her head.

"Meet me there tomorrow."

"So you can kill me?"

The old man's eyes were sad. "It's too late for that now," he said.

Sasha wiped her nose with the back of her hand. She looked as if she were about to speak, then turned instead and ran away from the bridge, her light footsteps smacking against the wet pavement.

BOOK FOUR

CHECKMATE

CHAPTER ONE

Ostrakov knew every route to KGB headquarters in Dzerzhinsky Square, so he knew that the driver of the car was not headed there.

"Where are you taking me?"

The man beside him pressed the gun deeper into Ostrakov's ribs. There were no more questions.

The car pulled up in front of one of the best apartment buildings in Moscow, just off the Kalinin Prospekt in the heart of the city. Like all the bastions of the rich in Russia, the building itself was a plain structure. Only an engineer could see that it had been constructed of materials far superior to those used in the great majority of dwellings built since the Revolution. There was a large doorman to discourage any would-be trespassers.

Ostrakov's companion pocketed the gun as he approached the door. "Comrade Badushenko's apartment," he said. The doorman nodded and pressed the intercom.

"Vladimir Badushenko?" Ostrakov whispered, awestruck. This had to be the city residence of the Politburo member. Who else could live in a palace like this?

The doorman waved them through. They entered a private elevator that opened onto a highly polished black-and-white marble floor adorned with an antique Persian rug of obvious value. Paintings hung on the walls, lit by their own spotlights, and an enormous blue-and-white Chinese porcelain vase filled with flowers sat perched atop a laquer pedestal. Ostrakov had never imagined an apartment that comprised the entire floor of a building.

"Is this all theirs?" he asked, like a child visiting a castle.

"Shut up."

A maid in uniform appeared and led them through a small anteroom filled with flowers and antique furnishings to a spacious living room, perfectly appointed in shades of mauve and cream. A wall of glass sliding doors opened onto a covered balcony green with exotic plants, flowers, and small trees.

Ostrakov had never seen anything like it in his life. He had heard that the rich, the truly rich, had access to undreamed-of luxuries. When he had held his former KGB post, he had himself received some special privileges, but this was even more than his imagination could have produced.

In the dreamlike pink room sat a small middle-aged woman whose face obviously had been carefully tended for so many years that her exact age would never be known. She was reading a magazine and gave the men hardly a glance.

Then Ostrakov saw a figure rise from a wicker chair on the greenhouse balcony and stand for a moment in the glass doorway.

"My God. The *Vozhd*," Ostrakov said.

"Comrade Ostrakov," Kadar said civilly. He extended his hand toward the woman on the couch. "Do meet Mrs. Badushenko. She and her husband have graciously invited me to be a guest in their home."

Ostrakov clicked his heels together and nodded formally. The woman did not rise. Although her eyes met Ostrakov's for only the briefest instant, he could see the pure hatred in them.

Kadar dismissed the others with a nod. "Shall we talk on the balcony?"

Ostrakov felt a violent need to urinate but was too afraid to speak. He followed Kadar into the greenhouse and obeyed his instructions to sit.

"I see you are still in uniform," Kadar said.

Ostrakov looked down at his gleaming brass buttons. Was it possible Kadar didn't know of his liaison with Pierlenko? Could he believe that Ostrakov hadn't been discarded with the rest of Kadar's flotsam?

As if reading his mind, Kadar said, "You've done very well for yourself, Comrade."

Ostrakov coughed.

"It was very perceptive of the Premier to single out someone with your abilities."

"Sir, I had to. My family was hungry. I—"

Kadar waved him down. "There is no need to apologize. You followed the vicissitudes of politics, that's all. Adaptability is the key to survival. Nature teaches us that."

Ostrakov looked stunned. "Yes, sir," he said quietly.

"Of course, there are some who have nothing to offer except their loyalty. But then, you wouldn't know about loyalty, would you? When Pierlenko took over this government, you went running straight to him."

"I didn't. I swear it," Ostrakov protested. "I was dismissed from the KGB and forbidden to work elsewhere. I could not support my family for two years. Then Comrade Pierlenko called me in to . . ." His voice drifted off.

"To what, Ostrakov?"

"I am not at liberty to say, sir."

There was a long silence before Kadar spoke again. "You know, loyalty is a funny thing, General. Some people are not politicians like you. I have many eyes and ears that watch and listen for me, even now."

"Yes, sir."

"Those eyes and ears tell me all about you. How, for instance, the Premier spoke freely in front of you, even in the presence of so high an official as the Director of the KGB."

Ostrakov colored. Even now he could not keep from

feeling the pride of his special status. When this meeting was over, if he was still alive, he would give it all to Pierlenko. Kadar's location, his spies inside the Kremlin, the role of the deposed KGB operatives. What a coup! He would get a promotion, a fat one, and enough money to live in an apartment like this one. Yes, he would use it all to his advantage. Not even Konstantin Kadar could best him. "He does confide in me on some matters," Ostrakov said, a sly smile playing on his lips.

"Then surely you know that the Director of the KGB is being dismissed."

The smile faded. "Dismissed?"

"Yes. The decision was made several days ago. How surprising you weren't aware of it . . . being such a close confidant of the Premier."

"He doesn't bother me with details," Ostrakov said lamely.

Kadar laughed. "You cretin." He said it with such good humor that Ostrakov smiled with him until Kadar fixed him with a cold stare. "Do you think the Premier of the Soviet Union would include a common soldier in his official discussions unless that soldier was expendable too?"

"Expen—"

"No. You do not think. That is obvious. Let me say it more plainly. *You are going to die.* Can you understand that much?"

"No!" Ostrakov protested, pouting like a child. "I helped him. I had a special assignment."

"To find Alexander Zharkov." Kadar didn't bother to look up, so he missed the look of utter astonishment on Ostrakov's face.

"Perhaps you should not be so zealous in your investigations," Kadar said. "The files you asked for in the research department all pertained to Zharkov. And did you find him?"

Ostrakov waffled. "He was found."

Kadar laughed again. "My dear fellow, you amuse me no end. Pierlenko probably keeps you around for your entertainment value. Unfortunately your demise will doubt-less seem less hilarious to you than it will to him."

"He wouldn't kill me! I'm in favor. He likes me."

"You had nothing to do with finding Zharkov. And how often has the Premier called you in to see him since?"

"Well . . ."

"Oh, stop being tiresome. You failed the assignment and now he has no use for you." He drummed his fingers on the wicker tabletop. "Have I given you enough gossip to take back to your master?"

Ostrakov started. "Sir, I assure you—"

"You really ought to think twice about where you place your loyalties, General, such as they are. You see, as much as Comrade Pierlenko would appreciate know-ing my whereabouts, it won't do him any good."

Ostrakov frowned.

"Come now, think. The home you are in belongs to Vladimir Badushenko, probably the single most influen-tial member of the Politburo. You will have to take my word that I would be equally welcome in the homes of the other members. Your dear Pierlenko would not. In a short time he will not be welcome anywhere."

"What do you mean, sir?"

Kadar sighed with exasperation. "The Premier is about to be deposed."

Ostrakov gasped audibly.

"Believe it, Comrade. The members are in a special meeting now to discuss the situation and decide on a successor."

"But why?" Ostrakov whispered.

Kadar shrugged. "These are matters of politics, my friend. But I do know the name of his successor." The doll-like eyes flashed. "You would be wise to follow him, General."

Ostrakov began to tremble as the realization struck him. "What would you like me to do?" he asked, his throat dry.

Kadar looked at him calmly. "That's better," he said.

"I want a favor from you. I don't believe you're such a fool as to stay with a sinking ship while there's still time to get off. Remember what happened the last time you served under a deposed head of state. That wasn't my doing, General. The machinery spit you out after I was removed from office. It could happen again if you choose the wrong side."

"What is the favor, *Vozhd*?" Ostrakov asked. His hands gripped the arms of his chair so tightly that his knuckles were white.

"A small thing," Kadar said smoothly.

The maid was passing by, carrying a tea service. Kadar called her over and whispered something. She nodded and was gone again.

"Call it a private joke between Premier Pierlenko and myself. I wish to have a message delivered to him."

"And I am to be the messenger?"

"Not even that. All you are to do is to escort the messenger. Introduce him to Comrade Pierlenko as your son or some such thing. He would grant you that small favor, would he not?"

"I don't know," Ostrakov said dubiously. Then he felt a shiver of fear. What if Kadar was planning to send an assassin with him? "The security around the Premier is very close," he ventured.

"Oh, I don't think the Kremlin guards will be unduly afraid of him. Here's my messenger now."

Siraj walked in and stood next to Kadar. He put his arm around the slim boy's waist. "Does that set your mind at rest?"

Ostrakov seemed to melt with relief.

"And by the way, the new administration will be swept clean. There will be a need for good men to assume positions of responsibility," Kadar said.

Ostrakov brightened.

"For one thing, Maxim Sterlitz's position will have to be filled very quickly." Kadar sat back. "Your talents have been wasted long enough, Ostrakov. Let's put them to use."

Ostrakov rose. "I shall be honored to help in any way possible," he said.

"Good, good." A slow smile spread across his face. "My boy will meet you at your apartment later."

"Yes, sir."

Kadar stood up and shook his hand. "You'll find your own way out, I trust."

"I will, *Vozhd*."

Kadar waited for the sound of the elevator descending, then turned to the boy. "When it's done, be sure to kill that buffoon."

CHAPTER TWO

The American embassy was in a state of chaos. The entrances were cordoned off, and armed personnel stood guard against the crush of foreign correspondents. No official word had been released by either the Americans or the Soviets, about the death of Mark Cole, but it had been impossible to keep the story under wraps. The body had been found in the middle of Gorky Park in broad daylight, and at least fifty people had seen it before the militsia had arrived.

One man was permitted through the barricade. The guards personally escorted him to the Ambassador's office, following orders given by John Downing himself.

This time Starcher wore no disguise. Even if it meant risking exposure, he had to present a good appearance. Ambassador Downing was not a man known for his imagination—one of Starcher's derelict disguises might just raise a lot of extraneous questions.

Downing looked just as Starcher remembered him from his own days as cultural attaché. As the Ambassador extended his hand in greeting, Starcher wished that he had spent more time in his company. The man had never been overly concerned with intelligence matters. Though he received regular reports on the state of the CIA presence in Moscow, it was doubtful that Downing had ever paid them much attention.

Until now. Starcher guessed from the frantic look on the Ambassador's face that he had read every Company document he could get his hands on in the few hours since Cole's murder had been uncovered. While he had largely ignored the details of field intelligence work, Downing was one of those diplomats who realized the importance of such work. Starcher remembered him as tough and hard, a shrewd and cool negotiator who had headed the American mission to Moscow for almost a decade.

"What have you got for me, Starcher?" he asked. His voice was polished and serene, the result of years of diplomatic service.

"The truth," Starcher said.

"It's about time I heard it from somebody. I've been talking to Pierlenko, and I don't think he's been leveling with me."

"What did he say?"

"He said that this Zharkov they captured actually *is* the Peace Killer. That's what he called him. He said Cole was killed after Zharkov's capture by one of Zharkov's accomplices, but they know who the man is and they'll pick him up right away."

"Your hunch is right," Starcher said. "He's lying to you."

"What is going on?"

"First of all, Zharkov isn't the so-called Peace Killer at all. The man behind all the killings is Konstantin Kadar."

"Kadar? You must be mistaken, Starcher."

"I told you I had the truth, Ambassador. Do you want to hear it?"

Downing sat down. "I . . . of course." He ran his hand over his face, shuffled a pile of papers on his desk.

"Kadar had an underground hideaway, outside Moscow, about sixty miles southwest of here. It was very large. My guess is that he built it while he was Premier, some kind of bunker."

He paused to let the information sink in, but Downing waved him on, momentarily speechless.

"There, he brought together a gang of ex-KGB operatives who'd been dismissed when Pierlenko assumed office. They've actually been carrying out the killings."

"Why?" asked Downing.

"To weaken Pierlenko's position," Starcher said. "To oust him, if possible."

Downing was expressionless for a moment. Then a weak, dry sound somewhere between a laugh and a cough escaped from his lips. "Are you saying that Konstantin Kadar is planning a coup against the Soviet government?"

"Yes, I am, sir. I was able to observe him under close circumstances, and it's evident the man's unbalanced. He believes Pierlenko's soft on the West and that unless Russia moves fast to gain supremacy, the balance of power will shift our way. He wants a nuclear confrontation."

Downing decided it was not too early for a martini. He mixed one quickly and downed it in one draft. "Interesting as all this is, Mr. Starcher, I'd like to know what it has to do with the business at hand. How would killing our people help him get back into office?"

"Politics. He wanted to make Pierlenko look bad, bring some pressure from the West, create some bad blood. Then, when Kadar took over, he'd have a reason to escalate the bad feelings. Pierlenko was desperate to find the killer, to appease Washington. So when he raided Kadar's place and found only Zharkov, he had Zharkov take the fall."

"And then Kadar killed Cole, just to humiliate Pierlenko further?"

"No," Starcher said. He looked at the floor. This was going to be tough. "Kadar didn't kill Cole. My operative did."

"*What?*" Downing rose from his chair.

"Cole was a double, working for Kadar. His name was Sumonov. He was Kadar's protégé back when Kadar was Director of the KGB."

"What proof have you?"

"There's no way to check absolutely, sir. The KGB's too thorough with their deep-cover operatives, especially someone who's been groomed for a position like Cole's. If he'd lived, we might—"

"But he conveniently died," Downing said.

"What's that supposed to mean, sir?"

"It means that the only evidence you've got against a dead man with impeccable credentials—credentials cleared through every level of the CIA—is the word of the man's murderer." He sipped his drink slowly. "I'm no spy, Starcher, but my common sense tells me you've got one hell of a dangerous agent on your hands. Who is he? We've got to get him picked up."

Starcher waffled. "By whom? There's no one to question him here."

"The militsia can help. Say we want him for some internal matter. Punching an embassy employee or something. He is an American, I presume."

"No. A Russian."

Downing blanched. "Let me get this right. You've been using a *Russian* as your assistant here? A Russian who's murdered the CIA Head of Station? God Almighty, you've been fostering the Peace Killer!"

"Mr. Ambassador—"

"Do you want to know something?" Downing shouted. "Cole thought you were dangerous. Now I think he was right. Your damned agent . . ."

Starcher left.

He was alone in this now.

The angina didn't start until he was back at the safe house. The pains weren't bad; Starcher had suffered worse in the years since his first heart attack. He lay down on the floor on his back and waited for it to pass, fighting off the urge to smoke.

When the pain lessened, he sat up and lit a cigar. There was no sign that Sasha had been in the house at all that day. What if she didn't show? For all he knew, she'd run straight from the covered bridge to Kadar.

The Ambassador had seen through her immediately, even though Starcher hadn't told Downing she had admitted to working for Kadar, that she had openly confessed to being a double. How much more proof of her treachery did he want? Suddenly he felt like a fool for believing her at all, for taking her story to the Ambassador.

Forget it, he told himself. John Downing was a diplomat with no experience in intelligence work. Things weren't always what they seemed. Yes, Sasha was a Russian, and yes, she had a background with Kadar and the KGB, and no, there was no way to confirm that Mark Cole had been an enemy agent, but that didn't mean . . . didn't *necessarily* mean . . .

Damn it, Starcher, you have to trust someone. He had an instinct about the girl. She was clean. She had been duped into cooperating, and she hadn't cooperated much. She couldn't still be KGB.

Could Rudolph Abel? Could Kim Philby or David MacLean? Doubt nagged at Starcher. The Russians were good, real good. Never mind the bumbling thugs at the bottom of the KGB ziggurat. At the top, their operatives could fool anyone.

Like Cole.

Or was it Sasha?

He stubbed out the cigar. The shooting pains had started again, and he jumped when he heard the door open.

"Andrew!" Sasha said, dropping the parcel of groceries she carried and kneeling beside him. "You're as white as a ghost."

"Some heart flutters, that's all," he said. He was unable to look at her.

"Let me help you into bed." He let her lead him. "I brought you some things for your dinner tonight. I didn't think your plane would be leaving until tomorrow at the earliest."

"Bullshit," Starcher exploded, slapping her hands away from the sheets on his bed. "Last night you murdered the CIA Head of Station in Moscow. I'm not going anywhere."

She sat down beside him. "Please, Andrew," she said, "whatever you think of me, or anything that's happened, stay out of things. Go home. Kadar will find you here. And your own government won't help you. Leave now, before it's too late."

"After what you've told me about your association with Kadar, I'd say it was already too late, wouldn't you?"

She closed her eyes. "I made a mistake by believing him," she said softly. "And you've suffered because of me. But I've suffered, too, Andrew. I paid for it for many years in advance. Now it's over. My parents are gone. I only want to see you leave this country alive."

Starcher listened quietly. Finally he asked, "Did you call the KGB in for the raid on Kadar's bunker?"

She nodded. "When I saw what he'd done to you and Justin, it was the only thing I could think of to get you out. I waited until they came to throw you the rope."

He picked up his cigar and studied it. "The American Ambassador thinks you're the Peace Killer," he said. "Should I believe him?"

Sasha sighed. "I guess you'll believe what you want to believe. Look, Andrew. Turn me over to your government if you like. In time the truth will come out. I have time. You don't. Kadar has already set his plan into motion."

Starcher's eyes flashed to attention. "In what way?"

"I walked here today through the Kalinin Prospekt. Vladimir Badushenko lives there, in one of the high-rise buildings. I was invited there to a party once. Badushenko's a member of the Politburo—"

"Yes, yes."

"There were men standing around outside. I recognized one of them from Kadar's place, one of the guards. *Kadar's* man. I don't think he saw me. I checked for a tail all the way back here, but no one followed me." She searched his face. "Don't you see? Kadar is with Badushenko. He's getting the Politburo to align with him. They'll force the Premier to adopt Kadar's policies."

"That's ridiculous. Kadar's policies are insane. *He's* insane."

"I don't understand it, either. Maybe it's nothing. Kadar doesn't have any hold over the Politburo anymore. Does he?"

Starcher got up. "I'd better see for myself."

"Andrew, no."

He walked heavily to the broom closet and took out a black wig. "I'd be a damned fool to trust you now," he said. "For all I know, you *are* the Peace Killer."

Ambassador John Downing placed the call himself, making very sure that the deskman at the militsia station understood who he was.

"There's a man we'd like you to pick up for us," he said in flawless Russian. "An American named Andrew Starcher. An embassy employee." He described him and added, "But he may be wearing a disguise."

"A disguise? What has this man done?"

"It's nothing serious," Downing said quickly. "Just some internal problems. But we'd appreciate it if you could keep an eye out for him."

"We'll do what we can," the policeman said, and hung up. He put the note on a spindle stacked almost to its point. "Those Americans," he muttered to his deputy. "They think everyone around them is a servant just living to cater to their whims. This one even says he's the Ambassador."

The deputy shared the laugh and picked up the note. "What's he want?"

"Oh, some other American. Probably a drug pusher at the embassy. They can't control their people at home, why should they do it here?"

The deputy read the particulars. "A disguise?"

His superior rolled his eyes. "Incredible, these people." He snatched the note away and crumpled it into a ball. "As if they haven't given us enough trouble. Now there's been another murder. It's a way of life for the

Jankis. I wish the lot of them would pack up and go home."

The deputy smiled and walked away. At the pay phone outside the station house, he dialed a number.

"Badushenko residence," a woman answered.

"Please give a message to your guest," he said. "Tell him Andrew Starcher is on the loose. And his own embassy wants him arrested."

CHAPTER THREE

General Sergei Ostrakov was embarrassed. He had pleaded with the Premier's receptionist for Pierlenko to meet his "nephew," whom he explained was a leader of the Young Pioneers. Pierlenko had agreed to meet the boy for two minutes. It had been a small enough triumph, but now Ostrakov wasn't sure the man had even remembered, because he had been waiting with the boy in the Premier's antechamber for over four hours. It was almost six o'clock.

Finally Ostrakov approached the hard-faced, uniformed woman outside the Premier's office. "Comrade, are you certain—"

"The General Secretary will see you when he sees you," she snapped.

"Yes, Comrade." He slinked back past the two armed guards to sit beside the boy.

Siraj was waiting patiently, not a wrinkle in his Young Pioneers uniform. He sat straight, never looking at Ostrakov.

"You're a very well-behaved young man," Ostrakov said. "I will remember to tell our friend about your good deportment."

Siraj ignored him.

"You may go in now," the woman announced. "But be quick. Two minutes. The Premier is a very busy man."

"Yes, Comrade," Ostrakov said. He bowed low, as if she herself were the Premier, and hurried the boy inside.

Pierlenko blinked impatiently as they entered. He got up from his desk with reluctance, but seeing the boy, the politician in him took over.

"Sir, I present my nephew, Siraj," Ostrakov said with what he hoped sounded like pride. "Siraj, this is my good friend and our great leader—"

"Delighted," Pierlenko said, interrupting, then extending his hand toward the boy. Siraj sullenly put his hands behind his back. Pierlenko looked confused. Ostrakov glanced away to hide his embarrassment.

Pierlenko tried again. "Your uncle tells me that you are one of the Young Pioneers," he said. "A great organization to build the leaders of tomorrow."

The boy answered, "A stupid pack of stupid people."

"What?" Pierlenko said.

"The Young Pioneers are stupid and so are you," Siraj said.

"Ostrakov," Pierlenko snapped. "I don't appreciate this joke. Get this surly brat out of here."

Ostrakov took a step toward the boy, then froze in his place as the boy turned his strange eyes toward the Premier. Pierlenko reached for the telephone on his desk. But before he could touch the receiver, his hand turned back in toward his own chest, where it clutched so hard at his shirt that two buttons popped off. The Premier gave a little cough, his face reddening.

"Sir," Ostrakov said, panicking. His arms pumped up and down at his sides as the man squirmed, staggering. Ostrakov approached the Premier, backed away, approached again, as if helping him were a matter of protocol. The boy said nothing, staring at the man in his agony.

"What . . . what . . ." Ostrakov began to lumber

toward the door, but the boy snatched his arm, his eyes never leaving Pierlenko.

"Be still," Siraj said.

"But the Premier . . ." He watched, astonished, as Pierlenko fell to his knees. His body convulsed once, then lay sprawled face down on the carpet.

"Get him back to his chair," the boy said quietly.

Ostrakov stood frozen.

"Quickly!"

Shaking, the fat man dragged Pierlenko's body back behind his desk and propped him up in his chair. The boy put the Premier's arms on the desk and lowered his head on top of them. Then he walked out. Ostrakov followed, his face white.

The uniformed woman never looked up from her work as they left.

"What have you done?" Ostrakov said raspily as they neared the subway entrance.

"Stop the car."

"Here?"

"Get out."

"We could have helped him, called the guard, something. Now everyone will blame us. We were the last—"

"I said get out."

Ostrakov obeyed. They walked toward the steps leading down into the subway.

"Surely you do not plan to flee," Ostrakov said. "Even though it was obviously a heart attack, there will be an investigation."

"Kadar will take care of that," the boy said calmly.

"But . . . but . . ." A searing pain shot through Ostrakov's head. He reeled backward, bumping into a crowd of people coming up from the subway. There were mutters and the scraping of shoes on concrete as they pushed him back, but Ostrakov could not right himself. Another pain came, worse than the first. He vomited, spraying the crowd, cradling his head in his trembling hands as people scrambled to get away from him. He slipped on a step, reached blindly for the guardrail, and missed. As people shrieked, horrified, Ostrakov fell down the long flight of cement steps, his arms stuck out in front of him, until at the bottom his skull hit the pavement with a crack. And then, with a last feeble twitch of his fingers, his heart stopped beating.

The boy walked away, smoothing the sleeves of his Young Pioneers uniform.

Starcher stood on the far side of the street, watching the men in front of Badushenko's apartment. Sasha had been right; the man with red hair who had picked them up at the chess tournament was among them.

Like the others, the red-haired man seemed to be idling in front of the place, a cigarette dangling from his lips, his hands in his pockets. Anyone venturing near the building, Starcher noted, was ordered to produce identification. Only residents were allowed to enter.

Starcher watched the men for some time. It was clear that Kadar himself was somewhere inside, and it seemed likely that he was with Badushenko. But why?

He didn't have to wait long for an answer. A couple talking excitedly walked out of the building and crossed the street, brushing past Starcher as they hurried away.

"I can't believe it! A heart attack, of all things. And such a young man. Will the May Day ceremonies be canceled?"

"Don't jump to conclusions. We don't even know if it's true yet."

"I just wish I could get Irina Pierlenko on the phone. They haven't been answering for days. Something's obviously going on. Look in front of their building. Maybe he's been dead for some time and the news just hasn't gotten out. . . ."

Starcher couldn't follow the rest of the conversation. He didn't have to. "Oh, Jesus," he whispered.

As Starcher left, the man with the red hair nodded to his companions, tossed his cigarette away, and followed. Starcher sensed him, in the way deer sense a predator. Without looking back, the American took a meandering route through the alleyways of the city, discarding his disguise piece by piece as he went. The black wig went into a trash barrel. The coat, a threadbare thing, was left behind in a pile of debris on a construction site. He was leaving a trail, but there was nothing else he could do. Finally, when he no longer sensed the chase, he ducked into the doorway of a restaurant to catch his breath.

There, through the curtained window, he saw the red-headed man turning the corner, coming straight for him.

He ran. Negotiating the alleys in a large circle, he brought himself back to the construction site and loped through the dust to a spot behind a pile of freshly cut lumber. He looked behind him. A high wooden wall, too daunting for him to climb in his condition, loomed ahead of him. It was over. Starcher's last stand.

He could hear himself wheezing. The pains in his chest were coming back, sharper than before. He opened and squeezed his eyes shut several times, trying to dispel the ringing in his ears.

If I can get back to the safe house . . .

Then what? The red-haired man wasn't going to stop until they'd killed him.

Starcher grabbed at his chest. *Doesn't matter. Get to the house.* He would figure out what to do later.

Maybe.

Nothing was clear anymore. The pain was clouding his mind. He knew he couldn't go to the American embassy. He didn't have a chance there. No friends. The Ambassador was a fool. Mark Cole was dead. And Sasha . . .

Did Sasha murder Cole to keep him from talking? Starcher thought suddenly. How much of what she had told him was the truth? Did she work for Kadar, as she'd confessed, in an attempt to save her parents? Or was that story a careful fabrication in case Starcher found her out? For that matter, did she even work for Kadar at all? If she had lied to him, how many layers deep was the lie?

Sasha, Sasha, my golden child.

He glanced at the entrance to the construction site.

"Oh, Christ," he swore to himself when he saw that there were two of them.

The red-haired man had been joined by a thug with broad shoulders and a flat, sullen face. They both held guns as they moved slowly into the fenced area where Starcher waited behind the pile of lumber.

The old man groaned as he forced his way around the stack of lumber. He would have to take his shot now, before they spotted him. He pulled himself into the open, assuming the best firing stance he could. He blinked hard. His vision was blurring, and he felt his hands beginning to tremble from the numbing pain in his chest. It wasn't going to stop, he knew. He would have to fire now or forget it.

The bullet took the red-haired man in the shoulder. He spun around, staying on his feet like the professional Starcher knew he was, but the return shot missed Starcher by more than a foot, cracking against the lumber pile. By the time the second man fired, Starcher was back behind the stack of two-by-tens.

Too late to get the second one, he thought. Too slow. He had hoped he could pick off both of them by surprising them with a charge, but he just didn't have it in him anymore. His legs were too old and the pains in his chest were too strong. He lay behind the lumber pile, gasping, waiting for them to come and put a bullet in his brain.

But there were no bullets, no footsteps coming toward him.

Catching his breath, Starcher rolled onto his stomach and peered around the corner of the lumber pile.

There was a third figure in the yard, who stood behind the two men and softly called in Russian, "If you want the old man, you'll have to take me first."

Starcher thought he recognized the voice. It can't be true, he said to himself. This had to be a mistake, a delusion from the pain.

The redhead crouched and turned, aiming his weapon with one arm as the other oozed blood. The heavyset man beside him swiveled toward the voice with remarkable smoothness, drawing his gun to eye level. Then Starcher saw the third man's face.

It was no delusion. The Grandmaster had returned.

Before they had a chance to fire, almost too fast for Starcher to follow, Justin jumped between them. His arm shot around the heavy man's neck. The gun was jerked into the air, then clattered to the ground as the thug's hands fluttered helplessly. Then, even at the distance between them, Starcher heard the crack of bones as the man's neck snapped. The heavy man slid to the ground in a heap.

Now that he had a clear target, the red-haired man behind Justin started to squeeze the trigger, but Gilead's right hand closed over his. The gun never fired. Instead Justin's elbow knifed under the red-haired man's chin. A flow of bright blood shot out of the man's mouth as he dropped.

Starcher fell back. A moment later Justin was beside him.

"Are you all right, Starcher?" he asked.

Starcher nodded. He tried to see Justin's face, but the sun behind it was too bright, and the pain now seemed to wash over him in waves. That didn't matter. There was a strong pair of arms around him, and he could hear Justin's soft, deep voice speaking. Starcher knew he was safe.

CHAPTER FOUR

The news was released with a speed virtually unknown in Moscow: Nikolai Pierlenko, General Secretary of the Communist Party, Premier of all the Russias, was dead of a heart attack in his Kremlin office. The twelve members of the Politburo, in an extraordinary telephone conference, had named Konstantin Kadar as acting Premier. That was what the Party press reported. Everyone even remotely connected with Soviet politics knew that Kadar was more than a temporary fill-in; his ties were strong, and there had not been a single vote cast against him. Within two hours of Pierlenko's death, the *Vozhd* had moved into the Kremlin.

The foreign diplomatic corps was swept with wild rumors.

He's going to cut diplomatic relations with the West.

He's going to expel all foreigners from the country.

He's going to call for an immediate summit.

At ten o'clock that evening, only two hours after returning to power, Kadar appeared on national television. Diplomats throughout Moscow huddled around television sets to listen to every word and to try to read some meaning into what was said.

Kadar expressed his regrets to the Pierlenko family.

He said that Pierlenko was a good man with noble ideals. But, he added quickly, the late Premier was leading Russia down the wrong path. Pierlenko had talked of peace, but what he had meant was surrender. Konstantin Kadar, once again entrusted by the Russian people with the leadership of their great nation, did not have the word *surrender* in his vocabulary.

"Much has to be done and much will be done. The Soviet Union will no longer allow itself to be manipulated by the West. The Soviet Union will once again stand on Marxist principles, the backbone of our progressive lives and the future of all men on this planet. The Soviet Union will no longer turn the other cheek to insult and threat."

The *Vozhd* smiled across the television. "There is much to do, but we begin immediately. I will have more to say about our plans at the May Day celebration. Let me make one thing perfectly clear, however: Those who stand for peace in the world will have nothing to fear from our leadership. Those who have cast themselves as implacable enemies of our great country will find themselves crushed. That is our policy and program."

When he finished speaking, the screen went blank, as Russian television shut down for the night.

No one knew exactly what Kadar had in mind. Not even the Politburo members who had swept him into power knew what Kadar's May Day speech was going to contain, but those who knew him well looked toward the West with apprehension.

The Kremlin buzzed with activity. Those who had left their jobs at five o'clock, an hour before Pierlenko's death, returned to sit uneasily at their desks. Many remembered Kadar from his earlier tenure as Premier. They remembered that Kadar, when not hidden in his darkened office, was fond of rambling around the Kremlin alone, paying surprise visits and firing anyone who displeased him in any way.

Rumors flew in the Lubyanka prison clinic where the

entire staff had come on duty to watch over five dying patients. One of those patients was Alexander Zharkov.

"Did you hear what happened in the kitchens?" one of the orderlies asked, casting his eyes toward the swinging double doors. "It wasn't clean enough for him, so he had the kitchen manager fire every employee, down to the pot scrubbers. Then he fired the manager."

"Kitchens," a nurse said with a snort. "I hear the Minister of Agriculture can't even get an appointment to see him. He was told to try again in July. I suppose the General Secretary was busy in the kitchen."

"Quiet," the orderly said. "They say he's shaken up the KGB too. Some of the top officials have disappeared from their homes. That's what the talk is."

Zharkov listened, pretending not to notice the pitying expressions on the faces of the hospital staff who tended him. He knew what they thought. Here was a man called in by Pierlenko, himself, just before he died, a man they had been ordered to keep alive. What chance did this man have of living now, with Pierlenko's enemy in office? Would their care for him reflect on the clinic? Would they, like the entire kitchen staff, be dismissed on a whim?

The charged atmosphere in the clinic became electric with tension when suddenly the doors swung open and Kadar walked through.

The staff stopped in their tracks, even those administering to the four other critically ill patients in the room. The Premier was not alone this time. There was a boy with him, a slender youth with strange blue eyes. Some of them had heard gossip about him. He seemed to spend his time in Kadar's office regardless of what the Premier was doing. Was it possible, the staff asked each other with their eyes, that the *Vozhd* openly kept a pleasure-boy with him?

"Out, all of you," Kadar said. Some of the staff left immediately. Others waited around, thinking they had misunderstood the man who now walked around to the beds, scrutinizing the patients. "Wait a moment. Him.

Get him out of here." He pointed to a man with tubes coming from his sides. His entire midsection was swathed in bandages. Despite obvious sedation, the man's eyes opened wide in terror at the sight of Kadar.

"Sir, this man has just had surgery to remove part of his stomach. We have to watch—"

"He's conscious," Kadar said. "Watch him elsewhere. Remove him."

The nurse was about to protest, then thought better of it. Quickly the patient's bed was wheeled out, apparatus and all.

"I'll tell you when you can come back."

"Yes, sir."

This raving lunatic is running one of the biggest powers on earth, Zharkov thought, half smiling. *And no one is stopping him.*

But then, he realized, it wouldn't be the first time. Russia had had a long history of mad Czars who ruled with absolute sovereignty. The Revolution had changed nothing. Russia's people would always be subjects, running willingly into the arms of anyone strong enough to control them.

As Kadar and the boy slowly approached his bed, Zharkov stiffened.

"Well, well," the *Vozhd* said. "Here we have the infamous Peace Killer."

Zharkov sneered with contempt. "Whatever you call me, I am innocent. Another American was killed after I was confined here," he said. "You can have me murdered, but no one will believe I killed those people."

"But you're mistaken, Colonel. That last unfortunate victim was killed by one of your accomplices in a desperate effort to secure your release. The public need not fear. We will soon have that person in custody. And you both will pay for your crimes."

Zharkov felt his face drop.

"Who will dispute it? I have a signed confession from you in my office. After all, no one knows what Alexander Zharkov's signature really looks like."

"I can prove it at my trial."

"Trial?" Kadar chuckled softly.

Siraj stepped forward. "You betrayed us."

"You see?" Kadar said, placing his hand on the boy's shoulder. "This one is young, but he understands loyalty. When the jackals came for me, only Siraj remained. For his loyalty I give my own allegiance in return. I am a man of my word." He turned to Zharkov again. "I wanted you to know that. Because I give you my word now that you will suffer for your disloyalty. You will suffer a long, long time."

Zharkov turned away in disgust.

"We will see how proud you remain at your new home, Colonel Zharkov." He bent over low to speak one word: "Kyshtym."

Zharkov showed no expression, although he had heard of Kyshtym. In the past he had even arranged for a few men to be sent there himself. He remembered the look in their eyes as they heard their sentences.

No one ever left the Kyshtym prison camp, except in death. And there were many ways to die there.

CHAPTER FIVE

The chest pains eased enough for Starcher to sleep. Justin sat by his side in the dingy safe house apartment, listening to Kadar's address on the radio.

As the speech ended, Starcher opened an eye sleepily, then struggled to a sitting position.

"He's gone off the end," he said to Justin. "He *is* going to start a war."

"It looks that way," Justin replied without emotion, not wanting to get Starcher upset. "How are you feeling?"

"Like a million dollars," Starcher lied. "I just needed a nap. I haven't been getting much sleep these days." He smiled broadly. "And now that Rip Van Winkle's come back to the land of the living, how about letting me in on how you found me in time to keep those Russkies from using me for target practice?"

"You were already gone by the time I got here, but I tracked you down, more or less. I lost you for a while before I spotted your coat in a trash barrel."

"I'm supposed to be hard to follow."

"Not for me," Justin said gently.

The old man snorted. "Or for those goons, either." His expression sobered. There was pain on his face. "I didn't think you were alive, son. I'd never have left you in those woods if I'd known. . . ."

Justin waved away the apology.

"Damn it, though, you seemed stone-dead. I checked you myself."

"Sometimes things like that happen," Justin said, fingering the broken pieces of the amulet in his pocket.

"Does Sasha know yet?"

"She was with me when I came to. I've been at her apartment ever since."

Starcher's jaw tightened. "Why, that . . ."

"She only wanted to keep you in the dark so that you'd leave the country before things got out of hand here," Justin said. "She didn't mean any harm."

"Didn't she?" The old man looked up sharply. "Sasha killed my control last night. She said he was a Russian agent." After hearing of Sasha's connection to Kadar, Justin just sat there, stunned. "There was nothing on the news about another American getting killed," he said numbly.

"Of course not," Starcher said. "Kadar and Pierlenko have already named Zharkov as the Peace Killer. Now that Kadar's in power again, he's going to keep this murder under wraps as long as he can. Then he'll call it an accident. He doesn't give a hang what America thinks of him. Any reprisals from us will only fuel his fire."

"And Sasha works for him."

"Worked," Starcher said, correcting him. "So she says. She's the one who blew the whistle on Kadar's headquarters. Apparently he was going to off us both, and Pierlenko as well."

Justin closed his eyes, then opened them again. "And Pierlenko's dead," he said.

Starcher blew out a gust of air. "I just don't know what to believe anymore." He looked around the grim, bare room. "Except that Kadar's going to start a goddamn war and there's nobody we can tell about it. And we can't stop him because he's buried in the Kremlin under ten layers of guards." He coughed. It made him wince in pain.

"Get some rest, Starcher."

"That's a great solution," the old man growled, although his eyelids were already heavy.

"Sometimes it is," Justin said.

After waiting an hour for Starcher to come back, Sasha had gone out to look for him. When she didn't find him at Badushenko's apartment, she began a thorough search in earnest. It had been hours now, and she had given up and headed back to the safe house, hoping Starcher had returned while she was out.

She checked her watch. The show at the circus would be starting soon. It was a shame, she thought, that yesterday's disastrous performance had been her last. She could never go back to the circus now. Kadar would not take long to figure out who had killed Mark Cole with a wire.

Turning the corner onto Starcher's street, she looked quickly behind her. No one was following. She went into the little grocery on the corner, dawdling over some shriveled oranges while she watched through the windows.

No tail. But someone was in front of the safe house itself. At first she had thought it was just a passerby, but the man, dark among the shadows, stayed close to the stoop.

She ventured out and walked closer. It was not a man. The figure was too lean and graceful. It was just a teenager, no one to be concerned about. . . .

"I've been waiting for you," Siraj said, striking a match near his face.

She thought about running, then remembered Starcher.

"What have you done?"

"To your friend? Oh, the old man's fine. I just wanted you here to watch this."

"Watch what?" she asked warily. As Sasha drew nearer, a faint, acrid odor wafted toward her. The match Siraj held was burning blue as he held it under a dry twig before tossing it into a clump of bushes in front of the house. Then a horrified look stretched across her face as she recognized the smell.

"No!" she screamed, rushing forward.

But it was already too late. The flames went billowing, fed on gasoline, like bright orange balls. The boy caught her.

"I *loved* you," he said. "Couldn't you see? That's why I saved you that time when you almost fell. You were the only one, ever." For the first time she saw something human in his eyes. "I never had a friend, never knew anyone I could trust. But I trusted you. It was going to be us, just us." Behind her, she heard flames crackling.

"And you tricked me," the boy said. "You betrayed Kadar and you ran out on me."

"Trust?" she said. "You never trusted me. I never even knew you worked for Kadar until I saw you at his place."

She struggled to get away, but he held her fast in a surprisingly strong grip. "I'm glad you didn't die, Sasha. I was mad at you before, but I'm not now. I want you to come back with me. Back to my own world. Will you do that, Sasha?"

He pulled her face toward him. Sasha lunged and bit him on the cheek, then whirled around and kicked him. She ran toward the flames.

The boy caught her on the crumbling steps. Grabbing her by the ankles, he dragged her down, then pinned her on the sidewalk. Her face was bloody from the fall, and pieces of broken concrete were embedded in her cheek.

"I'll still take you back," he said, touching her face tenderly.

She moaned. "Oh, my God." She looked toward the flames. They were spreading now to the other frame houses on the block, and she could hear the first screams as people ran out into the street. Starcher was still inside.

Her eyes followed the path of the fire. There was still a chance.

She clasped the boy's hands. "Yes, all right. I'll go. But I've got to get my friend out of there first."

Siraj looked up. "There isn't any way. He's dead already," he said, as if he were trying to reason with a child.

"Let me try. Just promise me you won't kill him and I'll come with you. I swear it."

"How can I believe you?"

"Siraj, you don't care anything for Starcher. I do. If I leave, you can find me and kill me. And him. But if you destroy him, I'll kill myself. That I promise."

The boy stared at her for a long, silent moment that was suddenly punctuated by the *whoosh* of the exploding fire. "And if he's already dead?"

"I'll go with you," she said.

He released her.

The frame house was engulfed in the gasoline-fueled flames, but the adjoining house had only started to burn. In the distance Sasha could hear the wail of fire trucks making their way to the tenement. They would not be fast enough, she knew, not for Starcher.

Grabbing a blanket from a woman who had run outside, she threw it over herself and ran through the spreading flames of the building next door. The staircase was filled with smoke, but the fire had only begun to burn the dry wood. Sasha held the blanket to her face, ran to the building's third floor, and tossed open the side window.

It was there. A clothesline, neatly coiled and hanging from a large chrome screw eye. She yanked on the rope to test it. It was sturdy. Had it been left outside to rot in the harsh winter, the line never would have held her. But a good housewife lived here, and the rope was strong enough—for a while, at least.

She looked around the room. These old houses often did not have running water on the upper story, but there was a basin, half filled with water, on a dresser. She dumped the water onto the coiled clothesline. Then she let out the rope, doubled it once, and twisted it for strength before knotting it through the large screw eye.

Then she tested the line with her weight. It seemed to

hold, and she wound the cord around her waist and climbed onto the windowsill.

"Andrew!" she called. "It's Sasha. Come to the window. I can get you out."

But it was Justin Gilead's face that appeared, sooty and streaked with sweat. "He's too sick to move," he shouted. "Get help."

"There isn't time," she called back. "I'm going to try to get over there. Be ready to catch me."

She lowered herself onto the rope, clutching it near the end, and kicked away from the side of the building. For a moment it all came back to her, the terrible instant when she missed her swing and felt herself slipping toward the ground. Her foot slipped, and she banged against the building. Her hands were sweating.

"Sasha, don't," Justin commanded. "Get down. You won't make it."

Her hands were sweating.

"I've got to make it," she whispered, and kicked out again.

Then she was free of the corner of the building. With every swing she was able to move her body a little higher, playing the rope out further, until her body swung in a big arc between the two buildings.

Some of the evacuees gathered in the street below to watch the woman swinging back and forth, her face illuminated by the surging red flames.

"What's she doing?" someone asked.

"I know her!" someone else called out. "It's La Kaminskaya herself!" A few of them even cheered, but Sasha did not hear.

She was now almost soaring to the height of Starcher's window, but her body was facing in the wrong direction. She would have to turn around on one swing, in midair, then manage to gain enough momentum to push herself forward at exactly the right moment in order to avoid slamming into the wall.

"You've got to catch me when I say," she shouted.

"I'm ready."

She knew there was almost no chance that an untrained man could manage the split-second timing the catch would require. But there was nothing else to be done. She owed this much to Starcher.

She prepared for the turn, swinging regularly, forcing her mind away from the rope burns on her hands, from her fear of the fall.

This is for you, old man, she thought before she let her mind go blank and her body sail.

She twisted inside the loop of rope as, at precisely the same instant, she tucked in her legs and spun in a somersault for momentum.

"Now!" she yelled, and blindly released her arms, holding them outstretched in front of her. And for that instant she was back under the single spotlight in the circus, flying free, La Kaminskaya once again.

The clap against her flesh came at just the right second. When she looked up, Justin was there, and she sailed through the open window like a darting bird.

Cheers rose from the street below.

Sasha slipped out of the rope and hooked it to the nails outside the window while Justin prepared a blanket for Starcher, cutting two holes near the top with a knife. He tore a sheet and threaded the strips of muslin through the holes.

"I'll go back over first and connect the pulleys from there," Sasha said, knowing that Justin understood what she was doing.

Starcher was coughing from the billowing black smoke that filled the room. There was a creak of wood as the hall stairway began to give way. Sasha climbed onto the windowsill again, then suddenly reached back and kissed Justin. "I'll never stop loving you," she said. "Please remember that, no matter what happens."

Justin thought the tears in her eyes were from the smoke.

She bound her hands with strips of sheets and took hold of the rope, making her way hand over hand to the other house. There she wound the clothesline around the pulleys, watching Justin do the same on his side.

He bound the blanket to the rope and eased Starcher into it.

"Ready," Justin called. Together they moved the line holding the makeshift stretcher across the pulleys and Starcher inched toward the other building.

The hallway stairs crashed down, shaking the entire house. For a moment Starcher hung suspended, his stretcher swinging wildly. He banged against the shutters, cutting a deep gash in his forehead. Sasha leaned out the window so far that she almost fell herself, but she managed to take hold of his shoulders and pull him inside.

"How bad is it?" she asked.

"Just a scratch," Starcher said, despite the blood streaming into his eyes.

She blotted his face with her sleeve. "I'm sorry, Andrew. For everything that's happened. But I'm not with Kadar. Please believe me."

He smiled. "I do," he said. "Now quit worrying about me."

Sasha went back to the window. "He's safe," she called. The fire had quickly spread to the adjacent house, and the smoke was as dense as in the building they had evacuated.

"Go on ahead. Take him down," Justin shouted back.

Sasha shook her head. On the street below, she caught a glimpse of Siraj in the gathered crowd below, visible only intermittently through the thickening smoke.

"Come over," she called to Justin. "Hurry!"

Hand over hand, Justin came across the rope. Sasha hoped that the smoke would obscure any view of him, but just before he came through the window, a stiff breeze blew the smoke away, enough for the boy to see them. Siraj's face twisted in hatred. He ran out of the crowd, staring up at the window.

Sasha climbed out onto the sill as Justin entered through the window, putting herself between him and Siraj.

"Get off there," Justin said. "Let's get out of here."

But she knew she would never leave alive.

An unmarked car pulled up in front of the house, and two burly men in suits got out. Kadar's men. She recognized them from the bunker.

Below, Siraj raised his arms. His eyes burned into Sasha's, and she felt the first pain in the center of her forehead.

"Don't come near me," she said softly to Justin. "Take Andrew down the back stairs."

"Sasha, what's wrong?" He started for her.

Sasha felt the world swirling around her, circles of black giving way to circles of red. Then, suddenly, the bones in her legs seemed to shatter. She was no longer able to stand. "Justin, my love," she whispered, before she fell with an agonizing cry.

He dived for the window but was too late. The crowd screamed as the young woman, her blond hair trailing behind her, plummeted toward the pavement. Looking through the window, Justin saw her crash, her legs twisted at bizarre angles, like broken matchsticks.

For a moment Justin could only stare at the broken body on the ground. He no longer heard the screaming of the crowd, or the wail of the fire engines, or even Starcher's anguished wail.

With a rumble like a muffled explosion, the building they had just escaped collapsed. People ran, shrieking, from the billowing flames as tons of burning wood and plaster poured onto Sasha Kaminskaya's small body.

Justin stood motionless at the window for what seemed an eternity. Starcher coughed, tried to speak, couldn't, then brought himself to all fours with an effort. "Justin," he finally croaked through the choking smoke.

Gilead turned as if in a dream, but something caught his eye. In the doorway stood two figures, shimmering in the heat. They held wet rags over their faces. Their weapons were drawn.

"Kadar's men," Starcher said.

Later the old man would know he never again wanted to see the Grandmaster kill.

What he witnessed was not a fight. It was an execution. Moving at a speed Starcher had not believed possible, Justin threw himself at both men, willing them to shoot.

But there were no shots. Before his feet touched the floor, Justin spun around, kicking his leg straight out. His heel snapped squarely against one gunman's throat. For a moment the man's neck bulged like a question mark, then exploded, spraying bits of white bone and thick ribbons of blood. His head dropped forward, hanging by a stringy thread. When the body fell, the head disconnected and rolled into the flames. Then the Grandmaster moved on.

The second man, Starcher sensed, had tried not to pay attention to the grisly spectacle. He behaved like a trained marksman, moving swiftly, watching for an opening as Justin maneuvered himself out of his line of fire behind the other gunman. Like Starcher, he had been stunned, first by Gilead's sheer speed and then by the astonishing decapitation. But the man could concentrate. He hesitated no more than a second as his partner's neck burst in a spray of blood only inches from his own face.

Unfortunately he hesitated too long.

Justin grasped him by both collarbones. The man screamed once, a long, high-pitched wail, as Justin lifted him off the ground, his hands gripping jagged splinters of bone. When the scream finally died, the man was unconscious. Justin threw him on top of the headless body.

Fire crackled in the hallway. Starcher could hear the firemen in the street below. He looked to Justin. If they were going to survive at all, they would have to leave at once.

But Gilead had no intention of leaving. He stood over the unconscious man for a long moment, the expression on his face strangely serene except for the blaze of his blue eyes. In those eyes Starcher knew he was seeing pure hatred.

Gilead bent over the man slowly, examining his face

like a surgeon planning an operation. Then, with one stroke, he thrust both thumbs into the eye sockets. The man convulsed. Starcher turned away.

Shortly afterward Justin hoisted Starcher up onto his shoulders, kicked out the back window of the apartment, and eased the two of them onto the creosote-soaked utility pole behind the building.

Starcher looked back. The face of the second of Kadar's men pulsed blood. It would have taken an act of faith to believe that the pile of mutilated flesh had once been human.

The deputy in charge of the fire brigade had never seen anything like it. His men had been pumping water onto the burning building for more than an hour. It had fallen in on itself, into a pile of rubble, but the water seemed to fuel the flames. Nothing would extinguish the fire. Finally he shouted orders to one of his subordinates.

"Don't waste the water. Let it burn. Just wet down everything else so it doesn't spread."

He turned and saw that a young boy was standing behind him, inside the police barricades, staring at the burning mass with a ghoulish fascination. There was pleasure on his face. The deputy, who had seen too many people die in too many fires, was revolted.

"Get these people out of here," he yelled to a uniformed policeman. "Especially this one." He pointed to the boy.

Siraj was led away, behind police lines. Smiling.

CHAPTER SIX

Sasha's body was not claimed until two days later, when a construction crew was finally able to remove what was left of her from beneath the mountain of rubble.

Konstantin Kadar ordered her remains brought to the morgue at Lubyanka, where they were secretly buried. In the morning edition of *Izvestia*, Natasha Kaminskaya was named as Alexander Zharkov's accomplice in the brutal slayings of eight American nationals, including Cultural Attaché Richard Rand and his successor, Mark Cole. At Zharkov's trial, which lasted less than an hour, his signed confession was introduced as evidence, along with a letter from Miss Kaminskaya, implicating her in the murders. No mention was made that the woman was known as Sasha and had been one of the leading trapeze artists in the world.

Starcher carried a copy of the newspaper with him, along with a flask of black-market American whiskey, as he walked with Justin along the bank of the Moscow River. Although the night was warm, an occasional chunk of ice floated by on the water, illuminated by the lights of Luzhniki Stadium on the opposite bank. His head was still bandaged from the cut he had received during the evacuation from the burning safe house, but he was feeling well enough to leave the cheap hotel where he'd been staying since the fire.

When Justin came for him, Starcher didn't ask where he'd been living for two days. Justin had his own way of grieving, Starcher knew, and it was private. From the look of him, though, he hadn't slept anywhere.

The men didn't speak until Starcher sat down on a concrete platform jutting out over the river and lit a cigar.

"Those things are going to kill you before your time," Justin said.

"Who says it isn't my time?" the old man answered with a smile.

Justin stood beside him. In the river's reflection the stadium lights shimmered like streaks of silver, dancing on the water for a moment, then vanishing in the blackness. The lights were like Sasha, sparkling brightly in the night before being extinguished.

"What are you going to do now that you're officially a dead man?" Justin asked.

"Hang out with other dead men like you," Starcher said. "How long do you think it will be before they find out that those two bodies weren't ours?"

"The fire burned a long time, Starcher. If anything's left of Kadar's men except bones, I'd be surprised. We're dead as far as everybody's concerned." Justin ran his fingers through his gray-streaked hair. "She knew the boy was there," he said. "She put herself between us to protect us from him. She knew she was going to die." He looked away, his fists clenched at his sides. Finally he spoke, and his voice was tortured. "What do you say about someone like that?"

"You say thanks," Starcher said softly.

Justin's shoulders tightened. "You're in a filthy, stinking business," he shouted, as if the river could hear him. "You people don't care a damn for life. Not even your own."

Starcher took the flask from his pocket and drank deeply from it. "Sometimes that's the way it's got to be."

"Is that all there is to it? She loved you, Starcher. She loved me. She got killed proving it."

"It's the nature of the work," Starcher said.

"The work," Justin repeated with contempt. " 'Wet work,' I think you call it. Another of your euphemisms for murder Your work disgusts me. There's no difference between you and the KGB."

Starcher's eyes narrowed. "Now wait a minute," he said sharply. "You may not have noticed, but I haven't spent forty years as a hit man for some thug. What I did—all of it—was for my country, which, whether you remember it or not, is your country too."

Justin sat down beside him. "Sasha's death wasn't your fault."

Starcher touched his arm. "It wasn't yours, either," he said quietly.

"If I hadn't come back, she'd still be alive."

"Sure. And she'd be alive if I hadn't recruited her. Or if Kadar had stayed in exile. Or if that monster brat had never been born. Or if she hadn't taken it on herself to jump into the fire and save our sorry butts. You can talk yourself to death, kid. It still won't bring her back."

He took another drink, a long one. "I just wish it hadn't all been for nothing. May Day's the day after tomorrow. This is a hell of a time for me to retire."

"You've done everything you could," Justin said, as the lights across the river began to go out, one by one.

"Yeah. And nobody would listen." He sat still, watching Moscow go to sleep. "It looks like even the President's buying Kadar's story about Zharkov, or at least pretending to. I don't think America wants to believe Kadar's pushing for war. I can hear those damn liberals in Congress now. Don't rock the boat and the shark will pass by. They'll never see what kind of teeth the shark's got until it's bitten their fool heads off."

"Is Zharkov going to be executed?" Justin asked, picking up the newspaper.

"Kyshtym," Starcher said. "Prison camp. From what I hear, execution's better."

"Where is it?"

"Soviet Georgia, about fifty miles north of Chelyabinsk. There's an underground song about it: 'A hundred miles of wasteland, watered with blood,' it goes." He drank again. "Poor bastard."

Justin took the pieces of the broken amulet from his pocket. How ironic that Zharkov would end this way, he thought. Not by the lightning of Brahma but by slow torture at the hands of venal men.

He had once hated Zharkov with all the fury of his soul. Now the Prince of Death seemed no more than another broken brick in the rubble of Kadar's junk-heap empire. And Justin would die along with him, far away, yet another broken brick.

"It *was* for nothing, wasn't it?" Justin said, thinking of the Black Star that would soon rise over Russia and the rest of the world.

Starcher wobbled to his feet. "I'd like to propose a toast," he said, lifting his flask. Almost all the lights on the other side of the river had gone out, and the old man was feeling the liquor. "To the losers. To all of us who try and fail. To Sasha, who was too young to know we weren't worth the price of her beautiful life. To Zharkov, whose brilliance was finally eaten up by the maggot thugs around him. To you, Justin, forty-two years old and waiting to die because there's nothing worth living for. And to me."

He stood unsteadily. "To Andrew Starcher, the grand old man of the CIA. They're probably planning to hang a plaque with my name on it in the revered halls of Langley Center now that I'm officially dead. It will read 'In memory of the man who lost America because he was too old, too feeble, and too cowardly to try again.' Here's to me." He drained the flask and threw it into the river.

"We ought to get out of here," Justin said, putting his arm around the old man.

"No, no." He pushed him aside. "I'm not really drunk. I'm just . . . just tired of running on the blade. . . ."

"What?"

"Never mind." He took Justin's hand. "I don't believe I'm going to see you again, Justin Gilead."

"Don't be . . ."

"Oh, nothing like that. I'm going to try to get out tomorrow. There'll be a lot of confusion about May Day, and Kadar's men will be busy. I've got those airline tickets. I may just be able to get out if I do it tomorrow."

"You're sure that's what you want to do?"

"There's nothing else I can do, son." He extended his hand to Justin. "Take care of yourself."

"I'll go back to your hotel with you."

"No," the old man said, picking up the newspaper. "I think I'd rather walk back alone. Unscramble my brains."

Justin was swept by a terrible loneliness. "So long, Andrew," he said.

Starcher walked into the darkness. Just before he was completely out of sight, he turned and raised his hand.

"Good-bye, Grandmaster," he answered softly.

Then another light went out across the river and he was gone.

CHAPTER
SEVEN

Southeast of Moscow in the Chelyabinsk Region where Kyshtym Labor Camp Number YaV-48/7 was located, the snow on the peaks of the Ural Mountains is always visible, even in summer. Here, in the spring, the mountains loomed over the camp like silent sentries, casting their shadows over the bare ground. There were no trees in Kyshtym, so the rain, when it came, flooded the grassless land, turning everything to mud. In the heat of the day, the excrement of the prisoners, buried until the rain unearthed it, drew flies that seemed to coat every surface from the bars of the prison to the sweat-shining skin of the inmates. At night a raw wind blew off the mountains and chilled the bones of Kyshtym inmates.

More than two and a half thousand prisoners worked there, every day crawling down deep into the earth to mine uranium ore by hand. Their life expectancy was five years. Most succumbed to radiation poisoning. While they could work, however, they were fed, clothed, and housed. When the sickness overcame them, inmates were placed in a large barracks-style building without heat or medical care and allowed to die. They were the lucky prisoners of Kyshtym.

There were another five hundred prisoners who were

not so lucky. These were the inmates of Kyshtym and other camps who had incurred punishment. No efforts were made to keep them alive. They were expected to work and die, the sooner the better.

More than half of these five hundred would die within a year. No one cared and no one complained. There was no one to hear them if they protested, and there was no point in getting shot and killed before one's time was up.

Alexander Zharkov was one of the unlucky.

He was housed in private quarters, in a wood-and-tarpaper shack where the night wind swept through the broken boards. In the shack were a wooden bench that served as a bed, a coffee can for a toilet, and a pail of water Zharkov was allowed to refill once a day. There was no light in the place except for the sunlight that crept through the broken slats, but Zharkov was seldom inside during the daylight hours.

He was awakened at dawn, given a lump of soggy bread to eat, and escorted to his job near the rear of the camp compound. The other prisoners worked according to grade: those accused of the worst crimes against the state dug in the trench just inside the barbed-wire fence surrounding the camp. After forty years it was ten feet deep and fifty feet wide, but there was always work in the trench. Here the garbage and waste of the rest of Kyshtym camp was dumped every night and filled in the next morning while another section was excavated. When the rains came, the loose dirt turned to mud and had to be slopped out.

Higher-ranking inmates got better jobs, cultivating gardens or polishing stone, and the best of them worked indoors, cooking and scrubbing.

Zharkov was a special case. His orders stipulated that he was to have no contact whatever with other prisoners, and his job was never to change: Zharkov would dig the graves of the inmates who died in Kyshtym.

The graveyard was a vast, flat area of clay soil strewn with rocks. The graves were unmarked, and the stacked corpses so numerous, that Zharkov often dug all day, only to pitch his shovel into the decomposing remains of another body. It was impossible to tell what parts of the ground had already been used. Here, the rains had turned the soil into a slippery soup, and the rocks were so plentiful that Zharkov had to use the handle of his shovel as a lever to get them out.

While he worked, four guards supervised him. They were not the usual prison guards. Men who spent many years inside the camp, even on the side of the State, understood the hardship of the inmates and sometimes took small measures to make the prisoners' lives less arduous: a proffered cigarette, a little conversation.

Zharkov's guards were KGB men, insulted to have been posted to this stinking hellhole at the end of the world. They wore civilian clothes, smoked European cigarettes, and swore at the flies and rats that the regular guards took for granted. Their only diversion in the camp was their prisoner.

In the remote clay wasteland of the graveyard, they stood with nothing to do but watch Zharkov. They devised ways to amuse themselves. They took turns urinating on him. In the rain, they laughed while he danced on the slippery clay inside his hole, and they kicked him for the pleasure of seeing him fall.

Zharkov said nothing, betrayed nothing with his face or with his gestures. He would not permit himself to feel anger, because if he did, he would also permit himself to feel despair. And after despair, he knew, there would be nothing. He had seen it on some of the other prisoners, the numb nothingness that permeated their every movement, the vacant look in the eyes of those who had no spark of human life left inside them. Zharkov knew their faces immediately when he saw them in the pile of bodies stacked by the graveyard in the mornings, the faces of the dead who had long before ceased to live.

He almost forgot his vow not to anger when he saw Maxim Sterlitz.

The former KGB Director walked in behind the guards during the rainy morning, wearing a rubber mackintosh. "So here you are at last, Zharkov," he said.

Zharkov looked up at him briefly, then took his bread and ate.

"The great-grandson of a prince. How fortunate that your illustrious ancestors cannot see you now."

Zharkov started to walk away. Sterlitz thrust out the riding crop he carried and barred Zharkov's way. "You forget yourself, Colonel. You do not determine when you leave. Your movements are dictated by me." He held the crop at Zharkov's throat. "Why, you may not even swallow your own spit without my permission."

He laughed, and the guards laughed with him. "How do you like that, Prince? That is what I am told they used to call you in the army, you know. The Prince." He folded his arms over his chest and leaned forward to whisper.

"You will be no prince here, Zharkov," he said. "It is because of you that I no longer head the Committee. It is because of you that I am posted to this stinking hole. I will make you pay for that. Did you know we expect a rescue attempt?"

"There will be no such attempt," Zharkov said.

"Kadar has announced that you have been sent here. Your precious Nichevo will come for you. And we will get them. And I will move back to Moscow."

"Get out of my way," Zharkov ordered.

For a moment Sterlitz started, ready to obey, then his eyes squinted. "What did you say?" he asked slowly.

"I told you to get out of my way. I'm expected to work here."

"Work." Sterlitz laughed again, but this time it was loud and forced. "Oh, yes, Prince, by all means, we must not keep you from your important work." He glanced toward a broken slat in the wall. Rain poured in and spread in a puddle on the floor. Outside, the sky was as dark as twilight, lit only by spears of lightning. "Remove your clothes," he said softly.

The guards stared at Sterlitz for a moment. Then one of them began to laugh. So did the others. Only Sterlitz did not laugh. And Zharkov.

"I think you heard me, Colonel." He flayed his arm with the riding crop. The end of it struck Zharkov's face, where a red welt appeared.

The guards fell silent, watching. Slowly, his hooded eyes never leaving Sterlitz's, Zharkov undressed.

"Everything," the man said.

The four KGB men and Sterlitz led the man who had once been called the Prince to the graveyard, naked and cold in the late spring rain. Some of the men in the trench saw him.

"Will you look at that?" a prisoner who had been convicted of murder said. "Bare-assed as the day he was born and proud as can be about it too."

The guard standing over the trench glanced over. He had served in the army for twenty years before this posting and recognized the bearing of a military man. He had also been at Kyshtym long enough to know a political prisoner when he saw one. A *ponosnik*. A goner. But this man was no ordinary inmate. Anyone could see that by the way he held his head. While those whining KGB men and that toy soldier who headed them hunched under the pelting rain, the naked man in the center of them walked toward the graveyard as if he were master of the land.

No. He was no ordinary inmate. And his life would be very short.

A *ponosnik*.

CHAPTER EIGHT

Alone in his hotel room, Starcher tossed on the creaky bed, unable to sleep. The blue streaks of early morning were filtering through the dirty window, giving an eerie prominence to the few furnishings in the room: a folding chair, a dresser with one drawer missing, a naked light bulb dangling from the ceiling, a scrap of rag over the window.

Soon, he thought, he would not even be able to afford these poor accommodations. The money Cole had given him was almost gone. Starcher would just have to find some other way to live out his life.

It wouldn't be long. His heart was sending him signals all the time now. The episode at the safe house had passed, but lesser attacks had continued.

Of course, the story he had given Justin about leaving the country on May Day was nonsense. Kadar virtually had control of the entire KGB again. He would not be fool enough to ease security at the airport just because of a parade. But the fabrication might have been enough to get Justin away.

The Grandmaster had wasted enough of his life on Starcher and Starcher's business. Justin was right. It *was* disgusting, a series of rooms like this one from the beginning of your career to the end, no friends, no family, no security, and the kind of work that would make a normal person's stomach turn.

America was a hard taskmaster. It didn't honor its intelligence agents the way Russia did. It preferred to believe they did not exist. It sent them out and then turned its eyes away so that it could say that freedom just happened, miraculously, like a flower blooming in spring. Meanwhile agents rotted in places like this.

No, it was not the life for Justin Gilead. He was not meant to run the blade. There was something fine about him, something pure and innocent. He belonged on his mountain. There were enough Starchers in the world.

They just were not in the right part of it now.

If only he could have stopped Kadar. Starcher felt an attack coming on and consciously eased his mind away from the subject. There was nothing to do about Kadar. Starcher would be damned if he was going to die from just thinking about the man.

He might be able to get a job. His Russian was so perfect that he could affect the accent of any state or social background. He could pass himself off as a provincial, maybe steal some identity papers, get some menial work where Kadar's men wouldn't find him. It would be easy to disguise himself. God knew, he had had plenty of experience.

He laughed out loud. It had happened at last. He was about to become one of the shuffling old peasants he had pretended to be for so long. The disguise had transformed the man.

Well, why not? It was as good a way to live as any. Besides, however wretched the life, it was extra time. As far as the folks back home were concerned, he was already dead. There would be a big funeral with all the Starcher women attired in designer black, weeping earnestly for a relative they would not recognize if he passed them on the street. An enormous marble tombstone would be erected over an empty grave, and everyone would come to Langley in their limousines for the unveiling of

the plaque commemorating his heroism. All very fine
and clean. Because freedom just happened.

Suddenly he sat bolt upright. That's it, he thought. It
had been right in front of his nose. He was dead: In the
eyes of Kadar, the KGB, his family, the Company, and
everyone else, *Andrew Starcher no longer existed.* That
one fact changed everything.

He picked up the newspaper he had brought back with
him that evening. There had been something that caught
in his subconscious so that even in his drunkenness he
had held on to the newspaper.

On one of the back pages he saw it, in a box at the
bottom of a story continued from page one about the
forthcoming May Day celebrations.

WORLD WAR II VETERANS HONORED
A special detachment of veterans who served in
the Armed Forces of the U.S.S.R. against Nazi
Germany will march in the annual May Day Parade.

He had found the answer.

He got dressed again and went out. It would be hours
before he could start, but it was easier to think in the
open air. He walked around the city as the dawn bloomed
into daylight, and his legs felt as if they were twenty
years old again. As soon as the shops opened, he spent
the last of his cash on a handful of the biggest, blackest,
strongest Havana cigars money could buy.

His next stop was the bank. He walked up to the
revolving doors slowly, his back bent in his old man's
posture, mouth slightly open, eyes rheumy and dull, hands
trembling. No one would have questioned why he waited
so long outside. An old man forgot a lot of things. Then
he spotted his target, a vigorous-looking man in early
middle age with a good haircut and European clothes. As
he came out through the revolving door, Starcher stepped
in front of him. The door slammed into the man's back.
He lurched forward, howling, knocking Starcher to the
ground.

"Watch where you're going, you senile old fool," the man snapped, rubbing his back. Starcher gazed up at him in fright, his fingers splayed on the cement steps. When the man stomped away, Starcher got up slowly, turned as if he no longer remembered what he was doing at the bank, and shuffled into an alley.

"Bingo," he said aloud, a cigar already in his mouth as the alley opened onto a busy street. Twenty-three hundred rubles, well worth a fall on his rump.

Next he took a subway ride to the outskirts of the city, to an area populated mostly by Arabs and Middle Easterners. Even so early in the day the narrow streets were permeated with the aromas of lamb and saffron. Women, some of them wearing the veil and black chador robe of the Shiite Muslims, shopped amid bushel baskets of okra and chick-peas and almonds and beans, while the vendors extolled the virtues of their wares in loud, sing-song Arabic.

Starcher went into a small coffee shop where a row of swarthy laborers stood drinking espresso at a pockmarked aluminum-covered bar. The fat man behind the counter looked up sharply as Starcher entered. Starcher jerked his head toward the back of the shop.

"What do you want?" the man asked curtly, wiping his hands on a towel.

"Nine-millimeter. Anything Russian."

The man shook his head. The grease on his forehead formed pools in the furrows. Starcher had dealt with him before, in the old days, for emergencies. He was not an agent, just a greedy, small-time gun dealer who worked the fence that paid him best. But he did not inform for anyone since that would be bad for business, so every agent in the area, of whatever persuasion, trusted him. "No understand," he said in broken Russian. "You have coffee, we talk."

"I don't have time. I'll pay you double. Sixteen hundred."

The man considered. "Twenty-two hundred."

"Deal," Starcher said. "You thief."

The man sighed, as if he were letting himself get hood-winked, then beckoned Starcher into the kitchen. "Wait here."

He waddled down some stairs and came up with a Tulskii Korovin wrapped in the towel. "Clean,". he said as Starcher examined the automatic pistol. "Never used."

Starcher knew he was lying, but it did not matter. Arms did not get here unless they were virtually untraceable.

Starcher paid him and left.

It took him hours to find the next item. But finally, in the fifth secondhand clothing store he searched, he saw what he needed: a Russian corporal's uniform, circa 1940, complete with cap and squadron emblem. It was smelly and moth-eaten but basically the right size. He took it to a cleaner's, offered an exorbitant price to have it looked after immediately, and went into a bar to wait.

On the way back to his hotel he picked up a razor, a small cobbler's hammer, and a sheet of sandpaper. Then he bought himself dinner at the best restaurant he could get into, dressed as he was. He smoked all his cigars there, downed a bottle of French wine, ate rare beef smothered in sauce, and topped off the meal with two Cognacs. You might as well live once in a while, he reasoned. Especially when you're already dead.

That night he began his preparations. He shaved his head and was surprised to realize how lumpy his skull was. Without the shock of thick white hair it would be hard for even his own mother to recognize him.

But that wouldn't be good enough for the KGB.

Puffing the butt end of his last cigar, he patiently sanded his fingertips until all the grooves were gone. He checked them patiently under the light. They were sore to the point of bleeding, and he knew that in time his fingerprints would grow back, but he was measuring his life span in hours now, not days. The temporary confusion caused by a printless man would be enough.

Now the hard part, he thought. He sat on the edge of the bed, pressing the pillowcase over his face. Then, holding his breath, he slapped the hammer onto the bridge of his nose.

The pain was excruciating, but he had expected it. He lowered his head between his knees to allow the blood to gush into the pillowcase. Within a half hour the flow had stopped, and he dared a look in the mirror. The nose might not be broken, he thought, but it was sure as hell dented. The face he saw was one even he didn't recognize. His nose was red and swollen, and dark bruises were already beginning to spread under his eyes. He was bald, his head adorned with only the bandage over his right eye. As a final touch, he removed his false teeth. The change was total.

He piled the hammer, sandpaper, teeth, his razor, and the sweepings of his hair into the bloody pillowcase, placed it by the door, then slept like a baby.

CHAPTER NINE

He awoke early on May Day. His face came as a shock to him when he first saw it in the dirty window, but after a moment the surprise gave way to a certain satisfaction. This was the best disguise of his career. Just in time, he thought, for the biggest mission of his life.

He put on the uniform and cap, then picked up the pillowcase containing his rubbish and left the hotel. A few blocks away he dumped the pillowcase into a trash bin. The only items he had with him were his automatic and the remainder of the money he had stolen.

He would have no more use for the money, so he bought an envelope and a stamp, addressed it to the old woman who had taken him in on his return from Kadar's compound, and mailed the cash to her. No note, no return address. If she figured out who had sent it, she would keep her mouth shut.

The soldiers were already starting to assemble outside the Kremlin. Companies of enlisted men were lined up for blocks ahead, while more were spilling out of a mass of trucks.

Dozens of officers shouted orders to a horde of young soldiers amid the excited babble of a crowd of civilian onlookers. Other military vehicles circled around in search of a drop-off point. Starcher took advantage of the situation and picked out a young private who seemed to be waiting, then approached him with his dotty-old-man persona.

"You're supposed to be back there," the soldier said, gesturing back through the ranks.

Starcher cupped his hand to his ear. "What? Can't hear."

"I said, over there," the young man shouted.

"Who's riding with the *Vozhd*? I want to see Comrade Kadar." He moved in closer, grinning toothlessly.

"He's not riding, he's walking. Don't worry, you'll be marching right behind him."

"Near those men with the red ribbons?"

"Yes. That's the Premier's personal guard."

Starcher looked properly impressed. "Are they going to be on the tomb with him to review the parade?"

"Sure are. Better look sharp, sir," the private said with a smile.

"Oh, yes, yes." Starcher saluted him proudly, then worked his way through the crowd to the section near Lenin's tomb.

The men with the red sashes were Kadar's men. Starcher recognized some of them from the bunker. Kadar would walk from inside the Kremlin and up the wide stone steps to stand atop Lenin's tomb, flanked by his closest advisers. Starcher had seen the parade before. They never varied.

It was all he needed. He was ready.

The detachment of old soldiers was set to march when he joined it. Ahead, Kadar and his red-ribboned guard had already mounted the tomb to begin the ceremonies. They would culminate in a speech that might announce the end of the world.

The drums beat. The parade began, thousands of men and trucks and tanks. And among them was one nameless, faceless old spook who was about to march down the edge of the blade for the last time.

CHAPTER
TEN

May Day.

Justin could hear the drums. Moscow had a strange, deserted quality during the parade. The city clocks kept time, store windows displayed their goods, an occasional stray dog ambled through the arcades. But there were no people anywhere, as if all human life had been wiped out.

Soon all cities may look like this, Justin thought as he wandered aimlessly through the empty streets. The big bombs will be for the military installations and defense plants. But the cities would be wiped clean of their inhabitants by more sophisticated arms, so that the buildings would stand to serve the victor.

And on the day after the bombs, as on this day, perhaps a solitary, dying survivor would hear what Justin was hearing, the music of a military band in the distance and the thud of the conquerors' marching footsteps.

Could even Alexander Zharkov have conceived of a world like this, founded not on evil but on madness? Or was the Prince of Death, like Justin, no more than an anachronism in this age, a useless tool of defunct gods? Perhaps they were both like Starcher, too old and feeble and cowardly to try anymore.

The music was growing louder. Lost in his thoughts, Justin had wandered near the parade route. There was nothing else for him to do now that Starcher was on his way back to Virginia and Sasha was dead. He followed the noise until he saw the last stragglers trying for a view of the spectacle from behind a sea of people. He milled about with the crowd, allowing himself to be shoved and buffeted by the press of bodies, caught in the roar of cheers as the *Vozhd* came into view. Justin was one of them now, one of the *narod*, the masses who would die in Kadar's new world of destruction and chaos. He would watch and listen while Kadar marched to victory. There was nothing else he could do.

Justin stood a head taller than most of the Russians around him, so it was easy to see. The Premier was walking briskly, frowning as if impatient to reach his spot on the reviewing stand atop the tomb. Why not impatient? Justin thought. His words would change the course of the world. His action today would signal the beginning of the end.

He did not think much of it when one old soldier stepped out of formation and marched double time toward the red-sashed officers in front of Lenin's tomb. If it had not happened right in front of him, he probably would not have given the man a second glance. But the soldier pulled something from his uniform and crouched, and for a moment—just the barest fraction of a second before the screaming started—the cheers stopped and a hundred thousand people held their breath.

It was all very fast. Later, film of the incident would be replayed thousands of times around the world. It would be freeze-framed and blown up. Security would be analyzed in great detail. The bullets would be measured, the gun scrutinized. But there would be no clue to the actual assassin.

In that split second of silence, five shots rang out, as loud as cannon. Four of them had already struck Kadar before the red-sashed officers even guessed what was going on. The *Vozhd* sank to his knees, blood spurting out of a mangled eye. A bullet went through his head, erupting through the glossy skin of his skull like a bright flower. His hands clutched at his chest, blood pouring from between his fingers as he jerked out of his kneeling position and onto his back before the security officers swarmed around him.

Other shots came. The assassin took a bullet in the shoulder, fell backward almost to the edge of the crowd, grabbed another soldier, and wrestled with him. The assassin's hat came off, revealing a bald head that glittered in the sunlight. The bald man himself was then shouting, "Assassin, assassin," and pointing to the soldier on the ground.

There were more shots, and the soldier on the ground erupted in a spray of blood, splattering the onlookers, already panicked. They surged in all directions, running like wild game, screeching like animals, and trampling one another in the rush to escape.

Justin stayed. He was only a few feet from the bald-headed assassin, who was trying to lose himself in the crowd. More bullets plowed in the body of the defenseless soldier on the ground.

Then Justin recognized the bandage on the bald man's forehead. "Andy," he whispered, moving quickly toward him.

"Get the bastards away from me," Starcher said.

Without hesitation Justin ran away from the old man, pushing another soldier forward through the crowd. "Over here," he called, waving his arm over his head. "Here's the assassin. Over here!"

Some in the sea of people tried to follow him; others tried to retreat. There was an internal tension within the panicked crowd, which finally tore loose in two factions, screaming and shouting in a maelstrom of confusion.

A group of red-sashed officers came over to scoop up the dead soldier's body, leaving a red smear on the pavement. They shouted at one another, unaware of the few stunned hangers-on who still stood in obedient silence behind the civilian barricades.

The music finally stopped, the parade route in shambles. An ambulance swept through the ranks of soldiers to pick up the bodies of the Premier and the fallen soldier.

There was no sign of Starcher.

Justin heard the old man's words again and again, echoing like wind: *You say thanks.*

What a fool he had been, Justin thought, to believe that Starcher would turn tail and run back to Virginia in defeat. The old man had done what Justin should have known he would do. He had stayed to fight and die and finish his job.

Sasha. Starcher. Both had found, in their own ways, the courage to try, then, failing, to try again. Both had achieved what Justin, for all his divine promise, could never touch. And both had loved him.

His eyes filled. The smear of blood on the street spread inside his eyes and obliterated everything else.

A hand touched him gently on the shoulder. "Go along home," a man's voice said.

Justin looked up. The man was a stranger, a Russian who thought that Justin was mourning for Konstantin Kadar.

"Tomorrow will come again, eh?" the man said. He smiled kindly and patted Justin's back before walking away.

Tomorrow . . .

Justin looked at the street. Soldiers had broken out of formation and had positioned themselves along the barricades, anticipating a riot. Megaphones blared instructions, unintelligible above the din of the crowd. Surrounded by motorcycles, the truck bearing the dead soldier's body cut a swath through the melee.

There was no sign of Starcher, and Justin somehow knew that he was still alive.

Where would he go? The safe house was gone. Would he just walk the streets of Moscow until he dropped? Or would he throw himself into the river and hope his body washed out to sea without a trace?

No, if he survived his wound, Starcher would try to keep living. He would try to get back to America, through the embassy. He would try to live. It was what Starcher believed in.

Justin turned and walked quickly out of Red Square.

It might be the lung. The bullet had pierced his shoulder. Since he was breathing and able to move, Starcher thought he might make it. He had survived worse bullet wounds before. But the pain was almost incapacitating. A bone had splintered, and some shards had found their way into his lung.

His military cap was jammed inside his shirt over the wound to stanch the bleeding. He found a rag inside a garbage pail and tossed it over his shoulder to hide the seeping blood.

He walked heavily but with a sense of fierce pride. He had done it. A sixty-eight-year-old man with a bullet in him had averted a disaster that could have devastated mankind. And he'd done it alone. All in all, that wasn't too bad a day's work for a semiretired country squire, he assured himself.

It was a long walk. Near the end, he was almost staggering, trying to force himself by sheer will to get to the embassy. There he would tell them what he'd done and why, and then he would go home to face whatever charges would be waiting for him. It didn't matter anymore whether the ambassador believed him or not. Kadar was dead. There would be no war.

As he approached the embassy he saw extra guards on the gate, and he realized he was wearing a Russian soldier's uniform. That, his wound, and no identification guaranteed that he would not be admitted.

He walked slowly around to the back of the embassy compound, to the spot behind the high hedges where he knew there was a slim opening in the steel-barred fence.

He dragged himself through, stifling a scream as the fabric of his uniform jacket caught on the metal, wrenching his shoulder.

But he was inside. He paused on the side of the sweeping lawn. Only a hundred feet to go to the main embassy building. He could walk a hundred feet.

He stood and tried to breathe deeply, attempting to gather his strength for one last run to the back door of the building.

He started. He went three steps, and the pain crushed his chest as if a giant wrecking ball had swung into his body.

Starcher dropped. This time it was not angina. He knew the signs of a heart attack; he had had one before. He fell facedown to the ground. The grass smelled sweet, and he remembered other times, other places. He thought of Justin Gilead and smiled. In the end he had not let Justin down, after all. Maybe Justin would be able to get back to his mountain now. Maybe there would be a mountain for him to return to.

Starcher felt proud of himself. He had done his duty. There would never be a public ceremony for him, never a medal, but at least the Americans inside would bring him in and send his body home.

He would like to have smelled the grass one more time; cool, blue Virginia grass in the United States that he loved. He closed his eyes and saw it in his mind, rolling hills sprinkled with wildflowers, the sky clear and empty with a breeze that carried the scent of grass and horseflesh and a good cigar.

Then Andrew Starcher, sixty-eight, veteran of forty-five years of service in his country's defense, died on a small patch of American soil at the U.S. embassy compound in the heart of Moscow.

United States Ambassador John Downing had watched the shooting of Konstantin Kadar on television, and now a telephone call from the French ambassador had confirmed that Kadar was dead. The assassin was apparently a Russian soldier, although there were reports that there was another soldier involved. The second soldier had escaped.

Downing poured a martini from a pitcher on his desk, called the embassy guard station, and ordered beefed-up security at the gates until further notice. No point in taking any chances, he thought. Not until he saw how the Russians were going to respond to Kadar's killing and who they were going to publicly blame.

If what Andrew Starcher had told him was true, Downing thought, it was probably best that Kadar should die. But who knew? Who knew anymore who told the truth, who lied, who stood for peace, who wanted war? Who knew?

He walked to the window and looked out over the embassy grounds. He almost dropped his glass as he saw a figure lying on the grass, arms curled up under his head.

He shook his head in disgust, walked to the telephone, and dialed an outside number directly.

"Militsia station."

"Hello," he said, trying to keep the annoyance out of his voice. "This is Ambassador John Downing at the American embassy. I know you're busy, but I've got one of your people . . . some old drunk . . . sleeping on my lawn. Will you please come and get him out of here?" He hung up the telephone and finished his martini. Diplomacy was hell, he thought. Sometimes he had to do everything himself.

He was dead. Justin realized that as he saw the single uniformed Russian policeman struggling to carry Starcher's body from the embassy compound. Of course. Inside, they had not recognized Starcher, so they had turned his body over to the Russians.

What now? If he was not blamed for the assassination of Kadar, he would be treated like a bum, buried in an unmarked grave outside the city. That was the way his kind ended. Starcher had known that from the beginning; it had been a pact he had made with his beloved country.

The policeman unceremoniously dumped Starcher's body

into the backseat of his red automobile and clambered into the front. Just as he pulled away, Justin jumped into the backseat behind the driver.

"I have a gun on you," he snapped in Russian. "Just drive and you won't be hurt." The driver tried to turn around, but Justin gripped the back of his neck with fingers like steel and squeezed.

The man's head snapped forward. "Turn around again," Justin warned, "and you will never see another thing."

He stripped the driver of his gun an hour outside of Moscow and left him standing by the side of a dirt road. There were no houses in view. The man could walk or he could hitchhike, Justin thought. But in either case the man was no threat and did not have to die.

Justin drove east for another hour. Here spring had not yet confirmed its hold on the land. Cold and barren, the land had not yet sprung to life.

Justin parked the car behind a stand of trees well off the road. Inside the trunk he found a small folding shovel. He carried it with Starcher's body deep into the woods.

He dug in the ground, covered with soft pine needles, and gently lowered the body of Andrew Starcher into its grave. After he filled in the grave he covered it with pine needles. No one would find the grave ever again.

"I'm sorry it had to be here, Andy," he said softly.

Then he dropped to his knees and began to say the prayers for the dead. This time all the words came back to him, and he prayed in the words of Rashimpur for the soul of Andrew Starcher—and for all who had died and for those who were yet to die. He beseeched the god of creation to receive Starcher warmly because he was a good man who had died to save the lives of others and because he had shown Justin Gilead that a man did not do his duty only when it was easy but all the time, because it was obedience to duty that made men share the qualities of their gods.

This was faith, Justin realized. Starcher had never denigrated his own calling, whatever price loyalty. He had not accepted defeat and then waited helplessly for death to free him from his guilt. He had not allowed a monster to take over his world and then turned his back.

In his own way, Starcher had kept his faith.

Justin trembled. "Thy will be done," he prayed.

He drove another day, until he came to a road sign he recognized. Then he parked the car off the road and walked away in the direction of the road sign.

Kyshtym.

The sun had set and risen and set again, and he kept on, never looking back, afraid that if he did, he would see the smear of blood on the pavement outside Lenin's tomb.

He walked until he was exhausted. In the country he could breathe again. He was heading southeast, toward a prison camp that held the key to his existence, toward his own rendezvous with duty.

If the gods who had spawned the boy with the killing gift expected Justin to give up without a struggle, he would spit in their faces. He would live. He would keep his faith, as Starcher had. He would try again.

"Thanks, Andy," he whispered, sitting under a broad maple tree. Its sap was dark, its budding leaves like bright feathers. The Tree of the Thousand Wisdoms was waiting for him. After he found Zharkov it would be time to go home, where his real task awaited him.

"Thanks."

CHAPTER ELEVEN

Justin knew he'd found the prison camp by its smell. The odor of human waste was everywhere, emanating from the massive trench just inside the twenty-foot-high fence, where thousands of prisoners labored in a cloud of insects.

But there was something else, another smell that Justin would never forget. The smell of fresh death. He moved so carefully through the thornbushes surrounding the camp that not even a twig trembled on a branch. He peered out. The sight sent a wave of nausea through him. The head of a man was impaled on a bloody stake planted near the spiky barbed-wire fence. Blackened by flies, its eyes had been plucked out by birds. A placard with NICHEVO inscribed on it was nailed to the stake.

On the surface it would seem merely to be a bad joke: a dead man's head bearing the legend "Who cares?" But Justin understood. An operative of Nichevo had come for his leader, and this was what was left of him. Zharkov was alone.

Justin stayed in the thorns, keeping still so that his flesh was not hurt by them, until nightfall.

The spotlights came on as Zharkov was walking back

from the graveyard. The other prisoners were already at supper, but Zharkov did not take his meals at regular hours. The guards no longer paid much attention to him. They were chattering excitedly among themselves.

"It was an old man who really did it, I hear. My cousin was in the parade. He saw it."

"The Jews probably hired him. Or the Americans."

"They're saying he worked alone."

"Come off it, Pinchov. They always say that."

Zharkov sighed as the guards attached the manacle to his ankle. That was a new addition since Kadar's assassination on the orders of Maxim Sterlitz. It was attached to a cement cube on the floor. The cement had been poured especially for the chain. Zharkov's ankle was raw from it, even though he tried to keep still during the evening hours when he had to wear it.

"I'm not going to run away," he said wearily.

"You're damn right you're not," one of the guards said with a laugh as he snapped on the metal cuff. "Looks like your friend didn't do you much good."

"Don't joke about it," another of the guards growled. "I'm the one who had to take the head off and put the stake in the ground." He shook his head in distaste. "Sterlitz," he muttered. "He doesn't like this one, that's for sure."

The guard named Pinchov stared at his prisoner. There was no hatred in his eyes. "What did you do, Zharkov?" he asked.

"Where have you been? He's the bloody Peace Killer."

"I asked him," Pinchov said.

Zharkov looked up from his cot. For a moment he saw Pinchov, not as one of the KGB guards hired to taunt and terrorize him but as a human being with the capacity for understanding. A family man, probably. He wore a wedding ring, and his shoes were always old and scuffed, as if he needed his salary for other things. Zharkov was about to tell him that he was there now, living like a toy for cruel children to play with because he'd had the bad judgment to take Konstantin Kadar at his word. Because once he'd made an organization that was better than Kadar's mighty KGB. Because he had been a prince living among savages.

But even Pinchov, who was not so cruel as the rest, was still one of those savages. He had spit on him when the others had. He had beaten him and made him march naked to the graveyard. And when the last man of Nichevo had come for Zharkov, Pinchov had watched as the dogs tore him to pieces.

"I don't talk to maggots," Zharkov said.

The guards left. "See what you get for falling in love?" one of them teased Pinchov.

Sterlitz arrived about an hour later, carrying a plate with Zharkov's dinner. There was some salted fish and a boiled potato. No utensils were provided. None ever were.

"I understand you've been talking to the guards," Sterlitz said. "That's against the rules, you know. Especially for someone who tries to escape."

Zharkov did not answer. Sterlitz would use any response as a reason for punishment. But then, Sterlitz did not need reasons to punish him. This was his world, this filthy camp populated by doomed men, and in this world he was Zharkov's sole master. And the brave, foolish, young Nichevo man had failed, as Sterlitz knew he would, and Zharkov would be here forever.

"Hungry?"

Sterlitz proffered the plate. When Zharkov reached for it, the KGB man let the food fall to the floor. "Eat it there, Prince."

He stood back and folded his arms over his chest as Zharkov picked up the pieces of fish and tried to dust them off with his filthy hands before he ate.

"Prince. That's a good name for a dog." Sterlitz laughed. "Here's a piece you missed." He kicked over a morsel with his boot.

When Zharkov tried to stand, Sterlitz shoved him back to the floor. "Don't be insolent with *me*," he shouted, flicking the riding crop across Zharkov's face. "Get up. Guard."

Cradling a Uzi in his arms, Pinchov entered. Sterlitz took a key from his pocket and tossed it to him. Pinchov knelt and unfastened the manacle.

"You need some exercise," Sterlitz said, shoving Zharkov outside. He walked him toward the outskirts of the camp. "Get in the trench."

Zharkov lowered himself into the muck. Here was all the daily waste from almost three thousand prisoners, covered lightly with a film of earth. When Zharkov stepped into it, he sank to his knees. The stench made him retch.

Sterlitz raised his crop, pointing at the head of the Nichevo member. Zharkov recognized the man's face. He had been the youngest of them.

"When more come for you," Sterlitz said, "they will meet the same fate."

When more come . . .

There were no more. Not even Kadar had known how small Nichevo's leadership truly was. It no longer existed. There was nothing left. Everything Zharkov had worked for, everything his father had started, was gone.

He now understood the prisoners who walked like zombies around the camp without hope or purpose. They waited patiently to die because that was all there was left for them.

Zharkov knew he would never get a trial or a sentence. He would stay here forever, performing his dog tricks for Sterlitz, shackled like a beast on a tether while he slept, stripped of all his human dignity. His father, in the same situation, would have found a way to kill himself. Perhaps it was time for that. He knew now that he could die. Once he had thought that he would die only when Justin Gilead died. But it was all a cruel hoax, a joke of the gods, because he, himself, had laid Justin Gilead in his grave, and yet here he was, still alive, still facing an eternity of days just like this one.

"Move," Sterlitz commanded. Zharkov pumped his

legs mechanically. They made sucking noises as they pulled out of the ooze. Filth splashed on his face.

A whistle blew, and the dogs came out, straining on their leads. "Keep them tied," Sterlitz shouted. "I'm not through yet."

He bent over the trench. "Would you like me to have them set loose on you?"

Zharkov remembered what they had done to the young man who had come for him. They were Dobermans, rigorously trained and kept hungry. That had been the operative's mistake. He had even managed to neutralize the electric barbed-wire fence, but he had not counted on the dogs.

When he came over, the dogs pounced on him from the shadows, baying like banshees, tearing, killing, eviscerating.

"Answer me, Prince."

"N-no," Zharkov stammered. "Don't set the dogs on me."

"Then run," Sterlitz said.

Zharkov ran, straining to move through the muck of the trench. His breath came in rasps.

"Behold Alexander Zharkov, descendant of the Czars." Sterlitz laughed, holding high his riding crop. Against the white light of the background he looked like a statue of a proletarian victor, drunk with a sudden power he had never known before.

Yes, Zharkov thought, perhaps it is time to die.

Justin heard. He followed the voice, crouching low and moving without a sound on the far side of the fence. The trench encircled the entire camp. At the entrance gate was a guardhouse. It was lit inside, and Justin could make out the figures of two men. The road led past the guardhouse to the main administration building of the camp. Here were the floodlights, dotted all along the front of the building. Up the hill beyond it stood the barracks of the prisoners. Far to the west, nearly a quarter of a mile away from the prison, was a small, hastily built shack surrounded by four guards. This was where the official finally took Zharkov.

"The prisoner is secure," Sterlitz called, and the dogs were set free, baying and running in all directions, casting long shadows on the barren hillside.

Justin looked up at the sky. It was a cloudy night, starless and moonless. Without the bright floodlights the place would be as dark as Manjusri's cave at Rashimpur.

It was Justin's only advantage. Without the amulet of Rashimpur, he was no longer the Patanjali. He possessed no magic, but Eyeless had taught him to see without his eyes.

He crept to the guardhouse, moving as softly as a cat in the night. He snapped the neck of one of the guards and killed the other with a blow to the temple. It was accomplished in seconds. As the second man fell, Justin took the rifle from his hands and smashed the butt against the light inside the guardhouse.

He took one last, long look down the length of the buildings to Zharkov's shack, setting the distances and obstacles in his mind. Then he aimed the rifle and shot out each of the floodlights, one by one.

The dogs went wild. Justin could hear them coming toward the source of the noise. He took off his cloth jacket and wrapped it around the rifle and hurled it off to his left. It landed with a thud, and the dogs went after it as Justin scrambled in the other direction, toward the shack.

The lights in the administration building came on in a blaze, but there was still not enough light to cover the hillside, and by Zharkov's shack it was pitch dark. Justin kept near the trench. Even running at full speed, he did not make a sound. He had spent a lifetime learning to move in silence, and it came automatically to him. But now he would have to fight blind as well.

"Trust yourself," Manjusri had said. "There is no other way."

Justin closed his eyes.

"Nichevo," whispered one of the guards. He hitched

his Uzi rifle over his shoulder and prepared to fire, but by that time it was too late. Something had sprung out of the darkness at him and struck the side of his head with such ferocity that he hardly felt the pain.

Justin snatched the weapon from another, upended it into someone's chin, thrust it into the chest of the third.

Then he sensed the barrel of a weapon, felt its energy the way he had felt the monks' spears as they flew toward him at the cave mouth on Amne Xachim. He dropped to the ground as the guard fired and grabbed the man's legs. Shifting his weight, he threw the guard headfirst through the rough door of the shack. The man screamed.

Even before the door splintered and fell, gunshots sounded from inside. The bullets had killed the fourth guard.

Following immediately after the body, Justin dived into the shack, kicking at the sound of the gunfire. His foot made contact with a soft belly. A man grunted and rolled to the side of the shack.

"Don't shoot," a familiar voice said. Zharkov hadn't recognized him.

Justin opened his eyes. In the dimness he could see Zharkov fumbling through the man's clothing. He removed a key and unlocked the manacle around his ankle.

Sterlitz began to regain consciousness. Zharkov scrambled to his feet, preparing to stomp on his throat.

"No," Justin said, and at the sound of his voice Zharkov looked up sharply.

"*You,*" he said incredulously.

"Get into the trench. Hurry."

While Zharkov ran down the hill, Justin dragged Sterlitz outside. He was coming to, staggering on his feet. Nearby, the dogs were bounding in their direction, howling, teeth bared. Justin whistled, then pushed the KGB man toward them and dived into the trench.

Zharkov was a short way ahead, but Justin caught up quickly and pulled Zharkov along. "The gate is open," he said.

Behind them, Sterlitz screamed as the dogs tore his flesh apart.

"Now," Justin said. The two men ran in the darkness until they stood in a copse of trees.

"Are you injured?" Justin asked him.

"No," Zharkov said.

Justin turned to leave.

"Where are you going?" Zharkov asked, panting for breath.

"I have work to finish elsewhere."

Before he could walk away, Zharkov grasped his arm.

"Why?" the Russian snapped, once again a soldier. "Why have you done this for me?"

Justin's eyes met his. "I asked the same of you at Kadar's bunker."

Zharkov struggled visibly with his emotions. "This changes nothing between us."

"No," Justin said, smiling sadly. "Nothing can change what is to come. The game is not ours to play. We will meet again."

"And I will kill you," Zharkov warned.

Justin listened to the din of the dogs and the shouting guards and Sterlitz's piercing screams in the distance.

"Nichevo," he said.

CHAPTER TWELVE

At the base of Amne Xachim he saw the first sign, a pile of cinders on the blackened ground near the lake. In the ashes he could see a charred human skull and the remnants of other bones.

Another pile lay ahead on the rocky trail. There were still more ahead. Justin counted five such fires before reaching the second lake near the closed doors of the Rashimpur monastery. Some were still smoldering. Near one, stuck to the branches of a gorse bush, was a scrap of saffron-colored cloth.

The High Priest had come.

Justin stood frozen outside the monastery, dreading what waited inside. He had failed again. By losing his faith he had cost Manjusri and his followers their lives. Now he was too late. The circle of karma had closed outside of him.

As if sensing his despair, the huge doors of the monastery creaked open in teasing invitation. The very walls of the place now seemed darkened with evil.

Here it ends, he thought. Thy will be done. He walked in slowly.

There was no one behind the door. Of course not, Justin thought without surprise. Siraj had magic here. On this mountain was all the mystery of the god of creation, ready to be twisted into sorcery by the boy with the killing gift. It had all been waiting for him.

The Great Wall was still, as quiet as the cave where Manjusri had first given Justin the precious knowledge he could have used to save the legacy of Brahma. Instead he had destroyed the sacred amulet of the coiled snake by allowing the boy to touch it. He still had the broken pieces, but none of the medallion's magic remained within those lifeless scraps of metal. The magic had died when Justin surrendered the amulet to the High Priest in exchange for his friend's life.

Would he have acted differently, he wondered, if he had understood that the choice was between Andrew Starcher's life and the protection of God himself? And then he knew that he was not a holy man and that he deserved whatever death the High Priest saw fit to give him, because in his heart he knew he could not have sacrificed Starcher.

The Tree of the Thousand Wisdoms stood before him, dying. Even in winter, the Tree had always been in full leaf. Now it was bare, its branches as dry as kindling. Justin reached out his hand to touch it. Its bark, once as hard as iron, crumbled into brittle flakes.

"Your world is gone, Grandmaster," a voice said.

It seemed to come from everywhere at once, reverberating like an echo around the gilded hall. Justin walked farther and there, behind the tree, he saw Siraj.

Encrusted with precious gems, the great throne of Rashimpur had remained hidden behind elaborate gold screens for centuries, revealed only for ceremonies of investiture. Now it stood in full view, no more than a piece of furniture, and on it sat the boy.

Siraj was dressed in the rich ceremonial robes of the Patanjali. A diamond the size of a robin's egg rested on his finger, and a jeweled dagger hung from his belt. He looked at Justin in arrogant silence, then smiled and opened one arm to display the obscene panorama behind him.

Some of the monks were still alive, although they were emaciated to the point of starvation. They were tethered by their necks, the ropes attached to stakes nailed crudely into the polished stone floor of the hall.

In the center of them was a tall mound, waist-high, covered by a cloth. The monks sat clustered around it, like statues, saying nothing, looking at nothing.

"Behold your flock," Siraj said.

Justin could not speak. Inside his pocket he felt the two leaden pieces of the broken amulet. *This is what I have brought them to,* he thought.

"What? No greetings for your friends?" The boy sneered.

"Why have you done this?" Justin said hoarsely. "They could do you no harm."

"Oh, they tried. But the ones who immolated themselves on the side of the mountain taught a lesson to the rest."

"They are starving."

The boy shrugged. "Their suffering will end soon."

"Where is Manjusri?" Justin demanded.

Siraj nodded toward the cloth-covered mound in the center of the praying monks. "See for yourself. As their leader, he deserved special recognition. It was the least I could do."

Justin raised the cloth, preparing himself to view the body of his dead teacher. What he found instead filled him with horror and shame. The old blind man lay sprawled across the big prayer wheel used by the monks. His hands and feet had been nailed to the wooden spokes of the wheel, surrounded by bits of brightly colored paper. These were written prayers to Brahma, believed sent toward the god's heart with every spin of the wheel. Now they fluttered in the faint breeze, their colors splattered with Manjusri's blood.

The old man wore only a dirty loincloth, and his wrinkled skin hung loosely over his bones. Justin let out a sob of disbelief and anguish. The monks, with their necks raw from the ropes around them, did not look at him. Only Manjusri moved his head slightly.

"The Patanjali . . . has come," he croaked.

"Manjusri," Justin whispered. He reached for one of the metal stakes that pierced the blind man's hands, but as he touched it, the metal grew white-hot, blistering Justin's skin instantly.

The boy laughed. "They did that to him. His brothers. Your followers. Afterward they burned themselves on the side of the mountain in atonement. I did not have to force them to do that."

"The gods curse you," Justin said softly.

"Curse me with what? You?"

Manjusri's clouded eyes opened again. "We have . . . stayed alive . . . for you," he said.

"Then you have lived for nothing," the boy said. "This man has no magic. The amulet is broken. I am here because the Patanjali is a lie. He was too weak to keep the throne of Rashimpur from me."

Justin knew he was right. He was no god. But he was a man. He still had hands to fight with and legs to stand on and a heart to pump his blood until his life was taken away. What did it matter if it was taken by the boy or by Zharkov or by a passing stranger? He was a man and he would die a man.

Deliberately he wrapped his hand around the metal stake once more. From the throne the boy opened his hand, and the stake once again burned with the intensity of molten steel. Justin felt his hand crack and sizzle. The smell of burning flesh filled the hall. He yanked out the stake, then threw it on the floor. The muscles in his hand were exposed, red and bleeding, the skin around them withered. Ignoring the pain, he removed the other stakes until Manjusri's body slumped off the wheel and into his arms. One of the monks looked up numbly, his eyes vacant. Justin lay the old man gently over the monk's lap.

Justin felt something pull weakly on his sleeve. Manjusri's lips moved.

"See without your eyes, my son," he said. He raised his hand and touched it to Justin's forehead.

"Look at me," the boy demanded. "We haven't even begun."

Rage swept through Justin like a fever. "No, we haven't," he said. Justin leapt to the throne and kicked the boy on the side of the head. Siraj fell to the floor, his robes billowing around him as he stared in astonishment at the man with the blackened, bleeding hands who stood over him.

Justin came at the boy again, but Siraj was ready this time. From the tips of his fingers issued thin rays of black light, as fine as the filaments of a spiderweb. Justin felt them moving through space, as if they were real objects. Like the spears outside the cave, he listened for them with ears outside his body, touched them with a sense beyond his human capacities. The force of his own energy, the energy of Brahma the Creator, ran over him like sweat and then snaked out its tendrils toward the source of the killing gift, winding around it, stopping it.

The boy was still for a moment, but when he spoke again, his voice was filled with contempt. "Choose not to watch this," he said. "If you can."

Justin heard the sickening thud of metal slicing through flesh, and then the soft moan of an old man dying. When he opened his eyes to see, Manjusri lay on the stone floor, a gaping slash through his bowels. The boy stood erect over him, a jeweled dagger dripping blood, held high between two closed fists over his head.

Justin felt his heart constrict. "Do you think you can fight me here, you laughable little clown?" the boy said. "You could not kill me in the world of men where I possessed nothing but my own power. Here I own both the legacy of Varja and the magic of Brahma."

As he spoke, his whole body seemed to glow with the unearthly, dark light of the killing gift. His hair stood on end. From his fingers issued fountains of sparks that shot to the ceiling and then spread over the walls. The Great Hall was bathed in the oppressive light, as bright and hot as the fires of hell. And in this light, floating like tangible dreams, appeared the tormented images of the dead: Tagore, Justin's first teacher, mutilated and burned; Sasha, her limbs broken and twisted; Starcher, his giant heart finally given out; and finally Manjusri, not yet fully formed, his clouded eyes staring emptily through Justin.

"These are your accusers," Siraj said. "These have you killed with your weakness."

A ball of fire rolled off the boy's hands and exploded into Justin's shoulder. There was a terrible pain as the flesh opened up and a thick yellow pus oozed out. The liquid took shape, began to move. Then the wound opened wider. A swarm of maggots crawled out.

"That is what you are made of, Grandmaster." Siraj laughed as the images closed in on Justin. The dead raised their faces.

"No," Justin whispered. He backed away from them, shuddering, but there was nowhere to turn.

"Manjusri." The old monk's face wavered, as if under water. "Sasha," he rasped. "Tagore, my teacher." The forms twisted in the air. From Tagore's mouth poured a stream of black blood. Sasha's broken arm lifted. From her fingertips writhed five vipers, hissing and spitting.

"Starcher!"

The man who had been his friend in life now turned toward him. The eyes glowed red and then black, and from them shot the killing gift. Two rays of dark light merged and struck Justin in his stomach. He doubled over. Blood trickled out of his mouth.

"A slow death, I think, would suit you best," the boy said, but Justin could barely hear across the sea of pain that flooded him. The image moved closer, smothering him, filling him with the stench of death.

"Die," they chanted softly. "Die, Justin. It is what you have always wanted. There are none of us left. Only you, and you have failed. Come with us, Justin. Come with us into the darkness."

He felt another blow.

Die, Justin . . .

Die . . .

"No!" he cried out. "I will not die. You are lies. The true souls of the dead are not here. They are inside me. They live inside everyone they have touched."

The images wavered for a moment. Justin felt Manjusri's presence. "You are finding the way," the old monk whispered from a place deep inside Justin. "See it now, without your eyes. See the truth."

"I will try," Justin said, his voice cracking as he addressed the visions of the dead. "I will try, as they did. I will try because that is the only way to life, and life is more precious to the gods than all the magic in the universe."

He turned to Siraj. "Your evil cannot harm me," he said. "My flesh may be destroyed, as was theirs, as were the bodies of the holy men who kept this shrine, but our souls will live as long as men can look into their hearts and find light in darkness, hope in despair, and wonder at the beauty of their own creation. We will live forever, Black Star. Compared with us—with the spirit inside each of us which is God in His truest form—you are as nothing."

After he spoke, the yellow pall in the room was replaced by a white light, blinding in its clarity. The door of the monastery crashed open, and a gust of wind swept through, snatching the jeweled dagger from Siraj's hands. Still dripping with Manjusri's blood, the knife sailed upward to the gilt-domed ceiling of the Great Hall, then turned of its own accord in the air and whistled downward. Before the boy could move, it embedded itself in his heart.

Siraj groaned and staggered backward, gasping for breath as his back brushed against the Tree of the Thousand Wisdoms. He uttered a shriek, high and piercing. His body twitched as his feet left the floor and seemed to dance in the air. He was pinned to the tree, his head jerking on his thin neck, his eyes rolling.

Above him, the images of the dead dispersed into foul black smoke. It swirled above his head for a moment, then poured itself into the hilt of the dagger and, through it, into the body of the High Priest as it slid bonelessly down the trunk of the great dying tree. His fingers opened and closed once in a spasm, and then were still.

Justin watched him die, then went to the monks and broke their bonds. They brought themselves out of their prayers, touching the burns on their necks and looking up at Justin as he lifted Manjusri in his arms. He carried the blind man to the base of the tree and lay him down beside the body of Siraj.

Then Justin knelt between them. From his pocket he took the two broken pieces of the coiled-snake amulet and set them down.

"We are in Thy hands," he said, bowing his head. "Thy will be done."

He sat without moving while the light in the Great Hall dimmed to darkness. Then, as the monks watched, the dagger protruding from Siraj's chest erupted into brilliant white flame.

The fire spread quickly, engulfing the tree and the still figures around it with its tongues, the color of diamonds. The monks gathered around, moving slowly and awkwardly, their gaze riveted to the sight of Brahma's fire. Within the flames Justin remained, not a muscle in his face moving. His form distorted behind the heat of the smokeless blaze, then disappeared inside it. When the fire subsided, he was still there, whole, and clothed in the robes of Patanjali.

Manjusri lay beside him; the gaping wound on his belly healed without a mark. On the Grandmaster's other side, where Siraj had been, was a heap of ashes. The pieces of the amulet were gone.

The hall was absolutely silent. Even the breathing of the monks was stilled. Then the ashes began to stir.

Inside them something moved, giving off light as it rose to the surface.

They saw it then: a golden snake coiling out of the ashes of the High Priest. It slithered toward the Tree of the Thousand Wisdoms, wrapping itself around the massive trunk, rippling up its height. And as it rose, the Tree breathed with new life. Droplets of sap appeared on the bark, now strong again. Budding green leaves appeared on the branches.

Justin plucked one of the leaves and touched it to the old monk's eyes. Manjusri awakened. His eyelids fluttered. When they opened, the eyes behind them were clear and seeing.

The old man reached his hand toward Justin's face but dared not touch it. It was the face of a god now. He moved away to sit with the other monks and prostrated himself.

"Hail to Thee, O Wearer of the Blue Hat," he whispered.

"Hail to Thee," the monks repeated.

Justin rose.

The snake uncoiled from the Tree and curled inside the palm of his hand. It glowed for an instant and then vanished.

In its place was the golden amulet of Rashimpur.

EPILOGUE

At dawn the Patanjali stood on the cliff of Amné Xachim. He held two pieces of paper. On them were written the ancient and sacred prayers of protection for the souls of the dead.

Neither Sasha nor Starcher had shed their bodies in the rite of ritual fire. It was not the way of their gods or of their lives. Each was buried somewhere alone, away from the people they loved.

But their souls would be free. Brahma, in all his names, would accept them. They would come back, in other lives, in other times. Perhaps in better times.

And in those lives to come, the Patanjali thought, they might meet another, a person whose name had once been Justin Gilead, the Grandmaster, who had remembered them.

A breeze whispered through the mountains, carrying the scent of spring as the first rays of morning appeared on the horizon. The Patanjali opened his hands and released the prayers. They fluttered on the air for a moment, specks of color against the misty gray sky, and then floated away on the wind.

About the Authors

WARREN MURPHY and MOLLY COCHRAN are the Edgar Award-winning authors of *Grandmaster*. Husband and wife as well as bestselling literary collaborators, Murphy and Cochran have established themselves individually as well. Warren Murphy is the co-author of *The Destroyer*, an action/adventure series available in Signet editions, and author of the Edgar-winning *Trace* series. Molly Cochran has written several books, including the bestselling *Dressing Thin*. They live and work in Pennsylvania.